...erited from her uncle who is a very successful children's author. Languages were her forte at school, but she decided not to go to university after her A levels as she had had enough of education by then. Also she had met her future husband and had started making plans. Her desire to be a writer was put on hold for a decade while she got married and had her two children, but when they were safely at school, or tucked up at night, she started again.

Also by Beth Thomas

Carry You

BETH THOMAS

His Other Life

AVON

AVON

A division of HarperCollins*Publishers*
1 London Bridge Street,
London SE1 9GF

www.harpercollins.co.uk

A Paperback Original 2015

2

A catalogue record for this book is
available from the British Library

ISBN-13: 978-0-00-754484-4

Set in Sabon LT Std by Palimpsest Book Production Ltd, Falkirk, Stirlingshire

Printed and bound in Great Britain by Clays Ltd, St Ives plc

MIX
Paper from
responsible sources
FSC™ C007454

Acknowledgements

Thanks must go as always to my friends and family for taking the time and trouble to read this and shine a light on my failings, most notably Zachary Dann, Annika Dann, Suzanne Allen and Sue Harding. I'm in the dark without you.

I am also extremely grateful for my minor brush with the law, in the guise of Kieron McCarthy and Andrew McKeeman. Together, they conspired to give me plentiful and accurate information about missing persons procedures. If my use of the information they provided is not quite so accurate, this is not a reflection on them, only me.

To Chris Jefferson, for your enduring patience and extremely annoying reminders (which, ugh, did actually help me get it finished).

(Nick and JK are not getting a mention.)

Finally, a huge thank you again to the completely lovely Lydia Vassar-Smith and Laura Morris, for all your continued help and guidance. Don't know where I'd be without you both.

For my Babbagee.
You may be a sour-faced puss,
but it's not your fault.

ONE

There's a text on my husband's phone. It's lying on the counter near the kettle and I just heard it vibrate. He's turned the sound off, probably thinking I wouldn't hear it – that's the only reason someone would put their phone on silent, right? – but I still can. It sounds like an automatic gun; our neighbours probably heard it. Pam and Mike next door are no doubt up off their sofa already, frantically dialling three nines before you can say *Crimewatch*.

I look over at the phone but it's face down, probably so that it doesn't light up noticeably when texts or calls arrive. Bit of a pointless precaution if you ask me, given that it sounds like a horse falling downstairs. Maybe it's also a precaution against someone – well, let's be honest, *me* – getting a glimpse of the name of anyone who might call or text.

Eventually the glasses and cutlery stop rattling from the aftershocks and I glance over at hubby to see if he's noticed. Of course he's noticed; the house shifted on its foundations. But he's not going over there to read the message, or even check to see who it's from. Why is that?

'I think you just got a text,' I say über-casually, then pick up a tea towel and saunter over to the draining board. 'Want me to see who it was?'

He's working on getting a particularly stubborn bit of baked cheese off the side of the lasagne dish and doesn't look up: this job apparently requires full concentration. 'Oh, did I? No, no need,' he says lightly. 'I'll have a look in a minute.'

I nod slowly. 'Oh, OK.'

Adam finishes the dish, carefully rinses the soap off under the cold tap, then places it gently upside down on the draining board. He empties the washing-up bowl, turns it over, wipes its base, then wipes the excess water from the draining board. Finally he turns and walks to where I'm listlessly drying a wine glass. He's smiling as he reaches out towards me but I don't move. As soon as his fingers touch the tea towel in my hand, they stop approaching and intertwine themselves into the fabric, drying off.

'Great grub, Gracie,' he says, then grins and raises his head to look at me. 'And I'm pleased to announce that the Wife of the Year award goes to . . .' He performs a miniature drum roll with his index fingers on the kitchen side. 'Oh, well, no surprises there, she's been the hot favourite right from the beginning, it's last year's winner, it's Mrs Grace Littleton!' He raises his arms and makes whispery crowd cheering noises in the back of his throat, while glancing around the kitchen at his imaginary audience. I smile at him, charmed by his boyishness as usual, and, for the moment anyway, the mysterious text message goes out of my head.

'Come on,' he says, jerking his head towards the door, 'let's watch the lottery. Did you get the ticket?'

'Yep, it's in my bag.' I retrieve the ticket from my handbag on the kitchen chair and follow him into the living room.

Adam and I have been married just a year – today is our first anniversary actually. We exchanged presents over dinner. One year is paper – I know this because I Googled it a few days ago – so I bought him a book called *Keeping the Magic Alive: How to Get and Give Satisfying Lifelong Sex* by someone called Dr Cristina Markowitz. On the front there was a full-colour photo of a pair of gorgeous naked models pretending to be a satisfied married couple, and the whole thing was wrapped in clingfilm, presumably so that people couldn't sneak into Smiths when they ran into difficulties, read up on a couple of tips, then dash back home again to finish the job. There was a nasty moment when I was paying for it involving Chloe on the till holding the book up in the air and shouting at top volume down the store '*BRYONY! HOW MUCH IS THE SEX BOOK? BAR CODE WON'T SCAN*', but eventually I'd carried it home (in my fingertips, like a hot coal) and wrapped it in cool blue shiny paper, releasing a tense breath once it was finally sheathed. A small part of me half expected the steamy photo on the front to burn through the wrapping paper, like the lost Ark of the Covenant, leaving a naked-body-shaped scorch mark on the outside.

I'd grinned as Adam opened it earlier, hoping he'd get the joke. I thought it was absolutely hilarious that someone had written a book about it, and more than that, that somewhere people were actually sitting down and reading it. 'Ooh, look at this one, Steven, do you think we could manage that?' 'Oh I don't know, Barbara, I've got that presentation tomorrow. What else is there?' For crying out loud, people, stop reading books about it and do it!

Adam looked at me quizzically once he'd unwrapped it. 'Wow. Um, you trying to tell me something, Gracie?'

I broke eye contact as I answered. 'No, no, of course not, but don't you think it's hysterical? I mean, imagine Steve and Barb in bed together flicking through the pages . . .'

'Who are they?'

I frowned. 'No, no one, just imaginary people, I'm just pretending.'

'Oh right.' He opened the book at a random page and read in silence for a few moments. 'Very interesting,' he concluded, then closed it and laid it on the table. It practically sizzled when it touched the surface. 'Thank you very much.'

I was disappointed. He had completely missed the joke. 'You're welcome.'

If I'm completely honest, I was also hoping he might read it. The couple on the front looked like they were having such a tremendous time, and I so wanted to experience that. Even though we'd been married an entire year – or only a year, whichever way you look at it – Adam and I did not partake of the old horizontal refreshment all that frequently. From what I'd seen in magazines and films, newlyweds were supposed to be at it like they were stuffing turkeys every day, with great big grins on their faces and sweaty, shiny bodies. But this was not my own experience. 'Hardly ever' was closer to my magic number.

4

Of course, films are fiction, and those magazine interviewees could have been exaggerating, knowing that what they said was going to become public knowledge. They probably were – their mates would see it. But even allowing for that, I still felt short-changed.

My present was a gorgeous bunch of carnations, with guaranteed freshness for seven days. I'd put them in a vase immediately and placed them in the centre of the table. 'Lovely, thank you.'

He'd smiled, pleased with my reaction. 'No problem. Shall we eat?'

We haven't won on the lottery again. I never expect to, and would be happy to stop doing it altogether – it seems so greedy when we already have so much – but Adam always wants me to buy a ticket on the way home. 'It's fun,' he says, 'something for us to enjoy together.' I'm completely in favour of that, so I oblige, week after week, stopping in at the newsagents on the corner of our street on my walk home from town every Friday. The bloke behind the counter recognises me now, and has started to pre-empt my request with a 'Still not won, then?' remark. It irritates me probably more than it should.

After the lottery results, we watch a cheerful film about a man whose daughter is kidnapped and sold into prostitution, and then we decide to call it a night.

I'm in the kitchen finishing off the clearing up and, as I'm wiping down the tiles behind the sink, I remember suddenly Adam's text from earlier. He hasn't been in here since then so his phone must still be over on the counter by the kettle. I could have a very quick look at the preview, just to find out who it's from. I won't actually open it and read it, I'll literally just look at the name. Of course, the first part of the message will be visible in the preview as well anyway, so it won't matter if I read that bit – anyone could see it as it's on display so it can't be that private, and I won't be able to help it. I glance up at the kitchen door, listen carefully for a few seconds and, hearing nothing, I move quickly over to the kettle and start hunting around. The phone must be here, but I discover straight away that it's not where I remember last seeing it. I look behind the kettle but of course it's not there either. I check the entire length of all three kitchen sides, in the sink, behind the microwave and have a cursory glance into all the cupboards, but it's not to be found. Where the hell is it? Adam has definitely not come back into the kitchen since we left to watch the lottery earlier, so how could it have moved?

Unless. A dart of frustration shoots through me briefly. He did get up once during the film, to go to the loo. 'Ooh, pause it a second,' he said, 'need a wee.' Then he was up and out of there like his trousers were on fire. Strange for him to move like that, just for a wee. But now it's obvious: he must have suddenly realised his phone wasn't in his pocket, and rushed to pick it up from the kitchen on his way upstairs. Bloody hell, that was probably my only chance to find out who the text was from. Although the three times that I've actually managed to get my hands on his phone since I've known him, it's had an impossible-to-break screen lock code on it. No amount of combinations of his birthday, my birthday . . . well, they're the only two things I've tried, to be honest, as I have no other information to go on.

But I couldn't unlock it. It might as well have been in a box, locked inside a safe with a secret key, buried underground, for all the good it did me.

But there's always the chance that the lock won't be on. That's what keeps me going.

When I get upstairs, he's already in the bedroom, but no sound is coming from the room. I remember to step over the penultimate stair to avoid making it creak, then stealthily cross the landing and peep into the bedroom through the crack of the door. Sure enough, there is Adam, standing motionless at the end of the bed, staring down at the screen of his mobile phone, the light from it illuminating his face bluish white. He's not replying, not smiling, not reacting at all to what he's reading. Unless you consider his non-reaction as a reaction in itself. It's spooky actually, his complete lack of response to this message. He's utterly immobile, as if frozen.

'Ooh, it's a bit chilly in here,' I say, blustering in. I'm rewarded by him jumping guiltily and slipping the phone fluidly into his trouser pocket as he turns to me with a smile. I feel a small leap of hope: he didn't get a chance to delete the message.

'Come on then,' he says, as if nothing has happened, 'let's get into bed and warm each other up.'

A little spark of excitement fires in my lower belly at these words, and I shed my clothes in a single movement. This is it – it's our anniversary, when better to indulge in a little happy dancing than tonight? Once we're under the covers, he moves close up behind me, his knees just brushing the backs of my thighs. My belly starts squirming as I feel his hot breath on my neck, then I shiver as very gently he places his freezing hands flat against my back. Then he turns them over and presses their cold backs to my skin. 'Ooh, that's lush,' he murmurs, then turns them over again.

Everyone thinks Adam is out of my league. They don't actually say it – not to me anyway – but I can see it in their eyes when they look at us. Even my own mum, for God's sake. She kind of glances from me to him and back again, then gives a tiny uncomprehending shake of her head before turning away. She thinks I haven't noticed, but of course I have. My sister Lauren fancies him rotten and wouldn't hesitate to betray our sisterly bond if she ever got the chance. I'm not sure I'd even blame her. Adam is tall and handsome and successful and charming and everyone adores him, my family in particular. That's not to say they don't adore *me*. Of course they do. They're always 'Oh Gracie, you're so funny' and 'Isn't Gracie just fantastic?' and 'You look pretty today, Gracie.' But when I first brought Adam home to meet everyone on take-away night three years ago, it was a family bucket of shock and awe all round.

'Hi everyone,' I said proudly. 'This is Adam.'

They looked up as one from what they were doing – watching *Doctor Who*, I think – and stared open-mouthed at the golden Adonis that had dropped from Mount Olympus to stand at my side. There was a brief hiatus during which the Tardis materialised noisily, then Mum and my brother Robbie were scrabbling for the remote – 'Pause it, pause it, quick, who's got the thing, who's got the *cocking thing*?' 'I've got it, Christ, stop pressuring me, I'm doing it!' – Lauren was standing up slowly, trying to look like Pussy Galore; and Dad leaned back in his chair with a satisfied grin, as if to say, 'finally'.

Adam looked coolly at everyone in turn, appraising, taking in, sizing up; and then, with a slow nod, said, 'So. You're the ones.'

'The ones who?' was the general enquiry that came from everyone. He paused before answering, so his statement had maximum impact. 'The four people in the world who think *Doctor Who* is worth watching.'

Adam was my landlord. Don't worry, no impropriety took place, a tenant dating her landlord; I've Googled it and there's nothing that says it's inappropriate. It's not as if he took advantage of me while I was renting a room in his house or anything hideous like that. No strategic holes in bathroom walls, no cameras planted in my room, no sleaze; just a shop on the high street. I'd gone in there a few months earlier to enquire about a flat I'd seen advertised in the local paper. My friend Annabel Price had lived there after having her illicit baby when the rest of us were still in the sixth form, and we all used to pile round after school and pretend to be grown-ups, alternating between consuming coffee and cigarettes on the fire escape, and holding the baby; while somewhere in the background Annabel sobbed into her sterilising tank.

I knew that hideous little place, I knew its mouldy walls and its stained carpets and the latent nappy smell and when I saw it advertised a thrill of excitement went through me and I got a fatalistic sense that it had been waiting for me. I was twenty-four at the time, so it was aeons and aeons since I'd left school, and here was a chance to relive those heady days. I'd had no desire at all to leave my parents' place until that moment; but for Annabel Price's flat, I knew I could make the break.

Adam was sitting at the single desk in his tiny office, which was squeezed in between the East of India and the dry cleaners. It had a plate-glass front with his name, 'Adam Littleton', etched onto it in an arc, and underneath it said 'Estate Management'. It was very impressive. It was August and the sun was shining straight through that enormous window covering the floor with a gorgeous golden carpet, so inside was barbarically hot. As soon as I stepped through the door, my instinct was to run from the fire, but Adam looked at me and smiled, so I stayed. I did want that flat, after all.

'Hi, how can I help?' he asked straight away, standing up and coming around the desk, allowing no chance at all for the potential customer – me – to change their mind and leave.

I scanned the properties displayed on the walls, hoping to see the advert for the flat that had appeared in the paper. A small desk fan was rotating ineffectually on the desk. 'Um, I saw a flat, in the paper . . .'

'OK. Which paper was it?'

I blinked. I had been expecting him to ask which flat it was. 'I think it was the *Herald*. It was a one-bedroom . . .' But in that very small space of time, like a magician, he'd produced a sheet of paper from somewhere and was holding it out to me to check.

'Is this the one?'

I moved forward and took one end of the paper. 'Yes, that's it.' I looked up at him. 'Is it still available?'

He whipped the paper away dramatically. 'You don't want to live there,' he said, theatrically screwing up the sheet of paper and tossing it backwards over his shoulder, 'it's a dump.'

'Oh, well, no, the thing is—'

'Now, I've got something for you that's a lot more suitable,' he said, rubbing his hands together and opening and closing his fingers. 'A much nicer place, coming on in a few days.'

'But I don't—'

'Take it from me, you won't believe your eyes when you see this.' He focused on my eyes for a split second longer than necessary, rubbed his hands together again and flexed his fingers, then delicately reached into his top jacket pocket and pulled out a small, folded piece of paper. It was approximately the size of a postage stamp.

I stared down at it in the palm of his hand, then looked up at him and pressed my lips together. 'I'm sure it's lovely, but I don't think it's big enough for me.'

There was a second's pause, then he burst out laughing, throwing his head back and guffawing fruitily, then leaning forward and clutching his tummy. It all felt a bit . . . exaggerated, as if he was trying to give me the impression that he thought I was hysterically funny, rather than actually thinking I was hysterically funny.

As I waited for him to calm down, waves of heat started to pour over me and I could feel sweat beading out everywhere. Eventually he stood up again and wiped his eyes, puffing out a couple of 'whoo!'s and nodding appreciatively at me. 'Oh my God, that was hilarious!'

he proclaimed. 'You're very funny.' Incredibly, he still looked cool and dry, in spite of the heat.

'Thank you. Um, can I just find out about the—?'

'So this property is not even being advertised yet,' he cut in, and began unfolding the sheet in his hand. 'It's so much more you, if you'll forgive me. Classy, attractive, modern and stylish. I think you're going to love it.'

I tried to raise my eyebrows sceptically, to indicate that I was not the type to succumb to mindless flattery. But inside my mind was jumping up and down and squealing, 'He thinks I'm attractive!'

And he was right, the flat did look lovely. Obviously very recently decorated; new bathroom and kitchenette; brand new carpets everywhere; light, spacious rooms. It was definitely going to be far more than I could afford. 'There's no price on here,' I pointed out, searching through the information sheet. 'How much is the rent?'

'Same as that other place.'

I widened my eyes. 'No way!'

He nodded decisively. 'Totally way.'

I stared down at the photos. 'I don't believe it.' I looked up at him and found his eyes on me. *He thinks I'm attractive!* 'It does look gorgeous,' I said, holding out the sheet of paper towards him, 'but I'm not sure it's what I'm looking for.'

'In what way?'

He was so abrupt, I was a bit startled. 'Oh, um, only that it was that flat in the paper, on Hardwick Road, that I wanted specifically. I like it.'

'But why would you want somewhere shabby like that when you can have this beautiful new place for the same money?' He actually scratched his head. 'It just doesn't add up.'

I thought about it for a moment. He did make a very good point. But I had been so happy in Annabel's flat, all those years ago. 'No, well, it does for me. So, is it available?'

He leaned against the edge of the desk and put his hands down on either side. 'Look, um, Miss . . .?'

'Grace. Just call me Grace.'

'OK, Grace. I'm going to make an assumption about you, if you'll allow me. You're planning on moving into this flat on your own, right?'

'Well that's fairly evident, seeing as I'm here on my own.'

'Right. So you'll be living there alone. What will you do if you need to change a fuse? What if the pipes burst? What if the electrics cause a fire? Supposing you need to re-plaster somewhere, or grout something. What will you do?'

I shrugged, trying to look nonchalant, although a seed of anxiety was germinating inside me. 'Isn't all that down to the landlord?'

He smiled smugly. 'Not everything, Grace. Not decorating. Not emergency repairs in the middle of the night. Even if he does take responsibility, he's got to get there, hasn't he? What if you've got water flooding through the ceiling at three a.m., destroying all your belongings, soaking the carpet and the plaster, putting you at risk of a ceiling collapse? What will you do then?'

I hadn't really thought about any of that, and was now fully gripped by panic. But I certainly didn't want him to know it. I'd have to Google what to do later. 'I'll do the simple things myself and get my dad to do the rest. Why?'

He shook his head patronisingly, as if no way in hell was I ever going to cope with anything. 'Wouldn't it just be easier if you got a place that didn't need anything doing to it? So you'd never have to worry about anything or think about anything or pay for anything?'

Fifteen minutes later, we were looking round the new place. Turned out to be his own flat, just above the shop. I wandered around the large cream rooms and compared them mentally to Annabel's woodchip and cramped kitchen. I had to admit, this place was attractive. An hour after first walking into Adam's shop, I'd signed the contract and agreed to meet for dinner the following evening. Adam told me months later that as soon as I'd walked in, he wanted me to rent it. He liked me that much, that quickly.

The next day is Sunday and we have a long lie-in then wander round to the pub for their very reasonable carvery lunch. The broccoli is over-cooked, and the spuds are still cold in the middle, but it is so reasonable, and so convenient.

'How's your meal?' Adam asks me, enthusiastically forking turkey into his mouth.

I nod. 'S'fine.'

He nods back. 'I love this place. Don't you? I mean, it's so great. All this food, at this price, and just round the corner.'

When we come out after dinner, it's started raining so we run shrieking back to our house then snuggle up on the sofa to watch a romance about a woman whose husband gets killed so she slaughters everyone responsible.

The text message is on my mind all day. And all the next day, while we're both at work. All week, in fact. Repeatedly I try to get on my own in a room with the phone, but fail because the phone is always in Adam's possession. He doesn't let it out of his sight for four days straight. Then, on Thursday evening, he takes it out of his pocket to answer a call from his mum, and at the end, after clicking it off and closing it down, he distractedly places it on the kitchen table. I freeze. I am electrified, and my eyes immediately zoom in on it lying there as he walks away. It's exposed, vulnerable, and I need to attack. We move around it, preparing the dinner, back and forth across the kitchen, and I'm acutely aware of it the entire time. I can't stop thinking about it. It's permanently in my periphery, the only thing I can see. When will he leave the room? He must need the toilet eventually – surely he will leave it there when he goes? It would look very suss if he goes off upstairs for a wee and stops at the table on the way to pick up his phone. Surely he would want to avoid arousing my suspicion like that?

'Gracie?'

His voice finally breaks through my reverie. 'Hmm? Sorry?'

'Wake up, dolly daydream. I've asked you three times to put the kettle on for the gravy. You're miles away.'

'Oh, sorry, just thinking about Dad. You know his birthday is coming up. I've got no idea what to get him. What do you think?'

'Oh, I don't know, you're good at that kind of thing,

15

I'll leave it to you.' He turns away. 'Just popping to the loo.'

I nod, watching in horror as he moves back towards the table. 'Um, do you want a drink, Ad? How about a beer?'

He stops, turns back, looks at me. I hold my breath. 'Yeah, OK, thanks.' He turns back to the table and takes the final two steps to get there, then scoops up the phone and without breaking stride slips it into his pocket. Then he's through the door and on his way upstairs.

Friday night comes around again and I'm home first, as usual. We've already agreed we're having take-away tonight, so I've got no dinner preparations to make. The house is stifling, and the first thing I do is unlock the sliding back door and push it open. It makes no difference; the gentle breeze on the street hasn't made it to our enclosed garden, and the heat and I move around the yard sluggishly in oppressive waves. I head back inside to wash up the breakfast things, straighten the cushions on the sofa, twitch the curtains. I'm just killing time until he comes home, but I have literally nothing to do and I can't relax.

'You need some hobbies,' Mum is always saying. 'Why don't you take up knitting?'

Yeah, I know what that means. There's absolutely no way I'm having a baby yet. Not with Adam, anyway.

I stop, midway through a pointless wander across the hallway. What the bloody hell does that mean, 'not with Adam'? Who the hell else will I have a baby with? He's my husband, isn't he? I know I definitely want kids some day, so what am I actually thinking? That when the time is right, I'll go off and do it with someone else? Of course not.

Although the chance to get pregnant in the first place would be nice.

When the phone rings in the living room a few minutes later, I'm standing in the kitchen staring into the fridge for some reason. I slam it shut and move swiftly to the living room, grateful to have a purpose at last. Just as my hand reaches out to grab the receiver, I hesitate. It'll only be insurance sales after all; they're the only people who ring the landline any more. Well, pseudo-people. No actual fingers press actual keys.

The answer phone clicks on and plays its message, and after the beep I wait to hear the usual spooky silence of the computer checking to see if anyone is there and then giving up and going down the pub. But instead I'm shocked to hear the sound of a man's deep voice coming into my living room from the speaker.

'Hello *Adam*, it's *Leon*. Long time no see. Betcha didn't expect to hear from me again, did you? Come as a bit of a shock, has it? Ha, I bet it has. Just thought I'd give you a call, let you know I'm in the area – nearby actually. *Very* nearby. Would only take me two minutes to get to your place from here. Piece of cake. I'm gonna try to catch up with you *very* soon. Don't worry about calling me back, I'll be in touch.'

The phone clicks as *Leon* replaces the receiver, and the room falls silent. In my mind I could hear the italics in his voice, particularly as he said those two names, as if just in saying them he was trying to make some kind of point. But what point could he possibly be making?

And why? And, by the way, who the fuck is *Leon*? We've been married a year, how come *Adam* has never mentioned him to me before? I know everything about him, all his friends, all his old jobs, where he used to live, everything.

Ha ha ha. That's just me being sarcastic with myself. I, of course, know none of those things. A creepy phone call from a weirdo called *Leon* should not be remotely surprising, considering what I do know about Adam.

I don't have any more time to consider it now as I hear Adam's car on the drive. He's home. I walk away from the phone and go into the hall to greet him, as I always do.

'Hi there,' he says as he sees me. 'Good day?'

I nod. 'Yeah, not bad. You?'

He nods too. 'Yeah, good.' He starts up the stairs and I follow behind. 'Finally sorted out that three-bed semi in Whitlow.'

'Oh good.'

'Yep. The owner can't believe it. He thinks I'm a god!' He starts to change his clothes.

I sit down on the bed and watch as, god-like, he folds his dirty shirt in half, then in half again, then places it carefully into the laundry basket behind the door. As he straightens the creases in his trousers before hanging them up, I remember the call from earlier.

'Oh, there was a call for you.'

'Yeah?' He's dressed again now and heads back downstairs. Dutifully, I follow behind. 'Chinese or Indian?'

'Neither, actually. He sounded English, I think. Possibly London or home counties . . .'

I come into the kitchen where he's standing with the

East of India's menu in one hand and the Moon Hung Lo's in the other. 'What?'

'Oh, sorry, I thought you meant . . . Um, we haven't had Chinese for a while, have we?'

He bounces the menus up and down in his hands as he looks at me with a smile. 'No, that's true, but I'm really in the mood for a good curry tonight. What do you think?'

What I *think* is that we haven't had Chinese for a while, and actually I would run through our street singing 'Don't Stop Me Now' wearing nothing but a splash of perfume and three gold tassels for the chance to eat sweet and sour chicken balls, just once. But I nod and smile nauseatingly. I despise myself sometimes. 'OK, yes, curry would be lovely. Thanks.'

'Cool.' He puts the menu down on the kitchen counter and brings his phone out of his pocket. As always, I feel a stab of . . . *something* when I see it. Or at least, my eyes do. They kind of jolt to attention as it comes into view, like a dog spotting a squirrel. Adam scans the menu, looking for the restaurant's phone number. 'Did you say there was a call for me?'

'Oh, yes, there was. Someone called . . . *Leon* . . .'

His head snaps up, the hand holding his phone frozen in mid-air. 'Who?'

I manage to drag my eyes away from the phone to focus on Adam. His usual air of ease and nonchalance is gone abruptly, replaced by an intense stark alarm. 'What's up?'

'Who did you say called?'

I frown, hesitating before speaking to let him know I'm not pleased with how he's behaving. If I'm brutally honest, I also do it to torture him, just a teensy bit. 'It was Leon.'

He brings his face closer to mine. 'What did he say?' He's speaking slowly, his hands still not moving.

'Um, well he said something about being in the area—'

'Shit.'

'—and that he would see you soon.'

'Oh *shit*. Anything else?'

By now, the phone is back in his pocket and the take-away menu all but forgotten. My stomach notices this and gives a loud growl in protest.

'You can hear for yourself – it's on the answer phone.'

Adam bursts into life, turning and marching rapidly into the living room. Seconds later I hear the answer phone message playing, that deep gravelly voice filling our cosy living space like a bad smell. When it reaches the click at the end, there's the sound of a small move-ment, then the beep and the voice comes on again. 'Hello *Adam* . . .' At the end, Adam plays it a third time, and then a fourth, until my head is filled with that horrible raspy voice, pointedly saying my husband's name, over and over.

I walk quietly into the hallway and peer through the open door into the room; Adam is staring at the phone, unmoving, apparently frozen. Thinking hard? Undecided? Then in a sudden dart he looks up, catches my eye, and hurries past me, up the stairs. 'Who's Leon then?' I ask pointlessly, running after him. He strides into our bedroom, but before I can catch him up, he's out again, passing me on the stairs as he runs back down.

'Oh, no one. Just someone I . . . used to work with. Years ago.'

'Oh, right. So why are you so pissed off?'

He stops in the hallway and turns to face me. I'm standing on the bottom stair still, so for once we're about the same height. He puts his hand out and gently touches my cheek. 'I'm not pissed off, Grace. Not really. I don't like the bloke, we fell out at school and I wasn't expecting ever to hear from him again. That's all.'

'I thought you said you used to work with him?'

He puts his arm back down and puts his hand into his pocket. 'Yeah, that's right, I did, we worked together for a while after we left school, but we didn't really have much to do with each other.' The hand in his pocket reappears holding the car keys, and he jingles them a bit, distractedly. 'He's a bit of a prick, to be honest.'

'Oh.'

'Yeah. World-class knobhead.' He looks at his watch then back at me, and smiles fondly. 'OK, well, I'm off to get the food.' He leans towards me, one hand round the back of my neck, and kisses me. As we break apart, he stays close, his thumb gently stroking my neck. 'Don't worry about him, Gracie. He's nothing.'

I nod. 'OK.'

He stares into my eyes for a few moments, kisses me again, then draws away and moves to the door. 'Warm the plates up, sweetheart, I'll be back in a few minutes.'

He wasn't.

TWO

Twenty minutes after Adam left finds me pacing the living room. I've put plates in the oven, got some wine ready and selected a few DVDs for him to choose from, but that only took a minute or two. Now I'm walking from the back window to the front, lifting up the curtain, peering out at the street then turning and walking to the back again. There must be a long queue in the Indian. And of course we never actually got round to ordering the food so he will have to wait while it's prepared and cooked. It could take, ooh, at least, I don't know, half an hour. But it's already been . . . Never mind, never mind, if there's a queue he could wait fifty minutes, easily. An hour, even. It's possible. Maybe he's had to try a few different places. Maybe he's bumped into someone he knows and has lost all track of time. Maybe he's bumped into *Leon*.

After about two hours, I've stopped pacing and am now sitting on the edge of the sofa, rocking backwards and forwards and occasionally biting the hard skin around my fingernails. I've got my own mobile phone loose in my hand but it's as good as useless when the one, the *only* person I want to contact has apparently switched his phone off. That sodding phone of his, full of mysteries and unknowns, always *always* with him, constantly lighting up and vibrating all over the place; but now, when I really need to use it, when it will be of more use than it ever has been before – to me, anyway – it's in his pocket in complete darkness. Oh my God, why would he do that? Why would anyone? What's the arsing point of having an arsing mobile if it's arsing switched off, for arse's sake?

I did wonder whether it's not switched off at all, maybe he simply hit a black spot or whatever it's called, so I've texted, Facebooked and WhatsApped him too. That way, if he does happen to get a fraction of a second of signal, he'll see my messages. At least then he could try to call me from a phone box, to put my mind at ease.

But he's called me before from the East of India. Or rather, I've called him there before. I know I have, I remember it. He forgot to ask me what I wanted, so I rang to tell him, to make sure he didn't come back with a vindaloo for me like the first time, when he didn't know I don't like spicy food. Which means I know there's no black spot there. Which means he's turned his phone off.

Unless he didn't go to the East of India . . .

I jump up out of frustration, wanting to shout angrily at Adam, wanting to shriek at him, wanting to throw my head back and scream at the ceiling. But I don't. Of course I don't. I turn down the bubbling volcano of fury that's threatening to erupt and try to think clearly. Why would he be taking so long? Did he go somewhere else? Or has something happened to him? Something . . . *bad*?

I walk over to the answer phone and listen to *Leon* again. I don't know why, the message isn't going to tell me where Adam is. But I have to keep hearing it. It seems connected to his prolonged absence somehow. Or is it simply a pleasant message from an old friend, wanting to catch up? It doesn't sound like it to me, but then my opinion is not really objective. I have my own feelings about Adam that colour every interaction he has with anyone else.

I press play yet again. 'Hello *Adam*, it's *Leon* . . .'

Something about that unknown point he's making when he says their names now sounds a bit menacing. Or am I imagining things, bearing in mind *Adam* went out for food over two hours ago and still hasn't come back?

I start suddenly. A car. There's a car pulling onto the driveway. Oh, thank *God*. He's safe. A giant flame of rage roars into life in me suddenly, along with my almost forgotten hunger. But why the *fuck* did it take him so long? I clench my jaw, my fists, and every other muscle in my body. Even my eyelids go rigid. Ooh you secretive sod, do you have some explaining to do. I charge over to the window and yank back the curtain. It's almost completely dark by now and I have to press my face to the glass to see out. My own face, distorted by a vicious snarl, lunges at me in the blackness. Where's the car? Where's that prickish little car? There's nothing on the driveway yet so I look at the road, to see the silver Corsa with its reversing lights on. But it's not there. There's

24

only one car there and it's an ordinary blue car, simply driving past. It doesn't stop. It doesn't discharge my husband, rescued after a cam belt disaster. It doesn't yield anything.

I drop the curtain and drop my hands and a small sound comes out of me. The hunger disappears, forgotten again, but the anger doesn't. In fact, the anger starts to swell again and turn white, blinding white, expanding inside me until I feel I can't contain it any more and I put my hands on my head and shout 'AAARRRSE!' as loudly as I can. It comes out a bit screamy – 'AAAAAAAHHHHHSE!'

When I stop, the house falls instantly silent. Supernaturally so. Like all the things that usually make a noise also suddenly stop. The fridge isn't humming, no pipes are clunking, there's no creaking, clicking, ticking or cracking. Everything is completely and utterly still. The house feels like it's waiting.

That's it, I'm calling Ginger. I've wanted to for over an hour already but managed to convince myself not to; managed to convince myself I was over-reacting. But she's my best friend in the whole world, she'll know whether I'm over-reacting or not. I spend the next few minutes rooting through my handbag, then frantically running from room to room looking for my phone, before remembering that it's already in my hand. I close my eyes. I growl a bit at myself. Come on, focus.

Ginger isn't ginger, actually. She has gorgeous, shiny brown hair, and her name is in fact Louise, but because her baby brother Matthew once painted her whole head red with poster paint when they were tots, she's been

Ginger, or Ginge, ever since. She answers on the second ring.

'Hey, Gee, how's you?'

I open my mouth and a kind of whimpering sound comes out.

'Grace?'

'Ginge . . .' It comes out as a breathy sob.

'On my way,' she says simply.

There's a sharp pain in the side of my head and I realise suddenly that I'm pressing the phone too hard into my ear. I ease it away and my ear throbs with the rush of blood.

So now I have about fifteen minutes to wait until she gets here. It's a huge relief to wait for something that has a definite and predictable ending. Although Adam going to the Indian take-away was in that category originally. Now that he's been gone for over three and a half hours, I'm starting to wonder if . . .

I halt that thought mid-way. Of *course* he's coming back. That's just mad thinking. His car's broken down and his phone's out of battery. That's all. I'll feel ridiculous in about one minute when he arrives in a taxi. I pull the curtain back for the thousandth time, more slowly now, not really able to convince myself any longer that *this* time he will be there. Sure enough, yet again there's no taxi. No AA recovery lorry either. Not even a police car. No one at all.

'Right, so what's going on?' Ginge demands as soon as she's in through the front door. She's business-like and determined but when she looks at my face she falters. 'Good God, Gee, what's happened?'

'It's Adam . . .' I begin, but immediately she starts nodding meaningfully. I stop and frown. 'Why are you nodding like that?'

'What do you mean? How else am I supposed to nod? It's a fairly standard gesture. Internationally recognised.'

'No. Ginge. Why are you nodding *at all*?'

She shrugs. 'I don't know. I'm listening to you. What's your point? Tell me what he's done, for Pete's sake.'

I narrow my eyes. 'Why would you assume he's done something?'

She looks momentarily discomfited and moves her head back slightly. 'Well, hasn't he?'

I think for a second. *Has* he? Ginger moves her head forward again and raises her eyebrows, waiting. Suddenly, I feel like I don't want her there. She's irritating the crap out of me and, as I look at her freckly face peering at me, a very large part of me wants to slap it. I can actually feel my arm start to move backwards so I stop it and clench my fists.

'He went out to get a pasanda about—' I glance at my watch – 'nearly four hours ago.'

'And?'

I shrug. 'There is no "And".'

She frowns. 'I don't get it. Where is he now?'

'That's the point. I don't know. He hasn't come back.'

She stares at me for a second, her eyes widening. 'Oh, fucking hell.'

Within minutes she's made tea for us both and installed me on the sofa while she phones round all the hospitals in the area. There's only one in our town but she phones the two neighbouring towns too, just in case. I know he's got ID on him so someone would contact me if he's been admitted, but at least it feels like we're doing something.

'Dead,' Ginge says, clicking her phone off and palming it.

'Wha-at?'

'A and E. They're all dead. Nothing's happening anywhere apparently.'

'Oh. Right.' I'm not sure whether that's a relief or not. No, it is. I mean, yes, of course it is. A huge relief. Except I still don't know a single thing. At least I would have known . . . *something* if he'd been admitted somewhere. I look up at Ginge. 'So, what now?'

She fiddles with her phone for a second, then comes over to sit next to me. 'I think it's time to call the police.' She puts the phone into my hand and we both stare down at it.

'You suggesting we call Matt?'

Matt is Ginger's little brother. He's a local PC, or DC, or PCSO or something now. Last time I spoke to him he was a silent, skeletal seventeen-year-old with dyed black hair and a nose ring. According to their mum, Mrs Blake, he 'got in with the wrong crowd' back then and barely came home for a few years, then apparently turned things round and joined the force. The thought of speaking to a policeman is made a bit less terrifying if it's a geeky, awkward, slightly familiar stranger with pimples rather than an intimidating, black-coated stranger with a notebook.

Ginger shakes her head. 'No, I mean the real police.'

'What's he then? Toy Town?'

28

'No, silly. I just mean you need to report it. Officially. Not just get Matt round here for a cuppa.' She pauses. 'Much as I'm sure he'd be up for it.'

I think furiously for a few seconds. Ginger and I have known each other since school, back when we had to pad our bras and smoke to look older. Now we work together in a costume shop called DisGuys and DisGirls in the main pedestrianised part of the town. I've been there four years; she's been there six. She's kind of the assistant manager or something. Unofficially of course. She doesn't get paid a higher responsibility allowance or anything. She just has control of the keys and the cashbox when Penny is away. It's only a set of keys and a cashbox, but it gives her the edge over me when it comes to taking charge of a situation.

I push the phone towards her. 'You do it.'

'No, Grace, I can't, can I? It's your husband, you're going to have to do it yourself.'

'You could pretend to be me.'

She widens her eyes, as if in . . . revulsion. Or do I imagine that? 'No, I absolutely could not do that, come on now.'

I stare at the phone in my hand; its smooth, shiny surface and pleasing heaviness have never looked more menacing. I so don't want to do this. I'll feel silly, like I'm wasting their time. It's only been a few hours. I look up at Ginger. 'We can't report him yet though, can we? Doesn't he have to be missing for twenty-four hours first, or something?'

'What makes you think that?'

'It's one of those things that everyone knows, isn't it?

29

You have to give them time to get over their sulk, or affair, or secret surgery, or whatever, and come home of their own accord. We'll just be wasting their time.'

She shakes her head and looks at me the way a traffic warden looks at a car on double yellows. 'I think you've been watching too many crime dramas, love. It's not like that in real life.'

'How do you know? Have you reported someone missing before?'

She puts her hand on my arm. 'Hey, come on. You can do it. Just dial the number, say what's happened, and that's that.'

Turns out it's actually quite difficult finding the right number to ring. I'm thinking 999, but Ginger says that's emergencies only and I say well what the fuck is this if it's not an emergency and she says it only means it's for an urgent kind of emergency like a crime actually happening at that moment and I say well maybe it is how the hell can we possibly know that we have literally no clue what's happening or happened to him that's why we need to ring and she says actually I think we've both got a bit of an inkling to be honest haven't we and I say what the hell is that supposed to mean and she says nothing sorry didn't mean anything and then she goes into the other room to see if she can find a Yellow Pages in the kitchen drawer.

'I've rung them,' she announces softly, coming back into the room a few minutes later. I'm standing at the window again, peering out. A cat is brazenly washing itself at the end of our driveway, apparently very confident that it's not going to get flattened by a returning Corsa

30

any time soon. I turn to look at Ginger and nod, weak with gratitude. Thank God that's done and I don't have to face them or answer any horrible questions.

'They're on their way over,' she goes on. 'They want to ask you some questions.'

So twenty minutes later the police turn up and I tell them what happened with Adam and the East of India, and then they interrogate me about his likes and dislikes and habits and hobbies and friends and associates. Once I've explained his line of work and the location of his office, I know that there is very little more I can say, so I watch them closely as I answer: they're very nice and softly spoken and write down the answers I give in their little black notebooks, but I notice their expressions, the furtive looks they're giving each other, the barely concealed surprise or contempt or impatience with me as I tell them the things I know about my husband.

'OK, Mrs Littleton, I need to know who your husband's work associates are?'

'I don't know.'

'Just one or two of them, then. His main contact. Don't worry, we can probably find out the rest.'

'I don't know.'

'OK, not to worry. Who are his drinking mates? And we'll need their addresses, if you can remember them?'

'I don't know.'

'Oh. Well, just his best mate then?'

I shrug. 'I don't know.'

There's a very brief pause and the two officers glance at each other. 'OK, never mind. Where does he drink?

What are his hobbies? Where did he go to school? What sport does he follow? Which team does he support?'

I look at them both, and then at Ginger. 'I don't know.'

There's an awkward, slightly longer silence. Then the female officer leans towards me. 'Can you try, Grace? Think really hard. Has he ever mentioned anyone, or talked about a place, the name of a pub, a street even?'

I'm already shaking my head because I know I don't need to think hard about this. There's no point. He has kept everything about himself completely shut off from me, right from the very start of our relationship, right from that moment I stepped into his office looking for a flat to rent. I have tried and tried to find something out about him – asked his mum and step-dad, checked his post, tried to sneak a look at his phone – but I've never got anywhere. His mum and step-dad, Julia and Ray Moorfield, just say, 'Ah, you'll have to ask Adam about that, lovey.' All he told me about his real dad is that he's no longer around, then closed the conversation off definitively. 'What more do you need to know?' he said, when I questioned it. And then peered at me, as if I was under a microscope, somehow managing to make me feel horrible for asking. 'He's not around any more, that's that. Jesus, Grace, do you have to know every single minute detail about all your friends' lives? Is that who you are?' His post is always generic bills or advertisements. His phone is completely and permanently inaccessible. The absence of any information about him has become like a third person in our marriage. The single piece of information that I do have about Adam is that I have absolutely no information about him.

'Adam never talks about his past, or his work, or what he does when we aren't together. He just doesn't.'

'And you don't question that?'

'No. Why would I?'

'Well, doesn't it strike you as odd that the man you married apparently has no friends and no past?'

I open my mouth to answer, but close it again when I realise I have nothing to say. How can I tell them that it has struck me as odd every single second of our marriage? How can I possibly confess to the fact that I was so amazed that someone like him had chosen to marry someone like me that I was terrified to look too closely at any cracks in the façade? That I tried to ignore the nagging doubts about him that wouldn't leave me alone? That I made myself ignore them? Worse, that I *got used to it*?

Eventually I shake my head. 'Not really. We're happy, just the two of us.'

'So who was your best man?' the male officer barks at me now.

I turn to look at him coolly. 'Adam's step-dad.'

'Oh, you've met his parents then.'

'Look, I don't think we're achieving anything here,' Ginger butts in at this point. 'Why don't I take you upstairs and you can look at Adam's room and personal belongings? There might be a clue there.'

The male officer stares at her, then gives one curt nod. He gets up and follows her out of the room and we hear them going upstairs. I turn to look at the female officer and I can see that she's readying herself to use this opportunity to get more out of me that I might have been reluctant to admit in front of her confrontational colleague. She's wasting her time.

'Is there anything else you can think of, Grace?' she says very gently. 'Anything at all? A first name, a glimpse of something you might have seen on his phone? A street he was maybe interested in . . .?'

With a jolt I remember the answer phone. 'Oh, yes, there is one thing. I completely forgot about this. A man left a message on the answer phone today. A *Leon*.' I get up and walk over to the phone, then press play on the machine.

'Hello *Adam*, it's *Leon*.' That horrible, deep, gravelly voice seeps out of the speaker into my life again. 'Long time no see. Betcha didn't expect to hear from me again, did you? Come as a bit of a shock, has it? Ha, I bet it has. Just thought I'd give you a call, let you know I'm in the area – nearby actually. *Very* nearby. Would only take me two minutes to get to your place from here. Piece of cake. I'm gonna try to catch up with you *very* soon. Don't worry about calling me back, I'll be in touch.'

The officer listens raptly as the message plays. When it finishes she asks me to play it again and furiously scribbles in her notebook the entire time. Then she asks me if I can give her the tape. I blink and wonder how old she is.

'It's a digital machine.'

She stares at me, as if she doesn't understand what that means.

'There's no tape,' I elaborate.

'Oh, God, silly me,' she says, shaking her head. 'I'll need to take the whole machine then, please.'

34

I unplug it and put it in a bag for her and then Ginger and the male officer come back downstairs.

'Anything?' I ask them both as they arrive in the room. Ginger shakes her head but the male officer is looking expectantly at the carrier bag containing the answer phone.

'Something interesting?' he asks her.

'Could be,' she nods. 'Message on the answer phone, left this evening, just before Mr Littleton left the house.'

'Uh huh, uh huh.' He's nodding approvingly, looking knowledgeable, but I'm sure the answer phone message won't give them anything other than the overt words in it that we've all heard. Someone called Leon phoned and left a message. That's it, nothing more. Big dumb policeman is probably just showing off since there's really little point in taking the machine with them. No matter how many times they listen to it, that message won't tell them anything.

'We'll have a look into your line records,' PC Burly says suddenly, interrupting my train of thought. 'See if we can find out where that call came from.'

Of course. I didn't think of that.

'Has the phone rung or been used at all since that message arrived?'

'Um, no, I don't think so.'

'Well that's something anyway.'

'Right.'

'Last thing, Mrs Littleton. Do you know where your husband keeps his passport?'

'Why?'

He tries to smile reassuringly but it doesn't go very well. 'Let's just see if it's still there.'

'Yes, sure, it's in the same place as mine.'

35

I take them all back upstairs into the spare room and pull open the drawer in the bureau where the passports are kept and we all stand motionless as we stare silently down into it. Lying there amongst the travel insurance documents and the suitcase tags and some old pens and batteries and foreign plug adaptors is one single solitary passport, abandoned amongst the detritus, ungrabbed, unincluded, unwanted.

'That lying little *shit*,' Ginger spits venomously behind me, neatly summing up my thoughts exactly.

THREE

When I was fifteen, I had a friend at school called Kate. She joined our school in Year Ten because her mum found condoms in her dad's jacket. Kate was pretty unhappy about the whole thing – moving house, changing schools, arguing parents – and made very little effort to make new friends, but she was clever and pretty so inevitably she became popular anyway. She didn't pay much attention to me of course. I was good at French and English and she was good at tennis; I was friends with Ginger Blake and Maria Stavronopoulous, she was friends with Ryan Mitchell and Daniel Williams. But one day when Maria was away visiting family and Ginger was off sick, Kate came and sat next to me in Sex Ed. It was like Kate Middleton calmly sitting down next to you in the Asda café. She said 'Hi' to me so naturally it was like we were already close. So we started chatting and I found out that she was actually a really nice girl and we became good friends and stayed that way until we finished school.

Ha ha. That's my sarcasm again. Kate, I think, was

quite happy to be friends with me now and then, so we would get together at weekends and go out in the evenings and paint each other's nails. But when I really needed her, when Ajeet Johar snogged Stephie Morrison in the geography room, or when I was off school for six weeks with glandular fever, she was nowhere to be seen. By me, anyway. By all accounts Stephie and Ajeet saw plenty of her during those two six-week periods of black misery – known in our family history as The Dark Ages and The Dark Ages Two: The Return.

I wasn't really surprised and didn't even feel particularly let down. Her being friends with me was extraordinary, remember. I was so grateful that she had chosen me at all, even on a superficial level, that I was happy with what I had. Ginger and Maria came and sat by my bed and brought me magazines and chocolate and DVDs for both of my teenage crises, and that was fine.

Marriage, on the other hand, is a different story. By definition, it can't be superficial. I Googled the definition, months ago, so I know. Two people, choosing each other above all other human beings on the planet, to go through the rest of their lives with, to support, confide in, listen to, help. Or, you know, something like that. I'm no expert but that sounds like the opposite of superficial to me. I heard once that marriage is a gift through which husband and wife may grow together in love and trust, united in heart, body and mind, but I don't know if I believed it then, and I'm pretty sure I don't believe it now.

The funny thing about someone in your life walking out of it without telling you they're going is that you don't know how to feel. Or rather, you feel so many different things, they all get blended up together so nothing is distinguishable. You end up with a kind of brown plasticine of emotion. A sludge of feeling. I'm upset, of course, and hurt. But also empty, lost, scared – for him and for me – mystified, curious and angry. Furious actually. Curious and furious. I swing from screaming 'I HOPE THAT FUCKING SECRETIVE LITTLE TOSSER NEVER COMES BACK!' to thoughtfully pondering 'I wonder what on earth has happened to him.' I hate him with a pure, scalding stream of loathing; I love him like I never did before. I hope he stays away forever; I yearn for his return with every single molecule of myself.

I spend stupid amounts of time Googling 'missing husband'. Mostly there are news articles from around the world talking about murdered wives or bodies being found. One actually makes my toes curl as it describes a poor woman collapsing after finding her missing husband in the local hospital morgue.

A sound comes out of me and I'm not sure if it's a sob or a laugh. But then the air gets stuck in my lungs and my face crumples and I have to blink very quickly for several seconds to stop myself from believing that I have anything to cry about.

For the first three days I don't sleep, I don't eat, I don't go to work, I barely see anyone. I feel like I'm in suspended animation, like sitting motionless in HG Wells' time machine, watching the world spin by faster and faster, plants growing, dust collecting, things getting older and everything moving on and changing except me. It's like breathing in and not breathing out again. I'm tense with a feeling of imminent onrushing change, my adrenalin levels dialled up to maximum, my fight or flight reflexes poised and waiting for whatever is coming, to come.

But it doesn't. The only thing that comes is the police. A bland, quiet officer called Linda Patterson who says she's my family liaison person while the investigation is underway.

'If you can find a key to his offices,' she says, 'that would be very useful. We'll need to have a look through his paperwork. Also I'll need a full description of the car . . .'

I stand at the window staring at the street, watching the comings and goings of all the neighbours, all the neighbours' visitors, all the neighbours' deliveries and collections. But no one and nothing arrives here. Apart from a purse that I ordered last week on eBay. It's completely gorgeous, covered in black sequins.

On the fourth day I wake up alone in my – not 'our' – double bed, look at the empty space next to me and think, *The toad's not coming back, is he?* The universe answers with a resounding silence, which I take to be confirmation, so I get up, get showered, and go to work. At least, I go to the shop. It will be good to see Ginge, but frankly helping someone decide between the Abraham Lincoln or the Scooby Doo outfits has never seemed more trivial.

'Oh my God,' Ginger says when she sees me, and walks over to me as rapidly as she can in a narrow Nefertiti dress. 'I didn't expect to see you back for a few weeks. Are you OK?'

I shrug. 'No. Yes. I suppose so. Massively pissed off, a bit unhinged maybe, but OK. How are you?'

She stares at me, obviously weighing up the likelihood of me genuinely being OK versus the possibility I'm lying about it and likely suddenly to explode into a full-blown Hulk episode and smash the shop up. That would seriously piss off our boss, Penny, especially with the front of shop displays looking as good as they do right now. After a couple of seconds, she evidently decides I'm safe and may be allowed to stay. She angles her head as she concocts an answer to my enquiry. 'I'm not bad, considering I've been dead for three thousand years and feel like I'm going to tip over in this ridiculous dress.'

I glance around me at the old familiarity of the place – the shelves of plastic fangs and bloody daggers; the disembodied zombie heads; the grotesque Golem masks – and feel comforted. The world around me starts to reassemble itself into something normal, something recognisable, and it makes me feel more real. Then Ginger moves closer and assumes a serious expression. 'Seriously though, Gee. Do you honestly think you're up to being back at work already? I mean, what's happened is ghastly – do you think you can cope with this too?' She pulls on the Nefertiti head-dress and straightens the attached hair on her shoulders. 'I'm worried you might struggle.'

I shake my head. 'No, I'm sure I'll cope. I'm OK.'

'Really?'

I nod. 'Yes, really. I didn't think I would be, and I've had my moments the past four days, believe me, but I'm not broken, just a bit winded. Being at work will give me something to do and something else to think about. The bills still need to be paid, don't they? And if he ever does turn up again, nothing short of a kidnap and torture or serious amnesia would make me take him back.'

'Right on.' She pauses. 'How about two broken legs?'

I shake my head. 'He's got a mobile, hasn't he? And if he hasn't, someone else will have, broken legs or not.'

'Broken arms?'

'Hands still work.'

'Broken fingers?'

'Dictation?'

'Of course. What about a fever? You know, delirious with it, couldn't say his own name, let alone find his way home?'

'That comes under amnesia. No, I'm holding out for kidnap and torture. That's the favourite.'

'Agreed.'

She's distracted by a customer at this point and I go and change into the Texas Chain Saw outfit, thinking about how generally OK I am feeling. Naturally when I think about Adam and the missing madras (I really did want Chinese anyway) all the fury and confusion and resentment start to boil and fester inside me again, and there's a danger of it bubbling up to the surface and spilling out in the form of shrieky, shop-smashing rage. But the funny thing is, if I don't actively think about it like that, it's not at the forefront of my mind at all.

'Seriously,' Nefertiti hisses at me, eyeing my costume, 'is that really what you're wearing?'

I glance down, then nod at her. 'It felt right.'

I watch for the next twenty minutes as she totters in

teeny tiny steps backwards and forwards to the stock room for a Fred Flintstone, then a Mr Blobby, then a Men in Black, then back to Fred Flintstone again. The scene is completely absorbing. Ginger is smiling sweetly with her 'Here you go's and 'How about this?'s, but I know her teeth are gritted and it makes me want to giggle. Thoughts of Adam are in my mind, simmering, but they're not overwhelming and they're certainly not crushing me.

Eventually it's settled – London Beefeater – and the difficult customer leaves us in peace.

'So what's the latest from the police?' Ginger asks me as she puts Fred and Blobby back on the rail.

'Nothing much. They've got the car details and they're going through some of his business stuff from the office, but I get the impression they're not that bothered about it.'

'Really? Why?'

'Because he's an adult man who drove off voluntarily. No one lured him into a car with promises of sweets or puppies, there's no jerky CCTV footage of him getting into a taxi at two in the morning, they haven't found his jacket and shoes on the beach or by a railway line, his car hasn't been discovered at some M1 services with a sinister blood smear on the passenger seat . . .'

She puts her hands up. 'OK, yes, I get it. What I mean is, why are *you* getting the impression they're not bothered?'

'Oh, right. Well, they've only been round to see me once since that first time. There are no updates, no one calling in to check on me. I don't know, it all seems pretty half-hearted to me.'

'And you have plenty of experience of what happens

43

in these circumstances, do you? I mean, this is half-hearted compared with . . .?'

I think about that a moment, then nod slowly. 'Yeah, good point, this is probably just the way it's done. I don't know why I was expecting more.'

'Look, Gee, you don't know what's going on behind the scenes. Maybe they've set up an incident room or something. There could be a team of five or six people working on it, going door to door or sifting through his work stuff. There's probably far more happening than you're aware of.'

'I suppose so.'

'And maybe they're so busy they haven't had time to update you on anything. They won't update you until they have something concrete to tell you anyway, will they?'

'No, probably not.'

'Do you want me to ask Matt to pop round and see you? He'll probably be able to tell you a bit more. From the police perspective. He might even have some inside knowledge that the investigation team would never tell you.'

'Really? Wouldn't he get into trouble for that?'

She shrugs. 'Who's gonna know? And anyway, what's gonna happen to him, someone calls the police?'

I look up at her gratefully. 'That would be good. Would you?'

'Course I would, stupid. Happy to.'

'Do you think he'll mind?'

'No, I'm pretty sure he won't mind.'

'And you'll be there too, right?'

She smiles and rubs my arm. 'Yes, Gracie, I'll be there too.'

I give her a quick hug. 'Thanks Ginge.'

'No probs.'

'And . . . sorry for sulking . . . a bit.'

She rings Matt during her lunch break and he says he can pop over tonight. Lucky for me that he's free so soon. Ginge comes home with me after work to wait for him. And eat my food.

'I think it's only fair that if I cook something, I should be allowed to eat some of it,' she says around a mouthful of sausage.

'Totally.'

We're slobbing it – understandable in the circs, I think – and eating our dinner on trays on our laps. As we eat, Ginge is glancing around the room checking out all the pictures of Adam and me that are everywhere. Us at my sister's twenty-first birthday party last year; us feeding goats on our honeymoon in the Cotswolds; us having Christmas dinner at his parents' house. Something occurs to me suddenly and I slam my hands to my head. 'Oh my God!'

'Oh my God what?! What is it?'

'Adam's parents! I haven't even told them what's happened! Oh arses, this is terrible. He's been gone for four days, he could even be dead . . .'

'He's not dead.'

'. . . and they don't even know anything odd has happened.' I turn to look at Ginge, my eyes wild. 'They might even have heard from him by now! God, maybe they know something, maybe he's explained everything to them and told them to fill me in the moment I got in touch with them . . .'

'Gee . . .'

'. . . which he would have expected me to do that same night.'

'Gee, listen.'

'But I didn't, I completely forgot about them. Bloody hell, Ginge, what sort of person does that make me?'

'It makes you the sort of person that's going through a pretty terrible ordeal, that's all. It's completely understandable, given what you've had to deal with, stop stressing.'

By now I'm up off the sofa pacing the room, each fist clamped around a handful of hair. It's still attached to my head, don't worry. I'm not quite there yet.

'I can't stop stressing, I'm a terrible, awful, horrible person.' I lunge towards the phone but Ginger is already up and grabs my arm.

'Stop!' she says, almost shouting. 'Seriously Gee, stop acting mad.'

'I'm not acting mad!' I halt in my tracks. 'Am I acting mad?'

'Yes. Oh, I don't know. Just for God's sake calm down and listen.'

I do a 'relax' thing, making a concerted effort to breathe deeply for a few seconds with my eyes closed, and actively loosen my arms and shoulders. 'OK. What?'

'The police will have let Adam's parents know. You don't need to worry about that.'

I stare at her. Of course they would have. Relief floods through me. 'Oh, thank God. Yes, of course they would. Jesus, I'm such a plank!'

'No, you're not, you're just not thinking straight at the moment.'

'I'm really not.' Another sudden thought. 'Do you think they'll have let my parents know?'

Ginger bites her lip and breaks eye contact. 'I don't know. They might have. Depends if they've been round to see them already, I expect . . . But no, if they'd already been round there to ask questions, your mum would have phoned you after, wouldn't she? So they probably don't know yet. Good idea if you call them and let them know first. Otherwise it'll come as a bit of a shock when the boys in blue turn up on their doorstep . . .' She tails off and watches me. 'What's up?'

I'm pacing again, rubbing my head and face, and I stop and turn to face her. 'Ask questions? What do you mean, ask questions? Why would the police need to question my parents at all? I mean, Adam is just their son in law, there's no other connection, they're not going to be able to tell them anything. He just drove off, no one knows what happened to him – well, I expect someone does, somewhere, probably Adam himself in fact, the lying SCUMBAG!' – I shout the word out, as if somewhere he can still hear me – 'but my mum and dad certainly don't know, why would the police even bother with them?'

Ginger walks across to where I've stopped and takes hold of my upper arms. 'OK, now I want you to try and be calm about this. Will you? Are you calm?'

Her words shoot darts of panic into me and my agitated heart dials up a notch. 'Christ Ginge, what do you know?'

She shakes her head. 'Nothing, nothing like that. I'm only guessing here. Matt will be able to—'

'Guessing about *what*?'

She takes a deep breath.

47

'*What Ginge? What is it?*'

'Thepoliceprobablythinkyoudidit!'

There's a brief but grotesquely tense silence as her words and all their ramifications make their way into my brain.

Ginger is shaking her head, plucking at my arm. 'No, no, that sounds awful. I don't mean . . . What I mean is, it will be one of their lines of enquiry. That's all.'

The police probably think I did it. That's what she said. They think I did it. But Adam has disappeared, so what do they think I . . . did . . .? If anyone *did* something, the thing they think someone, anyone, *did*, must be . . . I feel all the blood drain from my face and head, and sway a bit where I'm standing. They think Adam is dead.

'Oh God, Gracie, I'm so sorry . . .'

I shake my head and frown at her. 'No no. That's not . . . He isn't . . .' I look up frankly into her face. 'You think they think he's been . . . done in? And that I was the one who . . . *did* . . . him?'

She shakes her head again. 'No, no, I don't think they think that. It's just one of the possibilities they have to consider, when someone—'

'Is that what you think?'

'Oh my effing God, no *way*!' She flies at me and seizes me in a tight hug. 'You think I'd be here right now, calmly eating caramelised onion sausages if I thought you were a violent, psychopathic killer capable of ending your own husband and coolly vanishing the body?'

'No, no, I suppose not.'

'Damn straight.'

I think for a few seconds. 'So you don't think I killed him.'

'I do not.'

'But you do think he's dead?'

She looks at me sidelong and gives a wry smile. 'Of course he's not effing dead. Although he sodding well deserves to be, after this. Little shit.'

I close my eyes and release a breath. 'It's such a massive relief to hear you say that. I mean, I've been feeling so sure he's alive, but if the police think he's dead, and then if you did . . .'

'Don't worry. Matt's told me it's fairly standard for the police to think along those lines when someone is inexplicably no longer around. They have to think worst case scenario, don't they?'

'I suppose so.'

'Yeah. But that doesn't mean that they necessarily really actually *think* it.'

A sudden loud bang on the front door makes us jump and we both turn to stare wide-eyed in the direction of the hallway. Goosebumps rise on my arms and shoulders.

'Who. The *fuck*. Is *that*?' I breathe, reaching out blindly to grab Ginger's arm. I can almost believe it's murdered Adam, head caved in and dripping with gore, returned from the grave to seek revenge on the one who ended him.

'It's Matt,' she says, and gets up to let him in.

I eat the last piece of sausage then put my knife and fork down on the plate, and the plate on the floor. It'll be nice to see Matt again. Haven't seen him for years and I was always fond of the kid, in a big sister kind of way.

'Here he is,' Ginge is saying, coming back in. And filling the doorway behind her, even without his hat on, is a giant policeman. I stand up, because my neck is aching looking up at him. It doesn't make much difference.

'Is this . . . *Matt*?' I ask the room, sounding painfully like an ancient auntie who hasn't seen him since he was four. He's recognisable, with the same black hair, brown eyes and large chin, but now there's stubble where before there was only razor burn. His piercings are gone, as is the eyeliner, and his neck and shoulders look vast. It's as if he's been in a grow bag since I last saw him, and reconciling the two images is almost impossible.

'That's me,' he says in a very deep, proper man's voice. 'Hi Grace. Long time no see. How are you these days?' He closes his eyes briefly. 'I – I mean, obviously I know that you're not . . . That is, you know, of course, you must be absolutely . . .' He stops. Takes a deep breath. Tries again. 'I'm so sorry about . . . you know, what's happened.'

'Thanks.'

'Sit down, Matt,' Ginger says suddenly. 'Grace and I'll make a cuppa.'

She grabs my arm and practically drags me out of the room into the kitchen.

'I can't believe that's the same gawky lad I used to know,' I'm saying as she bustles around getting cups out and filling the kettle. 'He's a lot taller in black, isn't he?'

'Look, I want to say something,' she says really quickly, rooting through the cupboard to find some tea bags. 'It's about Matt.'

50

'Right?'

'I don't want him to . . .' She breaks off, looks round, then steps lightly over to the kitchen door. She peers out into the hallway then silently closes it and turns round again to face me. 'Matt's already told me that the first thing the police will do is try to work out whether or not Adam is dead, and that they'll be looking principally at you.'

'Oh, yeah. I'd almost forgotten about being a murder suspect. Thanks for reminding me.'

'The thing is, he probably shouldn't even be here, let alone tell you anything.'

'Oh. Really? Why not?'

She widens her eyes. 'Coz you're a suspect. Matt's not directly involved in the investigation, it's not his section. But even if he was, he couldn't be because he knows you personally. And of course he's my brother and I'm the best friend. It's a link that could be used by a good solicitor to muddy the waters in the event of a prosecution.'

'Oh right. I see what you mean.' I pause. 'No I don't. Are you talking about if they prosecute *me*?'

'Well, yes, but it won't happen because . . .'

'Of course it won't happen because he's not dead and even if he was – AND I HOPE HE FUCKING WELL IS – I didn't kill him.'

'I know . . .'

'So this scenario you're talking about, where my link with the police, through you and Matt, is used by a solicitor to . . . what was it again?'

'Muddy the waters.'

'Right. What you're actually talking about is *my* solicitor. Getting *me* off.'

She shrugs. 'Yeah. But we all know that'll never happen because you didn't do anything.'

I stare at her and the absolute horror of what she's saying starts to sink in. The police could somehow, in some monstrous, inconceivable twist of misunderstanding, misdirection and *mistake*, decide that Adam is dead; and by disastrous coincidence after shocking inaccuracy, could find me responsible for it. And then, in an almost unimaginably horrific runaway trial involving spurious witnesses and mistaken identity, I could actually get sent down for it.

'Grab the digestives,' Ginger says, heading back towards the living room.

As we walk back in, Matt stands up and his bulk practically fills the room.

'You don't have to stand up whenever we come in, Matthew,' Ginger says, handing him a mug.

'No, hah, I know. Sorry.' He sits.

'So,' she says. 'Tell Gracie what's going on.' We both sit down facing Matt, as if he's the entertainment.

He nods at Ginger, then looks over at me and lowers his chin. 'There really isn't much to tell you,' he says, his voice reverberating around the room. It's the deepest voice this room has ever experienced. Adam's voice was much lighter. Not feminine, but much less . . . manly. He was more refined; but there was less of him.

Why am I thinking of him in the past tense?

'Right,' I say, to encourage Matt. So far, it seems like a waste of time him being here.

'But I can find stuff out for you, pop in on my way home if there's anything.'

'Great. Thanks.'

'Is that it?' Ginger demands. 'I thought you said you'd heard something interesting this evening.'

'Oh yes, I did. Sorry, I was forgetting you hadn't heard it yet.' He turns to me again and assumes a funeral face. 'They found the car, Gracie.'

The shock of this hits me almost physically and tea slops over the side of my mug onto the floor. For a second my throat seizes, but my brain can't formulate a coherent word anyway.

'Where?' I finally manage.

'Church car park in a little place called Linton. About three hundred miles from here.'

'Linton? Where the hell is that? I've never even heard of it.' I look at Ginger helplessly but she just shrugs. I turn back to Matt. 'What does this mean?'

Matt shuffles forward on his chair a little, bringing himself an inch nearer to me. 'Look, it's OK, it doesn't necessarily mean anything. All it tells us for sure is that the car is there.'

I raise my eyebrows. 'Oh, right. OK.'

'Matt,' Ginger hisses at him.

He glances at her and she rolls her eyes towards me, so he looks back. 'What I mean by that,' he says hastily, 'is that that is all it tells us *definitively*. I mean, yes, it could mean that he drove it there himself and abandoned it. Or he was taken there. Or he was meeting someone there and never got back to the car. Or is still intending to return to it, but something is preventing him.'

'All right,' Ginger interrupts, putting her hand up.

'Or,' Matt goes on, regardless, 'it could also mean that someone stole it, and has abandoned it there. I mean, it's unlikely that someone else drove it there, with him in it. That's quite a risky thing to do, if you're abducting someone . . .'

'Because of the DNA,' I whisper reverentially.

'It's more to do with the CCTV cameras actually. They're everywhere these days. And speed cameras. You can be caught dozens of times every day, more if you're going a long distance. Now they know roughly what route it was on, the face of whoever drove that car to that car park will soon be coming out of a full colour printer in the station. And if it's not your husband, things will . . . change.'

'What if he wasn't abducted? I mean, someone else was driving, but Adam went along willingly?'

Matt nods. 'Of course that's another possibility. They'll be considering it. They'll know much more when they get the photo of the driver.'

'What was in it?' Ginger says quietly. 'I mean, in the car. Was his wallet in it? The passport? Money, jacket. You know.'

Matt turns to her and shakes his head. 'Nothing, that I know of. I don't know everything of course. This is just what I've managed to pick up, chatting to people in the station. But no one has mentioned anything being left in it.'

'What about a curry?' I ask faintly. 'Was there any take-away curry in the car?'

Matt frowns and smiles at the same time. 'No, no, I don't think so. Why?'

I shake my head, then drop it into my hands. For some reason, that's the most upsetting thing about the car being found. If there had been cold take-away boxes in there, I'd know that he had been planning to come home again, but events had somehow prevented that. But the absence of even a whiff of steam or a splash of korma sauce on the upholstery means only one thing. He left the house that night knowing he wasn't coming back.

FOUR

'I get it,' Ginger says, reaching across and rubbing my arm. 'I totally get it.'

Matt's mystified. 'Well I don't. What's the curry got to do with anything?'

'I'll tell you later,' she says quietly and I can feel some movement above me, as if she's shaking her head emphatically, or making cutting motions across her throat to shut him up.

'Oh,' he says, 'right. OK. Listen, Gracie, I'm sure you don't need me to tell you this, but in these sorts of cases they almost always come back.'

I raise my head to find him staring at me earnestly. 'Really?'

He nods, slowly and sadly. 'Oh, yes, definitely. He's driven himself off, he took his passport and wallet, that was forethought. It's incredibly unlikely that he's been taken under duress.' He smiles encouragingly, but it doesn't quite reach his eyes. 'I'm sure he's fine.'

I move my head slowly from him to Ginger, lock eyes with her briefly, then turn and look back at Matt. 'I arsing well hope not.'

Matt stifles the flicker of a smile when he hears this. 'Oh . . . kay. Well, I suppose that's an understandable reaction.' He looks over at Ginge. 'OK to use the loo?'

When he comes back in a few minutes later, he doesn't sit down again but says goodbye from the doorway. 'Work in the morning,' he says. 'Really great to see you again, Gracie. I'm sure everything will turn out fine.' Ginge gets up to show him out, even though it's a very simple journey straight through the hallway to the door, and he's a policeman so really ought to be able to find his own way. There's some loud whispering from that direction for about half a minute, but I can't make out any of the words.

I stay in a state of – I don't want to say shock; let's say, severe disappointment – for the rest of the evening. Everything that I thought I knew about my marriage, everything I'd felt, was turning out to be absolutely true. My feelings of unease and lack of faith, feelings that I had tried to squash, telling myself I was being ridiculous because of my own insecurity, were spot on, it turned out. The mystery surrounding my husband, the lack of information, the apparent absence of friends or colleagues, was not just me being paranoid and could not simply be discounted. Who knew?

Ginger dumps our cold tea in the sink and opens a bottle of wine I didn't know I had.

'Get some of that down you,' she says, handing me a large glass.

'Are you sure it's the best idea in the world at this point to give alcohol to someone whose beautiful husband has buggered off to who knows where?'

She barely pauses. 'It's Merlot, not meths,' she says, 'chillax.' Then she tips her head back and pours in the wine.

We go back into the living room and Ginger curls up round her wine glass. She looks at me frankly. 'You do know why Matt's secretly pleased that your husband's gone, and secretly miserable that he's probably completely fine, don't you?'

I frown, trying to make sense of this. 'Not sure I do, actually.'

She shrugs. 'Well, if you don't know by now, I'm not telling you.' She takes another large slug of wine. 'I think you need to see Adam's parents.'

I'm still wondering about what she said about Matt, but the notion of seeing Ray and Julia sweeps it away completely. 'Yes, I know. And mine. Don't really want to phone them about this, better in person. I'll do it tomorrow. Is Penny in tomorrow?'

She shakes her head. 'Nope. Still in Italy.'

'Great. Do you mind if I don't come in? I can't believe I've left it this long.'

'Course not, no problem at all. Take as long as you want, I can manage on my own in the shop.'

I think it was the wine talking.

Ninety minutes later, she's in the recovery position in my spare bed, and there's a strategic bucket on the floor directly beneath her face.

'I'm sorry, Gracie,' she says quietly with her eyes closed. 'I'm really really sorry . . .'

'S'OK.' More to myself, really. She's already unconscious.

Finally I'm on my own. Back downstairs I open up my laptop and Google Linton to see if I can work out why Adam went there. Why he would blithely disinter himself and heartlessly abandon the life we built together to go off on his own for some foul, selfish and probably illegal reason, the lying, deceitful little—

Oh, it's lovely! A completely beautiful, picturesque little village in North Yorkshire, not far from Skipton, apparently. There's a stream with stepping stones, cottages everywhere, pretty little bridges and even a waterfall. I lean closer to the screen and narrow my eyes at the photos. This quaint, rural scene, full of sheep and fields and really wholesome bread, is hiding something evil. Lurking somewhere underneath, just around the corner, out of sight, are ugliness; treachery; pain. And possibly violence. I click on the map and print off directions; then shut down and go to bed.

My dreams are full of breaking glass and squealing tyres but when I wake up I can't remember anything specific. The clock says it's 06:34 so I definitely need at least another week of sleep, but apparently my body has decided it doesn't want to go through any more dreams like that so it actively refuses to go back under. After half an hour of trying, I pull the covers back, swivel myself round and stand up. I feel achy and unrested, as if I've spent the whole night tensed up and anxious somewhere. It reminds me of that old fairy tale about the princess whose shoes are always worn out when she wakes up in the morning because she's been secretly dancing all night without waking up. Except I feel more like I've spent the night waiting for surgery than at a party.

I trudge downstairs in my dressing gown and put the kettle on. I'm not looking forward to today at all. First thing I've got to do is ring both sets of parents and make sure it's OK to visit today. Then I've got to visit them. It's day five, and the ramifications of Adam's disappearance just keep on growing.

Adam's mum and step-dad are only a fifteen-minute drive away, but we hardly ever see them. I think they were last here for dinner about two months ago, and before that it must be a year. Adam is obviously not close with them, and that suited me just fine. His mum, Julia, is a bit odd, somehow. Like she's not really there. Or you're not. I was never quite sure which one of us she was oblivious to – it varied. Sometimes she would hardly acknowledge my presence and pay more attention to the blank wall behind me; sometimes she would be over-the-top gushing with affection and enthusiasm. 'Lovely Gracie, fabulous Gracie.' Made it very uncomfortable for me, on every occasion; I couldn't work out whether to try to interact with her or not.

'Is your mum OK?' I stupidly asked Adam after the first time I met them. That time she had been almost entirely silent and extremely distractible. Adam's step-dad, Ray, had cooked a lovely roast lamb and was serving it at the table while Julia threw three glasses of wine into herself. She was leaning for the bottle to refill again when her hand suddenly froze, mid-reach. I glanced at Ray and Adam, to see if they'd noticed, and they were both locked in position – Ray carving the joint, Adam pouring drinks

– but had turned their heads to stare at her. Ray had even said, 'Julia,' quietly, almost like a warning. Eventually she dropped her hand, and the two men relaxed again and continued with what they were both doing.

At that point in our relationship, I still expected Adam to be open with me about himself and his family. I thought he would put his arms round me and tear up while he told me sorrowfully that she had some syndrome or other, something on 'the spectrum'. Or that she was maybe bipolar or clinically depressed. On medication for something at the very least. Probably not a very tactful way of asking, but we'd been home for an hour by this time and he wasn't volunteering it.

'Yes, she's absolutely fine.' He flashed a brief smile at me, then turned directly back to the film we were watching.

Alarm bells started clanging instantly. He'd shut down – what became his go-to response for any enquiry at all into some part of his life that wasn't to do with me. A solid and unyielding rebuff. A dead end.

'Oh. Well that's good,' I said weakly. His closed-off demeanour – arms folded, head turned pointedly away – told me not to pursue it, so, mystified, I let it go. But I dreaded the next time we went and was very relieved that it didn't come up again for several months.

But she's his mum and I'm his wife, it's almost a requirement that we meet up and console each other in these circumstances. I wish I knew how to behave around her, especially now, but Google has been utterly useless in that respect. Of course Julia will be missing him too, and may even look at me as the last remnant of her vanishing son. Oh God. I hope she doesn't think that I think about her like that. That I'll want to snuggle in her arms and talk about 'Adam the baby' and 'Adam the handyman' and 'Adam the party animal' and laugh and then cry together. I have no inclination whatsoever to see her, but it would look odd if I don't go. So go I must.

From upstairs there's a thump followed by a kind of groaning sob. I grab a glass of water and go quickly up to the spare room to find Ginger kneeling in front of a small pool of red wine. There's a glass on its side beside her. She looks up at me like a dog in front of a fouled rug.

'I'm so sorry, Gracie,' she says quietly, and closes her eyes.

'No point asking you how you are today then?'

She answers very softly without opening her eyes. 'Let me sort it out. Got any white wine?'

I smile. 'Thank you for the thought, but I'm not bringing wine anywhere near you today.'

'Alka-Seltzer might be a better idea.'

'Haven't got any I'm afraid. Oh Ginge, what were you thinking?'

'I know, I know, I'm an effing idiot, don't tell me. How long had that bottle of wine been there anyway?'

'No, you're not blaming the wine. It's Adam's—' I pause, correct myself – 'it *was* Adam's, so it was definitely a good one.'

'Good God, Gracie,' Adam's voice says in my head, 'what the hell have you bought?'

'It's wine. I thought it would be nice with the—'

'No it isn't. Jesus, this will probably taste like nail

62

varnish remover, not wine. How much was it? A fiver? We're not drinking that.'

I smile at Ginger now. 'You tipped nearly the whole lot down your throat all by yourself. And half a bottle of gin.'

'Don't talk about it.'

I get her cleaned up and put her to bed on the sofa with some dry toast, a jug of water and the bucket. The shop will have to stay closed today. Penny won't mind; it's more of a hobby for her anyway, her husband is a multi-millionaire businessman supplying toner ink to dry photocopiers around the country. Besides, she's in Italy.

'What's Fletch up to today? Can he come and look after you?' Simon Fletcher known affectionately as Fletch by anyone who has any affection for him – is Ginge's current boyfriend. She always introduces him like that – 'This is Fletch, my current boyfriend' – even though they've been together over three years.

'What? Aren't you looking after me?'

'No, you know I can't. I'm going to see Julia and Ray today, then Mum and Dad. Shall I call him?'

She pouts from the sofa. 'No point, he's working.' Fletch sells drugs for a living. He works in telesales for a large pharmaceutical company. She rolls over and faces the back of the sofa, so I start walking out of the room to go and get dressed. A whispery voice reaches me at the door: 'Can you get my phone, please? I'll text him later.'

I wait until after I've showered and dressed before ringing Julia and Ray. Ginger is snoring on the sofa so I take my phone out into the kitchen to call, but spend almost half an hour procrastinating with the washing up and cleaning first. Eventually I give myself a mental slap and am just about to dial when my phone starts ringing all on its own, making me jump.

'Hello?'

'Hello? Sarah?'

I puff out a 'Huh.' Haven't been called that for a long time. Ginger and I became best friends virtually on day one at secondary school because her nickname was Ginger and mine was Grace. Long story, but there was a legendary incident when I was about nine when I knocked an entire display of soy sauce over in Sainsbury's. Kind of tripped multiple times. Hey, it got very slippery very quickly. My dad dubbed me Grace at that point, and it stuck. Ginger and I both corrected our Year Seven teacher at first registration, then caught each other's eye and grinned. I don't think anyone at school ever even got to grips with our real names, we used them for such a short time.

But no one calls me Sarah any more. Not even my family. I haven't gone by that name for sixteen or seventeen years, at least. I literally don't associate with *anyone* who still calls me that, and apart from my passport and marriage certificate, everything I have is . . .

Suddenly I feel cold tendrils snaking up my spine and my heart rate speeds up. There's something off about this call, and it can't be coincidence that my husband vanished into the night five days ago. This is it, I think to myself. This is the moment when I find out what's going on and my world crashes around me.

My fingers wrap around the phone more tightly and I press it to my head. 'Yes, speaking. Who is this?'

'It's *Leon*, Sarah. I'm a friend of your husband's. Is he there, by any chance?'

Ice-cold air seeps out of the phone and sends chills all the way through me. I think furiously about what this means. Should I answer him? Tell the truth? Lie? I have no idea. I had thought that Leon was involved in Adam's disappearance, because of the message left on the answer phone the day he vanished; but now he's ringing asking for him again, apparently not realising that he's disappeared at all. Is Leon just a coincidence, then?

Or is Leon lying?

'Hello?' the voice comes again. 'Are you still there?'

'Um, yes, sorry, I'm here.' I run my hand through my hair a few times as I think. What should I do, what should I do? Then something occurs to me. 'How did you get this number, Leon?'

There's a deep, throaty chortle. 'Sarah, you're starting to sound a bit suspicious of me suddenly. What do you take me for, some kind of criminal? Your husband gave it to me, of course.'

'Oh, right. Of course.' Now I'm thoroughly panicked. If Adam did give this person my mobile number, surely he would have said my name was Grace? He knows my real name of course, but only because I told him. He has never known me as Sarah, or called me that. It would be unnatural for him to tell someone his wife was called Sarah. That would just be weird, and of course nothing Adam did was ever weird. Ha ha.

But now there's a tremor starting somewhere in my belly and I'm not sure if it's anger, fear, desperation or hunger.

'I'm afraid he's not here at the moment,' I say, if only to end the awkward silence that's growing larger by the second. Leon must be thinking something's up by now. If he wasn't already. Which he obviously was. 'Can I give him a message?' God alone knows why I'm saying this. I can't give Adam a message any more than I can give him a punch in the kidneys.

There's a long pause from the other end, accompanied by some deep, slow breathing. 'I don't think so,' Leon rasps eventually. 'I really need to see him myself. When is he going to be in?'

I can feel my eyes widening and my breathing starting to quicken as fear-fuelled adrenalin floods my system. 'Um, I'm not sure . . .' I know I'm in fight or flight mode. Even though the perceived threat is on the other end of the phone, in an unknown location, the fear I'm experiencing is no less real just because Leon isn't in the room with me. Everything about this call feels like a threat, and I start to glance around me, planning my escape. Or looking for a defensive weapon. My eyes land on the knife block and just as my hand is closing round the large bread knife, there's a robust knock on the front door. I practically scream out loud where I am, right there by the toaster, and the knife block falls over with a clatter. I spin in place, heart thudding, to face the door. Through the opaque glass panels in the door I can see a dark, formless shape, indistinguishable as either man or woman, hunched and heavy. The top part of the shape swivels slightly as I watch, turning to look around it, observing its surroundings. Yet again it feels like the undead Adam, returning to me grey and cold and dripping with lake water.

'I'll get him to call you,' I manage to croak. I need to be free of this call so I can focus on my fear of the front door. One frightening thing at a time is all I can handle. If that, actually. 'What's your number?' I'm staring at the door as I advance slowly towards it.

'No, don't do that,' the gravelly voice says. 'I'll call again. Soon.' And finally, thankfully, the phone clicks off. I put it quickly down on the kitchen counter like a ticking bomb, then turn to face my next fear. I want to take the bread knife, but it could be awkward to answer the door holding it if it's the postman, so I leave it there. As I walk down the hallway, my gaze is fixed on the lumpy shape behind the glass, and when I reach for the door catch, the image of a bloated, sallow-skinned Adam comes back into my head, and my hand hesitates in mid-air. I close my eyes. It won't be him at all, in any condition, I tell myself, least of all a walking corpse. I'm just being ridiculous. My hand trembles a little as I'm opening the door, so I grab my arm with my other hand.

As soon as the door opens fully, I see it's the female police liaison officer that was here before, Linda. She smiles at me, then frowns as apparently I go a bit pale.

'You all right, Grace?' she says, stepping nearer. 'You've gone a bit pale. Are you poorly?'

'No, no, I'm fine. I just thought, when you knocked . . .'

She smacks her hand to her mouth. 'Oh my God, I'm so insensitive. I'm really sorry. Missing husband, unexpected visits from the police, of course you thought the worst.'

She has no idea.

'I really am very sorry.' She puts her hand out and gently

squeezes my arm. 'I did try to call your mobile from the car, but couldn't get through. Not that that's any excuse. I promise next time I will wait outside in the car until I've spoken to you on the phone. That way, you'll always know I'm coming, and then if anyone ever turns up unannounced, you'll know it's because . . .' She trails off and looks away. 'Ahem. Anyway, you'll know when I'm coming. OK?'

I nod wordlessly.

'Can I come in then?'

As we walk along the hallway, Linda starts to go into the living room because that's where we went last time she was here.

'No!' I almost shout, and block her path.

She looks at me sidelong. 'Something wrong?'

'No, nothing, just my friend, passed out drunk in there.'

'Really?'

'Yeah. She hit it a bit hard last night.'

'Any reason for that?'

Bloody hell, you can really tell she's a copper. I just manage to stop myself in time from saying that we had the news about Adam's car last night. Matt told me off the record yesterday, from what he'd overheard in the stationery cupboard or something, so I can't let on he's said anything because it will probably get him into trouble. 'Don't think so. Quite standard for her. Plus, you know, this whole situation . . .'

'Having a tough time, is she?'

I have no idea what that's supposed to mean. Would she be happier if it was me sweating red wine on the sofa in there? I decide not to answer and just shrug as we go into the kitchen.

'OK, well. I've got some news for you,' she says, sitting down at the kitchen table. 'Come and sit down, Grace.'

My heart starts thudding in a dart of panic, but then I realise that she's probably about to tell me officially about Adam's car. I arrange my features into what I hope says, 'Oh Christ what is this news you've come to tell me is it good or bad I don't think I can take any more,' and sit down in the chair next to Linda. 'What is it? Have they found him?'

She narrows her eyes at me then, as if she's found what I've asked a bit odd. Or is struggling to understand it. 'Nooo,' she says slowly. 'Why do you say that?'

'Oh, I don't know, maybe because my husband has vanished into the night and I was kind of hoping involving the police might lead to him being found.' I widen my eyes. 'Was I wrong?'

She takes a deep breath and releases it in a sigh. 'No, Grace, you weren't wrong, we're obviously doing what we can to find him. It looks like it's going to take a bit longer than we thought, though.'

'Why? What's changed?'

She presses her lips together and tilts her head on one side. I think she's trying to look like she's compassionate. 'We've made a discovery, Grace. It's what we were hoping for, a lead of some description, but now that we've found it, it's turned out to be a dead end.'

'Oh for the love of God, tell me already!'

She flinches a little, then resumes her calm, compassionate look. 'It's the car, Grace. We've found Adam's car.'

She freezes at this point, with her head still tilted, her

eyebrows still drawn together. I can tell that in her head she's hearing the *EastEnders* theme tune starting. But this isn't a cliff hanger, I already knew about it.

'Oh. Right. I see.'

She almost imperceptibly narrows her eyes again. 'Don't you have any questions?'

'Oh, er, yes, yes, of course I do. I mean, this is a bit of a shock so I'm, you know, I'm a bit . . . out of . . .' I pause. Come on, Gracie, get it together. 'Was there anything in it? Any evidence? A lead?'

She shakes her head. 'Nothing obvious, I'm afraid. It's being examined by our forensics team at the moment, though, so we might know more eventually.'

'Oh, right.' I nod thoughtfully, aware that she is scrutinising my reaction, not entirely sure that I'm coming across as convincing. 'No curry then?'

'No, love, not so much as a poppadum.'

'Right. The bastard.'

She smiles. 'Anything else you want to ask?'

Her face is enigmatic. It makes me think there is definitely something else I should ask. And if I don't ask it, this could be one of those disastrous coincidences or shocking inaccuracies that pile up and pile up and ultimately find me languishing behind bars for the next forty years. Come on, Gracie, think! What else do I need to know? What did Matt tell us last night? The car was found, it had no curry in it . . .

'Oh, I know,' I burst out. 'Where was it found?'

So she tells me about Linton and I ask where that is and she says North Yorkshire and I say I've never heard of it and hope to God she doesn't see the print-out of the directions from Google Maps that's lying on the kitchen side near the bread bin.

Just before she leaves, she tells me that there's been no break-in at Adam's work premises, so no lead in that direction either. I nod and say, 'OK', and eventually she goes. As I watch her little police Clio speeding off up the road, I spot Pam's head from next door looking out of her side window at me. She's not being remotely discreet as she spies, with the net curtain pulled all the way back so her shiny white china figurine of two people dancing is completely visible. What room is that? Must be a study, or possibly a side window in the dining room. Either way, she didn't just happen to be in there at ten o'clock in the morning; she's gone in there deliberately to have a good old look out of the window at the catastrophe that's befallen me so she can report all the interesting bits back to Mike later.

'Oooh, there was another police car there this morning, Mike, must be something really bad, mustn't it? For them to be there again today like that, can't just be a parking fine or something.'

'Yeah, you're right, love. She's probably executed him and hidden his dismembered body in black bags under the upstairs floorboards. Pass the gravy.'

I deliberately lock eyes with Pam to make sure she knows I've seen her looking, but she doesn't turn away in shame or embarrassment. She just keeps on staring, as if she's trying to memorise every little detail about me. Probably thinks she's going to have to give a description to the police at some point in the future. I raise my hand and wave sarcastically. She waves back, then glances at her watch. 'She waved at me, officer, it was exactly ten oh five.'

Christ. I shake my head and go back inside, closing the door behind me with relief. I actually do feel a bit like a murderer desperately trying to hide what I've done from a prying detective. I've got away with it this time, but I know I won't be so lucky in the future. It's time to move the body . . .

'Oh my fucking God, what the crying out loud is this?' comes suddenly from the living room, followed by some rather fat, throaty laughter. I hurry in there to find a newly conscious Ginger sitting up on the sofa and giggling delightedly over a copy of *Keeping the Magic Alive: How to Get and Give Satisfying Lifelong Sex* by Dr Cristina Markowitz.

FIVE

As soon as Linda has left, I realise that I completely forgot to tell her about Leon's phone call, so Ginge and I spend the next twenty minutes hunting throughout the entire house, swearing and stamping and throwing things around until I eventually find Linda's business card on the coffee table under the sex book.

'You must have put the bloody book down on top of it!'

'Well I can't believe you didn't look there!'

'I thought you had!'

'I distinctly remember you saying that you had.'

So anyway, I ring Linda's number and leave her a message about Leon calling me and ask her to ring me back to discuss it.

Which leaves me with some nice empty free time to call Julia and Ray.

Ginge makes herself a large bowl of Shreddies and goes back to the living room to watch *Raiders of the Lost Ark* on DVD. I take my phone into the kitchen and sit down to make the call. Julia answers on the first ring. Was she sitting by the phone, waiting for news?

'Hello?' Her voice is breathy, expectant.

'Hi Julia. It's Grace.'

'Oh. Grace.' Definite disappointment.

'Listen, I'm sorry I've taken so long to ring you. I've just been a bit . . . Well, you know. How are you doing?'

There's a very brief pause as Julia processes the fact that it's not Adam on the phone, or the police, or anyone with any information about what's happened to him or where he is. Then she takes a deep breath in, and starts to speak, and what she says next disturbs me almost as much as Leon.

'Oh, love, it's so kind of you to ring. It's so terrible, isn't it, this whole thing? I just can't . . . I just can't think . . . But listen, Grace, I've had an idea. About three this morning, I'm sitting in the kitchen, OK, and I'm trying to work out the answers to the crossword, only the coffee time one, I never get the hang of those cryptic ones, they don't make sense, do they? And of course the neighbour's dog is barking – must have been shut outside again. I hate that, drives me totally bananas. On and on it went, bark bark bark, and then the occasional howl. Poor thing. Good job I was awake anyway, otherwise it would've woken me up. Anyway, it goes on and on and suddenly it starts to sound different, not like barking any more but more like someone whispering to me, over and over, *I'm here, I'm here, I'm here*. What do you make of that?'

This is the most she's ever said to me. My ears are thinking, 'Hang on a minute, we weren't ready, can you start again?' I blink. 'Um, well, I don't . . .'

'It must have been Adam! Mustn't it? I was thinking, you know, that it was probably definitely him, wasn't it,

74

trying to contact me, don't you think? From the other side, or wherever he is, I mean. Because of course he would try to get in touch, wouldn't he, if he could. He'd definitely try and contact me, I know he would. I'm his mum after all, aren't I?'

I can't answer for a few moments. There are so many things about this outburst that have surprised me, I'm not sure which one to react to first. She called me 'love'. She thinks Adam's dead. She's not sleeping. She thought she heard Adam trying to contact her in a dog's bark. She thinks Adam's dead.

'Julia, he's not even dead.'

There's a brief pause during which I can hear pages turning, or paper shuffling. Sounds like she's looking through a newspaper. 'Oh, my love, no, no, no, I know that. It's just we have to, you know, consider every alternative, don't we? I mean, if he did try to contact me, somehow, from wherever he's been taken, I'd want to try and get back in touch, you know, to try and find out what . . . or who . . . you know . . .'

Ginger appears suddenly in the doorway and gestures at the phone, making 'Who's that?' movements.

I mouth 'Julia' at her, and roll my eyes. She grins and makes drinking motions with her hand, then crosses her eyes and sways. I shake my head and look away. Ginger's theory for Julia's erratic behaviour is that she's an alcoholic, or a drug-oholic, or sniffs glue or marker pens or air freshener. I don't agree. Well, I'm not sure what I think, but I'm pretty sure I don't think it's stimulants.

I remember my birthday last year, when we'd all gone out for a meal. Ginger was completely psyched-up about seeing what Julia was likely to get up to, and arrived at the restaurant in a high state of anticipatory tension. She kept looking around for Julia, longing for her to arrive, wondering when she would. She had brought Fletch along, of course, and they were being loud and demonstrably loving with each other, in a mutually abusive kind of way. Adam and Fletch always seemed to get on, in the way that men whose girlfriends are close are forced to. Adam used to smile and nod and clutch Fletch's shoulder, but I'd sometimes wished he'd join in with their banter a bit more.

'All right buddy!' Fletch always said when he and Adam met. 'Still alive then?'

'Hello, Fletch. How's things?'

'Living the dream, man. Doesn't get much better, does it, eh?'

'Damn straight,' Ginger cut in at this point, punching Fletch's arm. 'Just remind yourself every ten minutes how bloody lucky you are, you snivelling wretch.'

'Gotta love her, the whore,' Fletch said with an affectionate smile.

We were in the Harvester because it was simple food with large tables, not too intimate. The four parents sat together at one end of the table, while we four youngsters sat at the other end. Adam and I were in the middle, effectively screening his parents from Ginger and Fletch. A sour expression had appeared on Ray's face the second he'd heard the night before that Fletch was going to be there, and now that he could see him, it was only getting worse. His hands were starting to fist-up, probably without him even realising it. Ray watched Fletch; I watched Ray; Ginger watched Julia. Fletch and Adam, oblivious to all of it, had a conversation about Arsenal.

The reason behind Ray's hostility was that the first time Julia had met Fletch, something very odd and uncomfortable had happened. It was another occasion, someone's birthday – probably Adam's – and he'd brought Ginge and Fletch over to where Julia was standing, to introduce them. Julia had not even acknowledged Ginger. She had kept her gaze firmly locked on Fletch's face the entire time. And as Adam had said, 'This is Gracie's friend, Fletcher', she had sidled in very close to Fletch and put her hand on his chest.

'Fletcher,' she had breathed huskily. Fletch's head had moved back almost imperceptibly. 'It's so very lovely to meet you.' She had put her nose even closer, practically touching the skin at Fletch's neck, and had taken a deep breath in through her nose. 'Mmm, you smell lovely.' She hadn't moved then for another four or five seconds, but had carried on staring straight at Fletch's neck, which was just about at eye level for her, lost in some kind of trance. Or overpowered by his liberal use of Lynx. Ginger and I glanced at each other, wondering what to do, and I remember the panicked look in poor Fletch's eyes, like a small animal in a snare. He thought he was going to be consumed. Eventually, Ginger pulled on Fletcher's arm, saying, 'You can move, you know', and Julia had wandered hazily away.

'Oh my God, how gone was she?' Ginger had stage whispered, then giggled. Adam had tried, unsuccessfully, to eviscerate her with his eyes, before stalking off after Julia.

So a few months later on my birthday, Ginge had been fidgety with interest, waiting to see what was going to happen. 'Oh God, I hope she gets stoned again,' she kept repeating, much to Fletch's annoyance. 'Oh shut up moaning, Fletcher. Don't pretend you didn't enjoy it.'

'I fucking well didn't,' he snarled, and opened his mouth to elaborate on the awfulness of it all. Then closed it abruptly as Adam joined us.

'What are you all talking about?' he'd asked, taking his jacket off.

Ginger had grinned. 'Remember on your birthday?' she started, but I couldn't let her continue.

'Yeah, remember that delicious tiramisu I had?' I cut in. 'I was just wondering if they did anything like that here.'

Ginger had frowned at me, but I ignored it. Talking about Adam's family was completely off the agenda. Particularly his mother. I didn't need that lesson twice.

'Um, Julia,' I start now, not because I have anything at all to add to this awkward rambling, but just to cut her off so I can ring my own parents, 'do you want me to pop round and see you both? Today? So we can talk about this properly?'

There's a brief pause, then she's off again. 'Oh, yes, yes, it would be wonderful to see you, love. I want to talk to you about my idea, Ray won't listen, he's just gone into a trance, with his headphones on, you know, that's his way of dealing with things. But he'll definitely want to see you too. Yes, it will help to have you here. When are you coming?'

I close my eyes. I have never been to Julia and Ray's place without Adam. In fact, I've never been in their company without him. I offered to go out of duty, really, and didn't really expect her to take me up on it. She's never shown much interest in me before. But at least we'll have a good, solid conversation starter. 'I'll leave as soon as I can,' I tell her. 'Probably within an hour.'

After we've hung up, I realise I don't have any means of getting there as my normal ride is currently languishing in Linton, so I sit down on the sofa next to Ginger, who is now glued to *SpongeBob SquarePants*.

'Ginge, you've got to drive me.'

She turns to me with her thirteen-year-old's face and says, 'Why do I? And more to the point, where?'

'I'll tell you in the car. Come on, make yourself decent. You can use my toothbrush.'

Twenty minutes later, we're pulling up outside the house. I had to drive in the end, as Ginger claimed to be too ill. We get out of the car slowly and carefully – Ginge with a poorly head, me with almost overwhelming reluctance – then stand together on the pavement for a few moments, trying to get up the nerve to go in. At least one of the people inside that house is going to be sympathetic to Adam's position here, and I'm not sure I can stomach it.

'Don't just stand there like buffoons,' Ray says suddenly from the front lawn, 'come inside. Julia's desperate to see you.'

We both start a little, neither of us having spotted the grown man standing right in front of us. We both greet him with a dutiful cheek-peck, and follow him in through the open front door. As we enter, I feel immense gratitude for the fact that Ginger is here with me. I'm not one of those selfless kinds of friends for whom a descent into hell is made more bearable by the knowledge that at least all their friends and loved ones are not there to endure it also. I need as many people around to support me as I can get.

Ray leads us into the living room, and there in front of us is Julia.

I'm shocked at the sight of her and find myself staring to take it all in. She's absolutely immaculate. She is dressed smartly and conservatively as usual in navy trousers, a pale pink blouse and a navy and white patterned scarf looped loosely round her neck. Her hair is washed and smooth. Her make-up is flawless. Her hands, one on her chest, even have polish on the fingernails. There isn't one thing out of place. I am absolutely staggered.

'Hi Julia,' I hear Ginge saying next to me as she moves forward to kiss Julia's cheek and give her a brief hug. Oh, yes, good idea. Can't believe I didn't do that first.

'Hi Julia,' I say then, and move in to repeat Ginger's actions. 'How are you doing? You look very well.'

'Oh I'm not well, Gracie, I'm not at all well. How could I possibly be? I'm a complete wreck.'

She really isn't. 'Oh dear . . .'

'Well what did you expect? Of course I'm going to be a mess, my only son has disappeared off to who knows where, probably dead in a ditch somewhere, or dying, panting his last breath right now, this very second, wishing his mummy would just come and get him and take him home.'

'Now what would you two girls like to drink?' Ray cuts in jovially at this point and we both turn to find him grinning in the doorway. 'Tea? Or something stronger?'

'I'll have one, Raymond,' Julia replies, and I notice for

the first time that the hand not pressed dramatically to her chest is wrapped firmly around a glass. She holds it out to Ray. '*Water* please.'

Ginger glances at me as if to say, 'Water? *Really?*' but I think that's unfair. Julia's had a terrible shock and anyway it could well be water. I turn to Ray gratefully. 'A cuppa would be lovely, thanks Ray.' I go over to the sofa to sit down, and thankfully both Ginger and Julia follow suit.

'I've not been sleeping, I've not been eating, I must look like skin and bone by now,' Julia announces. 'I must look like absolute death.'

Ginger and I both make the soothing sounds of denial, while discreetly taking in Julia's healthy, fresh-faced youthfulness and groomed coiffure.

'No, no,' she insists, 'I look dreadful. I'm grey, I'm sallow, I'm shadowy and I'm thin.'

'You're really not—'

'I *am*.'

There's a brief pause while Julia tips her completely empty glass back as far as she can and sucks the air out of it, as if she might absorb some fumes from it that she's missed before. I'm longing for Ray to come back so that I can at least hold a cup of tea.

'Did Gracie tell you about my idea?' Julia bursts out again, addressing Ginger.

'Um, no, she didn't.' Ginger turns slowly to me. 'Why didn't you tell me, Gracie?'

'I didn't . . . I mean, I haven't . . . It wasn't . . .'

'I had a vision, you see,' Julia goes on, undaunted. 'Well, no, that's not right, it wasn't really a vision. It was more a kind of . . . auditory vision. If that exists.'

'An ausion?'

'Shut up, Ginger.'

'What was that? What did she say?'

'Doesn't matter, Julia. Go on.'

'Well. Yes, I heard this noise. During the night. I couldn't sleep. I haven't been able to sleep properly since . . . Well, since everything happened with, um . . .' She glances up at me and for a horrible moment I'm convinced she's forgotten her own son's name. 'Um . . .'

'Adam?'

'Yes, of course Adam, who do you think I meant? For God's sake, Grace, I know my own son's name.' She tuts loudly. 'It's going to take more than five days for *me* to forget him.'

At this point, an angel of mercy appears in the form of Ray bearing a tray with two mugs and a glass on it. He dispenses the drinks silently, gives me a smile and a wink, then retreats to the other end of the room. There's an armchair there with a lamp above it, and a low bookcase full of thick, difficult volumes. This is Ray's refuge; not for him the garage or shed.

Julia takes a large gulp from her glass of 'water', closes her eyes briefly and then looks back at us excitedly. 'So after I'd heard Adam calling to me during the night, I got this idea. I can't imagine why we haven't thought of it before, actually. All this time we've been wondering what on earth has happened, and the answer is staring us straight in the face.'

'He's only been gone five days, Julia,' I interrupt. She's acting as though he disappeared months ago and no one's done a thing to find him.

'Wait,' Ginger says quietly to me. 'He was calling to her?'

'I'll tell you later.'

She raises her eyebrows. 'Total fruit loop.'

'Look, anyway,' Julia goes on, her eyes getting wider and wilder, 'here's my idea. I've read about these people, investigators, they find people who're missing. Psychics.' She points vaguely across the room. 'They're in the paper, everywhere. We'll get one of them to maybe sniff his toothbrush or handle one of his biros or whatever it is they do and then they'll be able to sense him or something and find out what happened to him. Oh Gracie, this is the answer, don't you think? She'll be able to see where he went, and then we can find him. It'll all be over, Grace. Won't it?'

Ginger says, 'A psychic? *Seriously?*'

Ray says, 'Bloody ridiculous.'

I say, 'He's not dead, Julia.'

'No, I know, but—'

'What use is a psychic if he's not dead?' Ginger again.

'Julia, a psychic is not the answer, whether he's dead or alive.' I glare at Ginger. 'We just have to let the police do their investigation, the traditional way, with computers and cameras and evidence. No sniffing of toothbrushes or handling stationery need be involved.'

She's momentarily flummoxed, but then rallies and starts in again. 'No, no, no, the thing is they don't need to be dead for these psychic investigators to find them. They can find anyone, no matter how long they've been missing, whether they're alive or dead. It's just easier if they *are* dead, that's all.'

'I'm starting to agree with that.'

She continues as if she hasn't heard me. 'This is just perfect, though, Grace, you do think so, don't you? I mean, the psychic will be able to tell us whether he's . . . you know . . .'

'Still alive?'

'*Well*. Whether he's well.'

I sigh. 'So even assuming that this actually works and that some stranger has some kind of spiritual communion with his underpants or something and tells us that he's well. How will that help? What possible good can that do?'

There's a moment's absolute silence. Then, 'How can you say that?'

I shrug wearily. 'Oh it's simple, Julia. Finding out whether he's well or otherwise doesn't make things any easier, does it? We still wouldn't know where he is or whether he's coming back.' I look at her frankly. 'Or why he left in the first place.'

She gawps at me in apparent horror and, as flaky as she is, she still manages to make me feel like the worst person in the world. A family trait. I open my mouth to say something soothing, something conciliatory, but as I watch, her face morphs slightly into a harder, less pitiful version of itself. Her eyes narrow, her jaw sets, her lips thin. It's as if she's just drunk a potion of some kind.

'You actually think it won't do any good to find out whether or not he's well? As if it doesn't matter in the slightest to you whether he's alive or dead?' Her voice is low and quiet now, and much more measured. There's more than a hint of steel in it. She snorts out a puff of air. 'Well that just goes to show the absolute difference between a mother and a wife, doesn't it?'

'Well, yes, it does, Julia! Of course it's different for both of us.'

'Oh, really? Would you like to explain that to me? Because as far as I knew, we both loved him. Didn't we? Or maybe you think I didn't love him as much because he was my son, not my husband? Maybe you think he loved you more, because you were his wife? Or maybe you've given up on him?' She pauses a moment, then adds, 'Can't say I'm surprised.'

'Well that's unnecessary,' Ginger butts in. I glance at her nervously, then look back at Julia. She's swivelled her head and is now staring in fury at Ginger.

'You don't have a flipping clue,' she says in a voice so low it reminds me weirdly of *The Godfather*. I expect her to come over all Sicilian suddenly. 'You're not a mother and never should be. Us mothers know stuff about life that ordinary people like you can't dream of.'

I'm getting chills and have to fight the urge to look over my shoulder defensively. 'Julia, I'm not in competition with you . . .' I say, but I get the sense that what I'm saying is bouncing off her like vodka on wool.

'Anyway,' she goes on, turning back to me, 'as the wife, it was you he left, not me. You obviously failed him in some way. And now thanks to you, we all have to suffer.' She rolls her eyes, then takes a deep swig from her glass. Apparently the venom in her words has dried her mouth up.

'Julia,' I start to say, a bit quietly, if I'm honest. At this point in my life, I should be raising my voice, taking a step forward, maybe pointing a finger, defending myself. Adam's not here, I don't have to worry about upsetting him at this moment. But Julia's words have sliced into me, drilled directly down into my gigantic reservoir of insecurity, and it's bubbling up. A geyser of tears is threatening to erupt, and I sidestep towards Ginger. She turns her head, sees my face, and moves towards me too, so that our arms are pressed together. Right now, I feel, yet again, the most enormous gratitude for her presence in my life, and in this room.

'It's OK, Grace,' Ginger says between gritted teeth, her eyes locked on Julia's the whole time. 'It's absolutely fine. I'm sure in a moment Julia is going to realise how vile and unpleasant she's being, and how completely unfair and unjustified that appalling accusation is. Aren't you, Julia?'

Julia doesn't move or speak for a couple of seconds. Then she blinks, her face crumples and she staggers backwards, her hand to her mouth. 'Oh . . .'

Ginger coolly watches her, still without moving, but I step forward and grab her arm. Finally I feel like I'm some use. 'Come on, Julia, come and sit down.'

I guide her to the sofa and she sits down heavily, leaning her head back and immediately closing her eyes. 'I'm so tired,' she says on a long exhale.

'I know. You've been through a lot.' I hear Ginger 'pah'-ing behind me, but I ignore it. 'Why don't you try and have a little snooze now?'

Julia opens her eyes and shakes her head. 'I can't sleep,' she says quietly. She searches my face. 'He is dead, isn't he? Do you think he's dead?'

86

'No, he's not dead,' I say with certainty, 'don't worry about that. Have they told you they found his car?' She nods. 'Well, then, you know that there was nothing in it, no blood, no smashed glass, no vindaloo. His passport is gone. There's no disturbance at his office, nothing seems to have been taken, although they haven't finished looking at it all yet. But even before they do, it's pretty clear to me that . . .' I hesitate. I still can't decide whether Adam going voluntarily is better or worse than him being taken by force. From a wife's point of view, it's miles better if he was wrenched roughly away against his will, fighting against his captor, struggling with every part of him, desperate to return to his true love; rather than simply deciding to piss off and please himself. No, that's wrong, because surely a good, loving wife would selflessly want him to have chosen this? Because she would not be able to stand the idea of him being hurt? I find I kind of like the idea. Which is a paradox because if he has been forced away, and hurt in the process, there's no need for me to hate him. Is there?

Julia is still staring at me with desperation in her eyes. I put my hand on her arm. 'Don't worry, Julia. There's absolutely no doubt in my mind that he's completely well, given all the facts. That he left of his own accord, for reasons unknown.'

'But—'

'And anyway, no body has been found, has it?'

She gazes at me with liquid eyes, that lost-puppy look back on her face. 'Yet,' she says.

Fifteen minutes later, Ginger and I are back in the car, heading home.

'Well, it's not substance abuse, is it?' Ginger says, ending the five-minute silence during which we both absorbed what just happened. 'The woman is completely off her rocker.'

'Oh, don't say that, Ginge. I feel sorry for her.'

Her head snaps round to stare at me. I'm driving again, so I can't stare back. 'Do you? Really?'

'Well yeah, course I do. She's absolutely destroyed.'

'You think?'

I risk a sideways glance. 'Don't you?'

She shrugs. 'I think it's an act. I think she's faking the whole "I'm-so-upset-about-my-son-going-missing-I'm-turning-into-a-certifiable-dingbat" thing.' She pauses and I can see she's staring at me. 'Don't tell me you fell for it?'

'Fell for it? Well, if you call believing that she's genuinely devastated by Adam's disappearance "falling for it", then yeah, I guess I did. Why didn't you?'

Another shrug. 'I dunno, really. Just didn't ring true to me.'

'You think she's not upset at all? That she couldn't care less?'

'No, I didn't say that. Obviously she's upset. Who wouldn't be? I just think . . . I don't know. It almost seemed like she . . .' She moves her head a little. 'As if she *wants* him to be dead.'

'No way!'

She nods. 'Yeah. Didn't you get that? All that breathy, "He's dead, isn't he?" stuff. And almost wanting a body to be found. Bit odd, I thought.'

'Well, you'd be odd if you'd been through what she's going through.'

'No, I don't think I would. I think most people would be anxious as hell, but trying to keep hopeful.' She glances at me. 'Like you are. He's a grown man, after all. He's not exactly vulnerable.'

'But it doesn't make sense. Why would she want that? She's his *mother*.'

'Who the frick knows? All I know is, something was off.'

I think back over our strange encounter again, but all I can see is a woman deranged by some pre-existing problem that I can't identify, coupled with massive stress, sleeplessness and grief. But I've never been any good at reading between the lines, or spotting subtle things. I tend to believe whatever I'm presented with. Maybe I'm naïve. Maybe I'm stupid. Turns out I was stupid to marry Adam, that's for sure. Probably. Maybe I need to start questioning my reality a bit more. Maybe if I'd done that a year ago, I wouldn't be here now.

'Oh, and one more thing,' Ginger says now, turning all the way round in her seat to face me. 'This grieving, desperate mother, this woman who you want to believe is going mad with determination to cling to the idea that her son is still alive, still loves her, and will come home again one day.'

'Yes?'

'Well, why the hell would a woman like that refer to her son the whole time in the past tense?'

SIX

I have no answer for that. Initially, I was convinced that Ginger had got it wrong, but remembering my conversation with Julia just now, I realise that she's right. There's no sound in the car for a few minutes while I think about it and Ginger nods off.

'So what does that mean?' I ask eventually. 'Do you think Julia knows something we don't?'

Ginger jerks awake at the sound of my voice and looks around blearily. 'Whassay?'

'I said, your theory about Julia talking about Adam in the past tense. Do you think she knows something?' I remember her addition of the word 'yet' after I reminded her that no body has been found, and instantly my flesh contracts and covers itself with goosebumps. Again.

Ginger rubs her eyes, yawns at great length, stretches her arms out in front of her, then shrugs. 'I don't know. I doubt it, to be honest. I mean, what could she know? Where he is? What's happened to him? The fact that he's dead?' She shakes her head tentatively. 'Nah, doesn't feel right. I mean, to know those things she'd have to have been involved, and she doesn't come across as the type, does she?'

'What type?'

'Violent, murderous matriarch. She's just too "tickets-to-the-opera-darling", in her blouses and slacks and home-made chutney, to pull it off.'

When we get back to the house, Ginger decides that she needs to go home to bed, so she leaves me on the pavement and shoots off. I watch the car until it's out of sight, then turn and walk towards the empty, silent house.

I run upstairs to start packing a small overnight bag. I want to go and see my mum and dad anyway, to let them know what's happened, and it'll be so comforting to stay there for a few days. Who knows, maybe this'll all be resolved by the time I have to come home again. I freeze with my hand in my knicker-drawer as that thought occurs to me. What do I mean, resolved? What kind of resolution could there be, after a husband is absent for five days? Maybe when I'm next in this room, Adam will be here with me. Or maybe he'll be dead. Probably not in the room with me, in that case. I hope not, anyway. I shudder and close my eyes a moment.

A sudden noise downstairs sends a thrill of fear plunging through me and my hand instinctively curls tightly around whatever is nearest. I look down at what I've grabbed. It's a sports bra. That is not going to protect me from anything. Except saggy boobs, possibly. I turn, cringing, towards the door of the bedroom, dreading what I might see there, shuffling its way across the landing: grey, dead flesh hanging off its bones, jaw slack and loose, head twisted much too far around on its neck. I am almost paralysed with fear, nauseous with it, and my mouth floods with saliva as my stomach spasms. But the landing is as empty of walking corpses as it was when I came through it a few minutes ago.

Good God, what is the matter with me? I need to get a grip. And preferably on something a bit sturdier than a white Nike Pro Airborne with nylon strap stabilisers. If I'm going to be here on my own, I'll need a defensive weapon. I glance quickly around the room and completely fail to spot an automatic firearm or serrated hunting knife anywhere.

I let go of the bra and creep stealthily over to Adam's side of the bed. Maybe he's got some kind of Swiss army knife in his drawer. My heart is thudding still, and as I reach for the drawer, I see that my hand is shaking slightly. I'm unclear at this point whether that's fear of whatever made the noise downstairs or anxiety over being about to touch Adam's things.

'We need to get lockable cabinets,' he'd said at Ikea.

'Why?'

'So that, my little petal, we can lock them,' he'd replied, giving nothing away with the words but letting me know with his tone exactly what kind of idiot I was.

'Oh, right yes, I realised that. What I mean is, why would we need to lock them? It's only you and me going in that room anyway.'

'Huh. You hope.'

'What?'

He took a deep breath in and released it very slowly to demonstrate his unending patience. 'I'm talking about burglars, Gracie. People who come into your house uninvited and go into the rooms where they're not supposed to be. It's a very real possibility these days, you read about it in the paper.' He paused. 'Well, *I* do. The thing is, if we lock them, we know that all our valuables are safe and sound every day, even if we go away on holiday.'

I had shrugged and not responded. I was smarting a bit over his dig about how I never read the paper. We'd had words about that before, and he wasn't happy. As far as I was concerned, news and the papers were just another form of entertainment. I can't do anything about budget cuts or the NHS or kids today, so what good does it do to get stressed over it by reading about it constantly? *Strictly Come Dancing* or *Heat* magazine were much cheerier. Adam despised me for it. Thought I should make more effort to keep up to date with current events, but had never been able to give me a good reason why. It's one of the few things he hadn't been able to convince me of.

So he'd bought the cabinets with the lockable drawers, and as far as I knew, his had remained resolutely locked ever since he'd put it there. I had a key to mine, too, but I'd never used it. I don't think right now I'd be able to lay my hands on it: inside the drawer it's meant to lock, probably. But we didn't keep our passports in there, so it seemed pointless to lock a drawer containing only a tub of lip balm, a packet of tissues, a novel and a selection of biros. Burglars could have 'em, and good luck.

I reach out now and tug the drawer on Adam's side. Yep, still locked. At this point I have to be honest and admit that I have tried it once or twice before now. When

I've been in the house on my own. It became almost a habit of mine, actually. Whenever Adam left the house without me, I'd sprint upstairs, try the drawer, then sprint back down again to be completely engrossed in something innocent by the time he got home. The first time I'd tried, it happened to be about three weeks before my birthday, only a month or so after we'd got the cabinets. Finding it locked, I'd assumed my birthday present was in there, and felt plumes of excitement ignite in me. It must be jewellery; the drawer was too flat for anything more substantial to fit. So I'd left it alone, not wanting to spoil the surprise. Oh, I didn't. The surprise was that he got my present three weeks later, on the way home from work, and gave it to me the same day. Which was fine because it was my actual birthday, after all. And it's always lovely to receive perfume.

After that, I checked the drawer regularly. More and more regularly. Pretty much daily, actually. And every time I tried it, I got angrier and angrier and angrier.

Right now, I'm in a state of heightened anxiety, extreme pissed-off-ness, desperation and blinding terror. It's the work of less than a minute to seize the cabinet roughly and slam it down hard onto the floor four or five times until it breaks apart. Thank God for Ikea. The drawer part separates entirely from the cabinet part below it and I bend down to examine it all.

The first thing I notice is that there's a tiny gold key Sellotaped to the underside of the drawer. I stare at it for a few seconds, shooting hatred at it from every single molecule of myself. If I'd turned to the side and looked in the wardrobe mirror, I'm sure I would have seen an ugly snarl on my face. That's if I could have seen anything with my eyes narrowed into slits. I unpeel the key and try it in the drawer lock. And, yes. It fits. Of course it does. Never mind, this whole lot can go to the tip when I get round to it. I give the shattered carcass a fierce, satisfying kick for good measure, and am rewarded with its further disintegration. It's starting to look like a defeated enemy, mortally wounded on the battlefield, spilling guts and blood everywhere. The next thing I notice is that the drawer must have been virtually empty, judging by the lack of any spilled contents. I crouch down onto the floor and pick all the other parts of the drawer out of the remains and toss them aside, then turn back to the broken innards and shattered MDF bones of the cabinet itself. There are a couple of biros amongst the detritus, but nothing else. I scrabble through it like a hyena picking over the carcass of a slaughtered zebra, incredulous that a man, however secretive, would keep an empty drawer locked. There must be something else here besides broken fake wood. Eventually, thankfully, I turn over one of the final shards of compressed woodchip and a thrill shoots through me as it reveals, there on the carpet, a large, heavy-looking, silver key, three times the size of the little gold one. My frantic rummaging and digging and grabbing and shuffling stops at once; I reach out slowly and pick up the key, then hold it up to my face and stare at it in wonder.

A noise from downstairs freezes me where I'm crouched, and I look up quickly towards the door, cradling my precious key safe into my hands. No one is going to get this from me, now that I've found it. As I start to move, I catch sight of myself in the wardrobe mirror: hunched and crouching low, uneasy expression, my hands protectively around my treasure, the silver of the key glinting just out of sight. 'We needs to see who's downstairs, we do,' I whisper to myself throatily, then stand up properly, smooth myself down, and go back to the landing.

From the top of the stairs I can see a large dark shape behind the glass of the front door. The noise I heard was just someone knocking, that's all. I relax with relief, then shrink with horror as an image immediately returns to my mind: Adam with blank, dead eyes, body bent and broken, skull crushed, a small trickle of blood running out of his ear . . . I close my eyes and shake my head to rid it of that idea. I'm one hundred percent sure – well, ninety-nine – that Adam is not even dead, let alone *un*dead; he couldn't possibly be coming back to me from the other side because he's still on *this* side. Plus, of course, zombies aren't real, and probably couldn't ever happen. Google was quite adamant about that.

I open my eyes and stare fixedly at the normal, living, breathing, person-shaped mass on the other side of the glass to convince myself it really is a normal, living, breathing person. Will have to get a grip on my fear – I'm alone now, better start getting used to it.

After some seconds of deep breathing and picturing lambs galloping around sun-drenched fields, I feel ready to advance towards the door. Evidently this person has been knocking while I've been ferreting around in Adam's things, doing impressions of disturbed literary characters. Swiftly I unclasp the silver chain around my neck, thread the big silver key onto it, then put it back on and tuck the key into my tee shirt, out of sight. As I go downstairs, I can see finally that it's just Matt, Ginger's large policeman-brother. I speed up a little, wondering if there's news. Then I slow down again, wondering if there's news.

'Hi, Gracie,' he says with a smile as I open the door.

'Hi, Matt.'

I expect him to go on, with something like 'I've just heard that Adam's been spotted getting on a bus to Cartagena', but he just looks at me, smiling expectantly. We play chicken like that for a few seconds while each waits for the other to speak. Eventually it becomes evident that he's not going to volunteer anything, so I have to ask.

'Um, do you have some news?'

His face changes dramatically, dropping like a punctured beach ball. 'Oh, God, no, I'm so sorry, of course that's what you would be expecting, I just didn't . . . I didn't think.'

'Oh.'

'I was just passing on my way to . . . and I thought I'd just pop in, see how you are.'

I lean a bit nearer. 'Sorry? On your way where?'

'Oh, um, no, I was just, you know, going to the . . . I was just passing. Thought you could maybe do with seeing a friendly face today.' A smile appears briefly, but disappears again.

I frown. 'Is there a reason why I might need to see a friendly face today?'

'No, no, God, sorry, I didn't mean . . . There's no . . .' He stops. Takes a breath. 'Well, there is . . . one small . . .' He stares at me a moment, I guess wondering whether or not to tell me the thing. From the quick succession of expressions on his face, it's clear he's undergoing some kind of internal struggle. Frown; smile; glance down; look up. Then he releases a breath. 'The only news there is, that I've heard, is that the CCTV pictures from the motorway . . .' He tails off and glances to the side. I don't need to see her to know that Pam's cleaning her spare room window again. He looks back at me. 'Should I . . . come in? Maybe?'

'Oh, yes, yes, sorry. Come in.'

He steps across the threshold and I close the door behind him, then turn to face him and wait.

He smiles. Then looks away. Then presses his lips together. Looks back at me. I want to slap him. 'Um, sorry, Grace, do you mind if we . . .?' He looks towards the kitchen door. 'I'm just . . . I just . . . don't think I should give you this information . . .' he glances around, 'in the hallway.'

'Oh. Right.'

'I think . . . sitting down would be best.'

I don't want to sit down. I don't want to stand up though. I feel like I might suddenly fly apart in all directions, or implode, shrivel up to nothing and blink out. But I hold it all in, keeping it together, and walk calmly into the kitchen. I busy myself with the standard response to a police officer turning up at your home unexpectedly, five days after your husband mysteriously disappears: I put the kettle on. I don't want to. I just want him to tell me what he knows. But Matt stays resolutely silent as he watches me make us both a drink. He leans against various cupboards, being repeatedly moved along by me needing mugs, then spoons, then tea bags, then milk.

'Sorry, I'm a bit in the way, aren't I?'

I don't want to lie, so I stay silent. It's already half past twelve. I need to know what he knows. It's almost become a pain, like a toothache, nagging at me, needing to be extracted. And beyond that, I want to ring Mum, finish packing and hightail it out of here. Whatever it is he's got to tell me, I'm sure seeing my family will help. Or at least, being out of this house will help.

When the tea's made, I lead us back into the living room and we sit down. I stare meaningfully at Matt; he stares into his mug like a fortune teller.

'Are you going to tell me my fortune?' I ask him.

He raises his head. 'What? Sorry, what?' He glances down at the tea. 'Oh, you mean . . .? Ah, I see what you . . . Sorry Gracie. This is one of the things about this job I don't like.' He looks steadily into my eyes. 'I mean, I love my job. I absolutely love it. I love helping people and being someone they know they can rely on, and sorting out the good from the bad, then grabbing bad by the collar and shoving it into the back of the car – carefully, I hasten to add. It's all very health and safety these days.' He gives an enigmatic smile and I wonder whether he's glad about the strict behaviour code, or resents it for getting in the way of 'real policing'. Probably likes it. He's very young, never known it any other way. Madly, an image of an innocent person going down for something they didn't do because of a corrupt copper flashes into my mind. Shouting 'It wasn't me! I'm innocent!' as they're led away, struggling. Shunning their friends

99

and family. Refusing all visitors. Launching unsuccessful appeal after unsuccessful appeal. Descending into depression, madness and, ultimately, suicide. Bile rises a little as I realise that, in my vision, that person is me.

'Innocent until proven guilty, you mean?' I say, to remind him that I didn't kill Adam. My voice is barely above a whisper.

He nods. 'Oh, yeah, definitely that. But also, you know, being very careful with people. Good and bad. Regardless of what they've done, you still have to look after them. Still have to treat them with respect and dignity.' Another meaningful look comes my way.

'Right.'

'Even though a lot of them don't deserve it.'

'I'd imagine.'

He nods. 'Even though sometimes, you think that those people, the bad people, get far more than they deserve, and never really appreciate it.'

I'm not sure I understand what he's going on about, so I just nod slowly, even though what I really want to do is yell at him, *Just tell me!* Preferably while beating my fists against his chest. We both take a sip. The watch on my wrist is screaming to be looked at, but it always seems so rude to check the time when someone is doing something nice for you.

'So,' I say, to hurry things along a bit. 'This is an aspect of your job you don't like?'

He nods again. 'Yes, it is. Same for everyone in this job.' He puts his tea down on the floor and scoots forward on his chair a bit, looking at me the whole time. 'It's giving people bad news.' He gets a panicky look immediately and shakes his head, putting a hand up towards me. 'No, no, that's not what I mean. I'm not saying I've got bad news for you, please don't think that. It's not bad news. But it's still . . . it's news. Probably not the news you want, although it isn't the worst possible news, I mean, no one's dead or anything.' He stops. Collects himself a bit. Starts again. 'It's about the CCTV pictures from the motorway.'

I know this from what he said at the door. Also I was already convinced no one was dead. 'OK.'

Matt rubs the back of his head as he struggles to find the right words to tell me something I already know. 'The pictures show very clearly Adam in the driving seat, driving himself.' He pauses. 'No one else was in the car.'

'Oh.' I take a moment to absorb this. In my head I can picture the grainy black and white image from the CCTV camera of Adam sitting at the wheel. He's smiling. Laughing actually. Thinking what an idiot his wife is, for being so gullible. Congratulating himself for having everything his way. Relaxing and enjoying the drive as he appreciates how cleanly he's managed to get away. Gradually, I can feel the muscles in my body start to tense and my breathing speeds up. A small flame of anger sparks inside me with a '*whoomf*' like the boiler coming on, and the heat from it starts to spread out through my veins.

Then a sudden thought occurs to me and the rising rage subsides. There was no one else in the car. He was alone. That means there was no woman in the passenger seat. So he wasn't eloping, then. He didn't leave my side and drive off with some other dozy cow to embark on a new web of silence and reserve with her. So why *did* he leave? I feel myself frowning and when I look up I find Matt's eyes on me. He squints a bit. 'You understand what this means?' he says softly. 'He wasn't coerced or threatened or abducted . . .'

'Yes, I get it.'

He presses his lips together. 'And you know what the implications are?'

I nod. 'Adam's left me, yes, I get it.' It's surprisingly easy to say. Maybe because it's not a surprise.

'Right.' He nods thoughtfully. 'You just seem pretty calm about it.'

'Oh, no, I'm not really. I mean, my husband left me, voluntarily, for reasons unknown. That makes me bloody furious. I mean totally, incredibly, absolutely, screamingly livid. And hurt, and frustrated, and let down, and abandoned, and unloved. But mostly explosively, homicidally enraged.' His eyebrows go up. 'No, no, not homicidally. Obviously.' Must remember that series of cataclysmic mistakes that leads to me in prison.

'Obviously.'

'But, you know, at the same time, he was alone. And in a way that's a good thing.'

'How is that a good thing?'

'Because there was no other woman in the car with him.'

He stares at me. 'Of course.'

I shrug. 'I'm his wife, Matt. Of course I don't want to find out that he has some other life somewhere.'

'Of course.'

'Although . . . I suppose the fact that she wasn't in the car with him doesn't mean that she doesn't exist . . .'

He puts his hands up. 'No, no, don't go down that road. That way sadness lies.'

I offer him a weak smile. 'I just don't know what to think. It's so . . . confusing.'

'Confusing? That certainly wasn't what I was expecting.'

'What were you expecting?'

He shrugs. 'Well, don't forget that I remember when you were seventeen and Blue went on a hiatus.' He smiles wistfully. 'You were pretty severely upset about that.'

'Oh my God, I was, wasn't I?' I find a smile coming as I remember Ginger and my ridiculous histrionics over that piece of news. 'I think we sobbed on Ginger's bed for three hours straight.'

He shakes his head. 'Four and a half.'

'Oh God! Really?'

'Oh yes. When you eventually came downstairs, you looked so sad, shuffling around like you had this terrible burden, all white and delicate-looking, like a broken little flower.'

'Well they are the greatest English R and B group that ever lived.'

'Hm, that's debatable.'

'I don't think so.'

He smiles broadly. 'We're debating it now. Ergo, it's debatable.'

'*Ergo?* Matthew Blake, you've changed.'

'I certainly hope so.'

'Oh, yes, loads. I remember you back then, too, don't forget.'

'You do?' He grins delightedly.

'Yeah. You were this skinny little kid who never said

anything to anyone. All moody and sulky, stomping around with your pierced nose and your Doc Martens.'

His grin falters a little. 'Oh God, don't remember that, pleeease!'

Now I'm grinning. 'Don't worry, that's pretty much all I do remember. You stayed out of our way most of the time, didn't you, so you didn't really make any impact. Apart from that hideous nose ring.'

'It was awful, wasn't it?'

'Terrible. Like a bull. I mean, what possessed you?'

He smiles and shakes his head. He's a bit more subdued now. 'Don't know really. Wanting to be different, I suppose.'

The mood seems to have changed suddenly. We've gone from playful laughing to wistful sadness in the space of two seconds. I nod. 'I get that.'

'It wasn't real, anyway. Not pierced. It was just a clip thing.'

'Was it really? I didn't know that. How funny.'

'Yeah. I was too scared of the pain to get it actually pushed through, so it just pinched my septum extremely hard all day, every day. Excruciating!'

'Ha ha! The things we do for . . . I was going to say beauty, but it was the opposite of that, really. The things we do to be different. To stand out.'

He nods. 'Yeah. And it doesn't work anyway, does it?'

'What do you mean?'

'I mean, we still get overlooked and unnoticed, don't we?'

He's staring at me intensely and I feel sure that I'm missing something. 'Oh. Well, I suppose . . .'

'I'd best be off,' he says suddenly, standing up. 'Thanks for the tea.'

'Oh, right. OK. Well, thanks for coming, Matt. I appreciate it.'

'No problem. You'll get the official notification soon enough anyway, I should think.'

'Thanks.'

We go in silence to the hallway and, once there, he turns to me and pulls out his wallet. 'Look, Gracie, if you need anything, anything at all—'

'Matt, no, I'm fine. Seriously.' I absolutely will not accept money from him; that would be mortifying.

'—here's my number.' He hands me a small white card with his name and mobile number on it.

'Oh. Thanks. I thought you were going to . . .'

'What?'

'No, nothing. Forget it.'

'OK. Well, give me a call. I mean it. Anything you need, any time, don't worry about it, just call me. OK?'

'Thanks, Matt. I will.'

'Good.' He smiles, maintains eye contact for just half a second longer than necessary, then opens the door. Standing there on the step is Linda Patterson, the police liaison officer.

'Shit,' I say, before I can stop myself. Pam's window beyond the fence steams up instantly.

Linda blinks and I can practically feel the handcuffs going on. 'Oh, Grace, sorry, is it convenient?'

Matt's in uniform, so they nod to each other in vague recognition, but it's obvious they don't really know each other. He steps round her then turns back to me briefly. 'Bye Gracie.'

'Bye.'

Linda turns and watches him leave, then looks back at me with a bemused smile. 'Who's that, then?'

'A friend. Do you want to come in?'

'Hmm. Oh, yes, if you've got a moment.'

I pull the door wider and she steps in. 'I'm going to see my parents this afternoon, so I don't have very long.'

She looks at me, still with that odd smile. 'No, I understand, that's fine. We don't always have time for everything that's important, do we? One of life's great frustrations. But I'll only take a few minutes.'

She's starting to remind me of Columbo now and it's making me act all suspiciously. I even feel guilty, as if I have something to hide. I know I was coming across as a bit odd during her earlier visit, when Ginger was still asleep on the sofa.

'No, I don't mean that. Of course I've got time. Let's go and sit down.'

I lead her into the living room without offering a cup of tea. She glances around the room before sitting on the edge of the sofa. 'Friend not here any more, then?' It's as if she doesn't believe Ginger was ever here in the first place.

I look around too. 'Doesn't look like it.' She's making me act suspiciously, I can't even help it.

She nods. 'Well, I've got a little bit of news for you, about Adam.'

'Right.'

I realise, too late, that I haven't given the correct reaction again. Linda is watching me closely, no doubt mentally scrawling in her mental notebook something like 'Grace acting suspiciously, apparently disinterested in news of husband.'

106

'What?' I ask, a bit more urgently. 'Have they found something? Or him? Has he been found? I mean, has he turned up somewhere?'

She shakes her head. 'No, sorry Grace, it's nothing like that. I should have made that clear from the outset.'

'Oh, right.' At this point I remember that she said this morning that she would warn me with a phone call from the car every time she was coming to visit, so that I wouldn't worry when I saw a police uniform at the door. She didn't do that, only a few hours later, and it makes me wonder why. Trying to catch me out? Hoping to walk in and find me in the middle of burning some clothing?

'No, all it is, is the CCTV footage of Adam's car driving off. We've got numerous different sightings of it, all heading north, and he's the only person in the car.'

I nod. 'Right.'

She blinks slowly. 'So . . . you understand what that implies?'

'Yes, yes, he wasn't coerced or threatened or abducted.'

'That's right.'

'Which means that he's probably just left me, for some reason.'

'Indeed.'

It occurs to me now that she's not breaking this to me very gently, given that it's my darling husband we're talking about. We've only been married a year, we're supposed to be blissfully deep in the honeymoon phase. We still could be, as far as she knows. Why isn't she being a bit kinder? Again, I suspect I'm not giving the expected reaction, and my apparent lack of distress is going down in that mental notebook, and building a nice little stack of evidence against me.

Oh what am I thinking? Of course she's not building evidence against me. There isn't any.

Yes, but if she thinks I'm acting suspiciously and not reacting how one would expect in these circumstances, she's going to suspect me and start actively digging around for evidence against me.

Doesn't matter, she won't find any.

I think about the smashed cabinet upstairs, and the silver key round my neck. I don't want to tell her about that, I want to look into it myself first, I want to try to regain something I feel I've lost. Power? Control? Self-esteem? I don't know. All I do know is that my marriage and Adam's disappearance have taken something from me, and I want it back. But if Linda somehow finds out about it, she might well think I had tried to hide it from her. And she'd be right, of course, because that's exactly what I have done. But what she thinks are my reasons for keeping it to myself will no doubt be something else added to the stack in that mental notebook of hers. And, of course, if whatever the silver key unlocks reveals something about Adam's disappearance, it will be very difficult convincing anyone that I hadn't kept it secret to prevent that information from being discovered.

By this time my eyes are practically rotating in spirals in my head, and Linda is staring at me oddly. Although, to be fair, I am acting oddly.

'Are you all right, Grace?' she asks, then leans forward interestedly to watch my reaction.

I wonder for a tenth of a second whether I should try

to give a more appropriate response – weeping, angry, distressed – but then I think better of it. Whatever response I'm giving is the appropriate one, because that is the one I'm giving. I have nothing to hide, I am not guilty of anything. This is just what my dad calls 'Green Channel Guilt': the way you always start sweating and glancing around you furtively, while walking like you've got five condoms packed with heroin up your bum, the second you set foot in the green channel.

'No, I'm fine, actually,' I say eventually, nodding slowly. 'I suppose I must have accepted the fact that he'd left me of his own accord when we found that his passport was gone.'

'Ah, I see.'

'And the fact that there was no curry.'

'Yes.'

'There never was any curry. There was never going to be.'

'No, no, I see what you mean.' She takes a furtive look at her watch, which I find deeply insulting. I'm a hysterical wife here, on the receiving end of some potentially devastating information, and she's wondering whether she's got time for Sub of the Day on her way back.

'Am I keeping you?' It's out before I can stop it.

She looks up, suitably embarrassed. 'Oh, no, no, I'm so sorry, Grace, that was rude of me. Um, I got a message from you, something about a phone call?'

So I tell her about the call from Leon earlier and she writes it down in her actual notebook, although there's not really very much to write down. She nods and looks interested, though, which is nice of her.

'So your name isn't Grace at all, then, Grace?'

'No, that was the odd thing about it.'

'Yes, I see what you mean.'

By the time she finally leaves, it's well past three o'clock and I'm starting to feel like the entire day is getting away from me. I'm very conscious of the heavy silver key round my neck and the feel of it there reignites my fury and sets my jaw with iron determination; I will get to the bottom of whatever has happened to my husband and my life, no matter what it takes, where I have to go, or what I have to do, in a ruthless and relentless pursuit of the truth. But first I want my mum to tuck me into bed with a hot water bottle. I finish packing my case and drag it down the stairs, then quickly ring Mum from my mobile.

'Is everything OK, poppet?' she asks immediately on hearing my voice, and instantly I want to cry.

'Oh, Mum . . .' I start, but my throat aches too much to carry on. Isn't it funny how you can stop yourself from crying for ages, or even not feel like crying at all, until you talk to your mum? She's incredibly perceptive, though. All I had to say was, 'Hi, Mum,' and she's got her nose up, sniffing the air.

'Gracie, are you OK, love?'

'Not really,' I say now, my voice catching. 'I'll tell you when I get there.'

'Oh, my love, what's going on?'

'I'll tell you when I see you. All right?'

She tuts and sighs and is clearly not happy about waiting, but I want her to cuddle me as soon as I've told her. 'All right, love. Tell Adam to bring his spirit level, would you? Dad's got a—'

'Adam's not coming,' I interrupt, 'it's just me this time. No, Mum, Mum,' I have to raise my voice over her as she tries to cut in again, 'I'll tell you when I get there.'

There's a pause while she no doubt reaches a conclusion. When she finally speaks, her tone, if not her words, are very much 'I knew this would happen.' 'Right,' she says, 'I'll make coconut cupcakes.'

SEVEN

I'm actually not a big fan of my mum's coconut cupcakes. They're a bit dry and woody for me. I prefer something moist and squidgy that's going to coat the inside of my mouth with goo while I'm eating it. Mum's cupcakes tend to leave a fine layer of dust behind. But once, when I was ill with tonsillitis or flu or something, back when I was twelve or thirteen, they were the only things I could stomach. They became my staple for about a week, only because they were bland and dry enough not to make me heave. Over the ensuing years, their performance during that time of illness has gone down in Kelly family history. Their healing power has been exaggerated so much, the cupcakes have taken on the role of a revolutionary new cure to which all known germs have no resistance. The story gets repeated at every family gathering: every barbecue, every wedding, every funeral. 'Ooh, these cakes are lovely. Bet they can't save a life, though.' 'Shame old Uncle Bill didn't have one of Judy's cupcakes, we wouldn't be here now.' 'The wedding cake is coconut, actually. We're hoping it will make sure we're not ill on our honeymoon.'

So now Mum thinks they're the cure for every kind of ill or problem that befalls me. As soon as she catches a glimpse of even the slightest frown, she's off into the kitchen whipping butter into coconut flakes and caster sugar before you can say 'cholesterol'. Then thirty minutes later she emerges carrying a plate of confections like a crown on a cushion. Of course, I have to devour three or four, and then immediately declare an improvement in whatever it is that's ailing me at the time; and she sleeps well that night knowing that her maternal job has been done well and all is right with the world (leaving aside the fact that at that moment saturated fat is silently and stealthily lining her child's arteries and restricting blood flow).

But, having no car, it's an ordeal of a journey on the bus with luggage, so by the time I get there after what feels like fourteen changes, all I want to do is retreat to my old room, get under the covers, and talk on the phone to my best friend about boys and homework. There's the hint of warm coconut in the air, but I don't have the stamina for it right now.

'What's he done?' Mum asks me as soon as I'm safely over the threshold. I close my eyes. 'What's that look for?' she goes on. 'Obviously he's done something, otherwise you wouldn't be here.'

'Mum . . .'

'All right, all right. Shall I bring you up some soup and cakes?' she asks as I head for the stairs.

I shake my head. 'It's been a ghastly few days, and today has been one of the worst. I'm going to have a lie-down. I'll talk to you a bit later on.'

'But—'

'Later, Mum.'

My room is pretty much exactly as I left it when I moved out – cream walls, white bedding, a shelf of handbags, a shelf of books, that kind of thing. There's a rogue exercise bike that's crept in somehow, and a plastic storage box containing what looks like Christmas decorations, but other than that it's all mine. I haven't slept here in years, though; certainly not since Adam and I have been together. Right now, I dump my overnight bag on the floor and crawl under the quilt without even getting undressed. It's probably only about half past five, but I'm not here because I'm tired.

When I wake up some time later, I realise that apparently I was tired. I haven't slept well since Adam . . . disappeared? It seems much more accurate to say 'left' now. I haven't slept well since Adam left, so it's hardly surprising I'm tired. I do feel quite significantly better, though, after that little nap. It's a bit darker than it was earlier so I must have been out for a couple of hours at least.

As I'm on my way back downstairs, I notice that the house is mysteriously and intensely silent. There's no television noise, no talking, no sound of someone washing up, no kettle boiling or dishwasher rumbling. The hairs on the back of my neck start to prickle and my heart starts thudding. I head for the kitchen door; that's where most of the activity should be this time of the evening. At the threshold, I hesitate. There is still no sound or movement coming from behind the door. What am I going to discover on the other side? Has Leon from the phone followed me here and, for reasons still unknown, slaughtered my entire family and left their lifeless bodies in a

114

lake of blood by the laundry basket? When I open this door, whatever I see on the other side can't ever be unseen.

I close my eyes and push it open at last, then stand there a moment, not wanting to look, dreading the sight of the blood in all its various forms – upswing spatters across the expensive chandelier light fitting that Mum bought from Habitat (and Dad always said was pretentious); pools collecting around the breakfast bar and in between the legs of the breakfast stools ('completely unnecessary: we have a table'); drips and drops running down the door of the Whirlpool dishwasher ('at that price it'd better prepare the food and put everything away afterwards, too'). I take a deep breath to do what I can to prepare myself for the horror I'm about to witness, raise my hand in readiness to defend myself, and open my eyes.

'What the fuck are you doing?' My eyes get instantly wider and scan the picture before me to try to make sense of it. In the kitchen, sitting at the table reading the back of the cornflakes box while he munches, is nothing more than my little brother, Robbie. He's turned to look up at me with a grin. 'You look like a proper twat.'

'Oh, Robbie.' My relief is intense and I feel a bit dizzy with it. The only spatters and drips anywhere in here appear to be standard gravy. And a small pool of milk next to Robbie's bowl.

'Mum says you and Adam have split.' He shoves in another loud mouthful.

I frown. How was that the conclusion she reached, just because I arrived without him? 'She doesn't . . . That's not exactly . . . Rob, what's going on? Where is everyone?'

'Probs still in bed, what'd you expect?'

115

'Still?' I frown, then look up at the clock above the sink. Distractedly I notice that the old Mickey Mouse one from Florida has been replaced with a sleek, shiny stainless steel job with no numbers on it. It's difficult but I can make out that it's around quarter to seven. I look back at Robbie. 'Is it morning?'

He rolls his eyes. 'Well duh. What did you think it was?'

'Evening, dick head. What other quarter to seven is there?'

'All right, smart arse.'

At this moment, a small black cat wanders casually into sight from under the table. When it sees me it freezes and stares at me with saucer eyes. I stare back.

'Rob,' I whisper, 'there's a cat in here.'

He looks round the end of the table. 'Oh, yeah, that's Ripper. Hey Ripper.' He leans forward off his chair and puts his arm out towards the cat, which immediately starts in abject terror and skitters away, zooming past me into the hallway and up the stairs.

'Who the hell is Ripper?'

Robbie goes back to his cereal. 'Our cat, numbnuts.'

'Since when have we had a cat?'

'Dunno. Ages.'

'But . . . you can't have had it ages. I'd have known.'

He shrugs but says no more.

I move to the table and sit down opposite him, feeling more than a little out of kilter. I'm astounded that I've slept for over twelve hours. I'm astounded that my family have got a cat and I didn't know. As I look around the kitchen I notice other things askew: a new knife block on the side in the shape of a man, with all the knives protruding from his torso; a mug tree I've never seen before, festooned with white and purple patterned mugs; this table in front of me is unfamiliar. And now that I look more closely, I notice that the walls themselves have been painted. They used to be yellow; now they're lilac. I feel like a time traveller coming back to my own time to find everything changed.

But obviously I haven't just turned up from a trip into the past. Obviously last time I was here, I simply didn't notice these things. Probably because Adam would have been with me. That's all. Maybe I'm just weirded out now because of the cumulative lack of sleep finished off by a mammoth thirteen-hour sleeping jag. And who wouldn't have bizarre thoughts after what's happened?

It occurs to me, in the light of my strange, bloody imaginings just now, to wonder whether it's thoughts of Leon that have been keeping me awake at night. I hadn't believed I was all that bothered by those two odd calls, but it seems that I am. Here, back in the bosom of my family, I feel safe again. I glance across at Robbie, his head low over the cereal box, spoon poised mid-air, a dribble of milk on his chin. 'It says here,' he says, not looking up, 'that when snakes are born with two heads, they fight each other for food.' He raises his head. 'How cool is that?'

Yeah, not sure how much use he'd be against a ruthless assassin, but still.

'Why are you up so early, dog breath?' I ask him.

He looks at me scathingly with hooded eyes. 'Because it's Thursday, slug head. Some of us have to go to work.'

'Oh, really?' Robbie's got a *job*? I feel left behind again, like things here have progressed and got older and moved on, and I'm stuck in that moment immediately before I left, when Robbie was still at school and there was a Mickey Mouse clock above the sink. I know Robbie's twenty now, and works . . . somewhere, but I suppose it hasn't really sunk in.

'Yep. I'm a man now, Gee,' he says, nodding wisely. 'Got commitments and responsibilities, just like you.' Then he picks up his cereal bowl and drinks the last of the milk from it.

Gradually over the next half-hour the other members of my family appear in the kitchen, starting with Mum.

'Oh, there you are,' she says, as if she's been looking for me everywhere. 'How are you feeling, love?' She uses a tone that says 'I'm so sorry for you', and comes over to enfold me in a hug. I'm feeling so much better after such a long sleep, I find I don't actually want her sympathy any more. Not when I know she's thinking, 'It was only ever a matter of time.'

I return the hug, but after a few seconds I give a couple of gentle pats on her back – hug language for 'enough'. She moves away and looks at me with her head on one side. 'What happened? Has he found someone else?'

'No he hasn't found someone else, Mum, and thanks for the vote of confidence.'

'Oh . . .'

'What happened was, he went out for a take-away on Friday evening, and never came back.'

Mum's head snaps upright and her face opens out. 'Friday?' she says, aghast. 'He went on *Friday*, and you're only just telling us now? It's Thursday!'

118

'Well, you know, it's been a bit weird, the police have been—'

'*The police?*' She glances around her in panic. I wonder why, then realise she's probably thinking a team of armed officers on ropes are going to crash in through the windows at any moment and go through all her unpaid parking tickets.

'Mum, it's fine, it doesn't concern you.'

She breathes heavily a moment, then sits down at the table. 'Well,' she says, 'what a shock.'

'Yes, it was awful.'

She looks at me. 'Oh, yes, yes, of course, for you too.'

I roll my eyes and notice Lauren standing at the kitchen door trying not to laugh. She sees me see her and comes over to give me a squeeze.

'Older sibling,' she says solemnly, holding me at arm's length. 'Female sibling.'

'Younger sibling,' I reply. 'It's good to see you.'

She gets a cup out of the cupboard and puts the kettle on. 'Your choice. You could've seen me any time you wanted. I've been here, like, the entire time.'

'I know. It's just, you know, Adam was . . .'

Her head snaps round. 'Adam was what?'

'Oh, nothing. Bit of a homebody, that's all. Wanted to be at home all the time.'

She goes back to making her drink. 'Ooh, did I hear right? Has he done a bunk?'

'Shh, Lo,' Mum butts in. 'You'll upset your sister.'

'No I won't, she's clearly fine. So, come on, spill. What's happened?'

I spend a few minutes recounting the events of Friday

night, and each day since then, to the tuts and sighs of both of them, until finally Dad comes in.

'I see next door have got a driveway man in, now,' he says as he joins us. He spots me there straight away and a loving smile breaks out on his face. I'm so happy to see him, my eyes actually tear up as I get up and cross the kitchen to hug him.

'Ah, Gracie. Have you had something bad happen to you?' he says gently, wrapping his big old arms round me. It's what he's been saying ever since I can remember, for every bumped head and scraped knee, every disappointment or let-down over friends or boys or parties or plans. I stay there for a few moments, my head pressed against his sweatshirt.

'What's happened, puddin'?'

So I recount the story again of the missing madras and the passport gone and the car in Linton and Dad nods and makes soothing noises while in my periphery I can see Mum trying to raise her eyebrows at him.

'How long are you staying?' Mum says when I've finished.

'Are you moving back in?' Lauren joins in excitedly.

'Do you need to borrow my car?' Dad asks, looking at me closely. I smile at him gratefully. It's the only useful thing anyone has said.

'Mum, Lauren, I don't really know, but no, I'm not moving back in.'

'Can you manage your mortgage, though?'

'It's not mortgaged, Mum, it's rented. And no, I probably can't manage the rent on my own.'

Mum looks at Dad. 'I thought they'd got a mortgage, didn't you?' He shrugs. 'I could've sworn they'd decided to buy.' She shakes her head. 'Can't understand that, these days, renting. It's just money down the drain, with nothing to show for it at the end.'

'Yes, well, luckily my husband didn't hang around for that, and now I'm not stuck with an expensive mortgage all on my own, so it's worked out for the best, hasn't it?'

'Hey,' Dad says, but I've had enough for today, and it's only eight fifteen.

'Yes, I would love to borrow your car, Dad. Where are the keys?'

'In the pot by the front door.' He puts his hand out towards me. 'Do you want help with anything, love?'

I'm in the process of stomping past him angrily, but I stop at this point and look at him. 'Thanks Dad. I don't think so. Yet. But I'll let you know, if I do.'

'More like when.' That's Lauren. She's holding a mug about an inch away from her lips and is staring down into it. She moves it the final inch and takes a sip as I stare at her. She's pretending she can't see me; I'm standing right in front of her.

'So they're getting their driveway done, are they?' Mum says now to Dad. 'What a surprise. Not.'

'That's pathetic,' Lauren joins in. 'Do they think we're stupid?'

'Could be a coincidence,' Mum says. 'Maybe they were thinking about having theirs done months ago, before ours even started . . .'

'Yeah, sure, Mum.'

Everyone disappears at this point to get ready for work, and thirty minutes later, they've all gone. Lauren to the council offices, Mum to the primary school, Dad to

121

the solicitors'. I'm all on my own. Again. Should try to get used to it, I suppose.

I've brought my laptop with me, so I make myself a cup of tea, then install myself at the kitchen table and Google locksmiths. It's not much of an idea, but it's a starting point. Surely someone, a specialist in the field, might recognise the style of the silver key and be able to tell me what it fits? Google tells me there are three locksmiths in the town here, so I'll try them all. I feel energised, positive – glad that I finally have some constructive action I can take to try to discover something about Adam, and maybe find out where he is. Or at least, why he's gone. Finally, after three years of knowing him, I might actually *know* him. Or something about him, anyway, besides his favourite type of ice cream. Although given recent events, he may well have been lying about rum and raisin too. It always seemed a bit unlikely. Anyway, I'm just assuming, hoping, that the silver key holds, well, the key, and will literally unlock some answers about Adam. Crouching at the back of my mind, unacknowledged and unwanted, is the idea that it might not be significant at all. That it's simply the key to a cabinet full of back issues of *FHM*, or Julia's catalogue money. That would crush me. All my hopes at the moment are pinned to this key, and the key in turn is pinning me. If it turns out to be useless I fear I will fall off the world.

But then, when I think about that, it seems pretty doubtful. The key was in a locked drawer. The key to unlock that drawer was hidden. There was nothing else in the drawer, just a couple of pens. So Adam went to the trouble and expense of buying a cabinet with a lockable drawer for the specific and only purpose of locking this key in it. *Hiding* this key in it. Hiding this key from me.

I need to let Ginger know where I am, and tell her I won't be in the shop again today. I'm not sure when Penny is back from Italy, but I doubt it will matter that I'm not there, for now at least. I've been through – am going through – a terrible, traumatic time. I'll probably need at least three weeks off. Longer, even. I'm already in Google, so quickly I look up the length of time that's an acceptable absence after your husband fucks off without telling you. The results feature mostly some obscure song lyrics by failing bands, and some advice for managers about malingering employees; but then four or five lines down, I notice a free online dictionary definition of the word 'leave', and as a form of self-flagellation, I click on it and read all of the meanings. 'To omit or exclude'; 'to abandon or forsake'; 'to remove oneself from association with or participation in'. Yeah, that sounds like my darling Adam, bless him. He's a living, breathing dictionary definition. I've been omitted, excluded and forsaken. I wonder why it doesn't say 'generally fuck over' in there.

I slam the laptop shut in impotent fury, then immediately feel bad and open it a crack to make sure it's OK. The light comes on timidly, so I close it again, more gently this time, and walk away from it to give it some space to recover. I'll take this opportunity to call Ginge and let her know where I am.

'Why have you gone there?' she demands, when I tell her. 'I thought you couldn't stand it there?'

'No, no, I don't think I ever said I couldn't stand it . . .'

'Yeah, you did, you've been going on about it for months. How your mum pisses you off with her negativity, your sister is so nosey, your brother gets away with murder—'

'Yeah, all right, maybe I did, I don't remember.' It's a lie. I remember perfectly. They were originally Adam's words, said to me after we'd had dinner with my family to let them know we'd got engaged.

I was so excited at the prospect of telling my family my big news. It was pretty much the first thing I thought of when Adam proposed, after wondering for a brief moment how much the ring had cost. Oh, and living happily ever after with the man of my dreams, of course. Mum was never going to believe that someone like Adam had chosen me to spend his life with; *me*, over everyone else in the world. I literally couldn't wait to see the expression on her face.

'Let's go and tell them now,' I'd pleaded, gazing at my finger's sparkly new decoration. I wanted hysteria and shrieks of joy and impulsive cracking open of the champagne that's been in the fridge for three Christmases. 'Come on, it's not late, they're bound to be up . . .'

'Watching *Come Dine With Me* or something?' he'd said with half a sardonic smile. 'I think I'll pass, thanks.'

'Oh, come on, Adam, please? I really want to go now . . .'

'No.' He'd practically snapped it. 'Oh, now, come on, let's not argue. We'll do it properly, take them out for dinner, make a big announcement. OK?'

I had been mollified. Of course that was miles better. And if I had to wait a few days, I would. And if it meant

Mum got an inkling of what we were going to say, so I wouldn't get the full impact of the surprise on her face, well that was a small price to pay.

There was a bit of kerfuffle about the restaurant in the end. I wanted to go to Dimitrio's – expensive, classy, Italian. Adam preferred the Harvester. He always preferred the Harvester. He was right, of course, it didn't matter where we went, as long as we were all together. And one of the tables in the Harvester was close to a little fake stream trickling under a little fake bridge. You could almost imagine you were sitting in a picturesque setting, especially in the evening when the motorway traffic had died down a bit.

After we'd eaten our mains and sides and were waiting for our desserts (three courses for £14.95 each, very reasonable) Adam stood up and tapped his knife against his wine glass. I noticed it left little gravy marks on the side. Should probably have used one of the unused knives from the adjacent table.

'Ladies and gentlemen,' he began, then like Seb Coe at the Olympic Games closing ceremony he fell silent and waited for everyone to pay attention to him. Lauren and Robbie were squabbling over the last half a glass of wine; Dad was looking around for a waiter to clear the plates; Mum was fishing in her bag for a tissue. I gazed raptly up at my future husband, until I realised that his mouth was getting a bit thin, and risked a glance back at the others.

'*Mum, Dad,*' I stage whispered, and rolled my eyes towards the head of the table, where Adam presided.

'Oh, Christ,' Mum said, and snapped to attention.

'Sorry, Adam,' Dad said affably, and turned back round in his chair.

'You have it, then,' Lauren said, pushing the glass across the table.

'Cheers,' Robbie said, and quickly necked the wine. 'Right. Over to you, Adam mate.'

'Thank you so much,' Adam said, not entirely pleasantly. But I forgave him. He was so handsome and commanding and my entire family sat captivated in their seats and listened to his big announcement. It was obvious they'd kind of been expecting it, because they all behaved impeccably afterwards. Mum cuddled me tightly and dabbed away a genteel tear; Dad stood up and shook Adam's hand, then patted him fondly on the shoulder, before crushing me in a daddy-hug embrace. Even Robbie and Lo kissed us both sweetly on the cheek and wished us every happiness. It was a bit stilted, but I was very proud of us all.

'Christ, that was an ordeal,' Adam said, as we bustled together in the bathroom later.

My eyebrows flicked to a frown, then out again. 'Really?' I'd thought it had gone very well. Mum had been obsequiously attentive throughout the meal – to Adam, not me – and Dad had thrown secret winks to me every time she was in danger of fawning Adam to death. 'What do you mean?'

He turned to me and smiled. 'Come on, you know what I mean. Look, I know they're your family but they really are very difficult people.'

I'd felt a hot spark of annoyance but I damped it down determinedly. 'Oh, do you think so? Why?'

'Jesus, Gracie. It's so suffocating, I don't know how

126

you can stand it. Your mum is so negative all the time, and your sister's so nosey, demanding to know absolutely everything about everyone.'

'Well . . .'

'And your brother gets away with murder. It's so painful watching how everyone indulges him all the time. Christ, no wonder you were so desperate to leave home and get your own place.' He ruffled my hair up. 'Good thing I was on hand to find you the perfect little pied-à-terre, eh?'

At first, I wanted to tell him that Mum's negativity was just exaggerated cynicism that we all found hilarious; and Lauren's nosiness was a genuine interest in people; and Robbie nearly choked to death when he was eight, so of course we all held him like precious china. But I didn't say it. Any of it. Instead, I thought hard about what he'd said about them. And then, for the first time, I started to realise that Robbie swanned around acting as if everything he touched turned to gold; and Lauren never gave me any privacy or respect; and Mum hated everything and everyone and it was very wearing. How had I not seen this before?

'You certainly did,' Ginge says now. 'Even if you don't remember, I do. You said it was very wearing being around them and you were so lucky to have got that flat of Adam's.'

'OK, but no one can stand to live with their family when they grow up, it's normal. That is, until they get abandoned, omitted and excluded by their husband. When that happens, there's nowhere else you want to be, believe me. It's well documented.'

There's a short pause. 'Ohhh-kaaaay.' I imagine her at the other end of the phone looking at Fletch and making spiral motions with her finger against her temple.

'I haven't gone insane, Ginge.'

Another pause. 'You know, truly insane people think they're perfectly sane. It's the sane people that think they're going mad.'

'Yes, I thought you might say that. Anyway, look, do you mind if I don't come to work again today? Or for maybe the next two or three days? Possibly longer. Do you think you can manage?'

'Of course I can, my friend. Don't worry about it.'

'Thanks Ginge. Gotta go, speak soon.'

'OK.'

Right. Locksmiths. I go to the hall to pick up Dad's car keys and catch sight of my face in the mirror there. Then I put the keys back down and go upstairs for a shower and change of clothes.

The first locksmith I go to is also a heel bar and café. As I wait at the counter for the assistant to get his boss, I wonder how many people come in here to have a key cut and decide to have a Danish and a coffee at the same time. The café is only four or five tables, to the left of the key and shoe counter, but three have people sitting at them. Good thinking, Mr Smith.

'You've got a key you want looking at?' Mr Smith says now, coming to the counter.

'Oh, yes, hi. It's this.' I hand over the heavy silver key and watch his face closely as he takes it from me. I don't know what I'm expecting – some kind of huge reaction, a gasp, eyes widening as he reaches for his glasses and reference book. 'Oh my God,' he'll exclaim, 'this is the lost key to the ancient chest of Cador that contains the last broken fragments of Excalibur' or something. But he doesn't. He turns it over in his hands a few moments then gives it back.

'Yeah, fairly standard key to an old Churchill safe.'

I blink. 'A . . . safe?'

'Yeah.' He nods. 'Not many of them left around these days. Everyone likes the keypad type, or the magnetic fob. Or there are some that require the user's fingerprints. Like something out of James Bond!'

'Oh, right, well . . .'

'Much more secure, right?'

'Yes . . .'

'Wrong. Easy way round that. Corpses turning up all over the place with their fingers cut off, ha ha ha ha!'

'Yes. Ha ha. Well, thanks for your time.'

'No problem.'

I try the other two locksmiths too, to get second opinions, but they say exactly the same thing. Well, one does. The other one doesn't have a clue and seems to resent my presence in his shop. 'I'm not here to give free advice, love.' Anyway, the consensus is that it's a vintage, freestanding Churchill safe, probably about the size of a microwave oven, although possibly smaller. No one was very clear on that one, but it's a start. Thank goodness Adam chose one that uses a key. I'd have had a terrible time lifting his fingerprints off an old coffee mug using superglue fumes, or whatever.

Back at Mum's, I Google 'Churchill safes' and scroll through all the different types and sizes. They're all modern ones with touch pad locks, or much smaller keys than the big old silver thing I've got. What I do learn is that Churchill are the leading manufacturer of hidden safes, and they're absolutely perfect for secreting stuff away from your prying wife and keeping all your personal information completely inviolate. Their tag line should be 'Your Safe's Secret with Us!'

I'm feeling restless and anxious again. I want to start looking for this safe straight away, but I have absolutely no idea where to start. Well, maybe not no idea at all: our home seems like the most sensible place. But I don't want to go back there yet in case Leon is watching the house in black leather gloves. Anyway, I can't think of a single place in that house where something the size of a kitchen appliance could be hidden, where I wouldn't already have seen it.

Except . . . wait. I remember suddenly that there is one place big enough that I haven't seen.

It's in Adam's wardrobe. It's so obvious! He never let me look in there. I was allowed to see it while he was present and admire a new shirt or suit that was hanging up there, but I was forbidden from opening the doors while he wasn't there.

'Why, though?' I'd asked, not understanding. 'I'm hardly going to trash everything in there, am I?'

'Ah, my sweet sugarpuff,' he'd said, taking my face between his hands, 'of course you aren't.' He'd kissed me, still holding my face. Then had turned away to resume whatever it was he was doing.

'No, Adam, seriously, what do you think I'm likely to do?' I'd persisted, not recognising at this point that the conversation was over. We had only lived there a couple of weeks and he had just started laying down the ground rules. I had accepted most of them, and gladly. All paperwork, accounts, bills and anything like that were to be dealt with by Adam. He was the man of the house, it was his role. Fine by me. I was to open no post or try to deal with anything to do with the banking. Why would I want to? Dull, dull, dull. We would each have an individual bank account, and a joint one into which we would both pay a fixed amount every month to cover joint responsibilities, such as rent, food, electricity, and so on. Suited me fine. That way we could still buy surprises for each other without the other knowing about it in advance, or finding out how much it cost afterwards.

I'd nodded and smiled, thinking how lucky I was to have found someone who was prepared to take on the huge burden of household finances and correspondence without any assistance whatsoever. Right now, sitting here at my mum's kitchen table with a mysterious key in front of me, I understand why he was insistent on keeping all the paperwork under his control. Why didn't I see it at the time? Why didn't I think, 'Hello, that's a bit odd'? But I was happy to accept his terms, without question. Naïve me thought he was just being super helpful. I remember that the only, the *only*, ground rule that I objected to, and that only faintly, was the wardrobe embargo.

'I don't think you're likely to do anything, sweetie,' he'd said, turning back to me again with an oh-so-patient smile. Ah, bless her, little wifey trying to understand me. 'It's just that it's my wardrobe, full of my things. Why would you want to go in there anyway?'

'I don't, but—'

'Well there we are then.' He'd grinned, blown me another kiss, and walked away, leaving me feeling . . . a bit mystified, but nothing more. I'd simply shrugged and packed it away as one of those little idiosyncrasies that I could love about him and tell people about at parties. 'Oh, yes, my husband's so clothes conscious, he won't even let me open the wardrobe door if he's not there, ha ha ha!'

At the kitchen table, I lean forward and rest my head in my hands. If I had ever told that one to other wives at a party, they would have looked at me askance and said, 'Really? Christ, that's incredibly odd. There's probably a secret safe in that wardrobe that he doesn't want you to find.' But then, of course, we never went to parties.

I spend the rest of the day on the internet, Googling the best place to hide a safe. Naturally, none of the websites has advice for people with secretive husbands who want to hide an actual safe. Every one of them simply gives advice about where to stash valuables in the home where a burglar won't find it. The assumption is that if you have a safe, no one in the family is going to want to hide it from everyone else, as everyone else will be putting their stuff in it too.

By the time Lauren comes home from work at six o'clock, I've moved on to private detectives and psychic investigators. She leans over the screen and reads what I'm looking at, then slowly looks round at me.

'Wow. You seriously need a hobby or something.'

'Oh, don't you start,' I snap, slamming the laptop shut.

'Psychic investigators, though, Gee? Seriously?'

I shrug. 'Can't hurt, can it?'

She widens her eyes. 'Oh my God, it so can hurt! Don't you know anything? You start messing around in that stuff, you'll be waking up some, like, long-dead malevolent spirit that will bring down a terrifying storm of violence and destruction on you before you can say "Ouija board".'

I roll my eyes. 'OK, Lo.'

'So anyway,' she goes on, biting into an apple. 'Is that right, you and Adam never got a mortgage?'

'Oh for arse's sake, what's that got to do with anything?'

She shrugs. 'Nothing. We all just thought you had, that's all.'

'So what?'

Shrug again. 'Fancy a night out?'

'Not really.'

She comes closer and lowers her voice dramatically. 'Think about it for a minute, Gee. You're single again.' She nods, knowingly. 'You can pick up blokes for meaningless sex.'

Pause. 'OK. I'm in.'

EIGHT

I have no desire at all to pick up blokes for meaningless sex. But a night out would certainly help take my mind off things. Off Adam, that is. Off the absent bhuna and the secret safe. Off Leon, waiting in the wings with a weapon.

Lauren gets dolled up – skinny jeans, strappy top, heels – then knocks on my bedroom door to collect me. She walks in as I'm saying, 'Come in, Lolo.'

She looks amazing, as always. I've brought disappointingly few nice going-out clothes with me. I have a grand total of none in my overnight bag. Doesn't matter though, I can trail round behind Lauren in a black tee shirt and jeans and bask in her reflected sluttiness.

'Come on, you don't need to dress up,' she says, looking at her watch. 'We're only going round the Fives.'

Ah, the Bunch of Fives. It's been a few years since I was in there. 'Really? That place is a dive.'

She shakes her head. 'Nope. Got bought out. Completely revamped. It's a theme pub now.'

I give her the single raised eyebrow. 'Great.'

'Oh come on, stop being so grumpy. It'll be fun.'

It isn't. It's about as far away as you can get from fun before you start coming back again. It seems the Bunch of Fives is under new management, and apparently Hannibal Lecter has decided this is going to be his retirement fund. It's very dim inside, considering it's July, but then it always was because of the tiny windows. It takes a while for my eyes to adjust, but when they do, I wish they hadn't. Every wall is decked with twinkling implements of torture – clubs, saws, bats, knives, axes – all apparently dripping with blood, which is running down the walls to the floor in copious amounts and pooling at our feet. The floor is uncarpeted black boards, for this effect to work to its best advantage. And worst of all, there are body parts everywhere. Silent, screaming heads; severed hands and feet; in one case an entire, dismembered torso; all liberally spattered with the same rusty red paint that's all over everything else.

I look at Lauren. 'Oh dear God.'

'I know, right?'

As soon as we go in, Lo spots a couple of her friends and goes straight to where they're sitting. I'm introduced to Cat and Nellie.

'This is my sister, Grace. Her husband's just done a moonlight flit.'

I close my eyes briefly, then shoot Lauren a killer look. She's facing away from me, though, and doesn't notice it.

'Oh wow,' says Cat. 'No way.'

I nod sadly. 'That is one way of putting it.'

'So, where'd he go?'

I look at her, then flick my eyes quickly at Lauren and back again. 'I don't know.'

'Oh wow. Why'd he leave?'

'I don't know that, either.'

'Oh wow.' She takes a sip of her drink. 'How long'd he go for?'

I blink. 'Again, I don't know.'

'Oh wow. That's, like, so weird.'

'Yes, it is, isn't it?'

'I'll get us a drink,' Lauren says.

'I'll come with you.'

Sitting on a stool at the bar is a headless corpse. I have to stop myself saying 'excuse me' to it as I lean over to get the barman's attention.

'What can I get you?' he says cheerily, coming over.

'Out of here?'

'Ha ha! You don't like our theme?'

I look around me pointedly. 'What, blood-soaked torture instruments, body parts and corpses? Who *doesn't* like that?'

He leans a bit nearer. 'To be honest,' he says quietly, 'I hate it. Not relaxing, not pleasant, not comfortable. But, you know, I just work here. What would you like?'

Lauren gets a round in and we shuffle back over to join Cat and Nellie at the table. Within five minutes, I'm ready to leave. I lean closer to Lauren. 'I'm going home.'

She seizes my arm. 'Noooo, don't go yet. We've only been here five minutes.'

'Yep. More than enough. I'm off.'

She sags. 'OK.' She turns to Cat and the silent Nellie. 'I'm off, Gee wants to go.'

'Oh, no, Lo, it's OK, you stay. I'll be fine on my own.'

'OK then.' She livens up immediately, and pretty much forgets I'm there.

'It's only plastic dummies, you know,' the barman calls out as I head towards the door.

'Sorry?' I take the couple of steps back to the bar to hear him.

'I said, this is all just pretend. Plastic dummies, red paint, a bit of papier-mâché. Don't let it give you nightmares.'

My first instinct is to throw him a quick, half-hearted smile, turn away, and leave at top speed. But before I have a chance to do that, I notice his wide, engaging smile and a memory from last year pops into my head. Adam and I were out for our usual Sunday lunch, and on my way back from the toilet my path to our table was blocked by a bloke in a cream cable-knit sweater. He looked like a model from the front of a knitting pattern. As we locked eyes, he gave me a wide, engaging smile and said something – the only thing I heard was '. . . made my day.' It made me feel noticed, attractive, and slightly bubbly inside, so instead of side-stepping him and making my way straight back to Adam, I hesitated a moment, enjoying the eye contact and the exchange of smiles.

'Come on, Loopy Lou,' a voice broke in behind me, and I felt a gentle but insistent pressure on my shoulder. I didn't have to turn round to see it was Adam. Cable-Knit Guy stiffened, his face fell, and he turned away with a little regretful shrug. And my day resumed, a little bit grey, a little bit uninteresting.

But Adam is not here now.

I give a slow smile and walk all the way back to the bar. 'Well that's a massive relief.'

He inclines his head. 'No need to leave then, is there?'

'But it's so . . . dingy. You know? I mean, maybe if you got some nice yellow curtains, or some flowers, it would brighten the place up a bit.'

He's laughing now and it feels nice. 'Are you having another drink then?' He's got cute dimples when he smiles.

I check my watch, more out of needing to look like I'm thinking carefully before deciding. 'Oh, all right then, you've twisted my arm.'

'Bloody Mary?' he says, grinning mischievously.

'Sangria?'

He chuckles. 'Have you seen our cocktail list?' He hands me a sheet of laminated cardboard and I scan through the names in horror. 'Can I interest you in a Blood Clot?'

'Ugh! My God, this is disgusting!'

'Oh, no, they're all delicious.'

I stare at the list. 'What's a Bloody Brain?'

He looks up at the ceiling as he thinks. 'Um, peach schnapps, Baileys and grenadine.'

'Ooh, that does sound nice.'

He grins. 'One Bloody Brain coming up.'

The drink is delicious, if you can ignore the colour and thick consistency, coupled with its terrible name. But the barman – Greg – is great company. Lo looks over at me after about fifteen minutes and catches my eye, then nods appreciatively. She even raises her hands to make the 'worm going into the hole' gesture, but I look away quickly.

'Looks like your friend is trying to say something,' Greg remarks.

I shake my head. 'I definitely don't know her.'

In the end, the evening passes very pleasantly, culminating in Greg taking me out the back for a quick snog. Things are heating up nicely and I'm wondering whether I could do what Lauren suggested after all, when suddenly Greg pulls back.

'I'm sorry, Grace,' he says, rubbing his hand over his head. 'You're really lovely, but . . . I'm just not that guy.'

'What guy?'

'The guy that fucks other guys over. Sorry.'

'What do you mean?'

He looks down at my hand still resting on his arm, and we both stare at the fourth finger. Of course. There's a big beautiful diamond there, and a thick, gold band. I look like I'm very happily, very securely, married.

I shake my head. 'Oh, no, no, that's . . . that's not really relevant any more.'

He smiles sadly. 'No, I know. It never is.'

'I mean it!'

'I know.' He turns away and opens the door back inside. 'Come on, you'd best be getting home.'

There's no sign of Lauren so I trudge home on my own feeling humiliated and let down yet again by my presently absent husband. The worm. He spent three years of my life blocking out just about everyone from my life, and he's still doing it now, even after clearing off to God knows where without so much as a backward glance. In a

139

moment of tipsy fury, I wrench the rings off my finger and fling them across the street into the darkness. Except I don't quite fling them. At the last moment before releasing them, I decide not to, and shove them roughly into my handbag instead. They're probably worth a few quid.

The next morning, everyone has already left the house by the time I come downstairs. Good. Last thing I need is twenty questions from Lauren about what happened. She's probably told Mum that I stayed out all night shagging some random barman by now, but I don't care. I have a cunning plan today which I've spent some considerable time devising, and I'm rather pleased with it. First, I'm going to go back to the house and look in Adam's wardrobe. Genius plan, isn't it? If the safe's not there, I'm out of ideas.

I shower and dress quickly, without pausing to Google anything, and grab Dad's car keys. At least, I put my hand in the bowl, but there are no keys there. Oh arses! I didn't even think to ask him if I could borrow it again today. He must've taken it to work.

I go back to the kitchen table and Google taxi companies in the area, but I can acknowledge that's not a very sensible suggestion. Taxis cost money, and that's one thing I don't have much of. I have tried not to think about my financial situation so far, but I will have to face it soon. I suppose I must have blocked out the possibility that Adam wasn't coming back, but it's day seven now and there's no word from him. Rent will need paying, I expect, and money will be coming out of the joint account to pay for power and council tax. I have no idea when those payments are due. I will have to look into it. Soon.

Right now, I need to find out bus times. I Google the bus company, but I know it's going to take me well over an hour to get back to the house. I have to get on and off multiple buses between here and the end of Maple Avenue in an unfunny, boring and tiring parody of that old maths question. It's a hellish journey, and the prospect of another bus ride right now is filling me with misery.

'I knew you weren't up to getting the bus all the way there on your own,' Adam told me once, after I'd persuaded him to drive me to my parents' for a visit without him. 'It's a pretty long journey.'

But right now, I don't have much choice, so the bus it is. I got here on it two days ago, when it was my only option; I can do it again. I reach for my handbag and start rummaging through my purse, and instead of a decent amount of small change, I come across Ginger's brother Matt's business card. As I stare at his details, I remember what he said when he gave it to me. If I needed anything, any time, I should call him. I tap the card against my hand. Right now, I need a lift. Does that count?

'Gracie, wow, hi,' he rolls, in that deep, stranger's baritone that just doesn't go with the memory I have of him. 'Didn't think you'd call, actually. How's things? Are you doing OK? Is everything OK?'

'Hi Matt, yes, I'm fine, thanks. Staying with my parents for a few days.'

'That's a great idea.'

Something in the way he says it makes me wonder whether he knows something I don't. Like maybe Leon has been identified and they're tracking him even now. Maybe he's got previous. Maybe he's got mob connections. Obviously that's not part of the investigation they would need to keep me informed about, so I'll probably never find out what's going on. Unless Matt tells me, unofficially.

'Really? You think so?'

'Yes, definitely. You'll need their support.'

'Oh God, will I? Why?'

There's a short silence. 'Because your husband is missing, Gracie.'

'Oh, right, yes, of course. I thought for a moment that . . .'

'That what?' There's a second's pause as he realises what I was thinking. 'Oh, God, no, no, sorry, nothing like that.' There's a short puff of air, like he's snorting out a laugh. 'I really must stop doing that to you, mustn't I?'

'Well, at least it means that when there is eventually some news, I'll be primed.'

'I don't know about that. You'll probably be completely exhausted with all the false starts.'

'Entirely possible. When I do find something out eventually, I probably won't react at all. Everyone will think I'm a cold-hearted bitch.'

He pauses, then, when he speaks, his voice is quieter, softer. 'I don't think that that's very likely.'

I'm not really sure how to react to that. Is he paying me a compliment? Or is he simply saying it's unlikely that I won't react? I don't know, so I laugh lightly and blunder on. 'Matt, you did say, when you gave me your card, that if I ever needed anything . . .'

'Of course, Grace. I'm at your service. What can I do for you?'

'It feels really, really cheeky to ask this, but would you by any chance be free to come and pick me up and drive me back to my house today? I hate to ask, but of course the car is still quarantined up somewhere as evidence or something, which leaves me—'

'I can be there in twenty minutes.'

I release a long breath. 'Oh Matt, thank you so much. Let me give you directions to my parents' place.'

'No, no need, I remember where they live. Gladstone Road, right?'

'Wow, fancy you remembering that, after all these years.'

'Huh. I guess some things just stick. See you in twenty minutes.'

He makes it in closer to fifteen, which is pretty good going, given that it must be about fifteen miles, door to door. Although technically I don't know which actual door he set out from. He's not in uniform today, so I guess he's come from his home.

'Where do you live now, Matt?' I ask on the drive back.

'Oh, I have a flat, on Arron Drive.'

A flat. I process this information interestedly. Is that likely to be a family home, a flat? It sounds small, like maybe enough room for someone on their own. I wish I could remember if Ginger has ever mentioned a girl-friend. She doesn't talk about Matt much, just the odd snippet here and there. I wish I'd paid more attention. Arron Drive though – it's a nice area, classy. 'Oh yes? It's lovely there.'

He nods slowly. 'I like it. Not as nice as Maple Avenue though.' He glances across at me. 'Very posh.'

'Oh, we're only renting the place.'

'Oh really? Oh.'

He definitely wants to say more. His mouth even makes the shape of the next word – it looks like it starts with a 'w' – but he doesn't say it and I'm not asking. Our decision to rent a place was perfectly valid and I don't feel like I need to justify it to him or anyone else.

'We decided to rent because we weren't sure whether we would stay in the area or move back to be nearer my parents,' I burst out defensively. 'Or nearer his parents, or into town or whatever.'

He nods. 'OK.'

'It was only ever a temporary arrangement.'

'Right.'

'Because we didn't want to be tied to one place for ages.'

'Understandable.'

'Selling a house once you've bought it is so expensive, what with stamp duty, estate agents' fees, solicitors and so on. If you're not sure about where you want to live ultimately, it's sensible to rent somewhere first.'

He looks at me again. 'No, no, you're absolutely right.'

'I know.' I turn and stare out of the passenger window, furious for some reason. We drive on in silence.

I remember the conversation with Adam about this. I quite liked the idea of getting our own place, starting to buy somewhere, feeling settled and secure, without that uncertain feeling of knowing we only ever had until the tenancy agreement ran out, or less if the landlord suddenly decided to sell up and move to Dubai or Croydon.

'I agree about the security,' Adam had said, 'but it's so permanent, isn't it, buying somewhere?'

'Well, yes. That's what I like about it.'

He'd nodded, thoughtfully. 'Yes, you're right.'

I'd thought that was the end of the conversation, but he'd come back to it a few minutes later.

'I still feel that we'd be tying ourselves down to a specific area, straight away, if we bought somewhere.'

'Yes . . .'

'Which might not necessarily be a good thing, you know.'

'I suppose not. Why not?'

He'd smiled at me and touched my neck with his fingertips. 'There are all sorts of reasons, sugarpuff. What if one of your parents got ill, or worse? You'd want to be near them, wouldn't you? Or what if one of us changes jobs, or we decide to leave the area one day? Just the process of buying a house is expensive, let alone making the mortgage payments each month. There's a kind of tax you have to pay when you buy property, called stamp duty. And then there are the solicitors' fees. They do something called conveyancing, which is a legal process that transfers ownership of the property.'

I'd frowned. Sometimes I worry that I don't know as much as I think I do. 'Is that the same thing as the legal expenses? Or something else?'

He'd laughed out a huff of air. 'No, it's the same thing. But that just demonstrates how I'm the expert when it comes to this kind of thing. Aren't I? I mean, that's the business I'm in; of course I'll have a better idea about what's best than you do.' I must have looked a bit . . .

something when he said that because he stepped nearer and gave me a quick hug. 'It's nothing against you, sweetness. Not your fault, it's not your line of business, you can't be expected to be knowledgeable on the subject. But I am, and I know all about the pitfalls and hidden expenses of buying somewhere.' He pushed his lips out. 'You don't really want to get saddled with all sorts of hideous, enormous bills we can't pay, do you?'

I had to agree that he was the expert. Well, I didn't have to agree. I did agree.

'And there are some really gorgeous places available to rent right now,' he'd gone on. 'Look at all these, within our price range.' He'd presented me then with five or six properties' details that he'd apparently picked up somewhere in readiness. 'What do you think of the Maple Avenue one? I really love it. Move in there with me?'

He was right, Maple Avenue is beautiful. Lined, as the name suggests, with what I can only assume are maple trees, pavements wide enough for a bit of grass, and a nice car on every driveway. As Matt pulls onto our drive, I stare up at the gleaming white uPVC windows, the gorgeous colourful shrubs in the front garden and the neat little path leading up to the glossy door, and all I can think is where the arse did that slippery serpent hide the safe? I want to excise it, like a tumour. I wish at this moment that I could see an x-ray of the house and scrutinise its revealed skeleton without the hindrance of walls and furniture and carpets to hide things. Where in that structure would I find a small, grey metal box? I picture it, cradled in the rib-cage of the roof rafters; tucked behind the chimney breast-bone; snuggled into the bosom of the hearth; or even, it occurs to me, languishing under the pristine lawn. The garden was always strictly Adam's domain, like the accounting, and, well, the rest of the house, and he himself had laid the turf out there. Oh Christ, I've got some work ahead of me.

I get out of the car, then turn back and realise that Matt is still sitting in the driver's seat. Of course; this was only a lift. I acknowledge to myself that subconsciously I was hoping – no, expecting – him to come in and help me search. He smiles at me and shrugs.

'Take care then, Grace. Don't forget, if you need anything else . . .'

'Well, actually Matt, there is something.'

He's out of the car faster than I can say 'loose end'.

Inside, the house smells a bit sour and musty, like old vinegar, and our noses crinkle as we enter. It's only been empty for two days, but it already smells abandoned. Or is that just me? Ha ha. There are two or three letters on the mat so I grab them and shove them in my handbag, then go and open the back door to let some fresh air in. While I'm there I stare miserably at the lawn. It hadn't even occurred to me before now that Adam could well have buried his safe in the garden. It's not a huge lawn, but I really do not want to dig the whole thing up looking for something that might not even be there.

'Penny for them?' Matt's deep voice says in my ear, making me jump and spin round, heart thudding. He's standing so close to me, my face practically collides with his chest. 'Oh, God, sorry,' he says, taking a step back. 'Didn't mean to make you . . .' He tails off and looks suddenly sheepish. 'Crap. I've done it again, haven't I?'

I put my hand on my chest and smile. 'You're very good at it, I'll give you that.'

He nods appreciatively. 'Thanks. I studied Making Vulnerable People Feel Worse at uni.'

It makes me laugh. 'Really? That sounds fascinating. I bet you got a First?'

'Sadly not. Two one.' He looks down.

I laugh again. 'I'm surprised, you seem to be a natural. What went wrong?'

He looks up and grins. 'Yeah, I was disappointed. I think it was the final practical exam. I was a bit sensitive in the role play to a woman whose cat had been run over.'

'Oh no.'

'Yeah. Let my tutors down, let my family down, let myself down.'

It's so lovely to feel myself smiling. I didn't realise Matt could be such good company. Mind you, Ginge and I used to avoid him as much as we could at school. Although that wasn't easy: he was always popping up unexpectedly wherever we went. 'Never mind,' I reassure him, rubbing his arm, 'I'm actually in a bit of bother right now, so you'll have plenty of opportunity to get some practice in.'

'Excellent, that's good to know.' We smile at each other, then after a second or two he looks down at his arm and we both notice that my hand is still there. I snatch it back and move quickly towards the kettle.

'Do you fancy a cuppa while I tell you why we're here?'

'I'll just have a glass of water, please.'

It only takes a few minutes to explain about the bedside

148

cabinet and the key, and the locksmith and the safe. It takes a bit longer to explain why I haven't told the police. And even longer to explain why I'm not going to. Yet, anyway.

'I want to do this myself,' I tell him, trying to clarify what I'm not sure I understand. 'I suppose it feels like something I could do to . . . Not get my life back exactly. But maybe to . . .' I shrug, floundering.

'To prove to yourself that you aren't completely useless?' He fills in for me.

I flinch. 'Well, I don't think I'd have put it quite like that exactly.'

He closes his eyes briefly, then looks at me. 'Oh God. They should probably lock me away, stop me from doing any more damage.'

I smile. 'Don't worry about it. You're about right, actually. I want to feel competent again. It's been a while.'

His face straightens out as he looks at me and becomes more serious. 'Really?'

I nod. 'Sadly.'

His expression is quite intense, his eyes never leaving mine. It's a bit odd, how he's looking at me. No one's looked at me like that since . . . Well, ever, actually. Is this standard, or is there some hidden meaning behind it? I'm just starting to feel uncomfortable when he turns his head and peers out at the garden.

I take a tiny step away, trying to make my movements unnoticeable while at the same time extending the space between us. That almost felt like, I don't know, that Matt might have been trying to . . . I want to say 'kiss me' but that's completely ridiculous. Why on earth would

149

he want to do that? With me? I know very well how bloody lucky I was to end up with Adam – my family have pointed that out to me relentlessly ever since we met (not that I needed them to; was very much aware of the mismatch myself already) – so it's pretty unlikely that another great, charismatic bloke would look twice at me. It doesn't matter anyway because whatever it did mean, I'm still married, regardless of the whereabouts of the other half of that equation, and I still love the absent fuck. At least, I feel something. I'm no longer sure it's love, but it's close and either way it's commitment. A meaningless encounter with Greg from the bar is one thing, but this would mean something; this is Ginger's baby brother, the irritating little twerp in black eyeliner who was always at the next table in the coffee shop, or buying a drink at the bar we were in. Although he certainly does not look like a little twerp any more. As we stand together in the kitchen, I'm very conscious again of how big he's got now. Broad and tall, like a . . . I don't know, one of those huge trees you see on nature programmes. Redwoods? An image comes into my head from a long ago geography textbook of three people leaning comfortably against a vast expanse of tree trunk, like a building behind them. Matt really looks like the sort of tree trunk someone could comfortably lean on. And right now, I really need to lean.

'Are you OK, Gracie?' he says softly, bending slightly to make eye contact.

I'm staring at his chest, so I blink and pretend that I'd zoned out. 'Oh, yeah, yeah, sorry, just thinking about everything, you know? Shall we crack on?'

It makes more sense for us to split up and search two rooms at the same time, but we go together up to the bedroom, which is weird (although only for me, I'm sure).

'Well, you certainly did a good job there,' he says appreciatively, eyeing the splattered mess of the disembowelled bedside table. 'It looks like furniture zombies have been feasting on it.'

'Furniture zombies?'

He nods. 'Yeah, you know, old cabinets and sideboards that have been cast aside and roam the land, undead, looking for solid wood stuff to feast on?'

I nod slowly. 'Of course.'

He grins. 'Right. So. Where shall we start?'

I hesitate for about three seconds, then yank open the wardrobe aggressively and stare hard at the contents. In my head I'm shouting 'I'M LOOKING IN YOUR PRECIOUS WARDROBE, *ADAM*!' as if he might hear me somehow; but of course with someone else here, I keep decorously silent.

Immediately, the sharp tang of shiny black leather and shoe polish reaches me, and Adam is almost here again, standing somewhere just out of sight. For a fraction of a second, I am banjaxed by a stunning feeling of amazement mixed with the colossal relief of discovery, as if he's been hiding in the wardrobe for a week, and is about to say, 'OK, your turn.' My eyes instantly fill with tears. But the thought disappears almost as soon as it arrives. Ridiculous.

'Shall I go and look downstairs?' Matt asks gently behind me. I realise that it's been a few seconds since I flung the wardrobe doors open, and since then I've been standing completely stationary, just staring. He probably thinks I'm overwhelmed by sadness at the sight of all my husband's clothes lined up neatly like this. He probably thinks that I'm experiencing a fierce jolt of love and longing while I take in the colour scheme of Adam's clothes arrangement. He probably thinks my yearning for my beloved has never been stronger, and I need to be alone with the suits for a moment.

'The arse has put his suits in colour order.' I turn my head and look at him over my shoulder.

'I noticed.'

The suits are black at one end and grow lighter from left to right, culminating in a row of crisp, white shirts. 'What a prick.'

Matt inhales sharply through his nose, as if he's shocked by such language. In turn, I'm shocked by his shockedness. Quickly he clears his throat and coughs a little, probably pretending that his inadvertent expression of disapproval was just a tickle. 'Are they always like this?'

I shrug. 'No idea.' I turn back to look at the very annoying suits again.

'How come?'

'I've never looked in here before.'

'You've never . . .?'

I shake my head. 'I wasn't supposed to look, so I didn't.'

'You're kidding?'

I turn back to face him again. 'No, seriously. He said he didn't really want me interfering in his things.' I think back to that conversation again. 'No, it wasn't about me interfering. I said I wouldn't touch anything and I'm pretty sure he believed me.'

'So why . . .?'

'I don't really know. He was just very particular about his things. He told me it was only his things in here, he didn't want me going in, so I didn't. Like he said, it was only his clothes, why would I even want to look?'

He frowns. 'I don't get it. You said downstairs that you got into the habit of trying out the locked drawer in his bedside table every time you were in the house on your own.'

'Yes.'

'So why that, but not this? This one wasn't even locked, you could easily have opened it, had a look, and closed it again.'

I think about that for a moment, then shrug. 'I suppose it was for that very reason: because it wasn't locked. I knew what was in here. It was just clothes, Adam had said as much, and it was likely to be the truth because it is, after all, a wardrobe. With no lock on it. What else would be in there? But a locked drawer – it's slightly different, isn't it? I mean, you could literally hide anything in there. I wanted to know . . .'

'What?'

I've almost told him the thing that's bothered me more than anything else about being married to Adam, the thing I have never told anyone, not even Ginger. I look into his face, so familiar and yet so strange. It's a kind face, open, friendly. But more than that, it's a policeman's face. And I'm not sure whether that means I can trust him, or is a reason for me not to.

153

'What is it, Gracie?'

I close my eyes briefly. I gotta trust someone. And I'm already so tired of coping with this on my own. 'I wanted to know whether or not he was keeping a gun in there.'

There's a short silence while Matt absorbs this new bit of information. When I look up at him again, he's frowning. 'What made you think he might have a gun?'

I shake my head. 'Oh, God, no concrete reason, nothing definite, nothing you police would like. I know you all get a bit obsessed with that kind of thing, don't you? Always wanting to see it, or someone else to see it, to know it exists.'

He smiles. 'That kind of thing, as you call it, is known as evidence. And it's kind of crucial these days. We're not allowed to go on "hunches" any more.'

I smile back. 'Yeah, I thought you would say that.'

'You haven't answered the question, though. Why did you think he might have a gun?'

I breathe in deeply and release it. 'What you have to understand is that my life with him was littered with inconsistencies.'

'Such as?'

'Um, let me think. Well, he never talked about his past, or his family, or anything about himself before we met. He didn't ever use the landline phone. I wasn't supposed to open any post. Ever.'

He's nodding, but still frowning. 'Nothing completely out of the ordinary there. Most women would assume he was having an affair. Not that he was walking about with an illegal, unlicensed weapon.'

'Yeah, I know, it's a bit of a stretch, isn't it? I don't

know, there were just so many odd things about him – there were sometimes huge gaps in his day that he couldn't explain.'

He nods. 'Affair.'

I look at him and begin to feel ridiculous. These things have been pressing at the sides of my subconscious almost since Adam and I met, but I've refused to see them. Now, it seems unfathomable that I could live with someone, be married to him, without demanding to know what the hell was going on. 'But . . . he would go out in the morning and then be unreachable on the phone and not in his office or anywhere I could find him, sometimes for four or five hours. He would always say he was with a client, or looking at a property somewhere. And it was a black spot, so he . . .'

'. . . didn't have any signal,' Matt finishes for me, nodding again. 'Yeah, that all sounds very familiar. Exactly the kind of thing someone would say if they were having an affair.'

I think about it for a moment. 'I suppose you're right. I've never thought that, though. It's possible, but it just didn't occur to me. Maybe I'm just too naïve.'

He smiles kindly. 'You're not naïve. You're just very trusting. It's a good thing.'

'Trusting? I've spent all this time wondering if there was a gun in that drawer, and all it turns out to be is a key!'

'Yeah, but maybe it was easier for you to focus on the ridiculous possibility of it being a gun in there, rather than face up to the much more likely explanation of him being unfaithful. You avoided the affair by thinking about a gun, which you knew was actually ridiculous and very unlikely. So in the end you were able to dismiss the inconsistencies altogether. Or maybe not dismiss them, but avoid thinking about them. In any realistic sense, anyway.'

It seems a bit unlikely, but I nod politely anyway. 'Maybe.' I look back at the suits. 'You know what I want to do?'

'No. What?'

'This.' I seize a handful of suits and pull them down off the rail, then throw them all in a pile on the floor, next to the smashed cabinet. It's incredibly satisfying, so I do it again, and again, until all the suits are in a jumbled mess on the floor. The shirts follow, and once everything that was hanging is in a heap, I wade into the pile and kick and stamp savagely, messing and crumpling everything as much as possible. I might have grunted a bit while I was doing that. 'You're very untidy, aren't you?' Adam's voice says from three years ago, but this time I ignore it.

Now that the wardrobe is clear, I can see that Adam's shoes are all beautifully arranged on the floor – black ones nicely placed below where the darkest suits were, leading up to grey below the grey, and flip-flops separate at the end. I bend over and grab armfuls of shoes, then turn and toss them carelessly across the room, one at a time to begin with, but then I launch four or five at once, with a primal noise that sounds as if I should be tossing a caber, not a crepe sole. Saliva may have gone with them.

'Hey, hey,' Matt eventually says, putting his hand on my arm. I jump as he does so, and stop mid-throw.

It's a bit like coming out of a trance, and I'm suddenly

very conscious of the fact that I probably have spittle around my mouth. I drop the shoes I'm holding and look at him shame-facedly. 'Oops.' Quickly, I wipe my face. He's looking right at me, but I tell myself maybe he didn't notice.

He raises his eyebrows. 'Shall we take a break there?'

I'm actually a bit out of breath, and my hand shakes slightly as I drag it across my forehead. I'm not sure if this is from the exertion, or from the stress of holding back. Ha ha. 'Good idea.'

I move to turn away from the wardrobe, but just as I do, I am pinned by the realisation of one important thing: there's no sign of a safe anywhere inside it.

NINE

Well, that's me all out of ideas. I stare at the wardrobe for a moment, flicking my eyes backwards and forwards, from left to right and back again, just in case I failed to spot a squat, silver cabinet against the smooth, cream blankness of the wall the first two or three times of looking. Maybe I'm stressed and not focused properly; maybe it's there but it doesn't look how I expected it to look; maybe it's camouflaged. I lean forward so my top half is actually inside the wardrobe's dimensions and turn my head, scanning its quite clearly empty interior. I wave my hands through the space, side to side, in case there's some kind of optical illusion going on. Then I lean back with a sigh and turn to Matt.

'What is it?' he asks, stepping forward a little.

'You're going to think I'm insane – ha, more insane – but please just tell me: is there a safe in there?'

'No.'

I put my hands up. 'Hang on a minute, take a bit of time over it. Have you looked properly?'

He flicks his eyes at the wardrobe again. 'It's empty, Grace.'

'But have you *really* looked?'

He nods. 'Yes. I have. And so have you. There's nothing in there.'

I want to get inside the wardrobe and walk up and down it, swinging my arms and legs to make sure there's definitely nothing there, but at this point Matt grabs my arm and drags me away. 'Time to go,' he says, probably reacting to the madness in my eyes.

As soon as we get downstairs, the ordinariness of the hallway carpet and the kitchen utensils makes me start to feel calmer and my actions upstairs seem a bit . . . extreme. And embarrassing. Oh God, what on earth must Matt think of me, going all possessed like that? He's still here though, all tall and solid and reassuring, so I presume he doesn't feel in danger, anyway.

It's almost lunch time so Matt suggests going out for something to eat. It's a way to pass the time, so we walk down the road to the pub at the corner. This is the one Adam and I have been having Sunday lunch in most weekends for the past year; the one where I met Cable-Knit Guy – The Dragonfly. It's got a repugnant painting of a dragonfly's head in close-up on the signpost. It looks like something from that magical film about the scientist who falls in love with a reporter and then accidentally mixes his genes up with a fly. God knows why they didn't go with the traditional image of a dragonfly: brightly coloured body, iridescent wings, hovering over a pond somewhere on a bright, gorgeous summer's day. I guess this is memorable at least.

'Hell fire,' Matt says, looking up at it, 'that's the ugliest pub sign I've seen since I had lunch at The Rotting Corpse last week.'

I give a little laugh. 'Well, you've obviously never been to the . . . er . . .' My mind is almost completely preoccupied wondering where that bloody safe is. Matt has turned to me with an expectant grin, but now I'm floundering. I'm such a simpleton, thinking it would be in the wardrobe. Of course it wasn't going to be in the wardrobe. Everyone knows if you're going to install a secret safe somewhere, you don't put it inside a wardrobe that doesn't even have a lock on it. *I* knew I wasn't going to look inside the wardrobe – he'd asked me not to and I was always eager to please – but *he* didn't know I wouldn't. He didn't trust me not to look in it. Of course he didn't. If he'd trusted me, he wouldn't have needed the safe in the first place, now would he?

'The . . .?' Matt prompts, and I grab my attention by the shoulder and swing it back round to face me.

'Um . . . The Disembowelled Cow?'

He snorts kindly, but it was a lame effort, delivered out of time, and we both know it. As we go into the pub I feel my fingernails digging into my palms and focus on relaxing my clenched fists back into hands. If I'm going to find the safe and Adam and ever claw back some self-respect and his eyes out, I've got to start thinking like a secretive, slippery, self-obsessed snake; not like myself. Where would a suspicious, mistrustful muppet hide a safe in our house? And why?

'This place is dire,' Matt says suddenly. Well, it's not suddenly actually, we've been sitting at a table in silence for a few minutes, Matt reading the menu, me silently seething about the secret and unfathomable machinations of my elusive life-partner. 'Salads and sandwiches for lunch; fish and chips for dinner.' He looks up at me. 'Did you say you and Adam came here a lot?'

'Yeah. Most Sundays, for the carvery.'

He raises his eyebrows. 'Why?'

'What do you mean, why? Because we enjoyed going out for Sunday lunch. I think quite a few people do it these days – it's really catching on.'

'No, I mean, why here? I mean, look at it. It's so . . .' We both glance around at the brown carpet, electric lighting, gas fire and white, featureless walls. 'Dreary,' Matt finishes.

I shrug. 'I don't know, really. We always came here, I suppose. It's the nearest place.'

He shakes his head. 'The Black Cock is nearer actually. Have you ever been in there? It's really nice, full of character, kind of old-style and cosy, with a real fire, chatty old landlord, you know the sort of thing. And they have a fantastic menu – meatballs, salmon, steak pie, that kind of thing.' He waves the menu in his hand. 'Salads and sandwiches. Mostly ham.'

I think back to my most recent trip to a pub, last night with Lauren. 'Well, I'm just relieved to see an absence of body parts and gore to be honest.'

He stares at me. 'Wha-a-a-t?' He glances around him nervously. 'Are there usually . . .?'

'No! No, no. I don't mean . . . It's just, there's this place . . .'

He's already nodding. 'Yeah, I know it. The Bunch of Fives? Hideous.' He flicks his eyes up at the room. 'Even this banal blandness is better than that!'

'Exactly!'

He grins, then looks down at the menu. 'So, what are you going for?'

'I don't know. What about you?'

'Um . . . I think . . . Cheese and pickle.' He looks up at me.

I nod. 'Sounds good. I'll have the same.'

He orders them at the bar and brings us both back a drink. My mind is still whirring and buzzing over the ever-increasing list of things that are missing: 1) the curry; 2) my nebulous husband; 3) the secret safe. I've given so much thought to where they all are, I've barely given any time at all to the question of *why* they're missing. Matt takes a hearty bite of his sandwich and chews it enthusiastically.

'So how did you and Adam meet?' he asks, round the mouthful of food.

I'm aware of him there, talking to me. I'm even conscious of what he's asked. But it's like my brain doesn't want to get involved. It looks up, glances briefly at the current interaction, then dismisses it and goes straight back to what it was doing. It's pretty obvious that there will be stuff inside that safe that will give me more information about not only where Adam is now, but also why. Some letters, receipts, maybe a map. Unless . . . I'm suddenly gripped with panic as another possibility occurs to me. What if he opened and emptied the safe before he cleared off? What if I spend days, weeks, locating the damn thing, only to find it empty? I frown hard and look up at Matt in alarm, to find him smiling pleasantly at me, his eyebrows up expectantly. I wonder for a brief moment why he seems so unperturbed by this possibility, but then remember that, of course, none of that was out loud. And even if it was, he won't be as invested in finding Adam, the safe and the curry as I am, will he? I relax my features and think back quickly to what he's just said, but all I can remember him saying is the word 'Adam'.

'Sorry, Matt. I'm a bit distracted.'

'Yeah, I kind of got that.'

'Sorry. I will try harder.'

'Don't worry about it, Gracie. Honestly.' He blows out a small gust of air. 'You've got enough on your plate to deal with, without me in your face, trying to . . .' He trails off with a small shake of the head, then lifts his glass and takes a long swig of his Coke.

'No, that was unbelievably rude of me. I'm really sorry. You've been so kind, helping me out like this, driving me around. You didn't have to do any of it, and I really am very grateful.'

He smiles. 'Well, of course I'll help you. I'm happy to. More than happy.'

'I know, I'm your sister's best friend and you love her so helping me makes her happy which makes you happy. But even so, I'm very grateful.'

He's shaking his head with a dead serious look on his face. 'No, no, that's not the reason. I'd help you anyway, even if you weren't Lou's mate.'

'Yes, I believe you would, because you're one of life's nice guys.' I take a bite of sandwich. 'So, what did you ask me?'

For the second time today, he looks like he's about to

say more. But instead he inhales deeply then lets it all go. 'OK, well, I was just thinking, maybe it would be an idea to talk about Adam generally, about your history together, his life, your life, see if anything interesting comes up that might help us find the safe. You know, maybe we can *deduce* where it is, rather than physically taking the place apart.'

My fingers are twitching with the need to physically take the place apart, but I nod calmly. 'That's a good idea.' It certainly can't hurt, anyway, and will pass some more time.

'Great. So . . . Tell me about Adam. How did you get together?'

I tell him the story of the flat and the letting agency, and how Adam persuaded me to rent a much nicer place than the one I originally went in for. Matt listens carefully while I'm speaking, watching my face closely, nodding occasionally, giving the odd grunt and 'ah' of understanding.

'Did you go to his office much, after you'd got together?'

'No, hardly ever. Why?'

His eyes widen. 'Well bloody hell! That's where the safe is, then, don't you think?'

I think about this, and it's like a bomb going off in my head, spreading energy down into my arms and tummy and legs, making me explode from my chair. 'Oh my God, I can't believe I haven't thought of that before!'

He looks up at me excitedly and stands up too. 'Come on then, let's go!' Quickly, he starts gathering his things together – keys, jacket, change. I grab mine and am just swinging my bag onto my shoulder when he pauses, half bent over the table.

'What?'

He turns to me. 'I'm just thinking. It makes no sense, actually.'

I could stamp with frustration. 'What doesn't?'

He presses his lips together and lifts his shoulders. 'Why would he keep the safe in the office, but leave the key in the house?'

'I don't know, does it matter, let's go!'

But he shakes his head and starts to relax, pulling the chair out ready to sit back down. 'No, Grace, listen. He keeps the safe with . . . whatever is inside it – we have to assume it's incriminating in some way, otherwise why would he hide it? – so he keeps it at the office, to make absolutely sure you never find it. Why not just keep the key there too? He could put it in a locked drawer. Or better yet, keep it in the legitimate work safe. In a lock box. Hanging on a hook, even, it wouldn't matter because no one would ever think it was odd or be looking for it there.'

I feel that information start to move round my body like a sedative, slowing me down, draining me of all energy and enthusiasm. It makes sense. My shoulders sag as it sinks in. 'You're right. And of course, what if he needed access to whatever's in there? He's in the office, the safe's in the office, the key's at home. Very inconvenient.'

Matt nods. 'Good point. No, I think we can assume the safe is in the house somewhere, with the key.'

We both sit back down at the table and listlessly pick

at our food again. The task ahead of us seems hopeless – perhaps even more so than before we thought we'd worked it out. And really, could this mysterious safe's whereabouts truly be all that important? Adam will still be gone, even if we find it.

'So. You rented his flat off him?' Matt says, breaking the silence.

I meet his eyes and they wrench me back to the pub. 'Yeah. He said that he liked me so much, so quickly, he wanted me to rent his place and no one else.'

He breaks eye contact at this point and stares down at his plate for a while. I'm not sure why: it's empty now. Then he looks up at me frankly.

'Did you like the place you ended up in?' he asks.

'What, Adam's flat, you mean? Yes, it was nice.'

He shakes his head. 'I mean, did you love it? Did you feel at home there? Did you thank your lucky stars you hadn't ended up in the other place, the smelly place?'

'Um, well, no, I suppose not, really.' I take a dainty bite of my own sandwich and consider that for a moment while I try to chew bread into a moist pulp without making any noise at all. I only lived in that place for around six months before Adam asked me to move into Maple Avenue with him. He wanted to sell it anyway. But while I was there, what did I feel about it? I think back to that time, three years ago. It was clean and new and fresh and low maintenance; but was it homey? The lights all worked and the grey carpet was new and the kitchen steel was stainless and the paintwork was brilliant white, not yellowing and cracked. The hob had an extractor hood. But its fire escape didn't take me back to my school days, to Ginger and me, hunched on the metalwork stairs, laughing until we cried, or crying until we laughed, smoking and drinking coffee. Actually it didn't have a fire escape. It had a fully functioning lift, and a set of concrete steps at the end of each corridor that led to the fire exit. The door had a bar on the inside and made a satisfying *thwuck* sound when you opened it. But I was hardly ever there, as Adam already had a rented house and we spent almost all of our time in it. If we weren't together, I usually went to Mum and Dad's. I can barely think of one single time when I spent an evening alone in that place. If I had, I'm sure I would have felt very safe and draught-free.

'That's a shame,' he says now, wiping his fingers on the napkin. 'I mean, if you really wanted that other place, if it had such special memories for you, it's kind of sad that you didn't ever live there.'

I shrug. 'I didn't really mind. I'm not great at making decisions anyway, that's why Adam did all that kind of thing.'

'All what kind of thing?'

'You know, making the decisions. Where to go for dinner, what to watch on telly, what I should wear, that kind of thing.'

He blinks. 'What you should wear?'

'Well, yeah. He liked what he liked, you know?' Adam was quite definite about what he liked me to wear. Round necks, long lengths, nothing too tight or revealing. 'Don't want my wife looking cheap,' he'd say to me, unhooking tops and skirts from the rails in Dorothy Perkins. I was so lucky, I thought then, that I had a husband who took

167

such an interest in my clothes, and even came shopping with me. 'And he obviously could see better than I could what looked good on me.' I glance down at what I'm wearing today. It's a brown corduroy skirt, beige tee shirt, boots. 'This top, for example. He bought it for me because he said it suits me. It's my colour, apparently.'

'Well, I wouldn't have said that.'

'Really? Why not?'

He appraises me closely, then shakes his head. 'The point is not what he thought looks good on you. The point is you choosing your clothes yourself. Getting a chance to express yourself. I mean, do you really like this colour?'

I look down. The colour is inoffensive, kind of neutral. It goes with anything, and this skirt in particular. 'What's not to like?'

He laughs out a puff of air and smiles. 'Nothing, Gracie. Nothing at all.'

'What does that mean?'

He doesn't answer because at that moment my mobile phone starts to ring in my handbag. I rummage around quickly to find it and, when I pull it out, I find that it's Julia calling me.

'Adam's mum,' I say quickly to Matt, and he nods and stands up, then walks away to the bar. I press the 'answer' key. 'Hi Julia. How are you?'

'Oh, oh, Gracie, there you are, thank goodness. It's me, Julia. Listen, I've got to tell you something, something important has happened. I don't want to talk about it on the phone, it's really important and it's happening right now. There was a slot, just luckily by chance, so I said yes, that wasn't stupid, was it? Was it stupid?

168

Sometimes I just can't tell whether or not I'm being stupid. Can you come over? Are you OK?'

The urgent panic in her voice travels through the phone into my mind and instantly I feel alarm. 'I'll try, Julia, but I don't have a car, remember? I'll need to see if I can get a lift . . .'

'Oh, thank you, lovey, thank you so much. I really would like you to be here. I really *need* you to be here. It's in twenty minutes, so I'll see you then.' And she clicks off without saying goodbye, no doubt without even a smidgen of irony.

When Matt comes back, I look up at him pleadingly. 'Everything OK?'

I nod. Then shake my head. 'Oh, I don't know. She wants me to go over there, in twenty minutes. Apparently there's some kind of urgent thing she wants to talk to me about . . .'

'Well, come on then,' he says, pulling his car keys out of his pocket, 'let's go.'

I feel a swell of gratitude so powerful it actually brings heat into my eyes. I blink a few times to get rid of it. How ridiculous, it's only a lift. I put my hand on Matt's arm as we walk back to the car. 'Thank you for this. I really . . . appreciate it. More than you know.'

He grins. 'It's only a lift!'

I nod. Yeah, and I won't have to do whatever it is Julia wants me to do all on my own.

Matt's never met Julia and Ray before. I wonder whether I should prime him in the car, but in the end I decide to let him make up his own mind, without any preconceptions. It's possible I've been blowing things up

169

out of proportion because of my obsession with the other peculiar things about Adam. Maybe there's nothing odd about Julia at all.

She answers the door in her underwear. Next to me, Matt goes rigid and seems about to bolt.

'Good God, Gracie, what on earth are you doing here?' she asks, eyes wide in surprise.

'You asked me to come over, Julia, about fifteen minutes ago, remember? You said there's something important happening.'

'Oh, yes, yes, there is, in a minute. That's lucky, you'll be here for it. Come in, come in.'

We follow her into the hallway, then she darts to the left and up the stairs, so we continue into the living room on our own. There's no sign of Ray.

Matt turns to me, his eyes wide. 'Where in God's name are we?' he says quietly, but I can't explain anything as in the next few seconds Julia skitters into the room. We both relax with relief at the sight of a blue polka dot dress and navy cardigan.

'I'm in a right jittery state about this, you know,' she says, smoothing down the front of her dress. 'Can't seem to think straight at all. Mind keeps wandering all over the place. Forgot something really important just now.' She puts up a hand. 'Don't even ask me. I'm so embarrassed!'

Matt and I exchange a look. I think we both know what she forgot, but it seems she doesn't remember it was us at the door, which is fine with me.

'It's been a stressful time, Julia,' I say softly.

She nods. 'Oh, yes, yes, I know it has. I've been cleaning all morning.'

170

'So what exactly—'

I don't manage to finish asking the question, as at that moment there's a knock at the door. Julia glances down at herself quickly, then pats the front of her dress, obviously reassuring herself that she's in the proper attire for door-answering. Then she looks at me quickly, grimaces, and leaves the room.

'Wow,' is all Matt says.

'I know.'

'Is she always . . .?'

'Yes.'

He nods slowly. 'Wow.'

'I know.'

'What do you think this is all about?'

'I have no idea. It could be absolutely anything.'

'Something to do with Adam, though?'

'Not necessarily. Maybe she's bought a new kettle or, I don't know, got an appointment for a haircut.'

'Can't be the kettle,' he says quietly, 'someone's here.'

Seconds later, an unremarkable young woman comes into the room, followed by an anxious Julia. The girl looks around her, relaxed and comfortable and giving nothing away as to why we are all there. She's in plain blue jeans and a purple tee shirt and has mousy hair tied back into a ponytail. She must be around twenty-one or twenty-two, but in spite of her age she doesn't seem to be wearing any make-up. She doesn't need to, though, as her skin is flawless, like a doll. The most noticeable thing about her is her confidence and ease at being in someone else's house, surrounded on three sides by strangers. Oh, that and the one-year-old baby sitting on her hip.

I'm hit in the stomach with a sickening lurch. Immediately the presence of that baby, so young, so dark, makes me unbearably uneasy. Suddenly I'm finding it difficult to breathe normally as all the twos from the past three years of my life add inexorably up to four. I make myself smile questioningly and take a step towards her.

'Oh, hello. Nice baby. My name's Grace and this is my friend's brother, Matt. How old is he?'

A brief frown appears on that smooth face and is then replaced by a smile. 'Looks about thirty, I suppose. Is this some kind of test?'

'What? Oh, no, no, ha ha, I see what you . . . No, I didn't . . . What I meant was, how old is your baby?'

She nods. 'Yes, I realise thit. Just a joke. He's nine months.'

'Oh, right. Nine months. Wow.' I think back furiously nine months. Where was I? And more to the point, where was Adam? It's July now, so nine months ago . . . I start to count back, my brain tumbling like clothes in the dryer, but when I get to seven I forget where I am, and what I'm counting. Nine months, nine months, so nine months ago . . . No, no, that's the wrong nine months, idiot. If this creature was born nine months ago, I have to go back nine months before that, back to, what? January last year? February? What was happening then? Was it snowing? Was Adam acting strangely? Well, hah, der, course he was. That's pretty standard. So for him, not acting strangely at all. Oh, God, I can't think straight.

'She was recommended to me by someone,' Julia says suddenly, nodding. She makes a sweeping gesture with her arm, I'm guessing to indicate that we should all move to

172

the sofa and sit down, but I'm still fixated on the child. 'Would you . . .?' she says, almost beseechingly, and I drag my eyes away from the baby to focus on her. She's already seated, so after a glance at Matt, I go over there and sit down next to her. Matt sits on my other side.

'What's this all about, Julia?' I ask her quietly. 'Who is this woman?' I stare malevolently at the baby again. It smiles and blows a bubble. 'And whose baby is it?'

The girl bends slightly to bring her face level with mine. 'The baby is mine and my husbind's,' she says firmly. I notice that she has a faint Australian accent, and my mind seizes it. Was Adam in Australia nine months ago? Or eighteen months ago? Huh, like I'd know. But I would know if he was away or not. Think, think . . .

'I really don't get why you're being like thit with hum.'

'Oh, no, I'm not, I just thought . . .' I dry up. Hmm. Can't really tell her that as soon as I clapped eyes on her baby, I bounded at full speed to the conclusion that she had been shagging my husband and secretly birthed his baby. No. 'No, sorry, I was just . . . I wasn't expecting . . . I didn't . . .'

'We're a bit in the dark here, to be honest,' Matt says confidently next to me. 'Julia has asked us to come, without explaining anything, so we don't even know why we're here, or whether your lovely baby is part of it, or whether he was just at a loose end and decided to tag along.'

The girl grins and relaxes visibly and I release a tense breath. I feel myself leaning a little towards Matt, as if pulled by some invisible force, and our upper arms press together.

'Oh, ha ha, no, no, he's just tagging along,' the girl says, smiling broadly. 'He's called Max, by the way.' She places him down on his back on the floor where he immediately starts to look sleepy.

'Oh, hi Max,' Matt says, waving. 'It's lovely to meet you. I'm Matt. How's your day so far?'

Max breathes quickly through his mouth and lets his head drop to the side.

'Julia,' Max's mum says, and Julia jumps in her seat. 'Yes?'

'Shall we get on?' Julia nodes mutely, so the girl gives a tiny nod. 'Right. Before we staht, my name is Melissa. You should know thit this doesn't always work, but I have been pretty successful in the pahst. I'll go over what I'm going to do and what may or may not hippen and then you can ahsk any questions before we do the reading itself. OK?' Matt and I must be looking pretty befuddled – actually, I have a feeling Julia is too – so Melissa smiles. 'I'm a psychic,' she says, as if she was saying 'I'm a teacher.' 'Actually I'm more of a psychic troubleshooter.' She giggles girlishly. 'Thit is, like a problem solver. You know?'

'Oh I see,' Matt says, nodding. 'A psychic troubleshooter. So, are you saying you solve psychic problems? Bad signal, interference, sluggish spirits, that kind of thing?' I can hear the smile in his voice even though I can only see him in my periphery.

Melissa frowns. 'No, not at all. I mean I can help to solve your problems by using spirit to guide you.'

Beside me, Matt nods gravely. 'Spirit?'

Melissa nods. 'Yes. Spirit.'

'I see. So it's a name? Like vodka?'

Melissa rolls her eyes. 'I don't know. Anyway. Shall I go over what hippens?'

Matt spreads his hands. 'Please.'

'Thinks. Now, first of all I need to make sure you're all completely comfortable. Can't be doing with interruptions for the toilet, or someone needing a snack.' She dips her chin and peers at us like a teacher. 'Anyone need the loo, or a drink, or anything like thit?' I shake my head quickly. Clearly our Melissa's not a very good psychic. I mean, shouldn't she be able to tell *us*?

'OK then. Mobile phones off please. Think you. And no interrupting – you can ahsk questions in a minute.'

So the three of us sit in a row, one of us devouring it all with wide eyes; one of us listening dispassionately; one of us dismissing it all silently. I know Matt is dismissing it all by his repeated, muted sighs and not-so-subtle tuts. Melissa tells us that she will need to hold something belonging to the missing person, then we will all have to keep very quiet (in other words, no sarcastic sighing, ha ha) while she uses spirit to help her find the person and tell us what has happened. The thought occurs to me to ask her to help me find the safe afterwards, but I dismiss that idea quickly. Something tells me her expertise won't run to missing objects. In fact, technically the object I'm looking for isn't missing, as I'm positive Adam knows exactly where it is, why it's there, and how to get into it.

Quickly I force myself to refocus on what's going on, before I get lost wondering about the safe yet again. Melissa's voice is still going.

'. . . so, if you could give me something belonging to Adam . . .'

'Grace,' Julia says, not moving her wide eyes from Melissa's face.

'Oh, sorry, I thought the missing person was called Adam?'

'Yes, yes, he is.' Julia nods but still doesn't look at me. 'Grace. Something of Adam's.'

I start and turn towards her. 'Oh, God, Julia. I'm so sorry, I don't think . . .' I grab my handbag anyway and start rummaging through it, even though I know I don't have anything of his in there. I never have had. I shake my head as I look up at her again. 'I don't have anything of his with me. I'm so sorry, I didn't know. Why didn't you ask me to bring something?'

She revolves her head towards me, pins me briefly with a look, then turns back to Melissa. 'I mean, Grace *is* something of Adam's.' She jerks her chin towards me. 'Use her.'

And then, like the amazing Grace in the song, I feel like I can see properly at last. I'm not invited to take part in this farce, or even to support Julia while she goes through it. My presence is for a much more practical reason. I'm here simply as one of Adam's possessions. Because in Julia's eyes, that's all I am. All I ever was.

'Um, I don't think so . . .' Matt starts to say. He puts his arm partway across me as a kind of barrier as he looks from Melissa to Julia.

I touch his arm. 'It's OK, Matt. It's fine.' I give Melissa a look, who is, to be fair to the girl, looking a bit uncomfortable now. Then I turn to Julia. 'Julia, I'm not one of

176

Adam's belongings. I've got my own personality, my own thoughts and ideas. I doubt very much that he will have left much of a psychic imprint on me.'

'You'd be surprised, actually,' Melissa cuts in helpfully.

'Well, my personality will no doubt interfere with the—'

'Doubt ut.'

I fall silent. Both Melissa and Julia are studiously avoiding looking at me. Julia has discovered something incredibly interesting on her sleeve; and Melissa is clasping her hands together and looking beseechingly up at the ceiling. No doubt gathering the spirits around her or something equally fatuous. I glance at Matt and he flicks his eyes towards the door – 'Get out of here?' – but I shake my head. As stupid and pointless as this all is, I kind of want to see it play out now. I take a breath in and release it slowly. 'I guess I'll endure it. Where do you want me, then?'

'Right.' Melissa indicates the floor next to the chair she's sitting on. 'If you could come and sit over here, thit would be most useful.'

So I get up and move to the spot she's indicated, leaving poor Matt on the sofa next to Julia. He's scooched forwards now so he's perched on the edge with his hands clasped loosely between his knees. He keeps glancing around, jerking his head forwards as he notices things: the mini brass Buddha head on the mantel shelf; the cupped angel's wings holding a candle in the shape of a curled baby; the books on the power of *now* and the self-healing properties of a raw meat diet. He catches my eye and I realise I've been staring at him for quite a while, so I shake my head as if in disbelief. He grins and raises his eyebrows, as if to say 'What?' so I smile and make an 'I'm so sorry' expression, pressing my lips together and hanging my head. But he just shakes his head dismissively, which I take to mean, 'It doesn't matter.' But it doesn't make me feel any better. As I look at him, he glances over to Melissa, then back at me, and his lips twitch a bit. He even flicks his eyes in her direction a couple of times, as if to say, 'Can you believe this?' And it occurs to me then that he might actually be enjoying himself.

Melissa is now waving her hands around in a wafting motion towards herself, as if beckoning someone – or something – in her direction.

'That looks very complicated and important,' Matt says, his voice quivering just a little. 'Are you summoning spirit towards you?'

'Nah, I'm just really hot. OK, Julia, you ready? Shall we get started?'

Matt looks over at me again, his face a frozen, mirthless mask. But his nostrils flare just a little and it's obvious – to me anyway – that he's trying not to giggle. I look from him to Julia, but she doesn't seem to be aware of anything except Melissa, who is now very seriously and slowly reaching down to place a hand on top of my head.

'What happens now?' Julia whispers reverentially.

'I just need to focus a few moments, Julia love, while I hold the . . . er . . . the item, and see if I can pick anything up.'

'Right. So what sort of thing . . .?'

'Focusing, Julia.'

Gradually, the room falls into silence and now we're all

watching Melissa. She seems to have gone into a trance-like state, eyes closed, chin slightly dipped, as if she were staring at the top of my head. But she's completely silent and immobile. My legs are starting to get pins and needles but I can't move, I can't speak, there's absolutely nothing stirring in the room. Even Matt, it seems, has got caught up in the moment and is staring intently at the top of my head. I roll my eyes towards Julia and find her staring at exactly the same spot. It's making me a bit nervous, to be honest, as if there's a small fire starting there, or a tiny creature is hatching. It does feel oddly warm, hot even, and I find myself wondering if some mystical power is being conjured. I picture a bright, ethereal light emanating from me, and I wonder what I look like with that happening.

Then I give myself a mental slap round the face. Come *on*.

Suddenly Melissa sucks her breath in sharply, as if someone has put an ice cube down her back. Instinctively I jerk back and try to turn a teensy bit to see what's happening, but I can't move. The pressure on my head suddenly feels like a building is resting on me, pinning me to the floor. My left foot is now completely numb but I can't move even a tiny bit. Matt and Julia are still staring unblinkingly at the top of my head. The pressure increases further, making me feel like my head is being forced into my chest cavity, then suddenly releases – I presume Melissa removed her hand – and Julia and Matt relax and lean back into their seats. For a split second I feel like I'm levitating, rising up, and I start to panic; but then I realise it's simply the sensation of the release of pressure from my head. Quickly I get my foot out from under me and stretch it out, then turn to look at Melissa. She's smiling and looking very serene and superior.

'Well, that went well,' she says, nodding at us all with half-closed eyes. I want to slap her. We all wait to hear what she's about to pronounce, but she just sighs and stares delightedly at Max, snuffling and rotating his ankles on the floor.

'Great,' Matt says eventually. 'Are you going to let us in on it?'

A hardness appears in Melissa's beatific smile, just for a second, then she's all loveliness and calm again. 'Oh well, yes, of course.' She reaches above her and stretches her arms. 'Now, let me think. Ah yes, there was a lot of blankness to begin with, not much there at all.'

'What does that mean?' Julia's voice is virtually a whisper. It seems oddly theatrical after Melissa's matter-of-fact tone.

'Um, well ut just means that I couldn't find him for a long time.'

'Join the club,' I mutter, and Matt snorts a breathy laugh out of his nose.

'His trace on Grace is very faint,' Melissa goes on. 'He clearly hasn't touched her for a long time.'

'Well, he's been gone a long time,' I say defensively.

Melissa looks at me. 'Yes. Exactly.'

'Shh,' Julia says at me, then raises her eyebrows at Melissa.

'Yes, yes, with a trace as faint as that he's definitely been gone a while,' Melissa says, nodding. 'How long is ut? Four, five months . . .?'

'A week.'

180

Melissa turns and looks down at me. 'Seven days?' She frowns. 'Not months? Are you sure? It seemed to me he'd been gone a lot longer.'

'Really?' Julia says hungrily. 'Well, that's strange.' She turns to me with narrowed eyes, but I have no idea what she's accusing me of. She saw Adam herself a week or so before he legged it, so she knows full well he hasn't been gone any longer than I've said.

'Well, ut's either longer,' Melissa goes on, 'or there wasn't much of a connection in the first place.'

'So where is he now?' I ask quickly, cutting Julia off before she starts.

Melissa smiles at me indulgently. My hands clench into fists. 'Oh, I can't tell you thit, my love,' she says, blinking slowly. 'This isn't an exact science, you know.'

'Not even a science,' comes a quiet voice from the sofa.

'But isn't that the entire reason we're here?' I get my feet under me and stand up. 'I mean, what the hell was this all about, if not to find out where the fucker is?'

Julia flinches at my language and covers her ears, as if she doesn't live in the twenty-first century. 'Oh dear . . .'

Melissa is scowling now. 'No, my love, thit is not why we're here. If you thought thit, then maybe you shouldn't have come.'

'I didn't know anything about it!' I'm practically shouting now. 'I wasn't given the option of not coming. Believe me, Melissa, I would . . . not have come, if I'd known in advance what was going to happen.' I glance at Matt. 'Although you were extremely amusing.'

He touches his hand to an imaginary hat. 'Why thank you, ma'am.'

Melissa's serene demeanour is completely dissolving now, and she gets up angrily. 'Ah don't git what you thunk is so fanny.' Her accent gets broader as she gets angrier. 'Ah've connicted to spirut to hilp you in your loss, end ah'm only charging hahf price as ut was a cancellation . . .'

'Oh, right. Now it all makes sense,' Matt says expressively, standing up, and up, and up, in front of Melissa. She actually seems to shrink as he extends to full height before her.

'No,' she says quietly, 'there's no deciption here. Julia knows there's a fee, don't you love. She rang me, she booked me, ah haven't done nothing wrong.'

'Very telling,' Matt says darkly. 'Unlike your psychic ability.'

Max the baby is getting stressed at this point and starts to grizzle. Melissa bends down and deftly scoops him up, then bounces him a little on her shoulder. 'Ah don't know what you're talking about,' she says, gathering her things together. 'Ah done what ah said ah'd do, no more, no liss. This isn't an exict science, like ah sid, and clients do know thit you might not always git what you want to hear.'

'I think you'd better leave.' Matt's voice is low and almost threatening.

'All right, ah'll go. But before ah do, don't you want to hear what ah did pick up?'

There's a sudden sense of someone pressing the 'pause' button. We all freeze. Even Max stops whinging. We all look at each other in silence for a brief moment. Then Max starts up again and the moment is gone.

'Yes. Oh yes please.'

Matt and I look at each other, then turn to the voice. It's Julia, of course, standing up from the sofa, wringing her hands together. She's been so quiet, we'd kind of forgotten about her. Which is rotten, really, seeing as she's footing the bill. 'Please tell me. Please.'

Melissa draws herself up from her previous cringing position and beams around the room self-importantly. She approaches Julia and gently takes hold of her upper arms. I hold my breath. 'Well Julia,' she says, her voice irritatingly self-important, 'ah'm so pleased to tell you thit ah was able to see, without any doubt at all, thit your son is still very much ulive.'

TEN

She announces it like some kind of declaration, as if she's just decided to share with us the formula for turning lead into gold. I roll my eyes towards Matt and find him looking just as un-thunderstruck as I am. He catches my eye and raises one corner of his mouth in a half smile, then widens his eyes.

'Wow, Melissa,' he says, shaking his head, 'thanks. I mean, that was great. Really, really impressive. Wasn't she? Seriously, skills like that, you should be on telly.' He takes two giant strides and arrives at the door to the hallway. He turns back to me. 'Coming?'

'Right behind you.' I walk past Melissa's flummoxed face as she struggles to get a grip on what's just happened, but as I stride to the door, a sound from the sofa makes me stop and turn. Julia is there, staring at the floor, one hand on either side of her face, and her expression makes me stop where I am. At the door, I can just see Matt looking from me to Julia; and then he edges back into the room.

'What is it?'

I don't take my eyes from Julia's face. 'Not sure. Are you all right, Julia?'

She's gone completely white, and has just made a small whimpering sound. She starts rocking, her hands still on her face. I sit down next to her and put my arm around her shoulder. She's trembling. This isn't quite what I was expecting. I mean, she's just had what she must consider to be 'proof' that her beloved son is still alive (personally, the missing passport, car and curry were all it took to convince me), so surely she should be joyful? If anything, I would have expected a dance around the garden in bare feet singing 'Stayin' Alive' or something. Looking at her now, she's about ten Valiums past disappointed. 'Julia? What is it?' She doesn't look up, just continues to stare at the floor and rock.

'Well, ah gotta go,' Melissa says, heading swiftly for the door.

Matt intercepts her. 'Whoa, hold on a minute, you can't just leave when she's in this state.'

'Why not? 'S nothing to do with me.'

I raise my head to face her. 'It's got everything to do with you! She was – well, I won't say fine, but certainly more coherent than this – before your little charade, and now look at her. Doesn't take Sherlock Holmes to work out there must be a link.'

Melissa shrugs and hoists baby Max up a bit further. ''S not my problem if she cahn't take the news, is ut?'

Matt gets right up close to her. 'What do you mean?'

She steps back a little and coolly looks Matt up and down. 'Well, sometimes the client doesn't like what they hear. Stands to reason, doesn't ut? You want news from

185

the other sahd, sometimes ut's not gonna be good. Ah can't be held responsible for thit.' She raises her free hand, palm up. 'Ah'm just the missinger, right?'

Matt stares at her with narrowed eyes for several seconds. 'What do you mean, not good? How can what you've said possibly not be good?'

Melissa shrugs. 'Ah don't claim to understand ut.'

'Yes you do! That's exactly what you do claim!'

She shakes her head. 'Ah don't. Ah just receive information and pass ut on. What ah hear and how they take ut us not my responsibility.'

He stares at her wordlessly for a moment, narrowing his eyes. 'Typical necromancer.'

'What . . .?'

'Oh just leave, Melissa. Go on, get out of here.'

She doesn't wait to be asked twice, but scuttles immediately behind Matt and out into the hallway. Seconds later we hear the front door bang.

I look up at Matt. 'Typical necromancer? You met many?'

He shrugs. 'Not personally, but I've seen lots of films about it. Summoning the dead all over the place without giving a thought to the consequences.'

'Ah, right. I see.' I give him a sarcastic nod, then turn my attention to Julia. She's shaking her head now, and looks seriously displeased. 'Are you all right, Julia?'

She looks up at me. 'He's alive, then.'

'Yes, Julia,' Matt says. He moves a bit nearer and puts a hand on her shoulder. 'It's good news, isn't it?'

She stares at him for a few seconds. 'You . . . you're sure? He's definitely . . .?'

'Yes, according to Melissa, he's definitely alive.'

I want to give him a nudge, to stop him being so absolute about it, getting her hopes up, just in case. But that's ridiculous. He can be as firm about it as he wants, because Adam is definitely alive. He always has been. And then I'm hit by the extraordinary realisation that part of me wanted Matt not to be so definite about it. Does that mean I want Adam to be dead?

No, no, of course I don't. Definitely not. No one would want that even for a casual acquaintance, let alone for someone they have loved and lived with for three years. So why would I try to preserve the possibility that he is?

'But . . .?' Julia is searching Matt's face, looking for clues, perhaps, or trying to find answers. I can't help wondering what answers she's hoping to find there. Discreetly I angle my head to get a better look at it myself. He's got a nice firm jaw, a rough shadow starting to appear on it, dark eyes staring at her concernedly, hair flopping across his forehead. Yes, definitely a nice face – a very nice face – but no answers there really. I want to know what's happened to Adam as much as she does – well, nearly as much – but even I know that Matt won't know.

'Julia,' Matt says firmly, 'what's the matter?'

Her eyes stop searching and instantly still, narrowing as they focus on his eyes. Her lips thin and for a second she looks like she might be about to lunge towards his jugular. I want to yell, 'Cover your throat!'

'I'm not insane, you know,' she hisses. Her voice is low and throaty. 'It's just a bit of a shock, or a surprise really. I mean, I hoped he was alive, of course I did. Who

187

wouldn't? I'm his mum, I looked after him every minute of every day for thirty years, now that's a lifetime.' She breaks eye contact at last, then starts fidgeting, as if she wants to move. Matt straightens up and moves to my side, and we both look down at the woman on the sofa. She's glancing from side to side now, then around the room, at her lap, at the sofa, back to the floor, as if she's lost something. I think it's her marbles. 'It's just . . . Well, I'm just disappointed that Melissa couldn't tell us any more about where he is, that's all.'

It's a blatant lie! I'm no Jeremy Kyle, but even I could spot that one. Her eye contact is all over the place, she's rubbing her face, her tone of voice is almost . . . robotic. She's annoyed, definitely, but not with Melissa.

'Should we leave?' I whisper to Matt. Neither of us can take our eyes off her.

'Yes,' he whispers back. 'Definitely.' But we don't move.

Julia gets up now and walks straight to the dining table where she picks up a folded piece of paper lying there. She unfolds it and glances at it, then puts it roughly back on the table with a bang. 'Fuck that!' she exclaims, and I jerk in surprise. I've never heard her swear before, or anyone else while in her presence for that matter, so this feels like an electric shock. To hear this fragile lady in her dress and cardigan cursing like that is making me nervous. Next thing you know, there'll be an article in the paper about a woman driven mad with grief butchering two visitors on the living room carpet. Except, she's not mad with grief, is she? Because Adam is alive. She stomps away from us towards the other end of the room, and I take a resolute step towards the door. Matt notices and looks round at me smartly, then goes back to watching Julia. Obviously he's more used to the prospect of being sliced like ham than I am.

'Julia,' he says, and I close my eyes briefly. Now he's done it. I expect her to round on him with glowing red eyes, then come flying towards him with supernatural speed and tear him apart. Or am I thinking of *The Exorcist*?

'Yes?'

'Will you be OK? I mean, if Grace and I leave now.'

A brief frown flickers across her face. 'Of course I'll be OK. I'm not a child. I'm perfectly capable of continuing to live without you here.'

There's a pause. Then Matt says, 'I'll take that as a "yes".' He looks at me. 'Come on then.'

'Right.'

We both march quickly out of the front door and get back into Matt's car. Then we sit there in silence for a few moments. Eventually, Matt turns to me and we lock eyes.

'Well,' he says, his lips twitching. 'That was awkward.'

'Oh my God, I'm so sorry for dragging you into that, Matt. I honestly didn't expect that to happen.'

He's shaking his head. 'No, no, don't apologise. It was brilliant. I had a great time.'

'You did?'

'Hell yeah. I want to be there every single time you go to a psychic reading please. It was priceless.'

'I wonder what the piece of paper on the table was.'

He shrugs. 'I reckon that was Melissa's bill.'

'Oh, yes, I bet you're right. Julia didn't seem too happy with the service she got, did she?'

189

'No she did not. Which is kind of not what I would expect, given that it sounded to me like good news.'

'Mm, that's what I thought.' I shake my head. 'Doesn't make sense.'

Matt is staring at me. 'Grace, it was a psychic reading. Of course it didn't make sense.'

'Well that's true.'

We share a brief laugh, then lapse into silence. 'Shall I take you home?' he asks, starting the ignition.

'Yes please. And thank you so much for helping me today. I genuinely could not have done all this without you. I'm just sorry it wasted your entire day off.'

He looks at me seriously. 'It was the opposite of a waste.' His voice has gone soft and low and meaningful, but I'm not sure what the meaning is. I smile, and he looks away.

'Did you get the sense that Julia was a bit disappointed to hear that her beloved only son is alive?' I ask him.

'Mm, yes, it did seem like it, didn't it?'

'Weird.'

'So weird.' He takes me back to Mum and Dad's and leaves me there pretty quickly as he's working the night shift tonight. I watch his car driving away with a very odd sense of the end of a strange, surreal adventure.

But the adventure hasn't come to an end at all. I spend the evening curled up snugly in an armchair in the living room with Mum and Lauren, watching *Big Brother*. I haven't watched it for years – not Adam's sort of thing at all – and it's great. The armchair is new, a giant cream leather thing that I've never seen before, and I glance around the room and notice the new sofa, and new coffee table too. The walls are a different colour – very pale lilac, like the kitchen – and there's a print on the wall of a huge flower in different shades of purple. It's very pretty, very relaxing, and feels strange yet familiar in here. I remember reading on Google that lilac is a colour to relax to, so I do. It's obvious that Mum and Lo have watched this series from the beginning as they're full of comments like: 'Oh bless her, she's so naïve, isn't she?' and 'Christ, he's such a cock.' But I've seen none of it.

'That is marshmallow telly,' Adam said, when I suggested watching it once, a couple of years ago. 'Not only completely lacking in any nutritive value, but also actively detrimental to your brain. Your mind will switch off because it requires no activity whatsoever to partake of that dross. Avoid at all costs. Let's watch a film – I've got *The Dark Knight Rises*.'

I sip my tea and relax with the fun of the programme and how entertaining it is. Later on, Ripper creeps into the room, low to the ground, trying not to be seen, and curls up on a sock that someone left on the floor. He stares warily at the space in front of him for a long time, but eventually he too is soothed by the lilac walls and chilled ambience, and falls asleep.

'We're leaving early tomorrow to go to Ikea,' Mum says, standing up when the programme ends. Ripper is instantly up and out of the door. Mum watches him go with a fond smile, then turns back to me. 'Fancy coming?'

Ikea. Where Adam and I used to go together. As a couple. 'Oh, thanks, Mum. I'm not sure, though. I think I might bring you all down. Adam and I used to—'

191

'Oh, that's a shame,' she cuts in, heading for the stairs. 'Anyway, night night.'

I blink. Couldn't go anyway; got a safe to find.

The next day is Saturday again. I wake up in a single bed in my old room at my parents' house, like a cliché, but instead of rolling over and crying into my pillow before trudging around the house in my pyjamas eating ice cream for three weeks, I open my eyes wide and eagerly pull back the curtain by the bed to let the sunshine come flooding in. I've slept well, I'm relaxed and comfy, and I'm pleased that I enjoyed *Big Brother* so much last night. I didn't expect to, thought I'd gone off it completely, seeing as it's nothing more than mindless marshmallow that requires zero brain power, but I really did. As I pull the covers back and swing my legs over the side of the bed, I wonder with a thrilling tingle what else could happen now.

The first thing to happen is that I have a root through my old clothes, loyally hanging there in my childhood wardrobe. Bright colours, shorts, skimpy vests, they're all here. I get them out and lay them on the bed. They look like forbidden fruit.

'I don't know why you have these things,' Adam's voice comes back to me from three years ago. 'They're awful. Make you look so . . . I don't know, unspecial. Like every other girl these days.' He was helping me unpack my things into the flat when I'd moved in, three weeks after we'd first met, and was dangling a lovely pastel pink vest from River Island between his thumb and forefinger. 'Do you even wear them?'

I had done. I used to wear them all the time. Ginge and I got quite a lot of attention in them. But when he said that, I looked at them differently. Yes, I could certainly agree that most girls my age were wearing things like these – it's called a trend. Most girls my age were showing a lot of provocative flesh. Most girls my age liked the attention. But did I want to be like them? Did I want to be unspecial? I eyed the top, seeing it through his eyes, and realised that I probably did look pretty classless in it.

'Oh, God, no, not that,' I said, quickly, grabbing it from him and stuffing it into a black bin bag. 'These are all things from when I was eighteen, nineteen.' In went a couple more tops, several pairs of shorts, some mini-skirts, crop tops and short summer dresses. 'I'm older now, I don't wear them any more. I'll get rid of them.'

But I hadn't binned them. I couldn't. Instead, I'd dropped the sack into Mum's one afternoon when Adam wasn't with me, and Mum had apparently washed them, ironed them, and hung them all up for me. And I totally love her for it. Today, I'm wearing a pair of white shorts and a tight blue tee shirt, finished off with silver flip-flops. I give myself a grin in the wardrobe mirror – it's great to see the old me – or rather, the young me – again.

'I'm wearing skimpy clothes, Adam,' I say out loud, looking around me at the air. 'And, would you believe it, they don't make me feel unspecial? Not at all.' My reflection leans forward and whispers, 'I think it was just you doing that.'

Downstairs, the kitchen is empty, save for a collection of breakfast items on the draining board. I glance at the clock and find that it's around eight forty-five, so assume everyone has already left for Ikea. I stretch and yawn in the warmth of the sunlight beaming in through the windows, and make myself a coffee. There's no sign of Ripper anywhere – probably still in hiding, recovering from the terror of everyone having breakfast. While I wait for the kettle, I flip open my laptop on the table and Google Linton again. As I click through the photos, I wonder if I could take a little trip up there, see if I just happen to spot someone who looks and acts suspiciously like a bastard, playing pooh sticks off the stone bridge or catching fish from the stepping stones across the Wharfe. Or more likely dumping toxic waste in the river. Maybe I could rent a sweet little cottage for a week or so, have a really good look around. How much could that possibly cost? I open another tab and Google hotels in Linton, and find the Mopane Bush Lodge, located on the Mapesu Nature Reserve. Wow, it looks lovely. It has a swimming pool next to the bar, fire pit for outdoor eating, and you can go on a wildlife and bird watch . . . Ah, wait. That can't be right, can it? I think that's the wrong country. It doesn't say exactly which country it is, but I don't think North Yorkshire is known for its game drives. Damn you, Google. I go back to my original search, and this time I put North Yorkshire into the criteria. Ah, that's better. There are plenty, all looking like they'd be right at home in the north of England. Not a bongo drum or mosquito net in sight. There's a very nice one called Linton Lodge which looks like a listed building, so I click on it and go to the 'book now' page. Well of course it's completely booked up already, it's absolutely gorgeous. And incredibly expensive, so no doubt full of runaway husbands with pockets full of used notes from secret safe stashes. I go back and find a Travelodge. Fifty-six pounds a night, loads of availability. Right, I'm going to book it, just to go and have a look. A few days away from here exploring a secluded and picturesque part of northern England is just what I need right now. I reach for my handbag and rummage around for my purse, buzzing with a feeling of spontaneity and complete freedom. If I want to go to Linton, I damn well will. Who's gonna stop me? I can do what I want, go where I want, move as far away from here as I want, or just live with my parents if I want. Absolutely everything in my life is up to me to decide now, and I'm loving it. As my fingertips touch my purse, my hands brush against the three envelopes I picked up from our doormat yesterday, and everything screeches to a halt.

Like a hole ripped in the side of an aeroplane, I am abruptly and violently sucked out of the false security of my childhood home and back into the terrifying freefall of my real life. Back there, in Maple Avenue, my life as an adult, as Adam's wife, is continuing, even though my marriage apparently isn't. Back there, I have responsibilities that still exist even if I remove myself from them. Coming here hasn't wiped out everything there, and these letters are a rather unpleasant reminder of that. I pull them out, leaving my purse where it is. That will have to wait. These three envelopes might be important. They're all addressed to Adam, of course, but I'm used to that. What I'm not used to is opening and dealing with any post.

I put two of the envelopes down and turn the last one

over to tear open, but my mobile rings suddenly, making me jump. It's right there, on the counter next to the kettle. I drop the envelope onto the table and get up to go and grab the phone. It's Matt calling.

'Why good morrow, good sir. And what will be your pleasure this day?'

'Grace, they've found a body.'

It swoops into me, picking me up and dropping me again from a great height. The ground slams into my feet and rises up to meet my face and suddenly the floor tiles are inches away from my nose. I sit up but nausea overwhelms me and a roaring blackness presses in around me. I think I might be going to faint. I close my eyes and press my head against the cold floor, which helps me to feel more stable. 'They . . .?'

'They're on their way round to see you right now,' a deep voice in my ear says. Distractedly I remember that Matt is on the phone. 'What was that noise? Gracie? Are you still there?'

I nod and the room swims, so I turn my head so that my forehead is against the tile. 'Yes. Here.'

'Are you OK? I'm worried about you. Have you fallen over?'

I shake my head, but then realise that the floor tile is against my forehead, so I open my eyes and find myself lying prone on the kitchen floor. I close my eyes again. 'Oh. Yes. I think . . . so.'

'Are you OK? Shall I come over? I'm coming over. Shall I?'

'I . . . I don't know.'

'OK, concentrate, Gracie. Focus on your body. Is

anything hurting? Can you see any blood? Check your head.'

I lift my head gently and look down at myself, concentrating on each part of me in turn. Nothing seems to be bleeding and the only pain I can feel is in my hip, presumably where I hit the ground. I run my hand gingerly over my head but it's dry and free of gushing wounds. 'No. Think I'm all right.'

I hear a long breath being released. 'OK, good. Can you get up? They'll be there in a minute.'

'OK.' I draw my knees up and roll over onto them, then slowly get to my feet. I still feel not quite there, and a bit shaky, but it's easing off a bit. I keep my eyes closed and lean heavily against the counter. 'I'm up.'

'Fantastic. Go and sit in a chair for a bit. You probably just fainted briefly. It's the shock, lowers your blood pressure. You'll feel better in a few minutes.'

'OK.'

'Listen, Grace, try not to worry too much. The fact that they've found a male body of the right sort of age and build doesn't mean it's definitely Adam. Does it? I mean, if you can, try to take some comfort from what Melissa said yesterday. He's alive, OK?'

'Well, you're right about one thing, anyway.'

'What's that?'

'That was yesterday.'

When Linda Patterson shows up a few minutes later, she takes me into the kitchen and makes me sit down before telling me the dreadful news. A male body, just like Matt had said, right sort of age, right sort of build. There was no ID, no wallet, no driving licence, nothing to give it a name, so it needs officially identifying, before they can be sure . . .

'Do I have to do that?' I whisper. Oh please God say no, please say no, spare me from that horrific job.

'There's no need,' she says, patting my arm. 'Adam's parents have already volunteered.'

'Oh, right.' My shoulders slump with relief and I let out a breath, but then realise that Julia and Ray must have been informed about this before me. How is that right? I'm the wife, for God's sake, I'm the next of kin. Potentially.

'It's just geography,' Linda says, reading my mind. 'Someone went there, I came here. My colleagues got there first, just because Gladstone Road is nearer to the station. Mr Moorfield – Ray, is it? – offered to go back with the officers and identify . . .'

'Oh. OK. When is he doing it?'

She glances at her watch. 'Not long. He went straight there.'

'So are they going to tell you straight away . . .?'

She nods.

We sit and stare at each other for a few moments.

'Would you like a cup of tea?'

She puts her hand over mine. 'No, I'm fine, but let me make you one?'

'Oh, no thanks.'

We fall into silence again, just waiting for the phone to ring or Linda's radio to crackle, I suppose. Or will someone turn up here, to tell me? I have no idea. And how am I meant to feel, if it does turn out to be him?

Destroyed? Maybe. Shocked? Undoubtedly. Tearful? Wretched? Desperate? Relieved? Wait, what? How did that one get in there? Relieved? That my husband is dead? No, definitely not. Of course not. I love him, don't I? But relieved that my waiting was finally at an end? Maybe. At least I would know, one way or another, what happened to him, I suppose. At least I could start trying to cope with it. I wish I could Google 'wife's reaction on learning of husband's death'. I bet that's interesting. There's bound to be a ton of personal experience stories on there, with melodramatic accounts of fainting or vomiting or collapsing into arms or screaming and raising fists to the sky shouting, 'Why?!' And even if they don't give me any pointers of how to behave around Linda, to convince her I'm not guilty, it would at least help to pass the time.

Something occurs to me. 'Do you know how he died?'

'Not yet, Grace. We've got to wait for the post mortem.'

Is it my imagination, or do her eyes narrow at me a bit? Maybe my reaction is all wrong.

'Oh, yes, of course.' Adam's body, on a slab, with an electric saw cutting off the top of his head. I close my eyes but that only makes it more vivid so I open them again. Linda's face is there in front of me, staring at me interestedly. I wonder for a second how I must appear to her, in white hotpants and tight blue top. 'Do you know where he was found?'

'Um, yes. It was by the side of a road, in the industrial estate.'

'In Linton?'

She shakes her head. 'No, no, that's the main reason

why we don't really expect it to be your husband. It was the industrial estate here, only three miles from his home.'

It's another whooshing sensation, and I quickly put my head down on the table before the dizziness takes over.

'Are you OK, Grace?'

I lift my head. 'Yes, sorry. Thought I might pass out.'

'Do you want some water?'

'No. Why was he here? Why is his car in Linton, but his body is here?'

She puts a hand over mine. 'It might not be him, Grace. Try to remember that.'

I nod. 'Oh, yes, yes. Of course.'

But what if it is him? How can he possibly be back here if his car is in Linton? Why did he go to Linton in the first place? Or did he even leave? Was the car stolen? Did he go to meet someone? Or was he kidnapped for some reason and managed to escape? Oh God, maybe he's been trying all this week to get back to me, and just as he was within a few miles of home, the person, or people, who were pursuing him caught up with him and . . .

'What are these?'

I open my eyes and find Linda has picked up the three envelopes that I left lying on the table. 'It's post. Arrived, I don't know, yesterday maybe.' I reach out my hand. 'I was just about to open them.'

'Oh, right. OK. Well, could I ask that you let me know what they are, when you do? No need to do it now, of course. I wouldn't expect . . . But if and when you do, just drop me a line, would you? Let me know. It might be evidential, if it does turn out to be Adam.'

I suspect, if it does turn out to be Adam, that that is something I will probably forget to do. 'Yes, of course I will.'

'Thank you.'

She puts the envelopes, still frustratingly unopened, back down on the table and we lapse back into silence. I want to phone Ginger. I want to speak to Matt. I need my mum.

My phone makes us both jump by ringing again. As I pick it up, Linda says, 'Who is it?'

I frown at her but don't answer. Nosey bitch. It's Ginger, so I stand up and go out to the hallway. 'Hi Ginge.'

'Don't you "Hi Ginge" me, you awful person. Where have you been the past couple of days? I haven't heard a thing from you, I've been waiting and wondering and not knowing and you're all blasé and calm and "Hi Ginge" and I've been going out of my mind. What's going on? Is Adam back? Is that why I haven't heard from you? He's come back, hasn't he, all "please forgive me" and "it won't happen again", and you've welcomed him home with open legs and spent the past two days in bed?'

I shake my head silently, and unexpectedly my eyes heat up with tears. Right at this moment, I wish more than anything that I could tell her she was right. 'No, he's not back,' I whisper. I can see Linda fixedly staring at me in the kitchen, and no doubt listening to every word, so I move further away and sit on the bottom of the stairs. 'Ginge, they've found a body.'

There's a moment's shocked silence. Then, 'On my way.'

She arrives ten minutes later dressed as Elvis. She's obviously come straight from the shop, and has definitely been exceeding the speed limit. She bursts in through the front door, already talking, and hugs me fiercely.

'Oh my life, I must have been doing over a hundred on the bypass, thank God I didn't get clocked. Whose Clio is that outside? Oh Gracie, how are you doing, hun? Any news yet? Matt says you're looking for a safe? What's up? Why are you . . .?' Eventually she shuts up, even though I've been making cutting motions across my neck to silence her the entire time. She gets it finally, and glances over my shoulder at the silent police officer watching us from the kitchen. 'Oh, hi there!'

Linda nods. 'Morning.'

Ginge looks back at me. 'Looking for a safe . . . place to stay,' she says, quick as lightning. 'Understandable, given the circumstances.'

'Yes, that's right.'

She leans in close. 'Why didn't you tell me you had company?' she hisses.

There's the sound of a throat clearing in the kitchen.

I roll my eyes. 'Didn't exactly give me a chance, did you?'

'OK, OK. So. Is there any news?' She looks at me appraisingly. 'You look *amazing*, by the way.'

I wonder for a second what she means. Amazing, for someone wondering if the body that's turned up is her dead missing husband? Then I remember the hotpants. 'Thanks, Elvis. No news. Only that they've found a body, male, right age, right build.'

'Shit.' She whispers it. 'OK. Well, it's not him, is it? Bound not to be. He's in Linton, isn't he?'

202

'His car is in Linton. Or was. This man, whoever he is, was found here, near the industrial estate.'

She nods, as if this isn't a massive surprise. 'Well, it's definitely not him then.'

'How can you be so sure?'

'It's obvious. Why would anyone go to all the trouble of secretly disappearing on the pretext of getting take-away, then drive all the way to North Yorkshire, abandon the car, and come all the way back?'

As she finishes speaking, there's a crackle in the kitchen and we both jump and turn instantly in that direction. Linda glances at me, then stands up and tilts her head to the radio, turning her back to us in the hallway. She listens for a few seconds while we stare at her back, and I feel the reassuring pressure of Ginger's hand on my arm. Thank God she's here.

Eventually, the radio voice falls silent, and Linda acknowledges it, then turns back to us.

'It's all right, Grace. It's been confirmed. It's not Adam.'

ELEVEN

Madly, the first thought that goes through my head is, *Well, well, Melissa was right after all*. But then in a sickening rush I realise that an unspeakable horror has just brushed past me, and I sink down onto the bottom stair, all my breath gone. There's a roaring in my head that feels like spinning, like I've just jumped out of a plane. I can't get a grip on a single coherent thought and I drop my head into my hands to stop it from breaking up.

Then, like a dam bursting, thoughts of our wedding flood into my head in a disordered surge. The proposal, at that very posh restaurant, in the dress I borrowed from Lauren, which was a size too small and meant I had to sit up straight and take very shallow breaths the whole time. I remember Adam asking me, 'Will you?', but it's a blurry, indistinct memory, eclipsed by the awful bloated, breathless feeling I endured all evening. Then the wedding preparations, how easy it was for me with Adam taking the lead in organising, even the honeymoon in the Cotswolds. In my head, a muddle of images whirls around, each leading to the next, confused, crowded, chaotic – trying on the dress, the drive to the hotel, coming home afterwards, Mr and Mrs Littleton – and as I sit there in the hallway with this swirl of images spinning past, I see myself as a tiny, fragile doll caught up in the tornado that was Adam. Picked up, spun round and round for three years with no control, no power over where I was going and what I was doing, simply spinning; and then dropped, panting, by the roadside. Amazed to be still intact.

'Grace,' Ginger is saying, her hand pressing my arm. 'Come and have a cup of tea. You're in shock.'

I shake my head. 'No, I'm OK.'

Linda is there, looking at me, eyebrows together. She's flicked open her mental notebook and is jotting something down. I sway a little.

'Actually, maybe I will have a drink.'

Ginger sits me at the table in the kitchen and makes me a sugary tea, then starts ringing everyone up to tell them. 'Come home,' she says simply, when they answer. Mum, Dad, Lauren, Robbie. 'Yes,' she says to them. 'Please. As soon as you can.'

And so, an hour later, they return from Ikea and rush into the kitchen to see me, hugging and crying and not believing it and finding it all such a relief but also terrible and awful.

'I'm all right, actually,' I tell them. My eyes have been smarting a lot and I feel a heavy shroud of sadness draped over me, but I don't feel like I'm going to flip out. In fact I'm quite calm now. Linda has gone, thankfully, which means I can finally examine how I'm really feeling about this, and stop trying to act like I think she thinks I ought to be acting. I'm shocked, undoubtedly.

Someone has died. But not someone I was married to. Not even anyone I knew. Which sounds so cold and hard-hearted, but in the end it's what it comes down to. As sad as it is to see a bridge collapse in some far-flung place, and know that dozens will have lost their lives, they're not lives that we will miss. Mostly, it's made me think about Adam, and realise how intensely, how utterly, I want him to be OK. Even though I've had doubts about my feelings for him. Maybe even because of those doubts.

'Oh God,' Mum keeps saying, blotting her eyes. 'That poor man, whoever he was. I wonder what on earth can have happened to him? Oh God, Gracie, this is so terrible for you, I'm so, so sorry, darling.'

'I'm OK, Mum.'

'Oh, yes, I know you are, this time, and luckily for you – and for us – it wasn't Adam. But . . .'

'Judy,' Dad's voice warns from across the kitchen.

'Oh never mind, Jeff,' Mum says, waving her hand. 'I wasn't going to say . . . anything.'

'You're saying something right now,' Dad goes on. 'Just . . . stop.'

'It's all right, it's nothing she's not thinking herself.'

'What?' I ask them both. 'What are you talking about?'

'Nothing,' Dad says, at the same time as Mum says, 'Just because it wasn't him this time, doesn't mean it won't be him next time.'

'Oh for crying out loud,' Dad says, rolling his eyes. Then to me, 'Don't pay any attention to Mum, love. I'm sure he's fine.'

'Right. Thanks, Dad.'

'Jeff, you shouldn't say things like that,' Mum says in a peeved tone. 'You don't know. You can't guarantee anything.'

'Shut up, Judy.'

'Oh shush.' Mum turns back to me. 'Of course it's occurred to you, love, hasn't it? It's best to be prepared. One day, you might feel like you can't survive another moment and all you want to do is pull all your hair out and scratch all the skin off yourself.' She's holding my hand and rubs it absent-mindedly, as if trying to capture a memory of what it feels like with skin on. 'Oh Christ, it's going to hit you so hard.'

'Do you want a drink, sis?' Robbie says.

'Oh Jesus, Robbie, don't encourage her! She may well hit the bottle at some point, but you don't have to suggest it straight away!'

'Mum, I'm fine. Seriously.'

She nods, knowingly. 'Yes, I know, sweethcart. I know.'

I look up at Ginge, who is standing up by the cooker in a white shiny trouser suit studded with fake rhinestones, watching mc. She nods, then says, 'Grace, don't forget I'm supposed to take you down to the . . .'

I give a fleeting frown, not understanding. Ginger widens her eyes meaningfully, and I catch on at last. 'Oh, God, yes, yes, I forgot about that.' I stand up. 'We'd better get going.'

Mum stands up too. 'What thing? Where? Where have you got to go? Oh God, have you got to go and look at the body? To make sure it's not him? Oh Jesus, Gracie, that's so awful for you. Do you want me to come with you?'

'No, Mum, Adam's dad has already done that. I've just got to get to the . . .'

'Police station,' Ginger finishes for me. 'They need some kind of statement or something. I'm supposed to take her down.'

'Oh no,' Mum wails. 'This is all so unbearable.'

'Do you want the car?' Dad says quietly as I walk towards him.

'Thanks Dad, but Ginger will drive me.'

He nods silently, then reaches out his arms and pulls me in for a great big bear hug. I rest my head against his shoulder for a moment, then step back. 'I'm fine, Dad. You do know that, don't you?'

He nods. 'Yeah, I thought so. I didn't think you were in shock, to be honest.' He studies me for a few moments. 'You think he's just left you, don't you?'

My dad: Mr Perception. It's like a blockage has cleared, when he says that, and pure light is coming in at last. I nod and give him a little smile. 'Of course he has.'

He gives me a sad smile. 'What a great shame, love. I'm sorry.'

'Thanks. But don't worry, Dad. I'm kind of getting used to the idea.'

He nods and gives me a sad smile. 'We're here for you, love. You know that, don't you? Stay as long as you want, whatever happens.'

I give him a tight hug. 'Thanks. I think I might take you up on that. He's not dead, but I'm pretty sure I'm not going back to Maple Avenue.'

My dad nods in agreement, then makes a 'sshh' noise with his finger on his lips. 'The person who's going to feel this the most is your mum.'

We both turn to look at her. She's sitting at the table,

her head in her hands, blotting at her eyes, making little whimpering noises and shaking her head. The words, 'dressed as Elvis' can be heard above the sobs. Rob and Lauren are flanking her, rubbing her arm and gently tucking her hair behind her ear.

'Try not to let her find out Adam wasn't perfect,' Dad says gravely. Madly, I start to feel the need to tell my dad exactly how unperfect Adam was, so instead I head quickly for the front door.

Outside, we don't get into Ginge's car.

'Come on,' she says, 'I'm buying you a stiff drink.'

'But I'm OK.'

'I know, but it's still shocking and it will hit you eventually what's happened.'

The Bunch of Fives is the nearest pub, so we walk round there.

'Holy fucking God,' Elvis says as we go in. Dismembered body parts are glinting in the morning sunshine. I close my eyes, remembering the grisly theme. When I open them again, Ginge is peering at me concernedly. 'Shall we leave?'

'No, it's fine, let's just get a table.'

'Are you sure? I mean . . .' she glances meaningfully around at the faked scenes of violent death, 'this place . . . in the circumstances . . .?'

'Ginge, it's fine, seriously.'

She gets us both a drink and I see her chatting to Greg, the barman. Or rather, he's chatting to her. She wants to get the two drinks and go.

'Holy moly,' she says, coming back to the table, 'what is this place? Night of the living dead or something?'

'I think it's charming.'

'You're not serious? You have seen the appallingly bad taste décor? Whoever runs it must be sick in the head. And it has a very grabby barman. Wouldn't let me leave!'

I smile to myself. And there was I thinking he was just flirty with me. Fooled again.

'So.' Ginge takes an enormous gulp of her wine. I can't help glancing at the clock. 11:02. Oh well, it is a special occasion. My runaway husband is not dead.

'So?'

'So what do you think has happened to him?'

'What, Adam?'

'No, the fricking muffin man. Yes, Adam, who else are we likely to be talking about, two hours after you find out he's not dead?'

'Oh, yeah. Sorry. Not thinking straight. Erm, I really don't know.'

'Do you think that Leon is involved?'

'Involved in what?'

'Adam's disappearance.' She shrugs. 'It's a possibility, isn't it? We need to consider it.'

'Why do we?'

'Because you get a weird phone call from some throaty creep called Leon that you've never heard of, and literally hours later your husband vanishes without trace. Ipso facto.'

I'm wrenched immediately back to that day in Adam's office when I was signing the tenancy agreement to his flat. We had known each other for about three hours by this time, and I was so entranced by his flirtatious and charming attention that it had started to affect everything I said. Relentlessly, and apparently without any design or control, I tried at every possible opportunity to make a joke or a quip, or come across by turns as either delightfully sweet, or confident and strong. A large part of me suspected that I was probably starting to look and sound like a donkey on a roller-coaster, but that part of me was less than half, so sadly it was outvoted.

'So if you could sign here, here and here,' Adam said, having just taken half an hour explaining all the different parts of the contract.

'Oh, and just like that I sign myself under your power?' I'd asked, then cringed inwardly. Charmingly, he had smiled and produced an amused little laugh.

'Oddly enough, you kind of are. In a mere matter of moments, you will be mine forever! Mwah ha ha ha haaaaah!'

I'd giggled, I hoped prettily, and signed where he was pointing. I made an exaggerated full stop at the end of the final signature, and put the pen down dramatically, then raised my head to look him boldly – and seductively, I hoped – in the eye. 'Ipso facto.'

'You don't mean ipso facto, you mean QED,' he'd said immediately. Then the smile was back on and the charm returned. 'Why thank you, Miss Kelly,' he said with a small bow, then turned to file the contract away. It didn't stop me from smarting for the next half an hour.

'Are you OK?'

I refocus and find Ginge looking at me worriedly. She's not worried enough to put the wine glass down, it seems. As I meet her gaze and give her a reassuring smile, she nods slowly, then takes another swig. Her wine is almost gone.

'So what's your theory?' she says.

'About what?'

She rolls her eyes. 'About Leon. Why do you think he wants Adam? I wonder what their connection is? Maybe they did some kind of heist together and Adam betrayed him and went off with all the diamonds.'

'Christ, do you think so?'

She nods enthusiastically and places the glass rim against her lips. 'Or maybe Leon is some kind of assassin and there's a price on Adam's head.' She takes another gulp. 'Yeah, bet you don't hear from Leon again. He's found his target and is intently stalking it even now. He'll be on an island in the Caribbean by next week.'

'Jesus, Ginge, you're scaring me.'

She looks up at me and kind of realises I'm there. 'Oh, yeah, sorry. Getting a bit carried away.'

'Leon knows my real name. He can probably find out where I live.' An alarming thought occurs to me. 'He'll be able to find my parents eventually.'

Ginge shakes her head. 'No he won't.' She thinks for a while. 'No, no. He won't.'

I take a sip of my own wine but my stomach is starting to knot up and bubble with acid. I put the glass down. 'Shit.'

'S'OK, Matt's on his way here. He'll be able to explain a few things to you.'

The thought of big lovely Matt being here immediately reassures me. 'Did you ring him?' She nods, glass still at her lips. I release a held breath and glance towards the door. No sign of him yet.

'So what's all this about a safe?' she asks. 'You're looking for one?'

I nod. 'Yeah. I found a key and it turns out it belongs to a safe, but it's hidden somewhere. We think in the house, but it could be literally anywhere.'

'Have you told the police?'

This is an excellent point that has caused me literally minutes of worry. The safe and its contents will definitely be of interest to the police. If not now, then eventually, particularly if . . . No, I won't continue that thought. But Ginge is right: someone goes off in the night never to return, leaving behind somewhere in the house a mysterious hidden safe. How likely is it that the two things are connected?

'No. But don't lecture me, please Ginger. I will tell them, I just really want to find it myself first.'

She takes a pensive swallow of wine, then puts down her empty glass and picks up mine. 'No, I totally get that. You want to regain some sense of control. And how much can it hurt if you're looking for the safe while their team are following up some other line of enquiry? Will save time, if anything. You can tell them as soon as you've found it. Want me to help?'

I feel a mixture of gigantic relief that she doesn't disapprove and isn't going to make me tell the police immediately; and a surge of love for my wonderful best friend. 'Oh my Jimmy Choos, yes I do. You're a star, thanks.' I get up and go round the table to give her a hug. While I'm there, I retrieve my wine. 'Mine.'

'I'll get us some more.'

By the time Matt arrives thirty minutes later, Ginger is three-quarters pissed and keeps bursting into unnecessary giggles. I'm simply feeling very relaxed and at peace with everyone and everything. When he appears in the doorway, he stands there a moment taking in the scene: a wasted Elvis Presley and some cheap little tramp in unspecial shorts, surrounded on three sides by dismembered bodies. I give him a great big warm smile and get up to go and say hello.

'Helloooo Matthew Blake, Ginger's nerdy little brother. You're here. In this terrible, ghoulish, haunted pub.' I lean in close to him and whisper, 'I see dead people,' then lose my balance and stumble right into his personal space. A giggle snorts out of me. He feels very warm and comfortable and smells of clean sheets. 'Oop, sorry, ha ha, didn't see the . . . er . . .' I glance behind me and point at the floor, but it's clear, smooth wood, completely free of trip hazards and obstacles. 'Oh.' Over at the table, Ginger is practically falling off her seat laughing, so I grab Matt's sleeve and lead him over there. 'Come over here, come to the table, sit down with us. Come on. Let's all have a drink.'

'Um, no thanks,' he says, and he sounds a bit stern. 'And I don't think you should have any more, either.' I look up at his face, but he's not smiling at all.

'Oh dear, what's the matter, big ol' Matthew Blake? Has something bad happened?'

'Well, yes, you know it has, Grace.' He looks over at Ginger, who is still giggling. 'This is your fault,' he says to her, like a teacher. 'What the hell did you do this for?'

'No, no, it's not her fault, Matty Matt. She's just got pissed, which, well, yes, that is totally her fault. But I didn't really drink much, so you can't get angry with her.'

214

He looks back at me. 'Well, from here I would say you're both as pissed as each other. Which, under the circumstances, is quite understandable – for you, Grace.' He turns back to Ginger. 'But not for you. For God's sake, Louise, you're supposed to be keeping an eye . . .'

Ginger flinches under his stern tone. 'Hey, I am keeping an eye. Don't talk to me like a childiot.' She dissolves into laughter again. 'I mean an ild. No, chid. I'm not a chid or an ildiot. I'm keeping my best friend company, after she found out she's not a widow.'

'Oh God,' he says, and turns back to me. 'So it's been identified? The body – it's not Adam?'

I shake my head solemnly. 'No, it would seem not. They radioed to my family liaison woman and told her, and then she told me, and then went to Subway for lunch. Adam's step-dad went to the dead body place and had a look and it's definitely not him. He's definitely not dead. My husband's not dead.' My voice rises at the end, and from the bar Greg looks over. I catch his eye and nod slowly. Then I slap my hand over my eyes. 'Oh my God, what am I doing? I've just been left by my husband, I need to be all severe and serious for a while.'

'I really think you should go home,' Matt says.

I nod. He's right. My head is very swimmy and I can't focus my eyes properly. Well, I probably could, but my eye muscles are just so *tired*. 'Yes, yes, I want to go home. Back to my house, to my house with my husband. I need to find that safe. Let's all go there now, and have a look for it.'

'Sshh,' Matt says. 'OK, we'll go there. Might as well have a lie-down there as anywhere.'

'Ooh, a lie-down, Matthew. You do remember I'm married, don't you? Even though my husband is a total mysterious . . . er, mystery. Oh, and also, currently not doing very much of anything. Except hiding. Apparently very good at that.'

'OK, OK, let's get you both in the car.' Gently, he pulls me from my seat and wraps his arm tight around my waist. As he guides me to the door, he turns and looks back at Ginger. 'Don't you move,' he says, very seriously. In response, she becomes a statue. Matt rolls his eyes. 'Just stay there, I'll be back in a minute.'

Half an hour later, I'm dozing on my bed in our house. Our home. The place I shared with my missing husband. Matt practically carried me up here from the car, then scooped all Adam's scattered clothes and shoes off the bed before laying me down on it. I can barely keep my eyes open, but through the slit just before they close, I can see Adam's pillow, next to mine, and I wonder whether the incredible, extraordinary, almost unbeliev-able possibility could exist that he will never, ever lay his head on it again. Or open that wardrobe to hang up a shirt (in colour order). I fall asleep with the image of his body, naked and white, on a cold steel table, while a man in a green plastic apron cuts off the top of his head with a circular saw.

I wake up with a start and a feeling of thudding panic. Some kind of sound has just been made. It woke me up. It's almost still audible, and my ears strain to recover it. It was a kind of gasping, shrieking noise, the sort of sound someone would make when faced with something terrifying. I lean up onto my elbows and listen, but

216

nothing else comes. Gradually, my thudding heart calms down and slows, and eventually I realise that the sound, the terror-laden shriek that woke me up, was made by me. It's still bright sunlight outside and according to my watch it's half past three. I've been asleep for around three hours. Bloody hell.

I get up and go downstairs, and find Matt and Elvis – minus the wig now – sitting at the kitchen table, drinking coffee. They both turn and smile as I come into the room, and not for the first time I'm impressed with Ginger's awesome ability to cope with copious amounts of alcohol. While I feel like I've been pulled feet first out of a river, she looks like she's erupting with the joy of a new baby announcement or something.

'We've got some news,' she bursts out. She's practically bouncing.

'Adam's back?'

Matt gets up and comes and puts his hand on my arm. 'Shut up for a minute, Ginger. Jesus. How are you feeling?' His voice is gentle when he speaks to me. 'Hungover?'

I shake my head. 'No, not really. I can't believe I got so drunk. I only had two glasses of wine.'

'Ha!' Ginge bursts out. 'Try four.'

'Four? Oh.' I sit down next to her and help myself to her coffee.

'I'll make you one,' Matt says, and goes to the kettle.

'Thanks. So. What's this news?'

'We—' Matt starts, but Ginger cuts him off.

'I'll tell her, I'll tell her!'

'Tell me what?'

She takes a deep breath. 'OK. So when Matt drove us

217

round here earlier, after he'd got you settled upstairs, he noticed an awful vinegary smell in the house.'

'I noticed it the other day, actually,' he says from the kettle, 'but didn't like to say anything.'

'Why not? I noticed it too, it was terrible.'

He shrugs. 'Well at that point, I didn't know if it was the normal smell of your house, or something . . . external.'

'You're kidding? Oh my God, you actually thought that my house, the place where I live, smelled like musty old vinegar? All the time?'

'No, no, I didn't think that. But, you know, you can't ask someone when you go into their home for the first time if that terrible vinegar smell is normal. What if they say, "What vinegar smell?"' He widens his eyes. 'Hideous.'

I nod and give him a smile. 'OK, fair enough. So?' I look back at Ginger to find her gawping at us both with her mouth open.

'Have you finished? Because I'm trying to tell a story here.'

'Sorry. Go on.'

'Thank you. Anyway, there's this terrible sour smell. Really pungent. Matt says to me, is that smell always here?'

'Oh God . . .'

'And I tell him that I've never noticed it before. So we think, new smell, mysterious circumstances, can't be a coincidence.'

'Right.'

'So instead of looking for the safe, which could be anywhere, we decide we need to locate the source of the terrible smell first. You know, because it was truly gruesome. And neither of us really wanted to spend any time in the house looking for a damn safe, with that . . . aroma hanging over us.'

'So you . . .?'

'All right, I'm getting there. So, we split up and went round the house, room by room, sniffing. Like a pair of bloodhounds! Nothing downstairs, although your fridge whiffs a bit now. But it wasn't that. So we went upstairs, obviously couldn't go into your room as you're passed out on the bed, so we think we'll check everywhere else, and if we don't find it, we'll check your room when you wake up.'

I nod. 'But it's not my room, is it?'

They shake their heads in unison, and I notice how much they look alike. 'No it isn't. Matt tracked it down to the spare room. Finally. Bloody relief to find it, I can tell you.'

'So? What was it?'

'Oh God, there's this horrible big red stain on the carpet in the middle of the floor. Dried now, but still with a very powerful odour. What the frick was it? You spilled something there recently? Some kind of thick, heavy sauce? Sweet and sour, maybe?'

I stare at her and raise my eyebrows. 'Ginger! That was you!'

She jerks backwards. 'Me?'

'Yes! Don't you remember, the night Adam disappeared or left, or whatever the hell he did. You stayed over here because you were completely wasted. Kicked over a full glass of Merlot on my spare room carpet.'

'Oh Christ, Ginger . . .'

'Shut up, Matt, you've been drunk too, we both know that.' She looks at me. 'I don't really remember that.' Her face falls. 'I'm so sorry, Grace. That's awful of me.'

I shrug. 'Doesn't matter, really.'

She brightens. 'No, it doesn't! Actually, it's a bloody good job I did mess up your spare room carpet, because Matt wanted to get rid of the smell so we could concentrate properly, so he pulled the carpet up. And guess what we found in a hole in the floor underneath?'

She's grinning, and Matt's grinning, and as I look at them both their absolute delight in their discovery is practically tangible. It's like fireworks over a Disney parade and it starts to have an effect on me. For the first time in ages I feel hopeful and excited. 'It wasn't . . .'

She nods. 'Come and see!' She grabs my hand and drags me out of the kitchen and back up the stairs, Matt following behind, and there in the spare room, with the carpet pulled up and rolled back, is a neatly sawed little hole in the floorboards. Lying on the folded back bit of carpet is a square of wood, roughly the same size and shape as the hole; and down inside the hole, in the intimate part of the house normally reserved for electrical wiring and pipes, is a tiny, squat, black safe.

'Secretive little *shit*.'

TWELVE

We all stare down into the hole for a few moments, trying to understand what this means, what it's likely to reveal, wondering if we really want to know. Wondering if what's in there will cause more pain and upset. Wondering who exactly was Adam Littleton, and why did we marry him. Well, I'm thinking that. Ginger and Matt probably aren't.

Eventually Matt moves forward and easily lifts the little safe out of its resting place, reverentially placing it on the floor like the lost Ark of the Covenant. It's a bit dusty, but not massively so, and it's obvious it hasn't been sitting there untouched for years or even months. This little box has been accessed regularly. Its key is still around my neck on its chain, so I take it off and kneel down, then lean back on my heels and stare at it for a few seconds. It feels decidedly like this is the start of something, like an episode of a soap opera or the beginning of a dramatic film involving missing data and car chases. Except at that moment, as I'm about to violate my husband's privacy in the worst – and best – way, it's not secrets and lies that come into my head. It's our wedding vows.

I wrote my own vows to marry Adam. I know, I know, it's cheese, but I'd seen a gorgeous romantic film where the lead couple had done it, and I longed for Adam and me to be like that with each other, to be that couple. I considered just doing it, as a surprise for him, but in the end I acknowledged to myself that that wasn't enough. What I really wanted was for him to do it. To be thought of in that way by my handsome fiancé. In front of everyone who knew me.

I was stunned when Adam had agreed. He'd looked at me and nodded as I was explaining what I wanted to do, and said it would be a nice touch. I'd flung my arms round his neck, then dashed straight off to my laptop to get writing. I spent every spare moment in the run-up to the wedding consumed by the need to get the words just right, just perfect (although a large part of me was consumed by wondering what Adam was writing). I wanted my love for him to guide my pen and produce something that would show eternal love, companionship, an enduring promise to support and comfort each other. I wanted to write about a joining of souls. A togetherness that couldn't be broken. A partnership. It was a fucking nightmare.

It wasn't my love for Adam that guided my pen in the end; it was Google. I looked up 'husband', and 'harmony' and 'happy' and threw their synonyms down onto paper in an order that sounded loving. I didn't question at that point why my actual love for him hadn't helped me. I believed in it then, and his for me, and assumed I'd struggled just because it needed to be perfect. Eventually, I was fairly pleased with what I came up with. It wasn't exactly what I'd envisaged when I'd started out on the project five weeks earlier – a breathtaking, heart-stopping piece of poetry that would bring a tear to the eye of everyone in the congregation and make even horrible old Uncle Nigel believe in love again – but it was good enough.

Walking up the aisle to some stirring classical music (Adam's choice; I'd wanted 'For the First Time in Forever' but he'd vetoed it) I looked up to the front and watched Adam's back as I advanced. Ray was standing next to him, turning round beaming to watch me arrive; and everyone in the congregation had turned to look at me too. I caught a few of Auntie Helen's words as I glided past, 'Oh, doesn't she look . . .' but the rest was lost behind me. Any minute now, I told myself, any minute now he'll turn and it will be that character from that film's favourite moment, when the groom turns round and sees his bride for the first time. His face will explode in joy and a single tear will make its slow, solitary way down his perfect cheek (I did look quite nice that day). But he didn't move. Just continued stoically staring ahead, keeping his focus. When I finally arrived at his side, he turned his head to see me at last and said with an approving nod, 'That's a lovely dress.'

I deflated like a soufflé. But I swallowed down my disappointment and got on with the business of committing myself to him for life. He must be anxious about his vows, I thought. He must be nervous about his speech. He must be worrying about Julia, sitting in the congregation on her own. It's a big moment, full of emotion and distracting thoughts, of course it's not going to be how it is in the movies.

When it came to the vows, I went first. I had memorised them, and said them to myself at least once a day for over a week, to make sure I didn't forget them at the crucial moment, so it all went off exactly how I planned. Except for the part where no one cried. But that's OK. People were smiling at me, which was good enough. When I'd finished, I turned to Adam, my stomach churning with anticipation as I waited for him to fumble a ratty old bit of well-thumbed paper out of his pocket and unfold it shakily. But he didn't.

There was a moment's hiatus while we stared at each other – me waiting; him . . . also waiting, it turned out. Then he blinked a couple of times and faced back to Father Michael.

'Your turn to do your vows,' I stage-whispered, turning my head away from the crowd.

He nodded. 'I'm aware of that, Grace.'

'So . . .?'

He flicked me a quick glance, then faced forward again. 'It's OK, you don't need to panic. Father Michael will read them, we just have to repeat them.'

And so we resumed the standard service, and Adam simply repeated the pre-written vows that had been said a million times by a million other grooms. I felt ridiculous, like everyone had been sitting in their seats, wondering what the hell I was doing, straying from the standard text with my flowery nonsense. But Adam hadn't written any vows, so that was that.

Afterwards, before we all sat down to dinner, I asked him why he hadn't. He smiled indulgently down at me, like an Edwardian father. 'Oh, Gracie,' he said, practically patting me on the head, 'did you want me to do some too? I didn't realise, I thought it was just something you felt you had to do.'

'No, Adam. We agreed we would write our own, don't you remember? We agreed we would both do it. For each other.'

He shook his head. 'No, I never would have agreed to that, my love. I mean, it was very sweet, adorable, coming from you. But that sort of thing is not appropriate for me.'

Now, crouched over a hole in our spare room, I look up and find two wide-open, expectant faces with held breath peering down at me. They don't speak but their expressions are both saying, 'Go on, do it. Do it!'

'I can't do it.'

Their faces drop simultaneously. Ginger's turns into frowning, uncomprehending disappointment. Matt gives a small smile and starts nodding calmly.

'Oh God, why not?' Ginge bursts out. 'Come on, this is what you've been waiting for. Just do it, open it, find out what's in there!'

I shake my head. 'I can't. I don't want to . . . I don't know, find out stuff. Let stuff in.' I shrug. 'I don't know.'

'Let stuff in? What the hell? You're not letting stuff in, you plank. You're letting stuff out.' She jabs a finger at the safe. 'Whatever's in *there*. Let it out, Grace, for God's sake.'

In my mind, that's no better. She's just described Pandora's Box.

225

Matt turns to look at her. 'Come on, Ginge, don't pressure her. It's not as if there's a kitten in there, using up the last of the oxygen, needing to be got out urgently.'

Ginger and I both stare at him, then turn back in horror to the safe. Is it my imagination or do I hear a very faint, hoarse mewing sound?

'No, don't be stupid, you two,' Matt says, stepping away a little. 'It's not a kitten. Now come on, let's get this thing into the car and get you both home.'

Odd how we all silently acknowledge, by moving to the stairs and leaving the house, that he's talking about my parents' place.

When we get there, he lifts the safe out of the boot and carefully hands it to me. It feels like a ticking bomb.

'You don't have to open it,' he says quietly. 'But I think you'll want to. When you're ready.' He holds my gaze. 'I think it will answer a few questions for you.'

I nod. 'Thanks, Matt. For everything.'

'Any time. I mean it.' His voice is low and makes my spine vibrate a little. As we stand and look at each other, his hand lifts up and I think he might be going to touch me but then he just rubs the back of his head. He blinks a few times and looks around, then focuses back on me. 'I really do mean it, Grace,' he says softly. Then he steps in close, leans down and kisses me very softly on my cheek.

Before I go in, I stand on the pavement for a few moments, cradling my bomb. Next door's driveway is starting to look nice – a herringbone pattern in red bricks, with a smart grey-brick border. Mum and Dad's doesn't have a border. They won't be happy about that. Distractedly, I wonder how little old Mr and Mrs Martin can possibly afford to

226

have a driveway like that laid. Have they come into some money, maybe? As I look, I spot that they've also had their ancient windows and front door replaced with smart new uPVC double glazing. Maybe they won the lottery. Ripper is visible, nonchalantly cleaning himself on their porch. As I watch, he freezes mid-lick, looks up quickly in the direction of something inaudible, then darts across the lawn and under their car.

I walk in the house into the middle of a massive row.

'It's my bloody decision!' Dad is saying. Well, shouting really. 'I never wanted to do it anyway, you know that, so I think I'm perfectly justified in calling it off.'

'Oh, that's just charming,' Mum says. 'Try and do something nice for you and you scream and shout about how you never wanted it in the first place.'

'Oh, Christ, woman, you know that's not what I meant.'

'It is so what you meant, you selfish goat. This affects more than just you, you know. People are coming from all over . . .'

'I don't sodding care about them!'

I freeze mid-creep in the hallway. It's incredibly unusual just to hear my dad shouting, but he never, *ever* uses expletives. I can hear the shockwaves bouncing around the kitchen, making the utensils ding against each other and the cups rattle a little in the cupboards. Then everything falls silent. No doubt everyone is staring at Dad with their mouths open.

'Dad . . .' Lauren says quietly.

'OK, I'm sorry for that. Obviously I do care about them. And I'm sorry for swearing . . .'

'I should think so.'

'. . . but it's just not appropriate to go ahead. Not now, with Adam and everything. I don't know how you can't see that.'

'Go ahead with what?'

They all turn to me as I come in, and instantly all eyes flick to the safe in my arms.

'Doesn't matter, love,' Dad says, coming over to me. 'How are you doing?' What he actually means is, what in the name of matrimony is that?

'Fine and dandy. What are you cancelling? If you're cancelling it because of Adam being gone, there's really no need.'

'Told you,' Mum says, folding her arms. Dad shoots her a look, then turns back to me.

'It doesn't matter, sweetheart, because whether you're upset or in shock or not, it's just not appropriate to go ahead. Not in the circumstances.'

'Go ahead with *what*?'

'Ugh, Dad's birthday party,' Lauren says. 'We've been planning it for weeks. Now he reckons he wants to cancel it.'

'I don't *want* to cancel it, for crying out loud, it's just not right to go ahead. Why can't anyone see that?'

I look at him. 'Oh Dad. You don't have to cancel it. Honestly. A good old knees-up is probably just what we all need.'

He stares at me a moment, then throws his hands up. 'OK, fine, we'll go ahead, we'll have a party days after our daughter's husband vanishes into thin air. We'll even invite the grieving parents, I'm sure they'd appreciate a

228

chance to get wasted and dance drunkenly to "The Birdie Song". That's perfectly fine. I mean, who cares if people are shocked and think badly of us? It's only all our friends and relatives and everyone we care about, how important can their opinions of us possibly be?' He starts to walk away, then stops suddenly and performs a comedy head-scratch. 'No, wait . . .' Then he shakes his head and leaves the kitchen.

'That's settled then,' Mum says with a satisfied smile, heroically missing Dad's sarcasm altogether. 'All systems go. Lauren, get on to the rugby club and un-cancel it, quick. I'll give the caterers the thumbs up.' She looks at me with a grin. Then her face drops and she puts out a hand. 'Oh, good Christ, sorry sweetheart, I wasn't—' She stops herself in time. 'I mean, how are you doing now?' Her voice has gone all high and breathy. It must be the strong emotion.

'Forget how's she doing,' Lauren butts in, 'how about what's she carrying?'

'I'm feeling OK, actually, thanks for asking, *Lo*.'

Lauren lifts her hands, palm up. 'What? What did I do?'

'Nothing. Forget it. I'm going upstairs.' I turn back towards the door, then hesitate just before leaving the room. 'Oh, next door's drive looks great with that grey border, doesn't it?'

There's a pause as they turn to look at each other, then Mum bursts out, 'I knew it! I bloody knew it! Those bloody people, now we'll have to get the caravan. Jeffrey! Where are you? Jeff!'

In my room, I put the safe on the floor and sit down on the bed to stare at it. I do intend to open it, straight away, I just didn't want to do it in front of Ginger and Matt. I also know that the contents of this metal box could be explosive and will certainly be of interest to the police. A small part of me wonders what Linda will make of the fact that I didn't tell them about it straight away. A larger part of me doesn't really care. Then an even larger part actually does care, quite a lot, because Linda has already got a mental notebook chock full of evidence against me, and now I'm concealing stuff too.

OK. I'll open the post, and the safe, deal with the contents; and then ring Linda and confess to everything.

Once I've decided to do it, actually doing it doesn't seem quite so hard. Adam's letters are still in my handbag, so I pull one out at random and open it. This one is from a power company, presumably the one that supplies the house in Maple Avenue. There's a lot of information in there relating to the amount of each commodity that we use per year, and how much each unit costs in relation to the cost of it last year. At this point in my life, the relative cost of fuel compared to last year is simply not relevant. I skim over it and skip to the bottom line. It seems that the amount now owing is just under £150. I lay the letter down on the bed and open the next one. A similar thing, this one is all about some kind of insurance. Our policy is up for renewal next month and if we want another year of stress-free cover, all we have to do is nothing. Can't help wondering why they've written in the first place. I lay that one down too, making a mental note to ask Dad to explain it to me. The final letter is from a company called Foyle's Estate Management, and is telling Adam that the year's tenancy is up, and does he want another year? If so, is he interested in saving five percent by paying the year's rent in advance again, or would he like to break it down into twelve easy-to-manage instalments? I'm just about to toss it aside, assuming it's to do with his business premises, when I catch sight of the address under agreement: 12 Maple Avenue. That's our home. Was our home. So this letter relates to the rent of that place. I read it again, slightly more carefully. A twelve-month tenancy. Jesus. Is that all we had? No security, no permanence, just twelve months, year to year, with no guarantee that the landlord will extend at the end of that period. I close my eyes. More deceit, more surprises.

'We'll have the stability you want,' Adam told me when we – or rather, he – decided to rent that place. 'We'll get a nice long lease, five years or something. The landlord will love us, he'll never want us to leave. And after five years, we'll buy somewhere.' But instead of doing what he promised, Adam was renewing it every year, and apparently paying the year's rent in one go. I scan through the letter and eventually find the bottom line again. The rent is £950 per month. I blink. So for a year, that's . . . Can't do it. I round up. That's almost £12,000. In one payment? For three years in a row?

I let the letter fall onto the bed and feel a kind of shivery, juddery sensation, like something is inside me trying to get out. I stand up and walk around the room for a few moments, but that just makes me feel like a caged tiger. I can't keep still though, I'm so restless and twitchy, like Adam's betrayal is clawing at my skin, inside and out, shredding me from both sides. I take a deep breath and it doesn't occur to me what I'm about to do until the second before I do it. I fling my head back, open my mouth and . . . just about manage to stop myself from screaming at full volume, like an insane betrayed banshee. Jesus, that was close. If I'd done that, Mum might have had to cancel the caterers.

I drop down onto the floor and do some deep breathing exercises I learned once at the single yoga class I've ever been to. At least, I think this is how to do it. Either way, I'm breathing deeply, which I know is calming, so it's got to be good. I close my eyes and let my head fall back against the side of the bed, focusing on letting all my limbs get heavy and relaxed.

Ten seconds later, I'm done. I open my eyes and scoot forwards to the safe. The key is still round my neck so I slip it off for the second time today and insert it smoothly into the lock. Without hesitating, I turn the little knob and pull the door open. It opens easily, as indeed it should, having been opened quite regularly over the past three years, no doubt.

Inside there is a small green box with a slot in the top; and a bundle of papers. I pull it all out onto my lap.

'What the fuck were you up to, you slippery toad?' I whisper. 'No, toads are warty, not slippery. You slippery eel. Slippery snake.' I find myself smiling at that, and it feels good. He cheated and betrayed me, but I can still smile about it. Especially now I know it's not him who's dead. No one deserves to die. Except maybe Hitler. And Harold Shipman. Well, anyone who kills people, probably. But that's it. I can learn to hate Adam, and make myself glad to be rid of him. But I'm relieved he didn't die. He's far too young to be over. What age was he, anyway? He was thirty when we met, and he's had three birthdays. Distractedly I wonder if any of that is true. I've got no reason to think that it isn't, but now I'm questioning everything. A complete U-turn for me. I finger the bundle of papers and feel with absolutely no doubt that the answers are all in there. I need to pull them open and read everything. Instead, I lay the papers down and turn my attention to the little box.

It opens easily. Well, there's no need to keep it locked, is there, when it's kept hidden in a secret place, inside a locked, secret safe, that can only be opened with a secret key, which in turn is kept inside a locked drawer to which the secret key has been hidden. There's precaution, and then there's *paranoia*.

Inside the box is a solid wad of fifty-pound notes, held together with two rubber bands.

I close my eyes. 'Adam. What a cliché.' I pick it up and feel it in my hand. It's quite heavy, and pleasingly tightly packed, like a small brick. I bounce it a bit in my hand and wonder how much is there. Five hundred? A thousand? I put it down carefully and turn back to the bundle of papers. Then I pick the money up again. I don't have to leave it aside, like it's Adam's and shouldn't be touched. This money is mine now! The thought gives me an exciting thrill and, for a second, images of gorgeous black leather boots and silver earrings fill my head. What I could do with a thousand pounds! Quickly now, I pull off the rubber bands and let the fifties separate from each other. They fall onto the floor and I spread them out around me like a game of cards. There are quite a lot here. I'm thinking it's probably more than a thousand.

Long before I've finished counting them, I find I'm amazed at how much money you can fit into a small bundle like that. When I reach ten thousand I pause. The neat pile to my left, now loosely stacked, is the ten thousand pounds I've already counted. In front of me on the floor are still at least another twenty notes. It's a very strange feeling, looking at that much money. Considering what I could do with it. Suddenly becoming aware with absolute certainty that I'm not going to tell the police after all.

Eventually, I place the final note on the stack. It now totals £13,350. Enough to pay that electricity bill. Enough to pay the rent on Maple Avenue for another year. Enough to go to Linton.

I neaten the stack of fifties and bundle it up again with one of the rubber bands. I hesitate, then take ten notes out of the stack and put them back in the cashbox. I hide the remaining bundle in an old handbag shaped like a guitar that's still on top of my childhood wardrobe. No one will ever look in there.

The bundle of papers is much more disappointing. There is what looks at brief glance to be some kind of tenancy agreement, the main parties of which are someone called Ryan Moorfield and Mistvale Lettings. There are also a few bank statements for this Ryan, all of them showing a zero balance; and, perhaps most interestingly, Ryan's birth certificate.

I turn all these things over in my hands a few times, as if doing so will reveal their mysteries to me. But nothing comes. Ryan Moorfield must be somehow related to Ray – his son maybe? Unless it's a massive coincidence that they have the same surname. That's pretty unlikely though. The birth certificate shows that Ryan is two years younger than Adam, so the right age to be Ray's son, his own step-brother. But why would Adam keep this stuff hidden away somewhere that he no doubt thought was inviolate? Somewhere that, in fact, *was* inviolate, until Ginger did a Ginger and drank too much wine. More to the point, why would Adam have this stuff at all?

I don't have time to think about it any more as I hear Mum calling me down. Quickly I stuff all the papers back into the safe, lock it up again and push it up against the wall. The key goes back on its chain around my neck. I don't know why this stuff of Ryan's is in there, or why Adam felt he had to keep it secret, but I feel I need to do the same until I work it all out.

At the bottom of the stairs I see Mum's slippers disappearing speedily through the kitchen door. Standing at the open front door is the unreadable face of Linda Patterson. Immediately I remember I've got over twelve thousand pounds stashed in a silver guitar handbag upstairs, and I drop eye contact with her and start to look around me nervously and fidget with my clothing. No doubt my pupils are dilating and the moisture on my palms has increased by some minuscule – but evidential – amount. Thank God I'm not wired up to anything – I'd be in prison before you could say 'Jeremy Kyle'.

'Oh, hi Linda,' I say lightly, giving her a wide, relaxed smile to hide my guilt. Too late I remember that I should probably be fretful and low after the brush with death earlier, and quickly try to rearrange my features into what I hope is the standard 'my husband disappeared and I thought for a while that he was dead' face. I'm not sure I hit it right because she widens her eyes and starts frowning. I recognise that expression – it's her making-mental-notes face. 'Is there more news?' I say, to remind her that the reason I look like a mad person with confused emotions is because of my trip on the edge of dreadful I got just this morning.

She nods. 'Can I come in a minute?'

She looks serious. A bud of anxiety starts to unfurl inside me, spreading out across my abdomen and reaching tendrils into my chest. This is going to be bad. Although I've had no news that another body has been found, so it can't be that. Then what could be making her look like that? He has forty unpaid parking fines? He cheated on his income tax return? He lied about his age?

'Sure.' I step aside and she walks past me and goes into the kitchen. I close the door and follow her through. At the kitchen table, Mum and Dad are looking up guiltily from Dad's laptop. Christ, Linda's going to think they're in on it, the expressions on their faces. Without looking away from Linda's dark-clad form, Mum surreptitiously and slowly closes the laptop lid, and they then both pretend that it isn't there at all. Mum stands up with a smile.

'Oh, hello. Can I get you a cup of tea or something?'

'No, thanks,' Linda says. 'I just need to speak to Grace, if that's OK.'

'Of course,' Mum says magnanimously, as if she's in charge of doling me out to people. 'She's right there.'

Linda looks round at me, then back to Mum. They hold each other's gaze in silence for a few seconds. 'Alone?' Linda says.

'Oh. Right. OK. Come on, Jeff, off we go into the next room. I'm sure we can find something interesting to do in there.'

'Thank you,' Linda says, apparently as skilled at ignoring sarcasm as Mum herself. She looks at me and smiles gently. 'Come and sit down a minute, Grace.' I do as I'm told, and Linda sits down in the chair next to me, then angles herself sideways so she is looking directly into my face.

'I have some more information about Adam,' she says in a low voice. She's obviously going to break something horrible to me. I brace myself. No, I shouldn't brace myself. I should just let myself be devastated by it, so she can see my reaction. 'We got a lead, something significant. And . . . Well, we know – or rather, we think we know – where he is.'

It's what I've been waiting to hear. Longing to hear. *Craving* to hear. It seems so oddly quiet here in the kitchen for such a momentous announcement. Nothing explodes or crashes or lights up. There's no drum roll or klaxon. No one cheers or gasps or sobs or pleads. The only sound is the washing machine, pausing for half a second, then rotating again.

I nod. 'Oh.'

She blinks a couple of times. 'Do you want to know?'

'Yes, of course.' But do I? I frown, then realise I'm frowning and stop. But would I be frowning? Yes, I think I would. I frown again. 'Actually, I'm not sure.' She looks

237

surprised, taken aback. God. 'Yes, yes, that's stupid.' I shake my head. 'Of course I want to know.'

'Don't worry, Grace, it's perfectly understandable that you're in two minds about it.'

Well, thank God for that.

'No one is judging you.'

I'm sure that's not true. Someone's always judging you, no matter what you do. Particularly when your husband's missing and you're a suspect.

'You're not a suspect.'

She doesn't say 'any more' but we both know it's out there.

'So,' she goes on. 'Obviously since Adam disappeared, we've been keeping an eye on any credit card or bank activity.'

I nod wordlessly. Obviously they have. It makes perfect sense. But they don't know what I know about Adam's apparent penchant for cash transactions. I feel like I'm teetering. Any second now, words will come charging at me out of her mouth and slam into me and knock me over the edge.

'Yes. It's standard practice when dealing with a missing person.' She leans towards me a bit and puts her hand on my arm. 'We've just had notification this morning that his card's been used.'

A million images erupt and swarm in my head like a kicked hornets' nest. Adam swiping his card for petrol; Adam drawing out cash for milk and bread; Adam buying a new jacket, a pair of sunglasses, a newspaper. In all these images he's living a normal life, doing normal things, in a normal way. The final image that I'm left with, the one that burns onto the backs of my eyes like a bright window, is Adam calmly strolling along some unfamiliar pavement in the sunshine somewhere, whistling, completely oblivious, or indifferent, or both, to the distress he's causing everyone.

Linda's still watching me. I haul myself back into my parents' kitchen and focus on her. She nods. 'Grace, he bought a ticket for a flight leaving this morning. To Ecuador.'

THIRTEEN

She braces. She takes a deep breath. She closes her eyes. She opens them again. She leans forward. She searches my face. She's being so melodramatic about it, I want to shove her off the chair.

I don't, though. Of course I don't. After a few moments, I move my hands off my mouth, wipe my face and eyes, and nod. 'Oh.'

'Are you all right?'

I think about that a moment, and consider this new information. Has Adam returned? No. Has he still left me voluntarily? Yes. Does the fact that he's in some far-flung country (I mean, Ecuador, who's ever heard of that? I don't even know where it is) make even the slightest change to my circumstances? No. I still don't know where he is. I look up at Linda. 'Yes.'

'You sure?'

I nod again. 'I'm sure. I mean, it doesn't change anything, does it?'

'Well, it points to him still being alive. That's good news, isn't it?'

My investment in the well-being or otherwise of my itinerant husband is decreasing in direct proportion to the increasing amount of information I learn about him. 'Oh, yes, yes, absolutely. Very good news.' I'm aware, of course, that my reaction is probably not what it should be in these circumstances, but to be honest my relationship with my husband was probably not what it should have been.

'Does he know anyone in Ecuador?' Linda asks gently, and it makes me want to send her skidding across the kitchen tiles on all fours. She'd bang into the fridge and eventually come to rest, then turn her head round to stare at me over her shoulder and her frown and down-turned mouth would say, *Whatcha do that for?* 'Grace?'

For a second I think she's actually asking me. I blink and the image of her on the floor dissolves. 'Sorry, what?'

'Adam – do you know if he knows anyone in Ecuador? Or elsewhere in South America, perhaps?'

Oh, South America. Right.

'You really are very ignorant, you know,' Adam's voice says in my head. 'For a woman of your age.'

Ignorant. Yes, that is very true. That is me. I don't know where Ecuador is. And I don't understand the conflict in the Middle East. And I didn't notice the fact that my husband was secretly making comprehensive and detailed plans to leave me, and the country, and, it turns out, the continent, at top speed. Was that mysterious text he got last week something to do with his travel plans? Was the airline requesting his in-flight meal choice? Did he get a weather update on his destination? Was he doing his online check-in? How can I not have noticed?

241

That said, I have seen stories on Channel Four of people who successfully hide an addiction to sofa cushions for years, despite the dwindling size of the soft furnishings. 'Does this sofa seem a bit smaller to you, Mary?' 'No, Douglas, same as usual.' And Douglas nods and says no more because the alternative, that his wife of twenty years is slowly *consuming* the sofa, is unimaginable. Like me, Douglas doesn't notice what's going on because he chooses not to. Is that the same for everyone then, or just simpletons like Douglas and me?

Christ, I don't know. More mysteries. More answers conspicuous by their absence. Much like Adam himself.

'Are you sure you're OK, Grace?' Linda asks me softly, her face all pinched concern and – internally I roll my eyes – pity. I stare at her and realise – perhaps too late, perhaps at exactly the right time – that she's recoiling from my stare. Oops. I guess my look was more withering than I meant it to be. Or maybe it was exactly the right amount of withering.

'I'm fine.'

She smiles, then stands up. 'Good. I'll let you know anything else we find out as soon as we do.'

'Thank you.'

She stares down at me in silence for a moment. Is she expecting more? She won't get more. There is no more. 'Well, as you're here with your family, I'll leave you to absorb that information. It's a lot to take in, I know.'

I shake my head. 'No, no it isn't. I got it. I'm fine.'

She widens her eyes. Mental note-taking. But who cares? As if I needed it, here is yet more proof that my marriage was a sham. It was all pretend, every last second of it, from the moment I walked into his office to the moment his feet hit the tarmac. A complete fabrication. But was it his concept, or mine? The creative part of my brain, the right-hand side, convinced me I was marrying a nice, handsome, clean-cut, articulate, educated and successful businessman. My left brain, the analytical side, has probably shrivelled up and atrophied by now. It probably looks like the months-old avocado Mum found at the bottom of the fridge years ago. Except slightly less useful. If it had been doing the one job it's there to do, it would have noticed that what I was actually getting was an evasive, opinionated, judgemental prick with a flair for the dramatic and a killer case of wanderlust.

I was obviously out of my mind; but only one side of it.

'I'll get going, then,' Linda says, moving towards the hallway. 'Let me know if you need anything.'

'I won't.'

She's taken aback by my new hard voice but I don't care. I feel different. I feel tough, as if nothing at all can hurt me now.

'Well, OK, if you're sure . . .'

'Yep.'

She nods. 'I'll be off then.'

'Seeya.'

I don't see her out. Suddenly good manners seem utterly unimportant. Nothing seems important because nothing is real. Throw anything you like at me, world. Bring it on. Nothing will shock me, nothing will surprise me, this is the new Grace, a graceless Grace, who from this moment on is as hard and unmoveable as Vinnie Jones on death row after the zombie apocalypse.

'We've just bought a caravan!' Mum says ecstatically, coming back in. And I burst into tears.

With Adam quaffing cocktails in Quito (I Googled it), there's a lot of admin to do over the next couple of days: ending the tenancy agreement at Maple Avenue, paying off the remaining rent and power bills, selling the contents to a house clearance place. I don't do any of it. It feels much more important at this stage to celebrate the new Grace that I've just turned into, to revel in my new capable strength and independence. So I go to my child-hood bedroom in my parents' house and curl up and think about how strong I am and how I will never be suckered like that again and how nothing can possibly affect me now. And after two days of lying in the foetal position with old Jinksy the pink rabbit in my arms, I can honestly say that I believe it.

Mum and Lauren visit me periodically with food and drinks and updates. Dad's paid three months' rent for the house in advance with notice to quit, and settled the utility bills. Mum and Lauren suggest that I might like to go with them to the house before the tenancy ends to choose which pieces of furniture or crockery or framed prints I might want to preserve from my make-believe life of failure and lies. I just shake my head and roll over. How can they imagine that I want any of it? It's all tainted. If I look at that bookcase or that telly, I'll just remember Adam and me in Currys or Ikea, and I'll get all choked up and misty-eyed until I remember that he was pretending and then I'll want to put my bare hands around something and squeeze and squeeze until it stops struggling.

Oh my God, what am I turning into?

So after Dad and Robbie have packed up all my clothes and toiletries and brought them all back, a dude with a big lorry and an eye for bargain-inducing tragedies (and the other eye on the death announcements) goes to the house and loads it all up and gives me £3,800 for the whole lot. Good riddance. I bet Pam next door's head exploded when she saw that happening. She'll need a new hobby now that we've gone.

I put the cash into the silver guitar bag with the rest. In those two days on the bed regrouping with Jinksy's help, I've come up with a plan. It's not a cunning or complicated plan, it's simple, but brilliant, like the best plans always are. I'm going to find out from Ray and Julia who Ryan Moorfield is. I'm going to track him down. And I'm going to . . . ask him a few questions.

OK, maybe it's not that brilliant. But it's simple, it's my plan and I need it. Give me a break, I've only been strong and capable for three days.

The next morning, Lauren taps tentatively at my door, and when she comes in with my tea as she has for the past two days, she finds me not only vertical but clothed and in the process of applying mascara.

'Fuck me, it lives,' she says, taking a sip of my tea. 'Feeling better?'

I glance at her, moving only my eyeballs, then go back to the mirror. 'What do you mean, better? I was fine anyway.'

She nods. 'Oh, OK.' She drinks more of the tea. 'So what are you getting dolled up for?'

'Going shopping. Need new clothes.'

'OK. Well, some of us have got to work.' She takes a final slurp before putting the half-empty mug down and leaving the room. 'Have fun.'

'Wait! Lo?'

She comes immediately back into the room. 'Yes, sis? You OK? What's up?'

'What day is it?'

She widens her eyes. 'Seriously? That's what you want to know? That's what you called me back for, all panicky and hysterical?'

I shrug. 'I hate not knowing what day it is.'

She rolls her eyes. 'It's, like, Tuesday. Cloth head.'

Ginger is more than happy to shut up shop for the day and take me clothes shopping. 'You thinking about court appearances?' she asks me tentatively, as she drives us into town.

'No, bollocks to that. I need sparkly stuff for Dad's birthday party. It's tomorrow. You coming?'

She glances at me from the driver's seat. 'You're going ahead with it?'

'Yeah. Do you think we shouldn't? Dad wanted to cancel but I think it would be good for everyone. Lighten the mood, you know?' I don't add that I have an ulterior motive for wanting to get into a room where there is plenty of alcohol and a certain step-father. Of course, he and Julia might choose not to come, but if there's even the slightest chance that they do, I want to seize it. I'm not going to tell Ginger this, though. Not yet anyway. To let anyone else in on my plan would feel like yet more epic ineptitude. I need to solve this one on my own. Dad's party seems like the perfect opportunity to speak to Ray about Ryan Moorfield, if only because it's likely to be the only opportunity I'm going to get. There's no word yet on any further sightings of the invisible man, and anyway, I've thought about it and I'm not sure that the right moment is ever going to arise in the wake of their son's abdication to casually bring up someone else entirely.

Dad's party it is.

Ginger shrugs. 'Have you announced Adam's mad disappearance and even madder reappearance in South America yet?'

'Announced? What do you mean?'

'Just seems like a bit of an odd time to make an announcement like that, don't you think?'

'Well, I'm not exactly planning on making an announcement, Ginge. This is my dad's night, I will not allow Adam to ruin it.'

'OK.'

'Why'd you say it like that?'

'Like what?'

'You know, like it's actually the opposite of OK. All sarcastic and knowing.'

She shakes her head. 'I didn't. Have you invited Matt? Fletch and I can pick him up if you want.'

At the sound of Matt's name, I get a tiny clenching feeling in my tummy, like my muscles are all doing crunches on the inside. 'Oh, could you? Yeah, OK, that'd be good. Thanks.' I'm trying so hard to sound off-hand, I end up rousing Ginge's suspicion, and she looks at me sharply from the driver's seat. I turn away to look casually out of the window and accidentally lock eyes with a cyclist, so I flash him a quick smile. He jerks in surprise,

247

tries to smile back, wobbles a bit, starts to look disconcerted, frowns, wobbles some more, and is then gone as we pass him. I watch in the wing mirror as he bumps the kerb then dramatically squeezes the brakes – a bit too hard – and slams both feet onto the ground.

'So you've invited him?'

'What? Oh, Matt? Um, no, I haven't. Yet. But Mum said Lo and I could invite as many friends as we want, you know, to bulk out the numbers. Otherwise there'll be seven of us in the whole of the rugby club.'

She turns to look at me again. 'The rugby club? Is that where you're having it?'

'Yeah. I know. But I wasn't involved in the planning of it, I just want to point that out now.'

'What? Well why weren't you? You could have stopped this hideous travesty!'

'Come on, it's not that bad. They could have done a lot worse.'

'Yes, they could have booked that old concrete factory on the industrial estate.'

'Hah! Yes they could. Or maybe those public toilets next to the park?'

'Ooh, yes, the toilets. Your mum would have loved that gorgeous stained glass window over the door.'

'Mmm, yeah. Gives the place such a lovely ambience.'

'Imagine what the acoustics would be like.'

We giggle at the image for a few moments as Ginger is reversing into a parking space, then she pulls on the handbrake, kills the ignition and turns to me.

'Seriously, though, Grace. Why weren't you involved in your dad's party arrangements?'

Her voice has taken on that gentle, sympathetic tone people do when they're trying not to hurt someone's feelings by accidentally implying something that might hurt their feelings. I frown. 'What are you implying?'

'No, nothing, just wondering.'

I narrow my eyes. 'Ginge. This is me. What are you getting at?'

She takes a deep breath and releases it slowly. 'OK. I just think that you should have been involved in this one. It's your dad's sixtieth birthday, it's only going to happen this one time, it's important.'

I feel myself frowning. 'Well yeah, I know that. But Mum and Lauren organised it without me. That's not really my fault, is it?'

'No, I wasn't saying it was your fault.' She breaks eye contact and looks down at her lap. 'Not exactly.'

Cold prickles start to break out all over me. 'Not exactly? What does that mean?'

'No, nothing, forget it.' She reaches behind her and grabs her handbag from the back seat. 'Come on, let's get you all glad-ragged up.'

'No, hold on a minute, Ginge, that's not fair to say something like that and not explain it. I know I haven't visited Mum and Dad so much since Adam and I got married, but that's normal, isn't it? You start a new life with your husband and leave your old life behind.'

She puts her bag on her lap. 'Yes, I know, you're right. To a certain extent. But you haven't been back to see them for months.'

'Yes I have! Months! That's rubbish. Where did you hear that?'

She looks into my face a few moments. 'Lauren told me. She reckons she last saw you just after Christmas.'

'Well, she hardly knows what day it is, let alone how much time has passed since she last did anything.'

Ginger nods thoughtfully. 'Oh, right. That does make sense. I thought it was odd, you not visiting in all that time. Considering that you used to go every week.'

'Exactly.'

'Sorry, Gracie. I should've known. Come on then, let's shop till we stop shopping.'

As we start walking, I'm wondering why Lauren would say something like that. I remember that I visited just after Christmas because we were at Ray and Julia's on Christmas Day. Then we went to Mum and Dad's on the twenty-seventh, or something. Actually, Adam didn't come because . . . because what? Can't remember. Probably had to work. But he hardly ever came anyway, so that was normal. But I *know* I've been to see them since then. It was Robbie's birthday in February, I definitely went then. Didn't I? Something bad starts to uncurl inside me. Twentieth of February, that's his birthday. The whole family would have gone out for dinner. I would have been there. So why can't I remember where we went for the meal? Think, think. Where does Robbie like to eat? My first thought is McDonald's, but that was probably a few years ago. He turned twenty, where would he have gone? Maybe he didn't have a family meal this time, now that he's a proper grown-up. Or . . . Is it possible . . . that maybe he did, and I just didn't go? Is Ginger right about me? The bad thing inside me starts to unfurl its wings and stretch itself out wide, spreading loathing

250

through me like a poisonous river. Suddenly my mind is filled with so many images of things in the house that are different – the new clock in the kitchen, the new sofas in the living room. The random exercise bike in my old room. Mum and Dad in competition with Mr and Mrs Martin next door. The new driveways, the Martins' new windows. That old couple were in their eighties, there's no way they would be doing up the house now. These must be new neighbours, moved in in the past . . . well, however long it is since I was last here. Does that mean Mr or Mrs Martin has died? Or *both* of them? How could I not know about that? They used to babysit us when we were little. Made us peanut butter sandwiches when we got home from school. Gave us a fiver each, every Christmas and birthday. Where are they now? All these things have changed since I was last home, and the only plausible, logical, contemptible explanation is that I simply haven't been here. Things have been changing and happening and moving on without me, and not because I've been sitting in HG Wells' time machine. I haven't seen my family since that time after Christmas. I'm a despicable person.

'You do see a lot of your parents, don't you?' Adam's voice comes into my head. 'I mean, far more than anyone else I know. It's . . . odd.'

Suddenly I find tears threatening and quickly I blink them away. I'm the bad person here, any tears would be self-pity. Or guilt. Which is just self-pity in a fancy bag. I can't let Ginger see me feeling sorry for myself.

'You OK?' she says. Fuckit. Nothing gets past her.

I nod silently. Let her think I'm upset about Adam.

She stops walking and puts her hand on my arm. 'Look, I know this has been a fucking awful time for you, finding out all this stuff about Adam.'

'I'm OK.'

She nods. 'I know. At least, I think you will be. It's such a shock, everything that's happened . . .'

'Well, not that much of a shock, to be honest. I mean, I knew he was secretive and wasn't including me in his life, so the safe and all that is fairly expected really.'

'Yeah, I was talking about him being on his way to a new life in South America, Grace. You can't have been expecting that.'

'Oh, right. No, that was a bit of a surprise.'

We pass by a shoe shop and stop simultaneously to gaze at the contents in the window.

'I love those.'

'Which? The boots?'

'Yeah.'

'Mm. Lovely colour.'

'Impractical though. They'd be ruined first time they got wet.'

'True.'

'Anyway, it's a bit like that woman who gets a call that her husband has had a car accident and is in hospital, and then this hidden life of his starts to unfold.'

'What?'

She turns to me. 'That film. Can't remember what it's called. He's been leading a double life the whole time, and she only finds out because of where he had the accident. It's like, hundreds of miles away from where he was meant to be.'

I stare at her. 'Are you saying Adam has been leading a double life?'

'Could be. I mean, you knew next to nothing about him, did you? His past or even his present. Maybe that would explain everything.'

I think about it. I've been assuming that he was just incredibly private, or uncommunicative, but was secretly booking flights and buying paperbacks during the advert breaks. And possibly setting up a new life thousands of miles away. Fairly standard shitty husband behaviour, I suppose. But what if there's more to this? Even more to find out? I shut my eyes. 'Oh my God, Ginge. What if there's another wife?'

'That's the least of your worries. He might be a serial killer.'

My eyes fly open. 'Oh my God!'

'Did Maple Avenue have a basement?'

'No.'

She shakes her head dismissively. 'That pretty much rules out serial killer then. He would need somewhere like that to . . . keep things.'

'Oh shut up.'

'Maybe he was a sex pest?'

'Flip, Ginger, why would you think that?' She doesn't answer immediately, which sends my mind spinning. 'Bloody hell, did you mention serial killer first so that when we finally realise he's just a pervert, it's not so bad?' Another thought occurs to me. 'Oh my God, has he ever . . . pestered you? Sexually?'

'No, no, nothing like that, don't worry. Jesus, can you imagine what Fletch would do if he had?'

Fletch adores Ginger, but he's not the most motivated man I've ever met. His reaction would probably be to frown a lot and call Adam something foul when he couldn't hear.

'Or maybe Matt?' Ginge adds, thoughtfully.

Now that's a different story. My mind is suddenly filled with an image of a huge, furious Matt, barging into our house with clenched fists and stomping around the place until he finds Adam cowering near the back door in the kitchen. Probably in the process of fleeing the scene, as that seems to be his preferred method for dealing with things. Matt marches over and shoves Adam on the shoulders with the heels of his hands, so hard Adam staggers backwards. 'How dare you?' Matt says, between clenched teeth. 'How fucking *dare* you?' Except in a nonsensical dream-like way, he's suddenly not defending his sister's honour, he's defending mine.

'Anyway, it doesn't really matter in the end, does it? It's dreadful he treated you so badly . . .'

'Or did he? Maybe he was actually treating someone else badly by being with me?'

She pauses. 'Yeah, possibly. But in the end, it doesn't matter. He's out of your life now. Whatever he was up to.'

'You know what I can't stand the thought of?' I say to Ginger, pausing on the pavement.

She stops too. 'What?'

Tears fill my eyes again as the thought fills my mind. 'What if I never find out?'

It takes most of the day to find a dress suitable for Dad's party. We hunt in a team, like velociraptors. I head straight

254

in for the clothing rails, while Ginger comes at them in a surprise attack from the side. I don't tell Ginge, but what I'm looking for has to be the right mix between devastatingly sexy and devastated wife. I need to look breathtakingly beautiful and heartstoppingly sad. I need an air of mystery, coupled with an air of misery. I want Ray to see my pain; and I want Matt to see my . . . wonderful personality.

Eventually we find a gorgeous strapless LBD that makes me look exactly like the sexy, grief-stricken man-eater I'd been hoping for. Then it's just a question of shoes and a bag, and we're done. Fortunately, Ginger doesn't know how much it all cost: there might be questions about cashflow that I'm not prepared to answer.

'So do you want me and Fletch to bring Matt to the party then?' she says suddenly, driving back to Mum and Dad's.

'Oh, yes, please, if you don't mind.'

'OK. I'll see what he's doing.'

I thought we'd settled this already and part of me wonders why she's asked me again. But I've got so many other things to wonder about, I forget about that straight away. Also, I'm very glad she's brought it up. This dress would only be half useful if Matt doesn't come after all. Plus I really want to thank him again for everything he did for me, and buying him a drink at my dad's party seems like the perfect time to do it. It's a social occasion, there's alcohol, it could almost be considered a date. In a way. If both parties wanted it to be. But the beauty of it is, if one of the parties wasn't interested in looking at it in that way, it's purely a thank-you drink and can be dismissed by both parties without any shred of embarrassment or awkwardness.

I can convince myself of anything if I try hard enough.

FOURTEEN

As I walk into the party at the rugby club in my new dress the following evening – actually I'm sashaying in; the dress calls for it – it's driven home to me just exactly what a bad choice of venue this was for a genteel party full of elderly people in pastel colours and pearls. For starters, the walls are covered with photos of enormous muddy men gurning in shorts. The hallway that leads from the field back to the changing rooms and bar has more than one blood spatter up the paintwork. And when you walk in, the unnaturally high levels of testosterone in the air make everyone feel a bit territorial and aggressive. After five minutes there, I start rubbing my chin and scratching my balls.

'What do you think?' Mum says excitedly when we arrive. 'Do you like it?'

I glance around. The walls were probably white once, about thirty years ago, but are now speckled with countless black scuff marks and paint chips, no doubt from decades of alcohol-induced games of 'Let's all throw Briggie in the air, hoorah!' Two rows of migraine-inducing striplights ensure that no cobweb goes unnoticed; and the vinyl flooring is curling up in the corners. It looks like a party in a prison cell. In Turkey.

'Wow. Who booked this place?'

Mum and Lauren stare at me, while Robbie sniggers loudly and says something like 'Told you!' before wandering off to the bar.

'I did,' Mum says, frowning. 'Why?'

I shrug. 'What's the theme? *Midnight Express*?'

She smiles delightedly and squeezes my waist. 'Ooh, love, thank you. How romantic.'

She's not being sarcastic. She's literally never heard of it.

'Come on then, birthday boy,' she says, grabbing Dad's arm. 'Let's get a drink.'

They wander off into the growing melee of all their closest friends and family who have arrived to celebrate with them the joyful occasion of my dad's sixtieth year on the planet.

'That table's taken, mate.'

'Ow, you just stood on my toe, you oaf.'

'Don't push in, pal, we're all waiting to get a drink.'

'When's Ginger getting here?' Lauren asks, then shouts out, 'Oi, Beefcake.'

A young man by the door scanning the room turns his head towards her, grins, and walks over. 'All right Lola,' he says, then bends and kisses her. I look round, yearning for Ginger and Fletch to arrive. 'All right, Grace,' Beefcake says, and I look back at him, startled.

'Oh, hi, er . . .?'

'Grace, you remember Justin Webb,' Lo says, indicating Beefcake.

258

'Um . . .'

'Come on, he was in my year, bit of a nerd, always making Lego models of the Millennium Falcon.'

'Oi!' Justin says, grinning. 'I only did one.'

'Oh yeah.' She turns to me again. 'Also, like, a massive underachiever.'

'Oi, you!' he says again, and lightly punches her arm. 'What you playing at?'

'Oh I'm kidding, I know you also did the Death Star and Doctor Who's Tardis.'

'Yeah, too right I did.' He turns to me. 'Believe it or not, the Tardis was the hardest one to do of all of them. All that blue . . .'

'Right,' she says, 'get me a drink, and ready for dancing.' She tugs on his arm and they start to walk towards the bar.

'Is there gonna be dancing?' I hear him say as they move away.

'Oh yeah. When David Guetta gets here, they're gonna put on a Jumpstyle Trance playlist, and the laser display will start flashing.'

'Cool.'

Over at the door I spot Ginger and Fletch arriving, so I walk quickly over with a mixture of relief to see them, and excitement that I'll see Matt in just a few more seconds.

'Hi Ginge, hi Fletch, really glad you're here.' Ginge is stunning in a halter top and silver sateen skinnies. Fletch is wearing leather trousers and a goatee. I look casually behind them both. 'Matt with you?'

'Oh, no, sorry,' Ginger says, looking around, 'he already had something else on tonight.'

'Oh.' Disappointment descends, layer upon layer of it settling on me in a heavy mass. Matt's not coming. I bought this dress for nothing. He's probably got a girl-friend. He's no doubt gazing at her right now, madly in love. I can actually feel the weight of this let-down pulling me into the ground, dragging my head down, and it takes a lot to remain upright. It occurs to me to wonder, briefly, why I'm reacting like this, but then Ginger is taking my arm and walking me to a table.

'Fletch, can you get us a couple of drinks please, lover?'

That's unlike her. To say please, I mean. I look at her sharply as Fletch moves off to the bar. 'You OK?'

'What? Oh, yeah, yeah, I'm fine, just wanted to get rid of him.'

'Why? What's up? Have you had a row?'

'God, no, nothing like that. But I've just seen Adam's mum and dad outside. I can't believe they're here, actually.'

'Wow, me neither.' My heart, so recently lying face down with its arms over its head, suddenly sits up, pays attention, and starts thumping with anticipation like a dog's tail. Ray is here.

'God knows what she'll do in her current state,' Ginger is saying, and for a second, I have no idea who she means. *She?* But of course: Julia.

Automatically, we both look up towards the door and see a couple there just starting to come through it: him in dark navy suit, her in peach chiffon. In sync we both turn and look back at Fletch's retreating figure, willing the crowds to surge round and close over him to conceal him from the approaching peach surprise.

I turn back to Ginger. 'How long have we got?'

She shakes her head and bites her lip. 'Not long. He usually gets served quickly at bars because of his charisma.'

It's probably more to do with his height and corresponding arm length, to be honest, but I'm not saying that to Ginge. 'What shall we do?'

She thinks for a second. 'OK. How about you head them off, try to stop her from seeing him. I'll stay here until he comes back, then I'll hide him somewhere.'

I nod. 'Good plan.' And as well as saving Fletch, I'll also get a chance to chat to Ray.

'Right.'

We both stand up and before I walk towards Ray and Julia, Ginge grabs my arm. I turn and look into her eyes. She gazes at me earnestly for a few moments. 'Good luck,' she says, as if I'm just about to have brain surgery.

'Thanks.'

I strike out towards them. This is it, I'm thinking, in just a few moments I might have achieved stage one of my brilliant plan, and could know something that brings me an inch nearer to knowing something. I was almost sure Ray and Julia wouldn't come tonight, couldn't imagine them coming, but credit to them, here they are. They're walking towards Mum and Dad, who are still dangerously close to the bar – where Fletch is – so I speed up a bit to intercept.

Then I slow down. Actually . . .

This is Ginger's plan. All she wants to do is save Fletch the embarrassment of Julia's awkward advances. It won't hurt him, though, and I have ulterior motives, so why am I automatically going along with it? Especially now that

I am new Grace, less naïve Grace, graceless Grace who does not simply accept everything she's told. If I want to ask Ray about Ryan without Julia there, she would need to be elsewhere. Or heavily distracted. Or both. And right there, at the bar, is a heavy, leather-trouser-clad distraction. Which is a much better plan, surely?

'Oh hi Ray, hi Julia,' I hear Mum saying. 'How lovely of you to come. I really appreciate it, especially since . . . I mean, considering that . . .' She trails off, obviously reluctant to mention Adam's scarper-y behaviour.

'Seeing as you've had such a difficult time lately,' Dad finishes off for her, and everyone sighs with relief. Well, Mum does. 'Can I get you both a drink?'

'Oh, yes, we'll both have a G and T please,' Ray says, shaking Dad's hand. Standing a few feet away, I hold my breath and wait. All four of them turn in unison towards the bar, and there, just turning round with three drinks in his hands, is Fletch.

He freezes, like a child trying not to be seen by a caretaker, and the colour drains from his face. There's a moment's hiatus as Julia sees Fletch, Ray sees Julia seeing Fletch, Ginge sees Fletch seeing Julia, and Mum and Dad spot Granny arguing with Aunt Daphne about some old china.

''Scuse me a minute,' Mum says, gives Dad a meaningful look, then sidles away towards the fracas at the nearby table. Aunt Daphne has just stood up so fast that her chair has fallen over. Dad watches Mum go, then glances back at the bar.

'Oh, look,' he says, spotting Fletch – who is now inching very slowly sideways –'there's Fletch.' He turns back to Ray and Julia. 'He'll sort you out some drinks. Won't you, Fletch?' He catches Fletch's eye. 'Thanks, lad.' And he scuttles after Mum.

Now I need to strike.

Julia starts towards Fletch and I start towards Ray, but before either of us reaches our goal, Ginger swoops in suddenly from the side, seizes Fletch's arm and pulls him away, out of immediate danger. Julia stops moving and watches regretfully as her prey is snatched from her grasp and borne away to a distant corner. Then Ray catches her up and they go to the bar together. My sense of anti-climax is suffocating. Dammit.

I stand still for a moment under the weight of disappointment, wondering when such an opportunity might come again, wondering whether Fletch might be persuaded to sacrifice himself for the good of mankind, realising that Ginge would never allow it, when I sense the arrival of someone behind me.

'How are you doing, Grace?' a deep voice says in my ear, and an electric thrill shoots up my spine.

I turn and find Matt there in a light blue shirt and sand-coloured chinos. His hair looks different, more messy than usual, and his chin is dark with a touch of designer stubble. Yet again, acute disappointment morphs instantly into a thrill of excitement. How have I never noticed before how attractive he is? Well, apart from when he's in his uniform, of course. That goes without saying. My insides feel like they've just put on the Jumpstyle Trance Mix and the laser show, and it makes my face grin all its own.

'Oh Matt. Hi. I thought you weren't coming.'

He grins back. 'Well, I was supposed to be at the cinema with a colleague, but I cancelled it.'

'Oh, no, now I feel terrible for your colleague. Will she mind?'

Yeah, I know, obvious.

'No, not at all. *He* is going with a few other people anyway. I was just tagging along.'

'Oh.' Would he be going to the cinema with a group of colleagues if he had a girlfriend? He wouldn't. Would he? Maybe I'll ask Ginger later. Although knowing her, she'll immediately tell Matt that I asked her, and then he'll probably think that I like him. Which would be terrible.

'So, I heard the latest about Adam,' Matt goes on, leaning towards me. 'Jetting off to sunnier South American climes. Ecuador, wasn't it?'

'Actually, most of the country has a fairly constant cool climate due to its elevation and proximity to the equator.' I give a little smile, then cringe as the hideousness of this approach hits me. This is me trying to be flirtatious. God help me, I'm actually reciting facts from Google.

He leans back again and blinks. 'Well, that's interesting. Maybe that's what attracted him there.'

'Could be. Or maybe it's because it's about as far away as he can get before he starts coming back again.'

'Well, technically, that's not true. I mean, how far away is it? About five, six thousand . . .'

'Five thousand, seven hundred miles.' Oh dear God, I can't stop.

'OK, thanks. So almost six thousand. The circumference

of the earth is, what, twenty-five thousand miles? So in actual fact, he's only gone a quarter of the way round.' He leans in and gives a warm smile. 'Must be something there that pulled him; not something here he's trying to escape.'

His tone of voice is so gentle and kind and I feel a huge surge of gratitude towards him. I have no idea why Adam skipped town, but if the lure of Ecuador, with its World Heritage Sites, megadiversity and Inca history, was too strong to be denied, I kind of feel less . . . rejected.

Eventually Matt looks away and clears his throat. 'Shall I get us a drink?'

Julia and Ray are looking uncomfortable at a table far away from everyone else. As Matt and I reach the bar, I note with satisfaction that there are two empty glasses in front of both of them. Good. Hopefully Ray will get wasted and blab all over the place about Ryan Moorfield when I ask him. I glance at Matt, who is now leaning across the bar on his elbows, chatting to the barmaid. His shirt has rucked up a little at the back, and there is half an inch of skin showing above the waistband of his trousers. I tear my eyes away and force my head round to look at Ray again. I really must go and speak to him. In a minute.

'Here you go,' Matt says, smiling as he turns to me with a glass of bubbly pink wine in his hand. I smile back and take the glass. I can't drink too much if I'm going to wheedle information out of Ray later. Matt catches my eye over the rim of his pint glass. As he lowers it, he has a creamy line of froth along his top lip. There's no rush, I can speak to Ray later.

'Come and sit down,' Matt says, leading us to a table. Once seated, he looks me earnestly in the eye. 'How are you doing? Honestly.'

I shrug. 'I'm actually fine.'

He shakes his head. 'Well obviously you aren't. Your husband has disappeared without warning, dumped the car and was last seen boarding a plane to an alternative continent. No one would be OK if they found that out.'

'But I am. It's weird but it's like I'm suddenly aware of how close we weren't.'

Matt raises his eyebrows. 'How close you weren't?'

'Yeah. He kept himself at such a distance from me, which I was always kind of aware of, maybe just in a subconscious way, but it's really only becoming completely clear now. I suppose I didn't ever feel . . . I don't know . . . attached.'

'Attached? That's an odd choice of word. Do you mean, you didn't care about him?'

'Oh, no, no, I did.' I hesitate and feel a pull of sadness. 'I do.'

Suddenly I have an incredibly vivid recollection of one day last year, when I woke up to find Adam had already left for work. That familiar faint feeling of abandonment niggled at me, but then I got up and started to get ready for the day and blocked it out, as I usually did.

When I got downstairs, I found the kitchen table laid out with breakfast things – a bowl, a spoon, the box of Special K, a glass of orange juice, and a plate under a plastic cover. When I lifted it off, there was just a little note there saying 'Good Morning! X'. Such a simple gesture, minimal effort, minimal time required, but it

266

made my abandoned heart soften. Thinking about it now, and picturing him cheerfully checking his luggage in at the airport, I feel heat come into my eyes and my mouth starts to distort. I swallow a couple of times and blink rapidly. Mustn't cry at my dad's birthday party.

Abruptly, the image disappears and in its place I see the same breakfast table at Maple Avenue but this time the things are being put there by a two-dimensional silhouette, a nebulous shadow, flitting to and fro across the kitchen in ghostly silence. Goosebumps prick out over my skin and I shudder a little.

'You OK?' Matt says, peering at me. 'You've gone a bit pale.'

I nod. 'I'm fine.'

'Well you don't look fine.'

'Gee, thanks.'

He puts his hands up. 'Oh, no, no, I didn't mean . . . I mean, you most certainly do look . . . In fact, you look absolutely . . .' He stops. Blows out a puff of air. Rubs his hand over his head and rolls his eyes at the floor. 'Smooth, aren't I?'

'Like James Bond.'

He nods. 'I've been practising. To get it just right, you know.'

'Good idea. It's no good leaving these things to chance.'

He grins. 'Anyway, if you're sure you're fine, would you like another drink?'

While he goes back to the bar, I glance casually around the room so that I can take another surreptitious look at Ray and Julia's table, and am immediately panic-stricken to see that they're no longer there. I stand up hurriedly and start scanning the room, feeling a strong urge to start running around like a mum looking for a toddler. Oh God, why didn't I go and speak to them both together? Why did I wait? I could have spoken to them both together, I didn't need Julia out of the way. If Ray knows who Ryan Moorfield is, then Julia will too. And if he doesn't, then neither will she. Probably. Maybe having Julia present in the conversation would even have been an advantage, as Ray might have been distracted, worrying about what she was doing, and could have let slip something he might not have meant to say.

My thoughts flit around like an anxious butterfly, landing on something then lifting off again straight away. Why am I assuming that he's going to try not to let anything slip about Ryan Moorfield? Why would he be hiding anything? Why have I got it into my head that it's all a big secret?

Because Adam hid Ryan's details in a safe, in the floor, locked by a key that was hidden in a locked drawer.

And then disappeared.

I want to charge around the room, grabbing people and turning them round roughly, before discarding them with a shove when they're not Ray. But as I peer around the room, clenching and unclenching my fists, I spot Aunt Daphne in deep discussion with Mum and Granny; cousin Keira, with her gargantuan baby Hercules gently rolling around on the floor; Great Uncle Morris with his hands in his lap; Aunt Maureen bringing him a glass of Guinness. Elderly, powdery relatives are moving slowly and gingerly around the room in every direction, and it's obvious that I can't charge round furiously seizing people's shoulders and pushing them away. There would probably be more than one hip incident if I did. And anyway, the place is so sparsely populated, I can see easily that Ray and Julia are definitely not here any more. Unless they're both in the toilets at the same time, and that would be weird.

I sag back down into my chair, just as Matt returns with our drinks.

'Well that was an ordeal,' he says, dropping into the seat opposite me. 'Someone seems to have been buying drinks for an eight-year-old.' He glances back towards the bar. 'He's up there now, getting a bit antsy, elbowing people out of the way and trying to hit on the barmaid.' He turns back to me and grins. 'He called me "pal". "Don't push in, pal," he says, "we've all been waiting." I thought it was going to kick off.' As he looks at me, I smile back encouragingly. I mustn't let him see the wasteland of my distress. His smile falters a little. 'Has something happened?'

I close my eyes. Dammit. 'I never was any good at hiding things,' I say to him with a shrug. 'Unlike . . .' I shake my head. 'No. I'm not starting on that again, it's getting boring.' I look up at him, peering at me anxiously, the remains of his beer moustache still glistening on his lip, and feel suddenly very certain and relaxed. I've known Matt for so many years, surely I can trust him? I smile sadly. 'Sorry.'

'Hey, what are you apologising for?'

'Ah, you're so sweet. Thank you.'

He shakes his head. 'No, no, I mean it literally. What *are* you apologising for? I'm not being kind, you know. I genuinely don't know.' He blows out air as he gazes at me. 'You're a mystery to me, Grace Littleton.'

'Am I?'

'Oh yes. Always were. I've spent years trying to puzzle you out.' He breaks off and looks away, suddenly awkward. Then looks back at me. 'You are actually more capable than you think you are, you know.'

I have no idea how to react to that. Proving him instantly wrong. 'No I'm not. I'm exactly the amount of useless I think I am.'

He leans forward and extends his hands across the table towards me. 'No you're not! Jesus, Grace, look at you, coping with what's just happened to you, not falling apart, not on the floor wailing about how it's not fair and why me and all that self-pitying crap. You're incredibly strong, and clever and bright and interesting and amazing . . .' He stops talking and gives a little laugh, then leans back and slides his arms back towards himself. 'Ah . . .' Then picks up his drink and takes a sip.

I can't take my eyes off him, the hunt for Julia and Ray forgotten. There are signals here, waiting to be read, but I've never learned how. I can remember little Matt, when we were all much younger, following Ginger and me around, always there in the background, getting on our nerves, omnipresent in eyeliner. I always thought he was just bored or hero-worshipped his big sister or was a bit of a loner or, perversely, thought he needed to be there to watch out for her. Now it seems as if . . . I'm frowning, trying to understand the past twelve years.

'Stop frowning,' he says now, rubbing his face and shifting around in his seat. 'It's making me nervous.'

'Nervous? Why?'

He rolls his eyes. 'Christ, Grace, I've pretty much just

270

blurted out . . .' He locks eyes with me, then breaks off and turns away.

'Blurted out?' I repeat, still frowning, but he shakes his head and gives a tiny half smile.

'Have you seen your mum and dad doing "The Birdie Song"?'

'What?'

He jerks his head towards the dance floor. 'Over there. Hilarious.'

I glance over to the dance floor, completely fail to spot my parents dancing badly, then turn back to Matt. I want him to finish what he was saying. I want him to explain what he meant. I want him to know that I want him to say it. But he's turned away from me now and is tapping his foot to the music, pint glass in hand.

'Matt,' I start, but I don't get any further.

'Thank Christ for that,' a voice says to my right, and I turn towards it. Ginger is standing there, hands on hips, looking above our heads as she scans the room. Just behind her is Fletch, also looking around, although slightly more nervously than Ginger.

'What?'

She focuses on me, then takes in Matt, turned away from the table and staring at the dance floor. Then, in a heroic obliviousness to the frigid waves of 'don't join us' emanating from me, she pulls out a chair and joins us. 'Ray and Julia have gone.'

'I'm not surprised they've gone,' Matt says. 'I was surprised to see them at all, to be honest, after what's happened.'

'Yeah, me too,' Ginger says. 'I'm bloody glad they've

271

gone though.' She grins at Fletch. 'We can relax now. Fancy a dance?'

'No.'

She stands up and boogies round to Fletch's side of the table. 'Come on, come and dance with me.' She grabs his arm and pulls. Eventually he stands up reluctantly, and trails behind her onto the dance floor.

'I hate dancing.'

'No you don't, come on. This is a fab song.' She's wrong: it's 'That's Amore'.

Matt and I watch them go, then turn back to each other. The conversation we've just been having is right there between us, but like the last cupcake, neither of us wants to reach for it. I'm distracted now, too, thinking about my utter failure to speak to Ray about Ryan Moorfield, my naïve trust in everything everyone ever says to me, and my ridiculous ineptitude at life in general. I give Matt a smile, then focus back on the dance floor. Granny is shimmying in front of a panicked Uncle Martin.

'Hey,' Matt says, leaning across towards me, 'you look so sad suddenly. Something just occurring to you?'

'No, not really, just feeling useless as usual.'

'You're not useless! What the hell are you talking about? Seriously, Grace, how can you think that, after all this has happened?'

I turn away from Granny and focus on Matt's kind face. He looks so concerned about me and has been such a good friend these past few days. Just the fact that he's there, with his messy hair and his beer moustache, is making me feel less anxious. It's almost impossible to think that someone that poised, that self-assured, that together, could ever be attracted to an incapable and ridiculous mess like me, but I feel almost sure I heard it, just now when he said all those wonderful things. His eyes are still on my face, his eyebrows drawn in a bit, his whole body leaning towards me, and I can feel an unfamiliar heat flaring in my belly. I try to smile back but the heat has reached my cheeks now and guaranteed he can see me going red, even in the flash of the strobe lighting. I put my hand up and smooth my hair a bit to try to hide my face.

'I feel useless,' I say quietly, '*because* of everything that's happened. It doesn't make me fall apart, or wail, or go on about it's not fair or why me, you're right. But not because I'm strong and capable. Because of the opposite of that. I'm not moaning about what's happened to me because I know it's all my own fault.'

'Grace . . .'

'No, Matt, it is. It's all down to my own stupidity. Or naïveté. One or the other, whatever you want to call it. I deserve all this, everything that's happened, because I walked right into it.'

'That's not true . . .'

'It is. It really is. I was an idiot and I got taken in. But I know one thing – it's not going to happen to me again. I won't let it.'

He draws back a bit when I say this, and looks sad for a moment. 'I believe it.'

I nod. 'Hell yeah! I am never, ever going to let myself get drawn in like that again, and simply believe things. Not without tons of proof. From now on, I'm going to need solid, documentary . . .' I break off as something occurs to me. I look at Matt, searching his face. He cares about me, he must do, to have been helping me out so much the last few days. Could I confide in him about the safe? Would he be my confidant, or would he insist I tell the police everything about it, and the money, and my hunt for Ryan Moorfield? Would telling him be putting him in an impossible position? Would he have to choose between the girl he cares about, or the force he loves?

I sound like a movie trailer. Mentally I slap my own face. Come *on*!

'What is it?' he asks, leaning further across the table. The fingers of his right hand are millimetres from mine, so close I can feel my hand being drawn towards them, like disorganised particles near a mass. I stare at our hands for a moment, then look up into Matt's eyes.

'Matt, we're friends, aren't we?'

He draws back a little. 'OK.'

'No, I mean . . . I don't mean that I'm not . . .' I stop. 'What I'm trying to ask you is . . . if I tell you something, something pretty big, would you . . . keep it secret?'

He doesn't answer straight away. He looks down at his hands on the table, then slides them back towards himself slowly, and leans back in his chair.

'Grace, I do care about you. You must know that. What you may not know is exactly how much. But . . . I would be duty-bound to report any . . . wrongdoing . . . that may have—'

I put my hands up. 'God, no! There's no wrongdoing here. At least, I don't think there is. Not by me, anyway. I would never ask you to keep anything like that a secret, Matt. That would be awful of me.'

He breathes in deeply and releases it with a smile, coming forward again. 'Oh, thank God. I thought you were about to confess to . . .' He breaks off and looks away. Then flicks his gaze back to me, raising his eyebrows. 'You know.'

It takes me a moment, but I cotton on in the end. 'Oh God. You thought I killed Adam.' My turn to shrink away into my seat. 'You think I'm involved!'

'No no no, I don't, please don't think that. Honestly, Grace, I mean it.' He shakes his head. 'Bum.'

'Well then why did you . . . say that? Act like that?'

'It was what you said, about keeping a secret. I don't think you did anything, or are even capable of it, but you said you had a big secret . . . Look at it from my point of view. Your husband disappears without warning; then a week later he flees the country. Who's to say he and you haven't done something?' He puts a hand up to stop me from interrupting immediately. 'No, hold on, who's to say he didn't do something, and you found out about it? Maybe he's coercing you into something. Maybe he's blackmailing you . . .'

I'm suddenly chilled all over. This is it. This is how it happens. 'Oh my God. Oh my God. Is that what they think? They think my husband has carried out some kind of, I don't know, diamond heist? And I've helped him escape the country because he found out about some hideous thing in my past, and is threatening to tell people?'

Matt pauses and squints a bit. 'Well . . . when you put it like that . . .'

'It sounds ridiculous.'

He nods. 'Yes. It does a bit. But, you know, when there

are mysterious circumstances, and one of the main players says she has a big secret . . .' He shrugs.

'That's unfair.' I sound like a child, and I can practically hear how pathetic that will sound in a courtroom.

'I know. I'm sorry.' He reaches across the table again and covers my hand. 'Oh, Gracie, you . . .' He breaks off and looks down at our hands a moment. 'Anyway,' he goes on, 'it won't be a problem because there won't be any evidence pointing at you.'

I can't believe he's holding my hand in public. Or hasn't snatched his hand back again immediately, recollecting himself after a momentary lapse. I'd tensed instantly as his skin touched mine, waiting for him to realise and retreat, but he didn't. His hand has stayed right there, on mine, taking care of it and protecting it from everything. Eventually, my hand starts to relax and feel safe there; and so do I.

'Matt,' I say quietly, 'I couldn't even find out who his friends are, or where he went to school, or who his favourite Bond is. There's no way I could've known if he'd been masterminding a massive criminal act.'

He doesn't respond. It's rhetorical anyway. As I think about that, it seems obvious to me, and to anyone else who might give it two seconds' thought, that I should have known. I'm his wife – *was* his wife – and I lived with him. I saw him every day. We shared meals and floor space and our clothes went round the washing machine together. I should have noticed that something was amiss. How could I not?

No, no, that's ridiculous. He was brilliantly secretive. He made an art form out of it. He could have hidden a murder weapon from Sherlock Holmes. He's probably got that stolen Vermeer painting in some secret lock-up somewhere. I bet Lord Lucan came to him for help all those years ago.

I look back at Matt and find him staring at me intently. He smiles as our eyes meet, and it makes my tummy flip. My entire body is acutely aware of his big, warm hand still on mine.

'Sorry,' I say again, although I don't know why.

'Still apologising for no reason. Why do you do that?'

'I don't know.'

'Oh. Well, you're forgiven.'

I shake my head. 'Don't forgive me too quickly. When I work out why I'm sorry, you might regret it.'

'I won't. I'm sure of it.' His voice has gone all low and gravelly and makes my spine vibrate.

'Good. Well . . . I opened the safe.'

'Oh, right. Good.' He raises his eyebrows. 'And?'

'There was a huge stack of cash inside.'

He raises his eyebrows. 'Huge? Define huge.'

'Thirteen thousand huge.'

'Shoot the hostage!'

It makes me smile. 'I know.'

'Anything else?'

'I kept it.'

'Ah.'

'Is that wrong?'

He considers for a moment. 'That's a grey area. I'll think about it. Is there any clue as to where it's come from?'

'Nothing. Not that I could see, anyway. Just some

paperwork relating to a tenancy agreement, some bank statements and a birth certificate.'

'A birth certificate? What, Adam's?'

'No, someone called Ryan Moorfield.'

'Who's he?'

'I don't know. I'm guessing he's related to Ray somehow.'

'Ray? You mean Adam's dad?'

'Yeah, but he's not Adam's dad, he's his step-dad. So he and Julia are Moorfield. Adam was Littleton.'

I pause as it strikes me suddenly how easily I referred to Adam in the past tense. Didn't even hesitate.

'You're getting used to the idea,' Matt says, sending shivers down my spine.

'I suppose so.'

We both fall silent for a moment and sip our drinks.

'What happened to his dad?' he asks me.

I look at him helplessly. 'You're still not getting it, are you?'

'Getting what?'

'Adam. Me. Our relationship.' I lean forward and put my elbows on the table. 'Matt, I'm telling you that I know literally *nothing* about him.'

'No, I know, I do get it, but I only meant was he dead, or did he and Julia get divorced . . .?'

He trails off as I'm already shaking my head.

He raises his eyebrows. 'You don't know?'

'Nope.'

'O-o-oh.' He elongates the vowel sound, as if just realising something. But he isn't realising at all. 'Well then, does Ray have any children, or are there other fam . . .?'

278

He stops when he sees my expression. Looks down at the table, then back at me. 'You don't know?'

'I don't know.'

'Ray's former wife?'

I shrug.

'Adam's brothers, sisters?'

'Nothing.'

'Previous relationships?'

'Are you kidding?'

He nods slowly, looking pensive. 'OK. I think I finally get it. Properly now.'

'Well it's about time.'

'Yeah, I know. Slow on the uptake, me. I failed the Uptake exam three times at Police College.'

'Oh dear.'

'Yeah, I know. I felt really stupid, especially as my tutor had been secretly giving me the answers to help me get through. I just . . . didn't realise.'

I grin and a small laugh escapes me.

'Ah, that's good to see,' he says. 'You have such a great smile, and we haven't seen much of it these past few days.'

'I haven't had many moments that warrant it.'

'Well I'm very glad this was one of them.'

'Me too.'

We fall silent again for a few moments and both turn to watch the dancing. I notice that Ginger is dancing on her own now, swaying sensuously with closed eyes, so I glance around for Fletch. It doesn't take long for me to locate him, cornered a couple of tables away, listening to Granny telling him her relentless story about a rather seedy incident from her past that everyone in the family tries to keep quiet, but which she always recounts immediately to any new face.

'It was so sheer,' she's saying, as Fletch looks beseechingly towards the dance floor, 'you could pretty much see right through it. But I had a beautiful figure back then, you know, so it didn't really matter.'

I start grinning and Matt immediately turns to see what I'm looking at. Even from here, Fletch's anxiety and discomfort are lit up on his face like a red, pulsating sign, and he squirms in his seat as Granny describes everything in lurid detail.

'Light and billowy, and so tiny, a bit like a teensy little curtain . . .'

Matt swings back round to face me, his eyes widened in surprise. I nod gravely and he jerks his head, then turns back to Granny. We watch together in silence for a few moments, and I feel something smoothly click into place in my mind. This feels right, and comfortable, and relaxed. This is what it should be like. This is what I want – to share my family with someone; to share his with him. And it seems that I can almost, *almost* have it. I just have one cloud, one blot hanging over me that I need to banish, and then I can start a brand new, real life.

Eventually, with the words, 'photographed me for four hours' still ringing in his ears, Fletch makes his escape.

FIFTEEN

Eventually the cake is cut, some eight-year-olds have skidded across the floor in their socks, and Great Uncle Morris and the baby Herc have fallen asleep. At midnight, just like Cinderella, we are all kicked out, lest our carriage turns back into a pumpkin and our clothes to rags. Well, there's a big match tomorrow and they need to get the place ready.

'Like that's going to take a long time,' Lauren says as we all trudge towards the exits, some more sulkily than others. 'Tip a couple of the tables over and sling a few kit bags around – five minutes tops.'

'No, they'll have to wash all the glasses and clear up a bit, too, Lo,' Justin, aka Beefcake, says, completely un-sarcastically.

Matt glances at me but makes no comment.

When we reach the road, there's a taxi already waiting, so Mum, Dad, Lauren and Robbie get in, leaving Matt and me standing on the pavement. Mum smoothly gives the driver our address and it pulls away with the words 'Get the next one!' shouted from the back seat.

Matt and I look at each other, then turn back to watch the dwindling tail lights of the taxi. 'Well, that was odd,' he says.

I nod silently, and close my eyes. I'm definitely feeling the clumsy, clammy hand of maternal match-making, and it's making my skin shrivel. As soon as I get home, I'm moving out.

'It's OK,' Matt says, stuffing his hands into his pockets and waggling his elbows. 'It's a pleasant night – walk with me?'

I smile. 'OK.'

'Can I ask you something?' he says über-casually as we walk, and I feel the ominous sensation of something heavy draping itself over me.

'Really?'

He puts a hand up. 'No, Grace, don't worry, I'm not asking you to explain your whereabouts on the night in question.' He looks at me with an earnest expression. 'I mean it, honestly.' Then his voice turns harder. 'That would have to be done at the station, under caution.'

I look at him sharply, heart thudding, and he gives me a wide grin and winks. 'Matt! Oh my God!'

'Oh come on, you can't possibly believe that they're going to think you've done something? I mean, seriously?'

'That's exactly what I'm terrified of, you bloody sod.'

'No way!'

I nod emphatically. 'You have literally just drilled down directly into my very own waking nightmare.'

He stops walking, so I do too. 'No. Genuinely? You're not winding me up, to get your own back?'

I shake my head wordlessly.

'But that's so ridiculous, Gracie. I mean, look at you.' He puts both hands out towards me. 'You're one of the sweetest, loveliest . . . Ahem. You could no more plot something evil than, I don't know, spin straw into gold.' He laughs once from the side of his mouth.

'Miscarriages of justice do happen. I know, I've Googled it.'

'Then it must be true.'

'Are you making fun of me now?'

'Oh God, Grace, no, no.' He reaches up and rubs his head, making his hair stand on end. 'I'm sorry. I'm just . . . I don't know. Nervous, I suppose.'

I frown. 'Why are you nervous?'

He looks at me sidelong, smiles enigmatically, and resumes walking. 'So anyway,' he says, making it clear he has no intention of explaining, 'I wanted to ask you something. Unrelated to any as yet unexplained disappearances.'

'OK. But I'm not promising to answer on the grounds that I may incriminate myself.'

He huffs. 'Right then. The thing is, when I . . . touched your hand, at the table, earlier . . .'

'Oh, yes, right. Yes, I remember.' We're both studiously avoiding eye contact now. 'What about it?'

'Well, correct me if I'm wrong, but you seemed . . . Well . . . OK. Look, to be honest, it was a bit weird.'

'Weird? Why?'

He shrugs. 'I don't know. You seemed tense, like you tensed up instantly. Your skin practically went rigid.'

'Oh.'

'And then you kept looking down at our hands on the

table, as if you felt you had to keep an eye on them. In case they exploded, or something.'

I stop walking and put my face in my hands. 'Oh, God. Did I? How embarrassing.'

He comes near but noticeably doesn't touch me this time. 'You don't have to be embarrassed, Gracie. It's only me, remember. I knew you when you had braces on your teeth.'

I lower my hands and find his face very close to mine. Hastily he moves away, clearing his throat. 'The reason I was . . . weird,' I start, 'is because I'm not used to . . . being touched. Like that.'

'Like what? I mean, it was just hands . . .'

I shake my head. 'No, no, I don't mean . . . What I mean is . . . When I say "like that", I mean, in public.'

He widens his eyes and gapes. 'What? You're saying . . .? Adam never . . .?'

'No.'

'Never held your hand?'

'No, he did, he did . . . Just not in public.' I look away. 'He used to hate it. Always snatched his hand back if I ever . . . Like he'd been burnt.'

'Oh Gracie.'

'No, it's fine. I got used to it. Didn't bother me.'

'That's so sad.'

'Is it?' I think about that for a moment, as we resume walking. It doesn't seem so terrible, what I remember, to be walking around Ikea or Homebase or Sainsbury's, opening drawers, stroking wood, picking up bags of pasta, not glued together at the wrist. In fact I recall distinctly that there were lots of other couples doing exactly the same: wandering apart, checking things out on their own, then coming back together to discuss their findings. They weren't in physical contact with each other the entire time. Doesn't mean they weren't happy. I always felt happy when Adam and I were in Ikea doing that. I felt close to him there in a way that I didn't anywhere else. I've never been able to pinpoint why that was, and it didn't matter anyway.

But now with a jolt it suddenly occurs to me. In Ikea, where the other couples were wandering around independently of each other, I was like them. My marriage was like theirs. It was normal. Standard. My husband and I talked to each other about trivialities like metal drawer runners and voile curtains and scented candles and it was shallow and unimportant and banal but that didn't matter, there. It was what everyone was doing, there. I fitted in, there. But strolling along the beach on a sunny day, or sitting in the cinema, or snuggling in bed, I did not. We did not. Our relationship had almost no physical element to it, and the only place where I didn't feel this was in Ikea.

I turn to Matt again, feeling heat in my eyes. 'You're right. It was terrible.'

'Oh, Grace . . .'

I shake my head and blink the tears away. 'No, don't do that. Don't feel sorry for me. Like I said, it was my own stupid fault.'

'No, for God's sake, it wasn't. You can't blame a donkey for wandering into a sand trap and not being able to get himself out again. You didn't know what you were getting into. And once you were in, it's very difficult to think about how to get out again. But you can move on with your life now. Start again.' He looks down at me meaningfully, that sideways look back again.

'Yes. That's exactly what I want to do.'

'But?'

I stop again. 'I need answers, Matt. I can't forget about all of this and move on until I know what I'm supposed to be forgetting.'

'What happened to him, you mean?'

'Yes. No. Oh, I don't know. That's definitely part of it. But I don't know a thing about the man I lived with for three years. It's ridiculous. I feel . . . ridiculous. Kind of ashamed of myself. No, don't argue. That's how I feel. So, to feel better about myself, to get back some self-respect, I want to know . . . stuff. What happened to him, what he was doing, who he was. That kind of thing.' He's nodding slowly as I talk, hands in his pockets, his eyes focused intensely on my face. 'Do you . . . see what I mean?'

'Of course I do. Totally. Let me help you?'

I feel an intense and immediate surge of affection for him which makes me want to run towards him and wrap my arms round his middle. I rock forward onto my toes, the pull is that strong. But I manage to resist it, and give him a huge, grateful smile instead. 'I was hoping you would say that. Thank you, Matt. Thank you so much. I can't tell you . . .'

'Of course I will help you, Grace.' He smiles to himself and shakes his head. 'Now let's go and make a plan.'

When we get back to Mum and Dad's, the house is in silent darkness. Without even thinking about it, I turn

286

to Matt and whisper, 'Mum and Dad are asleep, we'll need to be quiet.'

'And just like that, I'm fourteen again.'

I giggle. 'Shall we sing into hairbrushes and dye each other's hair?'

He looks at me full on. 'Er, *no*.'

'Right.'

In the kitchen, I make us both a mug of tea and we sit down at the table in front of my laptop.

'What are you doing?' he says, eyeing the computer as I fire it up.

'I'm making a plan.'

'Wha . . . How? I mean, with your *computer*?'

'Well yeah. I'm Googling it.'

'Googling what?'

I stare at him. 'How to find stuff out, obviously.' I launch the engine and start typing, 'Finding stuff out.'

'You're kidding.'

I smile and raise my eyebrows. 'Yes, Matt. I am kidding.' I start deleting the words. 'You can't Google everything, you know.' I've already tried this one, so I know it won't work, but I'm not admitting that to Matt.

'Well thank God for that. I mean, I'm no detective, but even I could see some flaws in your plan.'

Now I'm typing in 'hotels in Linton' and he starts nodding appreciatively. 'Where the car was found?'

'Yep. Can't be a bad place to start, right?'

'No, no, that's a much better idea.'

'Thanks.'

The Linton Lodge hotel is still completely booked up, of course. Such a shame, it looks wonderful. Four-poster

287

beds, crackling log fires, intimate seating areas in tucked-away nooks. Perfect for two people to get to know each other better, set amongst the stunning natural beauty of the Yorkshire Dales national park, full English breakfast included.

Mentally I slap myself in the head. We're not going for a romantic getaway. We're going to root out information about Adam. I click away from the images quickly and move around the site, eventually finding one twin room available – the last one, it says – in a Premier Inn. I click on the 'Book Now' button before it gets snapped up. Then look at Matt. 'You are coming with me, right?'

'Course I am.'

'What about work?'

He shrugs. 'I can take leave.'

'Seriously? You would do that?'

'What, use a few days of my annual leave allowance? Yeah, I'm prepared to make that sacrifice.'

'OK. Good.' I navigate through the booking. 'When are we going? Today?'

He glances at his watch. 'If by today you mean later on because it's already nearly one a.m., then probably not. I need to check in with work and organise the time off. But tomorrow will be OK.'

Disappointment snags me for not being able to leave today, but I push it away. 'OK. How many nights?'

He shrugs. 'Four? Five?'

'OK.' I click on five. 'I can pay with that cash stash, so even if we come back early, it won't matter.'

'Gracie . . .'

Something in his voice makes me turn worriedly in his direction. 'What? What is it?'

He presses his lips together in a weak smile. 'I really . . . can't . . . I can't let you pay for me . . .'

I put my hand up. 'What, because you're the man and I'm the woman? Don't be so sexist. I've got money, it's my trip, I will pay.'

'No, no, I'm not being sexist . . .'

'God, Matt, you so are, and you don't even realise it. Because you think you're being gentlemanly or something, and it's probably the way you were brought up, and although it's very sweet and actually kind of adorable that you think you must pay, it's absolutely—'

'No, I mean, I can't let you pay for me with the money from the safe.' He shrugs. 'It could be part of the investigation, so the less I know about it, the better.'

I blink. 'Oh.'

'In fact,' he goes on, 'I would like us both to pretend as if you'd never told me about that money. So if you ever get asked, I know nothing. OK?'

'OK. Right.'

'You sure? I'm deadly serious, Grace. It could mean my career.'

I nod solemnly. 'I swear I will never let on that I told you about the skeleton money.'

'Skeleton money?'

'It's kind of what I've been calling it in my head. For finding skeletons. In closets. I need to get them out and destroy them so that I can forget about them. I know they're there, and all the while they're there, I can't move on. And don't forget, they're only there in the first place because of Adam, so it's only right that he should be footing the bill.'

'OK, well that's a bit screwed up . . .'

I look round at him. 'Oh, God, is it?' I bite my lip.

'Hey, don't worry, I'm only kidding.'

'Oh.'

'You really need to worry about things a bit less, you know.' He moves nearer, and his voice drops lower. 'Especially with me. I already know you. That's not going to change.'

'Sorry.'

'And stop apologising.'

'Sor—' He puts his hands up and I stop. 'OK. Fine. No more apologising. Ever.'

'Excellent. Oh, unless you tread on my toe.'

'Deal.'

'Do you promise?' he asks softly, and as I look back at him sitting there, leaning slightly towards me, his hair all messed up from his vigorous – if somewhat inaccurate – rendition of the cha-cha slide earlier, his brow slightly creased as his eyes pin me with their gaze, I feel calm again. I smile, and his face relaxes too.

'Promise.'

Actually booking the room could prove awkward but isn't because there's only that one twin room left, so there's literally no choice. I reserve it and fill in the details and get that tickly, bubbly feeling of going on holiday. Even though we're not.

'It's one thirty,' Matt says quietly. 'I'd better go. I do actually have to go to work tomorrow. And by tomorrow, I mean today.'

'Oh, God, I didn't realise. What time do you start?'

He glances at his watch. 'In about five hours.'

'Oh no! Sorry. You'd better get going.'

'Yes, I really must.' I walk him to the front door and open it silently. 'Night, Gracie,' he whispers, his face very close to mine.

'Night.' I'm leaning towards him and almost fall into his chest as I say this, but he's turning away at that moment and hopefully doesn't notice.

And he disappears into the night. Well, into a taxi. Leaving me to go and lie on my single bed and stare at the ceiling and think about everything that's happened. Well, I'll be honest, I'm thinking about Matt. Matt who touched my hand in public and didn't recoil. Matt who had an honest conversation with me about how weird I was being, and didn't find it awkward. Matt who agrees with me that recoiling from human contact is the weird thing, not me for wanting it. It feels like a curtain has been pulled away to reveal a pathetic old man pulling a few levers. Or a manipulative puppeteer, pulling a few strings.

Which leads me, of course, to think about Adam. It's obvious, really, now that he's sunning himself in South America, that he didn't love me. Not properly. Or at all. Yet another item to add to the list of things I didn't notice. It should have been obvious from the moment he interrupted me in his office three years ago to correct my Latin. From the moment he leaned in to kiss me after we said our wedding vows, and turned at the last minute to peck my cheek. From the moment he moved away from me that same night and said he was exhausted.

Everything about him and the way that he was with me was so different in every way to how Matt is. The difference between Matt's insistence on being there for me and Adam's almost complete avoidance could not be more stark.

But the real question that keeps me awake tonight is *why*? Why didn't Adam love me? I did everything he wanted me to do, his way, and I never asked questions. I seldom asked questions. Well, I asked questions but I didn't expect any answers. I stopped expecting answers. I went along with everything he said and everything he did and expected – and got – so little in return. So what did I do that was so wrong, to make him reject me so utterly?

It can't be answered. The only person who can answer, with any degree of accuracy, is determinedly not here. And lying there in my bed that night, my hands curl into fists and thump the mattress in impotent rage.

The next day is Thursday and apparently in anticipation of the aftermath of Dad's party last night, the fam have all taken the day off work to stay indoors and loaf around. Apart from Dad who has gone out to Homebase to look at garden ornaments. Next door have got a brand new tinkly little water feature – some kind of huge grey shiny ball with a trickle of water running over it.

'Have the Martins won the lottery or something?' I ask Mum, over breakfast.

'Oh, no, they've moved to Australia. About, what?' She looks at Lauren. 'Two years ago? Three?'

'Last February,' Lauren says round a mouthful of Weetabix.

'Bloody hell, Australia?'

I know I need to focus on what I'm going to do with my life, now that it's disintegrated under me, but a day of loafing feels like exactly what I need. Lauren and I put onesies on and watch *Frozen*, followed by *Jurassic Park*, while we drink hot chocolate and eat olives from the jar. Ripper sneaks in and curls up on the arm of the sofa nearest to Lauren, then darts back out every time someone moves or speaks or breathes. I need to tell Ginger that I won't be at work for a few more days; and more than that, I need to go back to work. But right now I feel like nothing to do with my future can happen or is important until my trip to Linton. It feels like a bridge, connecting my past to my future, and I can't access my future until I've crossed it.

During *Jurassic Park*, my mobile vibrates and when I look at it I see it's Linda Patterson. I pause the film just as Samuel L Jackson's severed arm appears on Laura Dern's shoulder.

'What—?' Lo starts, turning on me like a T-Rex, but I hold up a hand as I answer.

'Hello?'

'Hello Grace, it's Linda Patterson.'

'Hi Linda.'

Lauren gets up and leaves the room. I'm not foolish enough to think she's giving me privacy; she's gone to tell Mum.

'How are you doing, love?'

'I'm OK, thanks. You know, getting on with my new, single life.'

'That's a very positive attitude. I'm impressed.'

293

'Don't be. I mean, it's not like I have a choice is it, with my husband in South America. There's only so much you can do on Skype. Ha ha.'

There's an ominous silence, and I realise too late that she might not have understood the joke.

'Right,' she says now, no doubt scribbling away in her mental notebook again. 'The thing is, Grace, there's been a development.'

Instantly I'm covered in goosebumps. 'What kind of development?' As soon as the words have left my mouth, Mum's face appears in the doorway. I hunch over the phone and turn my back to her.

'Well, it's the credit card transactions.'

'Yes?'

'So you know we know that Adam bought a flight ticket?'

'To Ecuador, yes.'

'Right. Well, we went through all the CCTV footage of the passengers of that particular flight checking in. And what we found was . . . well, we couldn't find Adam.'

My skin feels immediately like it's shrinking onto my bones, pulling tight, constricting me. 'What?'

'I said, we went over the camera footage from the check-in desk, and Adam never actually checked in . . .'

Her voice trails off, getting fainter, as the words sink in and thoughts start to go off like fireworks in my head. He didn't check in. He bought a flight ticket, then didn't check in. Why would he do that? To throw people off his trail? What people? The police? Or . . . someone else? *Leon?* Does this mean he's not in Ecuador after all? In which case, where is he?

I'd been getting used to knowing roughly where he is. Knowing he's not in the country and there's no chance of bumping into him at the supermarket was liberating. Relaxing, almost. After a good long look at the streets of Quito on Google Maps, familiarising myself with the place, placing him there, I had been able to reduce the amount of time I spent thinking about him. Not stop thinking about him. But wind it down at least. But now, here I am again, thrown back into that confusing, maddening maelstrom.

'Why?' I manage to croak out eventually. Mum's head noses further into the room, like a raptor through a plastic sheet.

'It's simple,' Linda says. An objection forms in my throat and it's all I can think about, filling my head, no it's not simple, it's anything but simple, it's stupid and confusing and complicated, and I'm so angry with her for saying it, I almost don't hear what she says next. 'Adam didn't buy the ticket.'

'What?'

'Someone else bought the ticket, Grace. Not Adam. It wasn't him. He never left the country.'

'I . . . don't understand. You said . . . he'd . . .'

'All we knew was that his credit card had been used. Someone used it to buy a flight to Ecuador. But it wasn't Adam.'

'But then . . . who was it? Someone he knows?'

'We don't know. It could have been compromised. It could have been stolen. Or he could simply have lost it.'

'Lost it?'

'It's possible. We're not ruling out the possibility that

whoever bought the ticket knows him, and we're also looking into whether Adam did it himself as a diversionary tactic.' She pauses. 'Either way, it's a good solid lead. If the ticket was booked online, we should be able to track down where it was done and that should lead us to . . .'

I stop listening. It feels like a monumental cock-up to me, to tell me that he's in Ecuador, when he's actually on a number 19 bus in Clacton.

Eventually I notice that Linda's stopped talking, and I try to re-hear the last thing she said. I think it was something along the lines of '. . . be in touch.'

'OK,' I say. 'Thanks.'

'OK, bye Grace.'

I click off, then stare at the handset for a few seconds. Mum is almost completely in the room by now, so I look up at her. 'Oh, come in, Mum.'

'Was that Linda? Did she have some news? Have they found him?'

'No. In fact, it was the opposite of that.'

'How do you mean?'

'They've kind of un-found him. He's not where they thought he was. So we're back to square one.'

'Oh no.' She looks stricken, and sits down next to me, gently tucking a strand of hair behind my ear. 'Are you OK?' Her voice has gone all soft and breathy.

I give her a reassuring smile and nod. 'Yes, I am. There's no real change, so I feel exactly the same really.'

'Oh good.' Abruptly she drops her hand, stands up and leaves the room in one fluid movement.

I give Ginge a call in the evening.

'He's not in Ecuador.'

'Whaaaa-aat?!'

I tell her about the credit card and the flight ticket and the CCTV and the monumental cock-up, and wait for her to explode with rage on my behalf.

'Ah,' she says.

'What do you mean, "Ah"? There's been a monumental cock-up! They told me he was in Ecuador, when actually he's been on a bus or buying shaving foam or paying his council tax all this time. I'm about ready to make a serious complaint!'

There's a pause and I know she's thinking how best to put this. 'Grace, what did they actually tell you about the flight ticket?'

'They said he was on a plane to Ecuador, that his credit card had been used to book the ticket, and it had left that morning.'

'Are you sure that's what they said? Is it possible they didn't actually say he was on the plane? Maybe you thought you heard that, because you've been desperate to get some concrete information?'

'Yes, that's definitely what she said!' A pinprick of uncertainty appears in the fabric of my outrage, and starts to get larger. Light trickles in. Maybe that isn't definitely what they said. Maybe I've jumped to conclusions. Maybe I wanted to have the name of a place, any place, where he is, so that at least I would have that. 'Well anyway, it doesn't matter, he's not here so it doesn't make any difference, does it?'

'No, you're right. But horrible for you either way, to think you had some information and then realise that actually you don't.'

Bless Ginger. What a great friend. 'Yes, it's horrible. I feel really weird again, back to square one, not knowing anything. Ginge?'

'What?'

'Can you manage without me for another week or so?'

'Oh wh-yyy?'

She sounds a bit whiny and petulant and I almost feel like reminding her that my husband has done a bunk. But of course I don't have to.

'Oh, no, I'm sorry, Grace,' she says straight away, 'I didn't mean to sound all stroppy and babyish. Of course you take as long as you want, don't worry about it. I just miss you at the shop, that's all. It's no fun without you.'

'I doubt that.'

There's a moment's silence while no doubt she is thinking about the businessman in the giant clown shoes, or the granny wearing a cardigan and stripper boots. 'Yeah, no you're right, it's still fun.'

'Knew it.'

'So anyway, what are you going to be doing instead of working?'

'I'm going to try and find out some stuff about Adam.'

'Right . . . What stuff?'

'I don't know until I find it.'

'Right. So you're looking but you won't know what you're looking for until you find it? Assuming that you do actually find something?'

'Um, yeah. Pretty much.'

'Tricky, then?'

'Yeah. But . . . I need to know something about him, or what happened to him, why he left, why he was like he was, so that I can put it all . . . to rest. Properly. At the moment, I can't stop thinking about it and wondering.'

'I get it, hun.'

'Plus I feel like a completely feeble-minded fool, to have lived with him for three years and not known what was going on.'

'What *was* going on?'

'That's exactly my point, Ginge! I don't know, do I?! At the very least he was booking secret flight tickets. And even if he wasn't and lost his credit card, he must have planned his midnight flit in advance. And even if he didn't and it was impulsive and spontaneous, he must have had a reason for doing it. He hid absolutely *everything* from me, he must have had a reason for that too. There must be more to it, there must be something else. Because if there isn't . . .' I take a breath. 'If there isn't, it's going to turn out to be something about me that made him that way. And that's almost unbearable.'

There's a long pause. 'Hmm. I see what you mean. Very difficult.'

'I know.'

'Got any ideas?'

'Well, we're going to start in Linton, because that's where his car was found, so presumably he went there at some point . . .'

'Whoa whoa whoa. Wait a minute. Back up there a bit.'

'What? Where?'

'Linton. You said you're starting in Linton.'

'Oh, right, yes. It's a really lovely-looking little village in the Yorkshire Dales, I've booked a room . . .'

'No, not that bit, spongebob. I'm talking about the "we".'

'The what?'

'"We". You said, "*We're* starting in Linton . . ."?'

'Oh, yeah, I did, didn't I.' I start grinning as I think about it and feel the bubbly excitement of a trip away again. 'I'm going with Matt.'

'Whaaaaat???!!!!'

So I explain about the Linton Lodge and the Premier Inn and the plan that we've managed to come up with, which at the moment consists of checking into the hotel, then going for a wander around to 'get a feel for the place'.

'Good plan. Complex. Must have taken ages.'

I nod slowly. 'Hours. It's all in the timing.'

I don't tell her about the skeleton money.

Matt is picking me up at seven in the morning, so I get an early night, then lie there for hours thinking. There's a giant mass of information in my head, milling about making noise like a crowd, some parts shouting more loudly than others, and I feel like I could be about to get this unruly mob to shut up and line up properly at last. Finally they will make sense, finally they will speak to me coherently, and no way am I going to be able to sleep until then. But then I get an image in my head of Matt and his big hands on the steering wheel as we zip up the M1, and feel myself begin to relax. I will think about everything tomorrow. Because tomorrow, everything will become clear.

SIXTEEN

And so, exactly two weeks after I last saw my husband, I arrive in the place where he was last known to have been. What he did here, and why he came, is as unfathomable to me as nuclear physics. Which is to say that I know that someone somewhere knows the answers.

Linton is exactly how I imagined it would be. Well, the parts I imagined are exactly how I imagined them – the village green, the stone bridges, the falls. The people. The rest of it I hadn't given any thought to at all, so when Matt's sat nav tells us we've arrived at our destination, I gaze hungrily around me, drinking it in. Well, we're in the Premier Inn car park, but it's still interesting.

'Shall we check in first, then have a wander?' I say to Matt. That is our plan, after all.

He nods. 'Sure.'

'And you don't mind sharing a room?'

'You've already asked me that, Gracie.'

'I know, but . . .'

'And I said I didn't mind. I still don't.' He stretches his arms above his head and arches his back. His tee shirt rides up a little, showing his belly button and the trail of dark hair that disappears beneath his waistband. He looks at me and drops his arms, then gives me a wide grin. 'Enjoying the view?'

'Hell yeah. It is the Yorkshire Dales National Park, Matt.'

'Of course. You do remember this isn't Linton, right?'

Crap. 'Yes, I remember. Um, where are we, exactly?'

'We're in . . .' He looks at his phone for a few moments. 'A place called Grassington.'

'Oh isn't that lovely? And so appropriate!'

'How so?'

I shrug, feeling silly. 'Because it's so gorgeously green and lush round here, isn't it? Sounds like Grassy Town.'

A little smile appears on his lips, and he stares at me a moment. He seems transfixed, and I start to feel a bit paranoid, imagining my hair in spikes or drool on my chin from falling asleep in the car. But then he gives himself a little shake and turns away to open the boot. 'Come on then,' he says, hauling our little cases out, 'let's go and check out the room.'

He's like an excited child, springing across the car park and later up the stairs to our room. Inside he flings himself down backwards onto one of the beds like Lenny Henry and lets out a satisfied groan.

'God, that feels great,' he says, eyes closed. 'I'm so tired after that drive.'

I put my case on the other bed and open it up. 'I'll take this one.'

'Mm-hmm.'

I put my toilet bag in the little bathroom and get my

302

laptop out, and that's me unpacked, so I dump my empty case on the little wooden alcove by the door and fill the kettle up. Matt is snoring by this time, rather sweetly curled on his side with his knees tucked up, so I stretch out on the other bed and fire up the laptop. I'm so glad there's no awkwardness about us sharing this room. The gap between these two beds is obviously large enough to make everything comfy and relaxed. I feel completely fine lying here, with him there. Right there.

I tear my eyes away and focus on Googling the Yorkshire Dales. There's masses of information about them – hotels, holidays, photos, maps – and it's difficult to know where to start. Eventually I find a great page with a lot of interesting facts and figures about the National Park, and I snuggle down for a read.

When we stir two hours later, it's definitely time for dinner, so exploring Linton has to wait until the next day.

'But we have no idea where to start anyway,' Matt says over his feta and spinach filo tart. 'I suppose I was thinking that once we were here, something would happen or we'd see something or . . . I don't know, *something*, and we'd get an idea of where to look and what to do. It was great in theory, but now that we're here . . .' He looks at me frankly. 'I don't have a clue, Grace.'

'Ah, well, that's where I come in,' I say, smiling and laying down my cutlery. 'Did you know that over twenty thousand people live in the national park? It covers over seventeen hundred square kilometres and contains fifteen hundred kilometres of footpaths.'

'I think—'

'And,' I cut him off, 'there are nearly nine thousand kilometres of drystone walls, and over ten thousand buildings.'

'All right, Magnus Magnusson, you've scored nineteen points. But all that does is tell me that it's an enormous area full of people and hiding places. Which I already kind of knew.'

'But not in so much detail.'

He nods. 'No you're right, I was lacking details. But one thing is clear: our search here is going to be extremely difficult, lengthy, and probably pointless.'

I frown. 'Don't say that.'

'Ah, I'm sorry. I didn't mean to be negative. Where exactly was the car found? Let's start there.'

'Ooh, good idea. Um, I think she said it was a church car park.'

'Right. Do you know which church?'

I shake my head slowly. 'I kind of imagined there would only be one church.'

'Well, maybe there is. But we'll have a look tomorrow and maybe speak to the vicar or whatever.'

It's awkward going back to the room after dinner. We've both been avoiding talking about the awkwardness of sharing a room – or at least, I have; it's possible that Matt doesn't feel awkward at all. He simply sees me as a kind of honorary sister, as I've been friends with Ginger so long, and we've known each other since we were kids. I try to focus on that as I giggle uncomfortably at the door when we bang shoulders.

'Sorry.'

'Sorry.'

In the room, we tiptoe around each other as we wash and get ready for bed. Every time we almost crash in the bathroom doorway – and for some reason this keeps on happening, over and over again – I feel a small jolt of electricity, which is not entirely unpleasant. But then I just catch sight of Adam in my periphery, or he's disappearing out of sight in the mirror, and it doesn't feel right, to be experiencing any of these feelings I have for Matt. Adam and I were together for three years, after all, and married for one of them. And he is still my husband, which I'm very mindful of, no matter how secretive, sly and missing he is.

Totally accidentally, I catch sight in the bathroom mirror of Matt's smooth caramel back behind me in the room as he pulls his tee shirt off, and quickly I hop into bed and pull the covers over my head. 'Night.'

The next morning after breakfast we drive the short distance into Linton itself, and finally I find myself travelling through the countryside that Adam drove through that night. Or, given the distance away, probably the early hours of the next morning. It's surreal, seeing it, the sweeping fields, the hedgerows, feeling the sun on me and hearing the birds, enjoying the beauty and serenity of the place and imagining him here, polluting it all. In my head he's a crouching little imp, gnarled and ugly, creeping around the place like Gollum in his own patch of stinking darkness. It's hard to imagine what was going through his mind at that moment. Did he give a thought to me left at home? Did he dismiss me and our life together as soon as he stepped out of the house that night? Did he come here to meet someone? And why did he leave the car here, abandoned in a church car park?

But all these questions leave my head the instant we set off. The area is absolutely breathtaking. The road we come in on is edged with a low stone wall on both sides, and beyond that are hedgerows or long grass, and beyond that is rolling national parkland, flat or hilly, smooth or rough, stretching away to the distant sky in peaceful partitioned quadrangles. Sometimes the view is obscured by trees, hanging over the road, dappling it with sunshine and shadows; sometimes it's a clear, bright sight right to the edge of everything.

'Wow.'

'I know.'

I look at him. 'Have you been here before?'

He shakes his head. 'No. But I've seen it on *Location Location Location*.'

He slows down as we drive because it seems wrong to speed past. The lane is narrow anyway, but the entire ambience of the place is leisurely, relaxed gorgeousness. Birds are gliding around in lazy circles; rabbits are lolloping along slowly with nowhere to be; even the squirrels are taking a gentle stroll. To rush through this would be like wolfing down a gourmet meal, or running round an art gallery. I want to stop and drink it in, but there's no need: the scenery is perpetual, the beauty is everywhere.

'This is incredible,' I whisper. 'I kind of almost don't blame Adam for coming here.'

'Mm.'

'Except . . . He just dumped his car here. Who knows whether he even stayed one day?' I drag my eyes from the vista and turn to Matt again. 'Why would he do that? Take a perfect, beautiful, unspoilt part of the country like this and add an old car to it? Terrible.'

'Shocking.' He slows down further and brings the car to a standstill in the middle of the road. We've come to a crossroads and there's a sign saying 'Linton ¼ m' pointing right.

There's no other traffic around anywhere. He turns off the engine and we both listen for a few moments. Nothing, except the ticking of cooling metal.

'Shall we go up there?' he says, inclining his head towards the sign.

'Well, that's where his car was found, so . . .'

'OK.' He makes no move to turn on the ignition. 'Seems a shame.'

'Yeah, I know.'

We fall into silence as we gaze around us, and I imagine a camera panning out from Matt's car, getting higher and higher, the car getting smaller and smaller until it's just a little red blob, all alone in the expanse of silent, undulating green.

'We could be miles from anywhere,' I whisper.

Matt looks at me. 'Grace, we literally are.'

'Oh. Yeah.'

Eventually a car comes up behind us and waits good-naturedly while we start up and get moving again. No immediate impatient honking here. Matt takes the right turn and we start along the road to Linton itself.

The lane is very similar to the one we've just turned

off, but this view is not getting old. I can't get enough of looking at the landscape, the stone walls, the rustic beauty of everything, the inherent peace of the place. I bet the people never argue here. I bet there are no neighbourly disputes or car crashes or petty theft. It's all summer fayres on the village green, and home-made jam. I bet husbands never take their passports when they go out for take-away food. To be honest, there probably isn't a take-away place here anyway.

Shortly we come across our first building for ages – what looks like a farmhouse, made of beautiful yellowish-grey brick right next to the road. It has a sign on it that says 'The Arthur Anderton Memorial Institute and Men's Reading Room'.

'Wow, look, there's a men's reading room.'

Matt glances at it but we've already gone past. 'Probably isn't that any more. I expect the sign is from a bygone era.'

I stare at him, a wide smile on my face. 'You said "bygone era". I can't believe it!'

He grins back. 'I know. I think it's this place.'

'Yeah, you're right. It does kind of feel like we've gone back in time, doesn't it?'

'Definitely.'

'What's a reading room anyway?'

Further on there is another small cluster of buildings, obviously homes, with little lawns out front and washing in the back, all built from the same beautiful greyish stone; and on the left-hand side of the road is a sign nestled in the grass saying 'Linton', and a request to drive carefully through the village.

'I guess we're here.' Our voices have been very soft

since we started driving this morning, and now mine is barely more than a whisper.

Matt nods, but says nothing.

We carry straight on for a few more hundred yards, passing more beautiful houses, more stone walls, one or two parked cars tucked away under the trees, until eventually we glimpse through the greenery on the left the lovely little stone bridge I saw on Google all those days ago; and then the view opens out into what is obviously the village green.

Matt turns left here and quickly parks the car on the side of the green. Before us is the most idyllic picture of village life I've ever seen. Behind us, at the bottom end of the green, is the stream and little stone bridge that we saw earlier; ahead of us at the top end is a large, striking building, presumably an old stately home of some kind, built from the same greyish stone as every other building, with an imposing front, a wing either side and what looks like a bell tower with a weather vane on top. It's looking down on the green and all the villagers like a kind of benevolent giant, or overlord.

'Wow.'

'Yeah.'

Our mouths have literally fallen open. We sit and stare for a few moments, before eventually Matt says, 'Come on,' and gets out of the car.

On the other side of the road is a low, white building housing an old pub called The Fountaine Inn, and Matt jerks his head towards it. 'They'll know where the church is.'

'Plus we can have a drink while we're here.'

He turns to gaze at me. 'You're so . . . practical.'

I sit down at one of the tables on the pavement outside while Matt goes in. The sun is hot on my shoulders and there's not a breath of wind. In the distance I can hear the occasional shout of a child, presumably playing with a hoop in the nearby fields, interspersed with a variety of faint animal noises – baaing, neighing and barking; and, more rarely, the sound of a car going past on the road. They're always driving very slowly, there's no revving or speeding here. It's just gone eleven o'clock, so the place is pretty deserted, but a man walking past with a small black dog says 'Marnin'' to me. He's actually wearing a flat cap and wellies. I feel like I've just walked into *All Creatures Great and Small*, and smile back, not a hundred percent sure what he's just said. By the time I realise and say 'Morning!' he's too far away to hear me. Vaguely I wonder what jobs the people of Linton do. Obviously some work here, in the inn, but what else is there? There's no supermarket, no factory, no high street. I can't see any office buildings, or even imagine any here. Maybe they all make cakes and jams and sell them to each other.

'Farming,' Matt says, coming out and sitting down opposite me. 'There you go, try that.' He puts a tall glass full of cloudy pink liquid down in front of me, and takes a deep swig from his own.

'What about farming?' I eye the glass. 'Are we on the cocktails already? Matt, it's eleven o'clock in the morning!'

'And I'm still a police officer, wherever I happen to find myself. No, this is not a cocktail. It's pink grapefruit cordial. And it's bloody lovely.'

I take a swig – it's sweet and bitter and cold and delicious. 'Mm. I knew I'd like it. Thank you.'

'My pleasure, milady.'

I put my glass down. 'Why'd you randomly say "farming", when you came out?'

He shrugs. 'I could see you looking around the place and presumed you were wondering what everyone does for a living round here. I reckon it's mostly farming.'

'Wow, that's amazing. That's exactly what I was thinking. How did you know?'

'Elementary, my dear Grace. It's eleven o'clock in the morning on Saturday and there's not many people around. You'd have been thinking it's quiet, not many people, where is everyone, are they all at work at the weekend, what do they do. Simple.'

I stare at him in awe. 'It's like you can see my soul.'

He chuckles. 'I have known you for a very long time, Gracie.'

'I know, but still.'

'Well anyway, what do you think? Farming, right?'

I nod quickly. 'Oh, yes, the same, farming. Of course. Not much else they could do here, is there?'

'Well, yes, there'll be a post office and food shops somewhere. Hairdressing, car washing, doctor, definitely vet. All the standard things.'

'Mm.' I sip my drink. Definitely not telling him about the cakes and jams idea.

'So anyway, the woman in there says that the church is back the way we've just come. Apparently it's on Church Lane.'

'Of course it is.' I don't want to move right now, though. 'Did you ask about Adam in there?'

'No, just the church.'

'Maybe they'll remember him?'

'OK, we'll give it a go.'

'Actually, you know what I really want to do?'

He stares at me for what feels like a very long time, as if he's got something he wants to say, but eventually he looks down and picks up his glass. 'What, fair maid?'

I snigger at that. Something about this place is making us both feel so old-fashioned. 'What I really want to do is check out of that Premier Inn in Grassy Town and stay in there,' I nod towards The Fountaine, 'for the rest of our stay.'

He looks up at the building and nods. 'That's not a bad idea. OK. Shall we see if there's a room free?'

There isn't. There are only five rooms in the first place, and it being July, and one of the most idyllic settings in the whole of the Yorkshire Dales, and winner of the Best Accommodation Operator award 2014, there was never going to be any chance. Matt and I walk glumly out onto the pavement, feeling let down.

'Doesn't matter,' he says to me, brightening.

I brighten too. 'No, it doesn't.'

'It'd have been lovely . . .'

'But the Premier is nice enough.'

'Yes it is. And we're still here . . .'

'In this breathtaking area . . .'

'And we could always come back here one day,' he finishes softly, looking at me.

We lock eyes and I nod, absorbing the importance of what he's just said. 'One day.'

'Come on then,' he says, unlocking the car. 'Let's find this church.'

Church Lane is easy to find – straight over at the crossroads where we turned right earlier – and we follow it all the way down, past more homes made of the same beautiful yellow-grey stone, to the end. The further we get down this road, and the nearer we get to the church, the less and less bouncy and light I'm feeling. It's as if gravity is increasing as our distance from the church decreases. My shoulders feel heavier, and start to sag under the weight of the air; the light, easy smile I've worn since setting off this morning is slowly slipping; even my head bows slightly as we move. Outside, the sun is still shining, but somehow now it seems like fake brightness, like it doesn't really belong and was only put here to try to hide the darkness pressing in on us. I notice an ache in my hands and find I'm gripping the seat so tightly, my knuckles are white; and every muscle in my body is tensed and ready for . . . what? It feels like something bad is coming, and I am preparing myself to flee.

There's no actual car park, more of a turning area where the road simply ends next to the boundary of the church property, but there's one car parked here now. There is no sign of the owner, or of anyone, or that Adam, or his car, were ever here.

Matt parks next to the other car, and we both get out. I walk slowly around the edge of the road stump for a few moments, trying to picture Adam here, in the very early hours of the next morning after he left. He drives slowly down here from the crossroads, headlights on, tyres crackling on the gravel, swings the car across the road and pulls up there. He turns off the ignition and kills the lights, then sits in the driver's seat for a few moments, resting his forehead against the steering wheel. He is breathing heavily with the anxiety, and only now feels a modicum of relief. He's made it. After a minute, he lifts his head, looks around briefly, then gets out, leaving the keys in the ignition. Standing here in the grey half-light, he takes one last look at the car, the last vestige of his old life, his home, his marriage. He touches it briefly, leaves his hand on the roof as he closes his eyes and perhaps whispers, 'Bye Gracie', as he gently brushes away a single, solitary tear. Then he opens his eyes, removes his hand, and is off up the road like the dead are after him.

I shiver. This place feels like a graveyard.

'Nice graveyard,' Matt says behind me suddenly. 'It must be ancient.'

We walk through the churchyard to the church itself but see no one. The place is as silent as the graves. When we try the door to the church, it's unlocked, so we step gingerly inside. The smell is musty and cold, from aged pages and dusty old cassocks, achingly familiar from childhood and school services; but still there is no one around.

Matt looks at me as we stand at the front near the altar. 'What do you want to do?' he asks quietly. His voice booms around the silent church like an abomination.

I shrug. 'I don't know.' I'm whispering. It seems right.

314

'I thought . . . I don't know. I thought it would be obvious when we got here.'

He nods. 'Well, there is one other car here. Let's have a wander and see if we can find the owner, and maybe ask them if they remember anything.'

'OK.'

Back outside the sunshine burns our eyes like the seventh circle of hell. 'Christ almighty!' I blurt out, squinting and blinking and shielding my eyes with my hand.

'Yes?' Matt says in a deep, resonant voice at my side.

I look at him quickly. 'Matt, you can't do that. Not here. It's . . . illegal or something.'

'What is?'

'Impersonating . . . you know.' I mouth it silently. 'You could get struck down.'

'Oh, OK, so would it be all right if I did it somewhere else?'

'Of course!'

'Why?'

'This is holy ground.'

'But isn't God omnipresent?'

'Well yes, but—'

'And didn't God make the whole world?'

'Yes—'

'So surely any bit of this world that we're standing on is just as holy as any other bit?'

'Oh hello!' I call out, ignoring him. Over by the gate back to the road, I've spotted a woman in jeans and a purple anorak. She looks like she's making for the parked car. She turns round and I wave and start trotting towards her. 'I'm sorry to bother you, could you help me, please?'

'Ah'll trah,' she says, smiling at me. I'm very relieved to see this – she could have been forgiven for legging it.

'Oh thanks. Um, I was just wondering if you knew anything about the car that was found here a few days ago?'

She shakes her head straight away. 'No, love. Ah know nothin' abou' tha'.'

'Well, it's just, a car was found here, about ten days ago. It was my husband's.'

'Oh?'

'Yes. And, well, he's missing now, so . . .'

'Oh, ah'm sorry to 'ear tha'.'

'Oh, thank you. It's been difficult. But, the thing is, his car was found here, after he disappeared, so I was wondering whether . . .?'

She's shaking her head again. 'Ah'm sorry, love, ah honestly don' know anything 'bout a cah.'

'But he left it here, it was found, by the police . . .'

I feel a big hand on my shoulder and a breath in my ear as a deep voice says, 'She doesn't know anything, Grace.'

'But—'

'Come on, let's leave her in peace.'

Something in his voice reminds me of a public information film about road safety. I glance up at him and he's got his eyebrows up sternly, as if he was expecting better from me. I nod, and when I turn back to the woman, her face looks relieved. I hadn't realised until I saw her relaxed that she had been looking anxious. 'Oh. OK. Sorry.'

The graveyard is a dead end. Literally and figuratively.

I don't know what I was expecting, going down there. Answers in the gravestones? A grainy photo of Adam handing cash to a shadowy be-hoodied person? Adam himself? All ridiculous. We drive back to The Fountaine, because it feels too soon to leave Linton, but we have nowhere else to look.

I sit outside again while Matt goes in for sandwiches, and we munch them in desultory silence. Well, there's a dog barking somewhere, and sheep bleating, and a tractor rumbling, and a loud conversation between two men at the next table. But we are silent.

Eventually Matt says, 'I think this is a dead end.'

'Oh God, me too. I don't know why we came, really. There's literally nothing here.'

'It's the foremost setting in the whole of the Yorkshire Dales, actually,' a female voice says, passing our table as she collects the glasses.

'Oh, no, I only meant . . .' I start, but she's gone. Matt is chuckling. 'Stop laughing.' I struggle to stop myself from smiling, and eventually give in.

'I've got an idea,' he says, leaning forward. 'Let's just enjoy ourselves here for another day, walk round, make the most of it. Maybe talk to a few people. And if we see or hear something interesting, we can investigate that. And if we don't, it won't matter, we'll have had a lovely break in the Dales.'

I nod. The idea lifts me, gives me something positive to focus on. 'OK.'

'And then tomorrow, how about we go back home and look into that stuff in the safe a bit more? Find out where – what's the bloke's name?'

317

'Ryan Moorfield?'

'Yeah, him. Find out where he lives, or that address on the paperwork, or ask Ray or something. And see where that leads us.'

This doesn't sound like a particularly good idea to me. Going back home feels like taking a step backwards. And I don't think Ryan Moorfield, whoever he is, is going to know anything about where Adam is. He's probably just some dubious old partner of Adam's, or a dodgy business connection. I shrug. 'I dunno. Do you really think that will help?'

'At this point, Gracie, I have no idea what to think. All I know is, you want—' he closes his eyes and shudders – 'closure. Ugh, hate that word. And I don't think there's any to be had round this way.'

We both glance around. Two people have stopped to talk to each other on the green. They're too far away to hear, but I imagine each one is saying ''Owdoo' to the other.

'No, you're right. This place is too . . . rural to house the answers to mysterious behaviour and a strange disappearance.'

He blinks. 'Too rural?'

'Oh, you know what I mean.'

'Well, I think Agatha Christie would probably disagree with you.'

I smile. 'OK, too serene then. I don't know, it's just too . . . quiet.'

'This is the Yorkshire Dales, love.' The waitress is back to collect the plates. 'If you want loud, go to Manchester.'

She tuts and crashes the plates together as we each

stifle our giggles, then we watch her go, head high, flicking her hair indignantly.

'OK,' I say, turning back to Matt. 'One more day, then home.'

'Excellent.' He's so delighted, he practically claps his hands. 'Drink up, then. We're hiring bikes.'

SEVENTEEN

The next day, driving back, I feel the same sense of increasing heaviness the nearer we get to home. It's as if the trip to Linton was a beautiful break from reality, surreal and dreamlike, but now here we are, right back in the thick of it, forced to deal with things again.

Matt pulls the car up outside Mum and Dad's and turns off the ignition. Neither of us speaks for a moment, even though we've literally just finished a conversation about people who laugh very loudly in the cinema. My tummy is jumping, anticipating the awkwardness of saying goodbye – should I kiss him? Give him a hug? Revert to the standard grateful-arm-squeeze? It seems so dismissive, but kissing his cheek feels as difficult a prospect as jumping out of a helicopter on a piece of elastic. But then I remember that it's just Ginger's annoying little brother, and feel ridiculous. What am I feeling shy for? It's so weird to feel like this about someone I've known since we were children. I turn a little in my seat to look at him. Good God, no, it's not weird at all. Look at him, filling up the car with his shoulders and his arms and his eyes. I can't reconcile this image with Ginger's weedy little brother; this is a large, attractive man, wearing a scruffy old blue tee shirt with a smiley on it that says 'Hi' underneath. He's turned too, and is gazing at me steadfastly, a small smile on his lips, his right elbow on the steering wheel, his chin on his hand. As we make eye contact, his elbow slips off the wheel and he punches himself in the face.

'Ow!'

'Hey, there's no need for that,' I say, smiling. 'I'm sure we can sort this out amicably.'

We chuckle a bit while he rubs his chin comically, then he drops his hand and gazes at me again. 'Grace,' he whispers huskily, and my spine vibrates in harmony with his voice. He gently runs his hand down my arm and every nerve ending elsewhere in my body stops and turns to see what the commotion is. Come on, Grace, get it together. It's nothing more than his version of the grateful-arm-squeeze. He leans towards me a little. 'I've had a truly amazing time,' he says in a low voice.

'Me too.' I check myself. 'Well, you know, apart from the whole looking-for-information-about-my-mysterious-missing-husband bit, of course.'

'Oh, yes, apart from that.' His hand moves off my arm back to the steering wheel, and he clears his throat. 'I didn't mean . . . I mean . . .'

'No, no, I know what you mean.'

He smiles that sidelong smile again. 'Thanks.'

'No, thank you.'

'I said it first.'

'No, you definitely didn't. Anyway, you have no reason to be saying it. I do. So there.'

'It's not a competition.'

'I know that, but if it was, I'd be winning.'

He laughs a little and it has an air of finality about it. Time to get out of the car, it's telling me. I turn away from him and push the door open.

'You'll be fine,' he says, as if I'm never going to see him again.

I swing round to face him. 'What?' It comes out a bit panicky, so I take a deep breath. 'I mean, you are going to help me again, aren't you? With the investigation and everything?'

'I was hoping you'd say that.'

I release the breath. 'I can't do it without you.'

'You can. But,' he cuts me off as I start to object, 'I will see you in the morning anyway. OK?' His breath stirs the fine hair of my fringe.

I nod, and he visibly relaxes. 'Yes, definitely.'

'OK then. Until tomorrow.'

The instant I step inside the front door, I have reality shoved in my face. It seems there is some kind of row going on, judging from the sight of Lauren standing at the bottom of the stairs, staring up them, red and frowning.

'YOU'RE ALWAYS BLAMING THAT ON ME,' she yells suddenly. 'IT'S SO SHITTING *UNFAIR*! Oh, hi sibling. Where ya been?'

'STOP BLOODY WELL SWEARING AT YOUR MOTHER!' Dad's voice, distant, somewhere downstairs.

'Hi sibling. Just . . . away for a couple of days. What's going on?'

She sighs. 'The Golden Duo.'

I grin. It used to be the Golden Trio – Housework, Responsibility and Homework, rather than Harry, Ron and Hermione. Now that none of us is at school any more, the trio has lost a member.

'Still?'

''Fraid so.' She takes a breath and turns her mouth in the direction of the living room. 'WELL, SHE'S SWEARING AT ME, DAD. WHY IS IT OK FOR HER BUT NOT FOR ME?!'

'Because she's your mother,' I say quietly, at the same time as a shriek comes down the stairs, 'BECAUSE I'M YOUR SODDING MOTHER!'

Lauren looks at me and nods. 'Nice.'

'Thanks.' I desperately want to get upstairs to my room and close the door so that I can rummage through Adam's safe again. But it seems somehow disrespectful to push past a row and blithely get on with my life. 'Um, anything I can do?'

Lauren shrugs nonchalantly. 'Nah, don't think so. It'll be over in a minute.'

'IF YOU WANT TO BORROW THE CAR, YOU EFFING WELL CUT THE GRASS FIRST, THAT'S THE DEAL. Oh, is that you, Gracie?' Mum's voice sing-songs down the stairs now. 'Are you back then?'

Lauren looks at me and we stifle a giggle. 'Yes Mum, just got in.'

'How was your trip, love?'

'Very nice thank you.'

There's an extended pause while everyone waits for me to elaborate. Eventually Dad's faint voice reaches us from the living room. 'Was it useful?'

'Useful?' Lauren says, and a second later Mum's voice comes down from on high, '*Useful?*'

I told Dad where I was going and why; I didn't tell anyone else. I can just hear his voice now, quietly saying, 'Bugger. Stupid man.'

'Yeah, it was useful, thanks. Very relaxing. I feel much less stressed now.'

I imagine Dad's face, smiling to himself and nodding, thinking, 'Clever girl.'

'Oh that's good,' Mum says, a smile in her voice. 'Glad you're feeling better.' She follows this up with, 'WILL YOU JUST STOP ARGUING ABOUT IT AND GET OUT THERE AND DO IT!'

'Oh, whatever,' Lauren says angrily, and stomps up the stairs.

'So?' Dad says, coming into the hallway behind me. He glances up the stairs, then takes my arm and guides me into the kitchen. 'What'd you find out?'

I shake my head. 'Nothing, Dad. Well, apart from a beautiful little village in the Yorkshire Dales.'

'What about the car park?'

'Nothing there. Just a church and some gravestones.'

'Seriously? Nothing? But, I mean, surely . . .' He breaks off, exasperated, and takes a couple of steps away. Then shakes his head and looks back at me. 'Nothing at all? Not even . . .?'

'What?'

'I don't know. I suppose I imagined that you'd get

there and find something, and at that point you'd know what you were looking for.'

'Yeah, me too.' I go over and give him a hug. 'Never mind. It was a lovely place, breathtaking, so not a completely wasted trip.'

He looks me in the eye. 'So. What do you think you'll do now? Go back to work, try and forget about it?'

I know that's what he wants me to do. That's probably what everyone wants me to do. But I have a kind of snag in my head that the rest of my life is caught on. I can't get to it until this is resolved. I shake my head. 'Not yet, Dad.'

He sighs. 'Oh, Gracie love. You'll drive yourself mad with this. There isn't anything else for you to do. The police are on it. Just leave it to them.'

'Oh, no, I am. Don't worry.' They can look into Adam's desertion. I want to find out about his life.

As soon as I'm in my room I grab the little safe from the corner and heave it onto the bed. Then I ring Matt.

'Hey,' he says, a big smile in his voice. 'What you doing?'

'Just about to open the safe.'

'Christ, you don't waste any time, do you?'

'Why wait? I want answers so I can get back to my life.'

'Totally get that. So? What's it say?'

'Hold on.' I lay my phone down on the bed and, after extracting the key from the chain round my neck, I unlock it. I pull all the papers out and spread them out on the bed, then pick up the phone again. 'OK, it's all here, the tenancy agreement, birth certificate, bank statements.'

'So the tenancy agreement must have an address on it? The property address?'

'I suppose so. I didn't really look at it the first time, just the name of the letting agent. Mistvale Lettings.'

'So have a look now.' He sounds almost as eager as I am.

'Already doing it.' I pick up the document and quickly read the details. 'It's a property in Didcot, looks like a flat. Derwent Avenue. Where's Didcot?'

'Didcot?' He sounds thoughtful and I get the impression he's doing something else in the background. 'Um . . . it's in . . . Oxford . . . shire. Quite near to Oxford, I think.'

'Oh, Oxfordshire. Well, how long do you think it will take to drive there?'

'Not sure . . .'

'Could we walk it? Because that would be a nice afternoon out, wouldn't it?'

'Um . . . possibly . . .'

'Or we could ride horses? Up the M1?'

'Er . . . no, you wouldn't . . . go on the M1. It would be the . . . er . . . M4 . . .'

'Matt!'

'Hmm?'

'What are you doing?'

There's a pause, then he clears his throat. 'Oh, sorry. OK. I'm done.' He pauses briefly. 'I was just reading . . .'

'What?'

'Sorry. Um. OK. A few days ago, I Googled Ryan Moorfield, just in case there was anything . . .'

I smack my head with my free hand. 'Oh my God, I

326

can't believe I haven't done that! I Google everything, why did this not occur to me?'

'Don't be too hard on yourself, you've had a lot to deal with recently.'

'Yes I know, but still . . .'

'Doesn't matter, Gracie. I've done it now.'

'Yeah, but, I don't know, it's kind of my thing. If I don't Google things, I'm not sure I even know who I am any more.'

There's a slight pause. 'Grace, I think, you know, following a traumatic event like this, you probably *are* going to find that—'

'Oh shut up, it was a joke. So? What did you find out?'

'Oh. Right.' I imagine him blinking and staring at his phone as if it's faulty. 'Well, not very much, in fact. Just a few links to some guy on Twitter and Facebook. Not interesting really, and no real information there.'

'Oh. Disappointing.'

'Well, to start with, yes. But then when you put in Didcot, and Mistvale Lettings, something very interesting comes up. Something . . .' He breaks off. 'Maybe you should see it yourself.'

'Really? Something significant?'

'I think so, yes. Have you got your laptop there?'

'It's downstairs. Don't hang up, I'm going down for it.'

'OK.'

I lay the phone down on my bed again and dart out of the room. On my breakneck journey down the stairs and into the kitchen, I get a snapshot of my family, frozen in those few seconds as I zoom past like a car advert. Robbie is crossing the landing with headphones on; Lauren is visible through the window pushing the lawn-mower; Mum and Dad are in the kitchen, Mum by the kettle, Dad sitting at the table holding his head over a conservatory brochure. I imagine myself to be moving so fast, I'm just a blur, a rush of air, rocking crockery or fluttering letters; then gone before anyone had even noticed, or was entirely sure that—

'Oh Grace, that policewoman called for you while you were away.'

I screech to a halt. 'What?' I turn slowly to the direction of Mum's voice. 'You mean Linda Patterson?'

'Is that her name?'

'It's Linda Patterson's name, yes. Is that who you're talking about?'

'The policewoman, the one who's been coming round.'

'OK, Linda Patterson. What did she say?'

Mum shrugs nonchalantly and pours hot water into two mugs. 'Nothing much. I don't think she had anything to report, actually. Bit of a pointless phone call, if you ask me.'

'But Mum. What did she actually *say*?'

Dad looks up from the catalogue as Mum pauses with the milk in her hand and turns to face me head on. 'Snapping at me isn't going to help, is it? She didn't say much because there wasn't much to say. Just about the investigation, you know. A tiny update. Nothing much.' She turns back to the mugs. 'Like I said.'

'OK, great, thanks, brilliant.' I grab my laptop from

the table and sprint back upstairs. 'I'm back,' I shout towards my phone as I enter the room.

'Did you look it up?' Matt asks urgently, as soon as I pick up the handset.

'No, no, I was just . . .'

'Thank God. You were gone so long, I thought . . .'

'Oh sorry, I bumped into Mum who chose that moment to tell me that the family liaison officer called for me while I was away.'

'Oh, did she? What about? Have they got some news for you?'

'I don't know. Mum wasn't very helpful there. Just kept saying "Nothing much" when I asked her what they'd said. So annoying that she doesn't remember things now she's got old.'

'Well to be fair, "Nothing much" is probably what the FLO said in the first place.'

'Oh. Well anyway, I need to ring her.'

'Yes, you do. Go on then, it's OK, I'll wait.'

'That's great, thanks. Except I need to use the phone to make the call . . .'

'Oh, God, yes of course you do.' There's a rustling sound, as if he's shaking his head. 'Stupid. OK, I'll hang up now.'

'OK.' I clutch the phone more tightly to my head.

'OK.'

'Speak later then?'

'Ring me back when you've finished.'

I'm smiling as I answer. 'Will do.'

'Straight away?'

I smile. How sweet that he doesn't want be disconnected for long. 'I promise.'

Eventually we both hang up and quickly I ring the number for Linda Patterson.

'Oh, hello Grace,' she says affably. 'How are you?'

I just manage to stop myself giving my standard 'I'm fine, thanks.' Might go against me mere days after my husband has mysteriously vanished. 'I've been better, thanks. Did you have some news?'

'Oh, right, yes. Um, it wasn't anything much, actually. Just to say that we're making progress with identifying the internet user who booked the flight ticket.'

'Oh. Really? Right.' That's something I hadn't given any thought to. Didn't think they would even bother with it. My mind is saying, he didn't use the ticket, that's the only relevant thing. How it was bought, or by whom, is not important.

'Yes. We've got our IT nerds to try and trace the – oh, I don't know the terminology, but they're confident they'll identify the individual.'

'Great.'

'Yes. We're also examining CCTV footage of the airport, on the day of the flight, in case he took an alternative flight and used the Ecuador ticket to distract attention.'

'Right. Good.'

'It's a basic error, you see. To use a credit card. If you're, you know, trying not to be found.'

'Oh, right, yes, I see.' Sounds like a hell of a lot of work to me, for not much result. Although, from their point of view, they probably have to pursue it, in case there's something criminal going on, I suppose. 'Thanks for telling me.' Although I'm frowning as I say it. Can't understand why I need to be kept informed of police business.

'Of course, Grace. No problem at all. I just wanted to reassure you that we will find the person. I guarantee you of that.'

'Well, thanks.'

'Believe me. At the very least, it's credit card fraud. At worst it's . . .' She tails off.

And suddenly I feel a wave of realisation break over me. Oh God, of course. They are letting me know about this because they have assumed, as anyone would, that I am desperate for justice, desperate for a person who may have been involved in my husband's disappearance to be found and face the consequences. And as I sit there on my bed looking at the contents of Adam's safe strewn around me, I realise that actually finding that person and making him – or her – face justice is not my top priority right now. Far from it. Helping him go, or at the very least using his credit card, doesn't change anything. I am more interested in finding out what Adam worked so hard to keep secret from me all the time I knew him; and why he did it. How he disappeared and who helped him rank somewhere around 'move out of my parents' place' and 'get new deodorant' in my priorities.

'Well that's a relief,' I say, cleverly hiding my disinterest under a thick layer of pretend relief. 'I'll sleep easier knowing the perpetrator is behind bars.'

There's a surprised silence and I wonder for a moment if I've accidentally sounded like an American gangster movie. 'Yes,' Linda says eventually. 'That's what we are aiming to do.'

'Good. Thank you.' Pleased with that, sounds from the heart.

'No need to thank me, it's what we're paid for.'

God, now I feel stupid. 'No, no, of course I realise that. I just wanted to let you know that I appreciate it . . .'

'OK. Well. Anyway, did you have anything you wanted to ask me? Or . . . tell me?'

I feel a lurch of panic. She knows about the safe. And the money. And already she's chalking them up in her 'Motive' column. I almost blurt it all out, but then realise that of course she doesn't know about them. The only people who know about the safe are my parents and Matt and Ginger, and they won't say anything. And no one except Matt knows about the money. 'No, nothing,' I say, maybe a bit too quickly. 'I mean, what sort of thing are you thinking about?'

'Nothing specific, just wondered if anything had occurred to you, or if you'd heard anything from anyone? Maybe friends of Adam, or business associates, that kind of thing?'

Apparently she still doesn't understand my relationship with Adam. 'No, no, nothing. Sorry.'

'Well, do let me know if anything turns up.'

'Will do.' But I had my fingers crossed when I said that, Your Honour.

As soon as she's gone, I ring Matt back and open up my laptop while it's ringing.

'Matthew Blake Detective Agency, on the hunt. How may I help you?'

I giggle. 'Wow, you have a high opinion of your detection skills, don't you?'

'Hey, I never said the MBDA was any good.'

'Ah, no, you're right, you didn't, did you? So anyway, what am I Googling?'

'Hold on a minute there, Miss Speedy. What did Linda Patterson say?'

'Oh, yeah. Nothing much.'

'No shit.'

I shrug. 'No, seriously. I'll have to apologise to Mum for accusing her of forgetfulness. But luckily she won't remember what I was talking about.'

His laugh rumbles down the line, making my tummy vibrate. 'Forgetfulness: the blessing of the old.'

'Ah yes, the foggy bliss of poor recollection. Truly their greatest joy.'

'That and SAGA holidays.'

We laugh together and again I get that sensation of 'right', of fitting in properly and slotting in smoothly with a satisfying 'clunk'. This is how it should be.

'So. I've got my laptop at the ready,' I say, turning to the keyboard. 'What do I need to Google?'

'OK, right. So put in Mistvale Lettings and Didcot and Ryan Moorfield. But be prepared, Gracie. It's pretty shocking.'

'Shocking?' I say, blasé, typing. I hit return and the page fills instantly with links. Links to Wikipedia, links to newspapers, local rags, national press, BBC news stories, blogs, articles, photographs. Links to Didcot Community Hospital, to gas consumption comparison websites, to plumbers, electricians, gas fitters. I blink as I try to take it all in, try to understand the connection between all these different sites. 'Whaaat . . .?'

'I know,' Matt's voice says quietly in my ear. 'What are you reading?'

I don't answer. I've clicked on one of the links to images, and it takes me to a black and white photo, apparently from a newspaper somewhere, of a woman lying in a hospital bed. The writing next to the image is too small to read, so I close it and go back to the results page. My eyes flick over the page incomprehensibly, not knowing which one to go for.

'What . . . is this?' I'm not really asking Matt; more thinking out loud.

'Try one of the newspaper articles,' a far-off voice says, but I'm already on Wikipedia, reading about the dangers to a foetus based on what the mother ingests. Most things are passed across the placenta directly into the baby's bloodstream and a relatively low level of toxin for the mother can prove fatal for a foetus.

'Look at the *Didcot Herald*,' Matt's voice says, 'from November four years ago.' So I come back to the links and scan down. It's not too far from the top, and as I read the partial headline on the results page, I recoil in horror. 'Baby dies in . . .' I stare at those words for a long time without moving.

'Gracie?' Matt says very softly. 'Have you read it?'

I shake my head. Not just to reply; also to shake off the horror, to make it not be happening, to take me back to the time before I had read those three words. 'Oh God, I don't want to.'

He breathes deeply a moment. 'I think you should. I think it's important.'

I stare at the words for a few more seconds, hoping

that when the entire headline is visible, it won't be what it looks like. Then I move the mouse pointer to the link, and click it.

BABY DIES IN HOME FROM CARBON MONOXIDE POISONING

A Didcot landlord has been handed a suspended prison sentence and ordered to pay costs totalling over £20,000 after an unborn baby girl died in the womb when her mother inhaled dangerous levels of carbon monoxide last July. Ryan Moorfield, 27 of Derwent Avenue, pleaded guilty to charges of failing to maintain gas appliances adequately under the gas safety laws, which directly led to the stillbirth of the baby of tenant Marie Parker.

On the evening of 23rd July, Ms Parker's partner Leon Grainger arrived home from a weekend away to find Ms. Parker unconscious in bed. Although Ms Parker recovered fully following treatment in hospital, the 33-week-old foetus she was carrying later died. An investigation by the Health and Safety Executive found that a gas boiler at the premises had not been . . .

I can't read any more. 'Oh my God.'
'Yeah.'
'What do you think this means?'
'I don't know. But Ryan Moorfield was responsible, and his bank statements and birth certificate were in Adam's safe.'
'Oh God. What . . . do you . . .?'

'I don't know, Gracie. It looks like Adam may have been involved somehow. Maybe he helped Ryan in some way, I don't know.'

'Do you think they were in business together? Do you think Mistvale Lettings was their business, jointly?'

'It's possible. Although Adam isn't mentioned in this article at all.' He falls silent and I imagine at his end he's doing exactly what I'm doing – clicking rapidly through the other links looking for Adam's name. I don't find it. I try a search of Adam Littleton with Mistvale Lettings and Didcot, but there's nothing, apart from what I've already seen relating to Mistvale and Didcot, but not Adam.

'He's not there,' Matt says to me at the same time as I reach the same conclusion. 'Maybe he wasn't involved.'

'But then why is he holding these documents for Ryan?'

'I don't know.'

Neither of us speaks for a few moments. Then Matt says, 'I wonder where Ryan is now.'

'In prison I hope.'

'No, no, I doubt that. He was given a suspended sentence, that means he skips prison time.'

'God, that's terrible. That poor woman, suffering that, and knowing that he didn't even go to prison.'

'The law is an ass.'

'Yes it is.'

'We need to go to Didcot.'

'We certainly do.'

'Tomorrow?'

'Definitely.'

EIGHTEEN

The drive to Didcot is quick and sombre. Matt is driving and although we chat the whole way about meaningless nonsense, the underlying tense atmosphere is not really penetrated by our half-hearted attempts at mirth.

'Did you know that the fingerprints of a koala are virtually indistinguishable from those of a human being?' he asks, joining the M25.

'I didn't know that. And more to the point, how does *anyone* know that?'

'Good question.'

'I mean, what possessed that person to take a koala's fingerprints for the very first time ever?'

'And, perhaps more importantly, why?'

I think for a moment. 'To eliminate it from their enquiries?'

'Ah, yes, of course. Maybe it didn't have an alibi.'

'Yes! Dabs everywhere, koala spotted nearby at the time of the incident . . .'

'Asked to appear to give sample prints.'

'Exactly!' I turn and look wistfully out of the window.

'I hope there are no koalas in the world languishing in prison for something they didn't do.'

He snorts out a puff of laughter, and glances at me quickly. 'You're so funny.'

We both fall silent for a few moments while we each think about crime scenes. At least, that's what I'm thinking about. I glance across at Matt. He has a small furrow between his eyebrows, in spite of our light-hearted conversation, so I imagine he's thinking about bad things too.

'How are your parents?' he asks as we join the M4.

'Oh, God, ridiculous as ever. Dad is descending in a spiral of one-upmanship with the new neighbours. Would you believe that he's actually just bought a water feature made of resin that looks like stone made to look like a hollow log, which lights up at night so you can appreciate the sound of the water twenty-four hours a day? It's called an oasis, apparently.'

'No! I'm staggered! This from the man who wanted a low-maintenance, no-nonsense garden so he could sit in a deckchair and read the paper in peace?'

I look at him. 'Wow, I can't believe you remember that.'

He glances across at me with a smile. 'Some things stay in your mind.'

'I guess so.'

He nods. 'Yes. He'd just arrived to pick you up from Annabel Whatsername's fifteenth birthday party, and we were all in the back sitting in their hot tub, drinking Seven-Up out of plastic glasses.'

'Ha, that's right!'

'You climbed out when he appeared on the patio, and wrapped yourself in a towel. It was a Disney towel, with a picture of Jasmine on it. And then I heard him mutter to you that it was pretentious and sleazy to have a Jacuzzi in your garden, and all he wanted was a nice quiet bit of sun to sit in and read the paper in peace.'

I'm grinning. 'He really hated that hot tub. But I'm surprised you found my dad so memorable.'

'It wasn't him that was memorable,' he says softly.

'Oh!' It makes me blush and I think back to that evening with the new realisation that nerdy Matt was watching me. Being silly with Ginger and the other girls, drinking too much, getting into the water. Getting back out again. Truthfully, I barely noticed him there, he was so quiet and in the background. I just have a vague memory of his little pale face floating on the water, white against the contrast of his dyed black hair, silent in the corner.

'You know, maybe we should have had a chat with Ray before coming all this way,' he says now. 'I mean, he might have been able to enlighten us about what happened. And what Adam's connection is to this Ryan Moorfield.'

I shake my head. 'Matt, we went all the way to the Yorkshire Dales without consulting him!'

'True. I was just thinking maybe we're making the same mistake again . . .'

'No, I don't think we are. I think that if Ryan's previous criminal history is linked in some way with Adam's disappearance, Ray would have told us, or the police, or someone by now. So either they're not linked, or Ray doesn't know about it.'

'There's a third option.'

'Is there?'

'Yeah. They're linked; Ray does know about it; but he's keeping shtum.'

I think about that a moment. It's almost impossible to think of my affable, cultured, unassuming father-in-law, bimbling around amongst Tchaikovsky LPs and leather-bound tomes of classic literature, as a sneaky and dishonest fraudster, hiding a sinister secret. Keeping something from everyone – the police; me; even Julia. No, actually, easy to imagine him keeping it from Julia. He probably keeps most things from her. Bank balance; magazine subscriptions; sharp knives. That kind of thing.

But let's be honest here. If Ray was hiding something massive under his spectacles and smoking jacket, the last person in the world likely to notice it is me. I'm right at the bottom in the league table of spotting weirdness in the home. And Julia's own particular brand of weirdness always eclipsed everything else, which made me even less observant – if that's possible.

We arrive in Didcot just around lunch time, so stop in the first pub we come to for a prawn mayonnaise jacket potato and lemonade. I keep looking around me, as if I'm going to find answers in the large flowery dress of the woman serving the food, or the old black and white photos on the wall.

Back in the car, the sat nav directs us off the A34 onto Broadway, under the railway line and into an attractive housing estate. Derwent Avenue looks very pleasant, well-maintained, peaceful.

'Wow,' I breathe. 'It's quite nice, isn't it?'

'Why wouldn't it be?'

'I don't know. Because of what he did. What he caused. The fucking terrible thing he let happen.'

'What did you expect? Darkened skies? Withered trees? Cracks in the concrete leading straight to hell?'

I puff out a laugh. 'No, of course not.'

No need for him to know that a large part of me was expecting exactly that.

The address on the tenancy agreement leads us to a low-rise block of flats, only three storeys. Matt parks the car and we get out and stand there for a few moments.

'I don't want to go,' I say, staring towards the building.

'We don't have to . . .'

'Yes we do. He knows Adam. He is literally the only person I have ever heard of who knows Adam. He also did something terrible. He must know why Adam . . . left.'

'He may not . . .'

'But he might. We have to at least ask, don't we?'

He nods slowly, then turns to look at me. 'Are you sure you want to come?'

I hesitate. My distaste at speaking to this man is rising like acid in my throat and churning around in my stomach. My reluctance to leave the car and walk to his front door is so strong, it's like a current, dragging against me, pulling me back in the opposite direction. He is no doubt an unpleasant, lazy, careless, disgusting oaf with no sense of public duty or responsibility, who recklessly lets out properties to innocent young mothers with no concern for their safety or well-being. The only thing on his mind is the cold hard cash he can get out of them each month for minimal effort or expense. I can feel my lip curling

341

as I think about it and my breath comes more rapidly as I start to descend into a hot fury. The idea of approaching him and being civil to him repulses me in every possible way.

'Hell yeah,' I answer Matt. 'I'm not missing this.'

Matt looks surprised for a moment. 'Wow,' he says, admiration in his voice. 'You've really changed, you know.' At least, I think it was admiration. Could have been disbelieving horror.

I dip my head and look at him, lowering my voice into a menacing, gangster growl. 'In that flat is the man responsible for the end of an innocent life. It may not be exactly what I want to do right now, but I will not allow my disgust for him to deter me from finding the truth. Because then he gets to hide behind his despicable crime forever, and that repulses me even more than he does. Let's do this.'

'Oh hello there,' a cheery old lady says when we knock on the front door. 'Have you come to collect the parcel? Hold on, I'll just get it for you.' And she walks away into her home, leaving two strangers standing at her open, unguarded door.

'And they say with age comes wisdom,' Matt murmurs. 'Hello?!'

'Just coming,' the voice comes back, and after a few moments she reappears holding a small box wrapped in brown paper. 'I hope you can read my writing,' she says, with a little smile. 'Can't hold a pen so well now, you see. It's the arthritis.' She holds the box out to Matt in swollen, distorted fingers.

'No, no, we're not here for the parcel,' he says, pushing

it gently back towards her. For the first time, she starts to look a bit discomfited.

'Oh. Well, then, why are you here?'

'It's all right, don't panic, we're just looking for someone . . .' Matt starts, and looks over her shoulder into the flat.

The old lady backs away and takes hold of the edge of the door in her free hand. 'I haven't got anything,' she says, her eyes darting about. I notice round her neck she has one of those panic alarms, to notify her loved ones if she has a fall.

'Oh, no, please, we're not here to . . .' I start, taking a step forward and reaching out. She darts – well, shuffles back further. Matt puts his hand on my arm and gently pushes me backwards. Then takes a step back himself and puts his hands up, palm out, in a surrender gesture.

'How about you close the door and talk to us through it?'

She looks momentarily relieved and tries a smile, but I can see she's struggling with herself. It would be so *rude* to close the door in someone's face like that. 'Oh, I don't think there's any need to . . .'

'No, you should definitely do that,' Matt says now, more forcefully. 'We're not here to hurt you in any way, but obviously you will be safer, and feel better, if your door was closed. Please do it, Mrs . . .?'

'Williams,' she says now, blithely giving away her name, when we already have her address.

'Right, Mrs Williams. Please close the door. If it makes you feel better, you can open it again straight away, but please make sure you put the chain on first.'

'Oh, all right then.' She disappears behind the door, which then closes. There's a rattle of the chain, then the door opens again. 'Now. How may I help you?' She's cheery again, obviously feeling relieved to have so cleverly avoided being burgled.

'We're looking for someone,' Matt says again. 'He used to live here, I think. About four years ago?'

'Oh, well, I've been here almost as long as that myself, so I'm not sure I can help you.'

'So you live here alone?'

'Yes, all alone, since my Ernest died fifteen years ago,' she says. Then catches herself. 'Oh, but I have a grandson. He's twenty-five, he visits me all the time. He's in the army, you know. He's very, very fit. And tall. And strong. In fact, he's here now.' She turns her head slightly and calls out, 'It's all right, Darren, I'll be back in a moment.'

She's adorable! I can't help smiling, but I'm worried that might seem patronising, so I try to stop it before it happens. In the end, I look away and leave it to Matt.

'Oh, really? That's great, I'm glad you're not on your own,' Matt says. 'I'm sure Darren takes good care of you.' I feel a surge of affection for him as he pretends he's fallen for it, and have to stop myself instantly giving him a huge squeeze. 'But do you know what happened to the person who lived here before you? A man called Ryan Moorfield?'

She shakes her head. 'No, no, I'm afraid I don't. He was gone before I got here, you see.'

Matt nods, so patiently. 'Yes, I thought he would have. I just wondered if you had any idea where he moved to?'

She shakes her head again. 'No, I thought I'd already said, I don't know.'

344

'Well, have you had any post delivered here for him, since you've lived here?'

She screws up her face and juts her head forward. 'No, no, no, for the last time, no. I don't know him, I've never heard of him. Now please leave me alone before I call the police!' Her voice is suddenly a bit high and panicky, and she slams the door roughly, hoping it would bang. She fails to muster enough strength, though, and it clicks shut smoothly. I turn quickly to see Matt stepping back from the door in surprise.

'Well, I didn't see that coming,' he says, eyebrows up.

'That was very odd, wasn't it?'

'Yeah. Dear, sweet little old thing.'

'So what now? This is kind of the only lead we've got.'

He looks at me, smiling. 'Lead? OK, Nancy Drew. Let me think a minute.'

Something occurs to me. 'Do you think Darren the grandson is really here?'

He considers this, then nods. 'I'll bet if he isn't, his granny will tell us where we can find him.'

'And if he is here, I'll put money on him answering the door next time someone knocks . . .'

Matt nods, then turns back to the door and raises his hand to knock again; but before he can, the door is pulled open, and standing there is a young man of maybe twenty-five, in jeans and a snarl. Matt's raised fist suddenly looks as if it's about to punch him in the face, so he lowers it and smiles. 'Afternoon. You must be Darren?'

The man steps outside and pulls the door almost closed behind him. 'What the *fuck* do you want with Ryan?'

His voice is low, presumably so that the sweet little old lady inside doesn't hear him swearing, but to me it just sounds threatening and I start to feel a chill up my spine. I glance around but there is no one nearby. We are two strangers to the area, asking about someone with a horror in his past, now faced with an aggressive, fit young man in a secluded and deserted housing estate.

And at that moment, I get a flash of inspiration so vivid, I actually shiver. An image comes into my head of Adam, knocking on a door somewhere, asking questions about something. He doesn't know the area, he doesn't know the person, he's just . . . investigating. He stirs up something nasty, something almost everyone wants forgotten, something no one wants to talk about. I imagine him in this situation; the person at the door swearing in his face; Adam – gentle, helpless, slightly nerdy Adam – stepping back in shock; he shakes his head, puts his hands up, OK, no, I'm sorry, I didn't mean to pry; but the person at the door is angry now, *furious*, doesn't want his secret to get out, can't let it get out, *won't* let it. He darts forward and seizes Adam's jacket, taking him completely by surprise, and pulls him roughly back into the flat, into the dark unknown space behind him. The door closes behind them both, leaving the porch still and silent and empty of people. And now all on the street is quiet and peaceful once more.

I blink, as if waking from a hallucination, and look urgently at Matt. He's nose to nose with the man now, not looking small or nerdy or helpless at all, and I focus on their conversation.

'. . . that little fucker that we don't want anything to do with him any more, you got that, pal?'

Matt nods. 'I can assure you, my friend,' he says politely, pulling himself up, dipping his chin, clenching his fists and curling his lip, 'that our intention is not and never has been to cause hurt or upset to anyone, including your lovely grandmother.'

'You better not . . .'

Matt is slightly taller than the other guy, and is staring fixedly into his eyes. 'Definitely not. All we want to do is find Ryan so that we can ask him about an unrelated matter.'

'What unrelated matter?'

'This lady's husband,' they glance quickly at me in unison, like Irish dancers, then go back to each other, 'has disappeared, and she wants to know what's happened to him. We think Ryan and he might know each other.'

'Why d'you think that?'

Matt gives a winning smile and juts his head closer to the other guy. 'It's a long story, to be honest, and it will take quite a lot of your time to explain it all. It's nothing whatsoever that might affect you, or your grandmother, because until this very moment, I didn't even know you existed. I'm just looking for him, that's all. Do you know where he is?'

There's an extended hiatus, during which I see a vision of two possible futures: Matt's car is found in a few days' time parked in the churchyard of some random village deep in the Yorkshire Dales, no sign of either of us anywhere, but Matt's credit card is used a few days later to buy two tickets to Johannesburg; or Darren the grandson backs down from Matt's imposing politeness and frankly giant proportions and gives us an address.

I bite my lip and wrap my arms around myself. Time passes so slowly I can practically feel the earth rotating. After eight hundred years, Darren the grandson gives a microscopic jerk of his head in a gesture of 'you win but only because I just can't be bothered with this any more'.

'He's got a place out on Park Road, other side of the railway line. Rented place.'

Matt nods. 'Thanks man, 'preciate it.' He looks at me briefly, then back at Darren. 'And I give you my personal guarantee you will never see or hear from either of us again.'

'Better not,' Darren says, and with a final snarl, he closes the door.

Unfortunately, Matt has to knock again immediately to ask him which number on Park Road. 'But now, you will never see or hear from us again.'

In the car, Matt sets the sat nav to the new address, while I tell him my just forming theory.

'What if Adam stumbled upon something, you know? What if he's not mixed up in any of this at all, not shielding Ryan or helping him at all, but more, I don't know, looking into things? What if he's the good guy?'

Matt looks as me as he swings the car round. 'Looking into things?'

'Yeah. I mean, maybe he doesn't know Ryan Moorfield at all, but heard about what happened on the grapevine . . .'

'The property management grapevine, you mean?'

'Well, yeah, maybe. Anyway, maybe he somehow found out that other people, other landlords, were being equally slack with their gas safety stuff. Maybe he found out that corners were being cut, lives were being put in danger.'

'What, and someone's vanished him, to keep him quiet?'

'Yeah!'

He thinks a moment, and glances at me. 'Sounds a bit ITV drama, to be honest.'

'Really?'

'Mm. What made you think of it?'

'It was while you were chatting to Darren. We were there, on this housing estate, miles from home, miles from anyone who knows us. Darren gets a bit antsy, doesn't like our line of questioning, pushes us off a flyover.'

'Fuck!'

'Well it's possible, isn't it? This kind of thing does happen, now and then. Not as often as Channel Four makes out, admittedly, but crimes do happen. Maybe Adam was asking too many questions. There are laws being broken, remember. And money is being made. People can get quite jumpy with those kinds of enquiries.'

He looks at me again, then pulls the car off the road and kills the engine. He swivels in his seat to face me properly. 'You know what, that's not a half-bad idea.'

'Isn't it?' A broad grin spreads across my face. 'I mean, yes, I know.'

He shakes his head. 'This is amazing. What if you're right? What if Adam has been killed?'

The thought makes me go cold. It's the logical conclusion to what I've been suggesting, but I hadn't followed my thoughts all the way to the end. 'Oh . . . God.'

He looks at me gravely. 'Grace, this is significant. We need to let the investigating team know what we're doing. What we've learned.'

'But we haven't really learned anything yet, have we?'

He thinks. 'Well, have you told Linda Patterson about the documents and statements that Adam had in that safe?'

I don't meet his eyes. 'No.'

'What about that they relate to someone who was convicted of causing a death? Another landlord?'

'No.'

'Well then, that's what we need to tell them.'

I don't want to tell them. I want to find stuff out myself, reassert myself as a valid human, a capable adult. It's not fair. I glance at Matt and he's peering at me with a quizzical expression on his face.

'You don't look happy about that.'

'No. I'm not.' I know I'm pouting and that it's not an attractive look, but I can't help it.

'This isn't a game, Grace. We're not doing this for fun.'

I glance at him, then look away again. 'I know.'

He leans nearer and tucks a strand of hair behind my ear. 'Ah, Gracie. You're so charming when you're sulking.'

'I'm not sulking.'

He smiles and sits back a little. 'You're so charming when you're not sulking.'

I won't smile. I'm stressed and unhappy. I want to find stuff out and it feels like we've just about got there, and now he wants to take that away and give it to someone else.

He leans in again. 'Grace,' he breathes and I feel it warm on my face. 'I know this is so important to you. I understand that.'

My insides have gone all jiggly and I feel like I want to smile, but the possibility of Adam having been killed is still there, drenching everything in fear.

'But we do need to fill Linda in with everything we know. If it's murder, they need to look at it in those terms.'

'I know.'

'But, charming girl, before you ring Linda I want you to look where we are.'

I look up and see we are parked on a nice-looking residential street. I was so absorbed telling Matt my new theory, I didn't notice us getting here. Just ahead is a left-hand turning called Rutherford Place. I look at Matt. 'OK, I've looked. Where are we?'

He raises his eyebrows. 'Where do you think?'

I look out of the window again, then turn quickly back to him. Now I'm smiling. I'm grinning actually. 'It's Park Road, isn't it?'

He smiles back and nods, like a godmother saying it's a 'go' for the ball. 'Sure is.'

'Oh, wow.' I fling my arms around his neck and hug him tightly. His arms close around my back and hold me and I feel safe, like I'm in the right place. 'Thank you.'

'OK. This is the last one before we call it in, and I think we need a plan.'

I lean back and look him in the eye. 'I agree.'

He stares into my eyes for a few moments, not moving. Then he blinks. 'Sorry, um. Right. A plan.'

'Yes. Maybe we shouldn't barge in there asking questions about Adam. Just in case, you know . . .'

'Agreed. So . . . what?'

I shrug. 'Couldn't we have just broken down or something?'

'What, ask to borrow their phone?'

'Yeah, why not?'

He rolls his eyes. 'Because the last time that happened in real life was *never*. Even in the fifties, when cars broke down all the time and mobile phones hadn't been invented, people didn't do that.'

'I bet they did.'

'Well, maybe they did. But they don't any more.'

'No. OK. Fair enough. Have you got a better idea?'

He thinks. 'OK. We'll just ask if they've seen our cat.'

'Terrible.'

'You're right. Delivering leaflets?'

'Nope.'

'Spreading good news?'

'Jesus!'

'That's what I said.'

'No.'

'OK, I give up. What have you got?'

I raise my eyebrows. 'Nothing. Shall we just knock and say we're making enquiries? See what happens?'

He looks resigned. 'I'm not terribly happy with it, but I suppose it'll do for now.'

'Great.'

We get out of the car and walk a few yards up the road, as Matt hasn't parked right outside the house Darren told us about, as a precaution. It's a quiet, suburban estate but on that long walk from the car, it feels exactly as if it's waiting, as if something is expected and everyone in the entire neighbourhood has decided to stay inside with their doors bolted and their curtains closed.

At the gate, we hesitate for the briefest moment, looking at each other. Then Matt just brushes my hand before lifting the latch on the gate and swinging it open.

It squeaks as it moves and the sound slices through the silence like a scream. I practically jump out of my clothes and look behind me quickly as if I expect to see . . . what? Undead Adam again, shuffling towards me with blank eyes, arms outstretched, moaning? Mentally I slap myself in the face and tell myself to pull myself together, while making sure I stay directly behind Matt so he can't see what a complete lamo I am. As I trudge up the path, I feel exactly how I imagine it would feel to be walking towards a guillotine. Again, intense reluctance pulls at my steps like a current and I have to force myself to keep going. Eventually after what feels like hours, I arrive next to Matt at the front door.

'Matt,' I whisper, and he turns to me.

'What?'

I look into his eyes for a long time. 'I'm . . . scared.'

He moves nearer to me. 'Ah, Grace, don't worry. I won't let anything happen to you.'

I'm shaking my head before he's finished. 'No, I don't mean that. I mean . . . I feel like we're about to find out . . . something. Like I might finally know . . . something. And I'm scared that . . .' My voice catches in my throat and Matt dips his head towards me.

'That what? What is it?' He looks genuinely concerned and his frown deepens, but I can't get this anxiety out of me.

I look at the door, then back at Matt. 'What if . . . *I* was his other life?'

We look at each other wordlessly for a few moments, then turn as one to the door.

'Here goes nothing,' he whispers, and rings the bell.

353

From inside comes the sound of someone coughing, and I reach for Matt's hand as we wait, curling my fingers around his.

After a few moments we hear some movement behind the door, footsteps coming down a hallway, a fumbling in the lock, and my breath comes faster and faster. This is the despicable person who allowed that poor baby to die. Could he also be responsible, somehow, for Adam's death? Are we about to look into the eyes of a cold-blooded killer? There's a rushing in my ears and for a moment it's all I can hear. My blood pumps faster and faster through my veins as my heart accelerates and as the door swings open all my senses dial up and zone in and I focus everything on what I can see when the man at the door comes into view . . .

And as I stare into the face of Ryan Moorfield, all the rushing and whooshing and thudding and pulsing just suddenly stops.

Because it's Adam.

NINETEEN

'Oh shit,' he says immediately.

'Shit,' I echo, but definitely for very different reasons. 'Wh . . .? Why . . .?' It feels like I've been punched in the brain. Suddenly a million questions are dislodged from where they've been hibernating for the past couple of weeks and now they're all awake and stomping around roaring like a hungry bear. In the melee, I can't identify the question I want to ask first. The thing I want to do first. I shake my head, as if that will help sort everything out and line it up neatly. 'You . . .'

'What is it?' Matt is saying, looking at me. 'Are you OK, Gracie?'

I hear his voice, and he doesn't know, and I should answer him; but my eyes are locked onto the face in front of me.

'You . . .' is all I can manage, as my mouth opens and closes like a landed fish. The whooshing in my ears has started up again – or is it shouting? – and I can feel my hands curling into fists. It feels good.

'Come in, quick,' Adam says, and I feel a hand take

355

my arm and guide me forwards. I walk alongside Matt, leaning into him, feeling the reassurance of his solid presence next to me. We go through the open doorway and into a darkened hall, which becomes immediately darker as Adam closes the door behind us.

'What is it?' Matt is saying in a low voice, bent over, his mouth close to my ear, and it's clear that he doesn't realise, he's never seen Adam, he can't know.

'Adam,' I breathe, looking at Adam.

Matt glances at him. 'What do you mean?'

I nod at Adam. 'It's Adam.'

'What?' He turns from my face to the other, and back. 'Are you sure?'

I nod wordlessly. I recognise him from our wedding photos.

Matt is now staring hard at the person in the hallway with us, turning slowly to face him full on, positioning himself a little in front of me, so he's between me and the other entity. 'What is this?' he says quietly, non-threatening. 'Who are you?'

'Adam,' I whisper again, but no one hears me.

Adam closes his eyes briefly and sighs. Then he says, 'You'd better come through.'

I look to Matt for reassurance, but he just glances at me and gives a little shake of his head. Then he takes hold of my hand as we walk along the hallway behind Adam and I focus on the warmth of his hand covering mine, its flesh and bone.

We follow the other man into a sitting room with two black leather sofas, a small black glass coffee table and some sturdy black shelving containing DVDs and CDs.

There are red curtains and red coasters and a small red rug under the coffee table which make it look chic and stylish and exactly like our old lounge at Maple Avenue.

I stare around me, open-mouthed. After a few moments I realise that my head is shaking, probably in disbelief. I feel like I've walked into the Twilight Zone. 'Wow,' Matt says beside me, obviously noticing the similarities, 'creepy.'

'Have a seat,' the entity says, and in sync with each other Matt and I lower ourselves onto one of the sofas.

'What's going on?' Matt asks. 'What are you doing here?'

'Isn't it obvious?' he says, a half smile playing around that familiar mouth.

I shake my head, and Matt says for me, 'Not to us.'

'Jesus, a baby could work this out.' Adam sighs and smiles again, then looks directly at me. 'Adam is my brother,' he says off-handedly, and it's like another hit to the head. Vaguely I'm aware that I'm reeling. Adam has a brother. I have a brother-in-law. This is the first piece of information I have ever learned about my husband.

'My twin brother,' the man adds, at the same time as Matt says, 'Twins?'

'Yes. Twins. Identical twins.' He gestures around the room. 'We like the same things, as you see.'

'So . . .?' Matt starts, but there are so many questions that need answers, he falters immediately.

'So,' Adam's brother goes on, 'my brother has left the country. Without telling anyone. The turd. We are all having to come to terms with that.'

'But, Julia . . .' I manage to get out.

'Oh, she speaks!' the brother says, turning to me. 'Welcome, Grace. Nice to have you with us. You were saying?'

I jerk when he says my name. We've never met, but he knows my name. Does this mean that Adam has told him about me? Why would he do that, when he's never told me about him?

Adam's brother is giving a knowing smile. 'Ah, I see you're wondering how I knew your name. Well, of course I've seen your wedding photos. Although,' and he looks me up and down appraisingly, 'you've got a bit more timber in the trunk than you had a year ago, haven't you?'

This brother is not like Adam after all. This brother is mean. Whatever Adam is – secretive, closed off, hiding a mean twin – he was never mean. Not overtly, anyway. 'Julia,' I struggle on. 'Why didn't she mention you to me? Why didn't Ray? Are you Ryan Moorfield? Why do you have Ray's name, but Adam doesn't?'

He puts his hands up. 'Whoa, there's no stopping you once you get started, is there? Let's deal with this one at a time. It'll be easier for you to cope with, right?'

'Just answer,' Matt says, and it sounds like his teeth are clenched together.

'OK, keep your cardy on, ha ha ha!' He snorts when he laughs, which is so peculiar and alien, coming from that quiet, dignified face. 'Ha, sorry about that. OK. Julia – Mum, I should say – and the rest of the family don't talk about me because of what happened. I presume you know about what happened, with that woman?'

I'm clenching my teeth now. 'By "that woman", I

assume you're talking about the poor lady who miscarried her baby? Because of your negligence?'

'Well, they called it negligence. Doesn't mean it was, though, does it?'

'That's exactly what it means,' Matt says, his voice low and monotone.

'Well, matter of opinion.'

'Definitely not a matter of opinion.'

'Of course it's a matter of opinion,' he goes on carelessly. 'The opinion of those people that gave a verdict doesn't make it actually true.'

'OK,' says Matt, and somehow he manages to sound like a volcano trying not to erupt. 'So what *did* happen?'

Ryan shrugs. 'Who can really know? The only person who was there has got good reasons to make something up. So . . .' He pushes out his bottom lip and shrugs with his palms out in a 'whaddya gonna do?' gesture.

'Reasons to make stuff up?' Matt bursts out. 'What possible reasons can she have? Oh, and by the way, didn't the medical report state categorically that she had carbon monoxide in her system?'

'Fuck, who are you, Rumpole of the Bailey? "The medical report states *categorically*". Prick. Yes, there was carbon monoxide in her system, but who can say where it came from? And of course she has reasons to claim it was her landlord's fault. Small matter of compensation payments? Heard of them?' He turns to me. 'Heard of that, Grace?'

Matt and I both ignore that. Or at least, we act as if we're ignoring it. Underneath, I'm cracking apart like rocks under pressure. 'So did she claim for compensation?' I manage to force out from a rigid jaw.

359

'Course she did. Are you paying attention, love?' He bends slightly in the middle and uses that despicable tone that some ghastly people use when talking to someone over the age of sixty.

I open my mouth to voice my objections to this flawed, weird, *insane* logic, but Matt's hand on my arm stops me.

'OK, well, whatever,' he says dismissively, and I realise he's right. This awful person is never going to accept even the possibility of any wrong-doing, let alone admit it and take responsibility. No amount of arguing and pointing out and objecting will change his thinking. 'Leaving all that aside,' Matt says, and inwardly I cringe to hear him refer to that poor woman's suffering as 'all that', 'maybe you can shed some light on another matter?'

Ryan looks bored. 'Fire away.'

'Why did Adam leg it?'

Ryan immediately breaks eye contact with Matt and crosses his legs. Then uncrosses them again. Then pushes his body weight further up the chair. Then crosses his legs again. He rolls his head on his neck and looks everywhere except at Matt and me. Then eventually he says, 'How should I know?'

'Because you're his brother. Because you were obviously in contact with each other because otherwise how would you know that this is his wife? Because he had your birth certificate in a hidden safe in his house.'

'Even so, I still don't know why. And he can't tell you, so . . .' He finishes with a shrug, which makes me want to leap from my seat and launch myself at him, roaring. I clench my fists by my sides and just manage to stop myself killing him with his own red curtains. Then as the red mist fades, I realise something. He wasn't even a teensy bit surprised to learn that his birth certificate had been languishing in Adam's secret safe all this time. Although of course I have no idea how long it was there. But from Ryan's reaction, he definitely knew it was there. And there's something else about that birth certificate that doesn't feel right, but I can't sort it out in my head.

'You really have no idea where he went? What he did? Why he left? Seriously?'

Ryan shrugs again. 'Nope.'

'OK, let's pretend we believe you . . .'

'Well, it's true, so . . .' He shrugs again.

Matt puts his hand up. 'OK, fine. We'll leave that. Would you just explain one thing, though? Why did you take your step-father's name, and Adam didn't?'

He shrugs carelessly. 'Oh, we're both Moorfields. Adam just didn't like it so he changed his name by deed poll. He thought Littleton sounded more sophisticated, you know? Like, urban, rather than rural. Thought it was better for his business, I guess.'

Deed poll! Of course, why didn't we think of that? It's so obvious, and it's the sort of thing people with their own businesses do all the time. I look at Matt, thinking that at least that aspect is cleared up, and we might as well leave; but he's just staring at Ryan, his head slightly forward, lips just parted. I look back at Ryan and he seems to be studiously avoiding Matt's eye, picking at an invisible dot on his jeans, checking his fingernails, looking up at the ceiling – checking for spider webs?

'Come on then,' Matt says suddenly, turning back to me. 'We've taken up enough of Mr Moorfield's time.'

'Oh, OK.' We all stand up and Matt and I go back to the front door.

'Well, thanks for . . . well, your time, anyway,' Matt says, and although I cringe a bit because it's rude, I kind of think Ryan Moorfield doesn't deserve common courtesy. He lost that right when he let that baby die.

'Yeah,' Ryan says, as we walk past him back outside. 'Seeya.' The door closes behind us, and we step into the unnatural stillness outside. Then instantly the birds start tweeting again, distant traffic can be heard, and wind stirs the previously stilled leaves on the trees. It's like the whole world is releasing a held breath.

'That was weird,' Matt says, looking at me.

'It was, wasn't it? It felt like the world was on pause for a bit, and someone just pressed the play button again.'

He stares at me, his mouth twitching. 'I meant Ryan Moorfield's blatant lies. What the hell were you on about?'

'Nothing.'

He blinks. 'Right. Well, anyway, what did you think about the lies?'

'I don't know. I mean, was he lying? How do you know?'

He unlocks the car and we both get in. 'It was obvious to me. Not knowing why Adam did a bunk, but his birth certificate being in Adam's possession? Adam changing his name by deed poll because Moorfield was "too rural"?' He shakes his head as he starts the engine. 'All complete and utter bollocks.'

'Oh, yeah, definitely. *So* obvious.'

He glances at me and smiles affectionately. 'Don't worry, Gracie. I actually think it's better to be naïve than cynical.'

'Better how?'

'Well, it's charming. Adorable.' He grins. 'Sweet.'

'Oh piss off.'

'Oh . . .'

'I'm serious, Matt. I hate this about myself. The only thing that's good about it is that I'll never have trouble getting someone to do work for me round the house because all the cowboy builders will be lining up outside.'

'Don't be so hard on yourself . . .'

'I'm not being hard on myself, I'm just being realistic. Anyone could tell me anything and I'd probably believe it.'

'You wouldn't.'

'OK, maybe I wouldn't.'

He nods slowly. 'Ah, yes, I see what you mean.'

'Now you getting it?'

He gives a little shake of his head. 'Anyway, I'm not happy with his story at all, it's full of holes. Something's definitely not right.'

'I believe you.'

We reach a junction and while the car is stationary, he turns his head and gazes at me a moment. 'You're so unusual.'

I frown. 'What now? What brought that on?'

He shakes his head, and pulls the car away as the light turns green. 'I don't know. Just . . . your sweet nature. You're so unspoilt. The cynicism and bitterness I have to deal with every day in my job, and you're . . .' He glances

363

at me again with a fond smile. 'You're like the scent of a rose after walking out of a sewer.'

It makes me smile, cheesy though it is, because straight away a memory of Adam pops into my head, grinning as he's shoving me and saying, 'Come on, Gracie, get with the programme!' It made me stammer and apologise and mentally slap my own face, feeling unbelievably stupid and gauche. Right now, sitting next to Matt, I feel charmingly child-like and adorable. And maybe a bit naïve. But it doesn't matter because he seems to like it.

'Well, you haven't seen my sewage side yet. I can be as sewage-y as the next person, you know.'

'I very much doubt it.'

A wide grin comes to my face. 'OK. Well anyway, the question is, what do we do now?'

'Yes, that is the question. Personally, I think we should go and talk to Ray. He definitely knows more than he's saying.'

I nod. Of course, this is absolutely the only thing to do now. Ray definitely knew that his wife had twin sons, not just one, and he'll be more able to grasp what's going on when we question him.

'Actually,' I venture, as a thought occurs to me, 'do you think it would be more use to talk to Julia?'

There's a moment's pause, during which I feel stupid again. But then Matt starts to nod and a smile spreads slowly across his face. 'Ah,' he says appreciatively, 'I was wrong about you. You do have a sewage-y part after all.'

And even though he likes my rose-scent part, the fact that he also likes my sewage-y bits makes me swell a little inside.

We don't hesitate or stop anywhere, but drive straight back down the motorway to Ray and Julia's. As we pull up outside, I feel as if I'm reaching the end of my journey. Adam's disappearance, his secret safe, the cash, the documents, the brother, it all seems about to be revealed. I have a sense of imminent discovery, like I'm teetering on the edge of a giant revelation when all things will become known. I stand on the pavement for a second, staring at the house, wondering if my brain will be able to take it, wondering if I'll cope with the knowledge, or if I'll implode or melt or break down. My life, currently stalled, may now at last be able to start up again.

'Grass needs cutting,' Matt says from the doorway.

We didn't discuss in the car how to get rid of Ray so that we could talk to Julia uninterrupted, but in the end it doesn't matter. He opens the front door already wearing a coat.

'Oh, Grace, lovey,' he says with a smile, and leans forward to give me a quick hug. 'I'm so sorry, I'm just off out for Hoover bags. Julia's in though, go on through.'

'Oh, thanks Ray.' Matt and I glance at each other quickly as we go in. 'Sorry to miss you.'

Ray nods. 'Ah, yes, me too, love,' he says sadly, then charges off up the path like he's fleeing the undead. At the road he turns and calls back, without even slowing down, 'Can I get you anything?'

'From Currys? No thanks,' I call back, at the same time as Matt says, 'Bring me back a nine volt battery!'

I nudge him playfully. 'Shush.'

'Stupid question.'

'He's just being nice.'

Matt shakes his head. 'He's not. He's legging it to get away from you, then felt guilty.'

I frown, and turn back to watch Ray's car speeding away off up the road with a squeal of rubber. 'You think so?'

Matt nods. 'Damn sure.'

'Sometimes I think you're a bit *too* suspicious.'

'You can never be too suspicious.'

As we go further in, the sound of Julia's voice comes from the lounge. Almost without realising it, we both slow our steps as we listen. It's obvious straight away that she's on the phone.

'. . . wouldn't help me,' she's saying, in a very emotional tone. Matt and I exchange a look, then hesitate outside the door for a moment. 'I mean, this has been so difficult for me, he knows that, but just like always, he uses some excuse to . . . No, I don't think so. It's not urgent, he could have waited.' Pause. 'All right. I will. Yes, I know. Me too. OK. Bye. Bye.'

Quickly Matt pushes the door open and we go in. Julia is just lowering her hand after ending the call.

'Hi Julia,' Matt says, and glances at the phone in her hand. 'Oh, was that Ryan?'

She shakes her head. 'No, it wasn't, it was . . .' She stops herself and puts her hand over her mouth. Then she says, 'Who's Ryan?'

It's all happened so quickly, I've barely even had a chance to enter the room. Matt looks at me with a knowing smile, then goes back to Julia. 'We all know who Ryan is, Julia. Grace and I have just come from Didcot. We spoke to him.'

'Didcot . . .' she breathes, looking aghast. 'Oh heavens . . .' Distractedly, she moves to an armchair and sinks into it. Then she looks up at me, her eyes brimming. 'So you know?'

I go and sit down in the chair next to her, and nod. 'Yes, I know. Why didn't you tell me, Julia?'

Tears are running silently down her cheeks now, but she doesn't seem to be aware of them. 'Oh, Grace, you have no idea what this has been like for me. It's been unimaginably hard. I mean, you're not a mother so you couldn't possibly understand it, but for a mother, it's a feeling of abandonment, or rejection – yes, that's probably a better way of putting it. The feeling of the years and years of devoted love you give to someone, absolute devotion, you know, that person is everything to you, there's nothing like it, nothing comes close, you'd do anything for him, and then they do this and it's all thrown back in your face. You can't possibly understand, you're not a mother, only a mother would know.'

It doesn't make sense, but then I didn't really expect it to. I want her to keep talking, though. I think she's making a connection between the secret existence of Ryan and the absence of Adam. Or has Ryan abandoned her in some way too? 'You're right,' I tell her, rubbing her arm, 'I don't know. I'm only a wife but for the mother in these circumstances, it's much more awful, isn't it?'

She's nodding vigorously before I've even finished. 'Oh, yes, yes, it is, you have no idea. I mean, there's the grief of course, you know, that he's gone now and you can't see him any more, that's so hard, it's unbearable, I just couldn't bear it. I mean, I was going mad, you see, I couldn't sleep or eat or anything and Ray was just, you know, being Ray and not much use, but he doesn't really know either. I mean, it's not the same for dads, is it? All they do is have a bit of fun right at the beginning. They don't carry him around in their tummy for nine months and feed him with their body and cuddle him in the night or kiss him when he cries. It's all those things, all those precious things that I did, that I wanted to do, that I loved doing, and it's all thrown back in my face. I mean, someone you love, going off like that, having to accept it, having to know that he doesn't really care about you any more. Oh, Grace, I'm so glad you understand, such a lovely girl.'

A quick glance at Matt shows me that his eyebrows are practically on the ceiling. I focus back on Julia, who's wringing her hands now. 'But he does love you, Julia. Of course he does.'

'Yes, yes,' she says impatiently, swatting my soothing hand away, 'I know that. Of course he does. But he still went. Didn't he?'

'Of course he . . .' I start. Then stop. Look at Matt. He just shrugs so I go back to Julia. She's a mother, devastated over her lost son, vanished and unfindable. And yet her face is giving me . . . peeved. Seething, actually. Her eyes and lips are narrowed and she's breathing hard through her nose. Suddenly I feel as though a chilly hand has grasped my shoulder and I turn quickly but of course there's no one there. Adam's not there.

Julia stands up suddenly and walks a couple of steps across the room. 'How could you do this to me?' she says, as if there's been no shocked silence. 'How could you have been so cold and heartless? So selfish?'

I open my mouth to remind her that *I* didn't go, but then I realise she's not talking to me at all. There *is* a fourth person in the room with us, she feels him there too, standing behind me, cool and dispassionate and silent.

'Well, that's just the start, though, isn't it?' she goes on. 'I mean, after that, you just stay away, don't call, don't visit, don't even *text* me, and I know you know I hate that but I wouldn't mind, it would be better than nothing, better than this silence.' She turns suddenly to face me, and I'm shocked by her expression. Her features are distorted – her mouth wide and square, her eyes huge and dark and pleading – by rage, or by grief, or by pain or by all three merged together in a giant raw emotional wound. 'It's more than anyone could stand!' she cries.

I glance at Matt and he's shaking his head, and I can see from his face that he feels just as sorry for her as I do. This poor woman, her son is gone, probably forever, and she just isn't accepting it. 'Julia,' I start, but she acts as if we're not there.

'I mean, at least it's not Ecuador,' she says, more to herself than to anyone present, or not present. 'That would be unthinkable. So far . . .' She makes eye contact with me again and stares at me earnestly. 'Not that it makes any difference. I mean, he could be in the next town, the next road, the next house. Wouldn't make any difference. I still can't see him, can I? Not if he doesn't want to see me.'

I open my mouth to ask something, but Matt lightly

touches my arm. 'Why do you think he doesn't want to see you?' he asks, then looks at me.

Julia turns towards him. 'Oh I don't know, do I? He'll have some reason. Some selfish reason. That's the lot of the mum, isn't it? Devote your life to someone and then they do something awful and you can't see them any more.'

My ears prick up when she says 'something awful', and I quickly look at Matt. He's interested too. His nose is practically quivering. I want to ask Julia so many questions, but Matt's hand on my arm stays me.

'I know they say that's what happens,' Julia is going on, 'that your child will end up hating you. But it still hurts. Like you wouldn't believe. And the fact that he knew what everyone was saying, about how he left me and didn't even care enough to say goodbye. He knew that, and still didn't . . .' She takes a deep breath in and releases it in a rush. 'Still didn't come back.'

Matt takes a step nearer to her and puts his hand out towards her. 'What happened, Julia?' His voice is almost a whisper, and he reminds me of someone gently coaxing a wild animal out of its hiding place. We want it to come out, it has to come out, but we all know that at any moment it will be free enough to explode from its hole and lunge at us with its razor teeth and sharp claws.

Julia drops her head and stares at her hands in her lap. There's a pause and for a moment my attention leaps to the sound of the clock ticking on the wall. In my head, it's incredibly loud, pounding away relentlessly, drowning everything else out. 'He said he was him,' she says eventually, so faintly I have to strain to hear it.

'He said who?' Matt coaxes, and my entire body tenses, sensing the danger, getting ready to fight or flee.

Julia looks up, glances at Matt, then focuses on me with brimming eyes. 'He said he was Adam.'

TWENTY

I'm hit with the limp stroke of anti-climax. I was expecting gigantic revelation: what I got was nonsense.

'Said who was Adam?' I start, putting my hands out. 'Who said it? It doesn't make any sense, he said he was Adam.' I shake my head. 'Adam's gone, God knows where, we'll probably never see *him* again . . .'

But she's coming towards me, a sad smile on her lips, shaking *her* head, tilting it on one side almost pityingly. 'Oh Gracie,' she says, 'but you must know by now, surely, that there *is* no Adam.' She takes a breath, as if to say more, but doesn't go on. I put my hands up to stop her. Stop her coming, stop her looking at me, stop her speaking.

'What? What do you mean?' There's something coming, something terrible, I can feel it mixed up in her words somewhere, it's there, shocking and inconceivable, squatting at the back like a troll with sharp teeth. And I know that if I keep still, if I sit down and think about it carefully, go back over everything that's happened and everything Julia has just said, I'll be able to make sense of it, to work it out, to coax this particular monster out of its hole. So

I start moving. Because *no way* do I want to get to the bottom of this. Instinctively, I feel that this particular beast is going to do a lot of damage when it's finally free. Maybe it's instinct. Maybe it's because way, way down at the bottom of my mind, I already know what's what.

I march purposefully to the door and yank it open. 'Come on, Matt, we don't need to be here any more, this is pointless, let's go.'

He grabs my arm. 'Grace, wait. Christ, didn't you hear what she just said?'

'What? Oh, yes, yes, I heard it, now come on, let's go, I'm really hungry. Ooh, you know what I fancy? A Cornetto. A mint one. Shall we go and get some from somewhere?'

'No.' His hand on my arm tightens. 'We have to hear this. You know we do.'

I'm already shaking my head. 'But . . . No, I don't want to.' He raises his eyebrows. 'No, I mean, I want to go. I want to go and get an ice cream.' Even to my own ears, I sound like a child. Matt wraps his great big arms round me and turns to the side to rest his cheek on the top of my head.

'Grace,' he whispers, 'this is important. I know it, you know it, Julia knows it.' He steps back and holds me at arm's length. 'I think you . . . you guessed this a while ago, didn't you?'

I stare into his face. 'No.' But it's barely more than a whisper.

'I don't believe that.'

I close my eyes, then nod once slowly.

'Thought so. Your brain has probably been working

it out, putting all the pieces together, without you even realising it.'

I don't say anything.

'So this is it. Here is your chance to hear it all, everything, from the horse's mouth as it were, and finally know, once and for all, what happened. And why.' He bends and peers directly into my eyes. 'You must want that, surely? I know you want that.'

Of course I do. It's what this entire investigation has been about, finding out a bit about Adam's life, why he was like he was, what happened to him. I can feel a frown but I nod in spite of it. 'Yes.'

'Right. So come back and sit down, and maybe Julia will explain everything.'

'She won't,' a voice says from behind me, and we all turn towards it, and there is Adam at last, standing by the door in that languid way of his, leaning against the doorframe, arms folded. Returned.

Without even hesitating, I check his hands to see if he's carrying a warm, aromatic white plastic bag full of take-away food. Then mentally I kick myself and slap myself in the face a few times. Of course he isn't. That take-away food never existed. Just like Adam. This is Ryan, and Adam isn't coming back. Adam was never even here.

'Ryan!' Julia says, launching herself at him. 'Oh, I'm so glad to see you!' He enfolds her in a hug and Matt and I stare awkwardly at them, and then at each other, and then at the floor.

Eventually they break apart and hold each other at arm's length for a moment. 'You came back to me,' Julia says quietly. 'I thought . . . I thought that dreadful man

374

might have . . .' She closes her eyes briefly, then brightens. 'But here you are! Back where you belong.' She throws me a smug look, then goes back to the armchair and sits down. Ryan faces me and gives a little, oh-so-familiar smile. 'Gracie,' he says in a low voice and my stomach lurches. My body is recognising him, even though my mind is struggling.

'So if Julia's not going to explain this,' Matt says, and everyone turns to look at him, 'who is? Are you?' he says to Ryan.

Ryan shrugs. 'You already know it all, I think,' he says, and his gestures and tone are nothing like they were earlier in Didcot. Now, standing in his parents' home, the parents of my identical but fictitious husband, where I've seen him stand so many times before, he's exactly like . . .

'We don't know it all,' Matt says quietly.

Ryan throws himself into a chair and crosses his legs casually. 'Well, you know the bit about the carbon monoxide accusations, and the unfortunate thing that happened. Like I said earlier, it could have happened anywhere . . .'

'Happened in your property, though,' Matt mutters.

'But she could have been poisoned anywhere. So I got my sentence and that was that. You know, paid my debt to society, as they say. Except that wasn't that. Because that woman had a partner . . .'

'The baby's dad . . .'

'The baby's dad? Oh, right, yes, I presume so. Well, he wouldn't let it go. Leon something, his name is.' My mind jolts. Leon. *Leon.* 'Nasty piece of work,' Ryan is saying, 'criminal record, ABH or GBH or something, so

. . . It wasn't reported in any of the articles at the time, but he stalked me. For ages. Followed me around, watched the house, kept calling me up. Wanted me in prison. Or the ground. Threatened to kill me.' He nods as he looks wide-eyed around the room at us all. 'Yeah, no one told you that bit, did they?' He looks outraged, as if he's just announced that someone's stolen his war medals. 'I was in fear for my life, so . . .' He puts his hands out to the sides, palm up. 'I had to hide.' He looks at me now. 'And where better to hide than tucked away in suburbia, living the dream?'

'Hide?' I manage to croak out. I don't want to ask any questions, I don't want answers. I just want to leave. My mind and body are obviously locked in a battle with each other to prove which is the strongest. I think it's my knees that are winning at the moment, bravely keeping me upright.

He nods. 'Yeah. It was a genius plan, really. Get a house, get a business, get married. Fake name, fake ID, easy enough to get hold of if you know people.'

A tiny pinprick of coherent thought ignites in my mind, and I focus on it for a moment. Ryan Moorfield is two years younger than Adam. Or at least, two years younger than the age Adam told me he was, and what was on his apparently fake passport. So they couldn't possibly be twins. I knew this, it was in my mind. Ryan must have known I knew it because the mere fact we were in Didcot meant that I had found and opened the safe. But he still lied to my face when we confronted him. He still assumed I wouldn't add up the pieces. Still relied absolutely on my stupidity. I'm not sure at this point whom I despise the most, him or me.

'So I decided to live out my life,' Ryan is going on. 'At least until everything had died down a bit.' He pushes out his lips. 'I was thinking maybe five years, then think about what to do. Nothing to stop me leaving if I wanted to. Or I could stay, depending on how I felt.'

'Nothing to stop you leaving?!' Matt explodes. 'What about your wife? What about how she felt?' He turns to look at me and doesn't look away. 'What about the life she thought she had?' His voice is softer as he says this. 'Didn't that count for anything?'

Ryan looks from Matt to me and back again. 'Of course it counted for something.'

Matt rounds on him again. 'But just not much, right?' He shakes his head incredulously. 'And what if you'd had children? Would they have been left too? What name would they have had? When you returned to your other life, would they ever have seen you again? Would they have been told that you'd died? What kind of life would that have left them with?'

Ryan's already shaking his head before Matt has finished. 'I'm way ahead of you, mate. There was never any danger of that.' He glances at my open-mouthed horror. 'I made sure of it.'

'Wha . . .?' Matt starts, then looks at me. I can't meet his eyes, and drop my gaze. This is torture. It feels like I've turned up at school with no clothes on. Except even that would have been closer to actually having sex than my passionless partnership with Adam. His distance, the reluctance, the rejections – it all makes sense now.

'Anyway,' Ryan goes on, 'no feelings have been hurt, have they? I mean, Grace didn't love me, that much was obvious.

We were housemates, really, that's all. She was like a . . .'
He snorts out a single fat laugh. 'Like a costume for me.
A disguise.' He shrugs. 'And I was the same for her.'

'How so?' Matt demands. 'As far as I can make out,
Grace entered into a marriage in good faith, to an Adam
Littleton. But she was marrying a complete lie. Everything
about you was . . .' He breaks off and rolls his eyes.
'Christ. Ray isn't even your step-father, is he?'

Ryan grins. 'You got it. Nope, he's one hundred percent
my real dad. But I needed to change my name, and how
else could I explain my mum and dad having a different
name to me? Boom, my dad becomes my step-dad. Easy.'

Matt is gawping at him, shaking his head. 'You really
don't care how many people you hurt, do you?'

'What are you talking about? No one got hurt. It was
the perfect plan.'

I gape at him. He must have worked me out the second
I walked into his office that day, looking to rent a flat.
My gullibility must have been like a bright green light
above my head, flashing and bleeping, letting people like
him know as soon as they looked at me that I would
be the perfect little stooge for his plan; that I would be
useful and easy to manipulate. Standing there in that
room, hearing the person I thought was my husband tell
everyone how convenient my stupidity was, I stop being
aware of the sensation of my feet on the floor or the air
on my face or the breath in my lungs. The world around
me fades out and I feel as if my body has stopped existing;
only my mind is left, suspended weightless in deep space
with no sensation.

'Someone did get hurt, though, didn't they?' I hear a voice

saying. 'It may have been a convenient disguise for you, but your wife was definitely hurt when you disappeared.'

My mind is floating and I can't really focus on anything, but I hear the words. Adam's voice says, 'Nah, she wasn't hurt. She was just . . . piqued. That's all.'

'Piqued?'

'Yeah. Of course. Who wouldn't be? As far as she was concerned, her husband had abandoned her.' There's a pause and I imagine Matt is staring at him open-mouthed. 'But think about it,' Adam goes on. 'She knows what our marriage was like. She knows it was a shallow façade. It was so obvious. No one would ever love someone, or trust someone, who behaved like that. Someone who wasn't really there. She may have thought something at the beginning, but after even a couple of months, she would have noticed. Look, all I did was I misrepresented myself a bit, and if she—'

'Misrepresented yourself . . .!' Matt explodes, his eyebrows practically leaping off his face. I bring everything back into focus and look at him, his livid rage, his furious expression. But then he stops, closes his eyes briefly and breathes slowly for a moment. When he opens his eyes, his eyebrows are relaxed and his face is bland. 'You're not going to take responsibility for anything, are you?' he says calmly.

Adam shrugs. 'Nothing to take responsibility for, is there? I needed somewhere to hide. Someone to hide me.' He glances at me. 'Then she walks into my office. It was a gift.'

'It was all coincidence?'

'No, it was not coincidence. Jesus. It was the brilliant

379

manipulation of circumstances. Getting married? Who could have thought of that? I did! I thought of that. It was perfect, until Leon somehow discovered my new identity. I've been gone for over three years, he was never going to find me.' He pauses and thinks for a moment. 'Except he did. So then Adam Littleton disappears too. Just walks out of his own life. A few days later, the car is discovered in some random remote little village miles from anywhere, stripped clean of any clues, and the next thing he hears is that I'm on a plane to South America, boom! He doesn't bother looking for Ryan Moorfield any more. It was a stroke of genius, that's what it was.' He cocks his head as he turns back to us. 'Everybody wins.'

'Wow,' Matt says. 'That really is clever. And so impressive. In fact, I'm amazed this Leon was able to find you at all, you know, with you being so clever and all. And not only find you, but your wife and her real name and mobile number too.' He blows air through puffed cheeks. 'How on earth did he do it?'

There's an extended pause, during which I imagine that Adam – Ryan – is seething with impotent rage. 'Well obviously he had contacts somewhere,' he says eventually. 'If you don't mind paying, there's always someone who'll take a bribe – at the phone company, the council, marriage registry. It's not that difficult.'

'Probably quite easy, in fact . . .'

'No,' Ryan interrupts quickly, 'not easy. I was really well hidden. It took Leon three solid years of relentless, dogged pursuit to track me down.'

'And yet we found your address in Didcot after one day of looking.'

'Yes, but you obviously had the stuff from the safe, didn't you? Leon didn't.'

'Ah,' Matt says, as if he's just fathomed something out. 'So when you saw us at your front door earlier, you must have known that we'd found the safe? And opened it? And got your address details?'

'Well yes, obviously.'

'So in that case, why did you make up that frankly ridiculous and unbelievable story of being your own twin brother? I mean, we'd found you. What was the point?'

'Oh, because of her,' he says, kind of tiredly.

'You mean Grace?' Matt corrects. 'Your wife.'

'Grace, yes. I realised that, against all odds, she must have found the key, and the safe, and got the address. But, you know, there was still a chance she wouldn't add everything up and work it all out.' He pauses briefly. 'A fairly good chance, actually.'

There's a loud tut, presumably from Matt. 'You talk about her as if she's stupid,' he says. 'She really isn't.'

'Potato, potato,' Ryan says. 'Either she was stupid to be taken in so completely, or I was just brilliant. You can't have it both ways.'

They lapse into silence and there's no sound for a while. Apart from the clock ticking. That one sound I am aware of. And then gradually other sounds fade back in – a car on the road outside, a far-off child shouting, a lawnmower. I start to notice that I'm standing. I feel my feet on the floor again and I'm aware of my own body, like I'm coming back into it, waking up from a long sleep. I look around me and see Matt staring wordlessly at Ryan, who is still lolling in the armchair.

'What about me?' My voice is so small and quiet, I'm not sure anyone's heard me. I'm not even sure they're aware I'm still here. I feel invisible.

But Matt turns, then Ryan does to see why Matt is turning. 'What?' Ryan says, at the same time as Matt says, 'Sorry, Grace?'

'I said, what about me? My marriage? Am I still married? Well, no, I don't mean that, obviously I'm not because you're not . . .' I wave my hand in Ryan's direction. 'But what I mean is, was I ever married?' I stare at Ryan unwaveringly. 'Was it ever real?'

He stares back. For a second we're locked together, eye to eye, each challenging the other to back down. But I don't look away. All my instincts are screaming for me to drop my gaze, to submit, but for the first time since I've known him, I don't. I'm stronger now, I'm not the weak, pliable girl he selected all that time ago. I won't be. He has changed me and I feel stronger and more determined with every second that passes.

And finally, after what feels like a century, he drops his eyes; and I start to smile.

'Are you OK?' Matt asks later in the car. We're on our way back to Mum and Dad's. I want to put my PJs on and drink hot chocolate with my mum in my dressing gown. Plus it's time I told them everything. Ryan, Ray and Julia are either on a plane to Ecuador by now, or in custody, but I don't care which. If they got away, I will never have to see any of them again.

Ray returned from wherever he'd sped off to just as Matt and I were leaving, and realised instantly that all the cats were out of their various bags. And right there in front of me he transformed from a bumbling old sweetheart into someone so ruthless and driven, he literally swept me aside with his arm.

'We have to get out of here,' he said, charging across the room. 'You two idiots have put us all at risk.'

'They found me,' Ryan says lethargically.

'Not those two,' Ray shouts from the stairs, '*you* two.'

'What?'

'You didn't have to fucking blab about everything did you?! Now get your stuff together, you stupid fuckwit. And be quick. We're leaving in half an hour.'

Matt and I crept out and Matt rang his colleagues from the car to alert them to Ryan's imminent flit. His marriage to me, all his business affairs, his accounts and tax returns, everything will have to be looked into, as it was all fake and therefore fraudulent. Ray will have to be investigated too, his involvement worked out. I don't really care what happens after that.

Now, I look across at Matt's big hands on the steering wheel, guiding it effortlessly around corners or keeping it straight, and think about what he's just asked me. Am I OK? Mentally, I check myself all over, as if I'm just emerging from a traumatic experience. But then, my husband was missing, then in South America, then not missing, and now not even my husband. That's quite traumatic, really. And after all that, I wasn't even married. I'm right back where I was before I met him. Only better. Grace, Version two point oh. I'm a bit battered, a bit bruised, but like the skateboarder who falls, and falls, and falls, and then doesn't, I have learned a lot. I nod. 'You know what? I think I am. Yes.'

Matt grins and looks at me quickly. 'Great.'

'I've never been someone's disguise before.'

He shrugs. 'It ain't all that.'

Which makes me giggle. 'No, you're right. Don't think I'll bother again. Weird though, that Ryan thought he was my disguise too. What on earth do you think he meant by that?'

'I don't know. Maybe just deluding himself that the arrangement was reciprocal, to ease his own conscience.'

I nod. 'Yeah, maybe.'

But I know that's not right. Ryan Moorfield doesn't strike me as someone with a conscience. The way he can dismiss the death of an unborn baby, exonerate himself in his own mind. The way he could use me, delude me, then drop me when I was no longer any use. Those aren't the actions of someone with morals. So what did he mean, he was my disguise? I can't make it out.

'So what happens now?' I ask Matt. 'I suppose I should ring Linda Patterson, let her know my husband's not missing any more.' I catch myself. 'Never was a husband. Huh. Never was a wife.'

'It's OK, I've asked that she be notified,' he says. 'They'll need a statement off you at some point. Ryan is bravely overlooking the fact that fraud is against the law.' He glances at me. 'This is probably going to go on a long time.'

'Oh God.'

'Don't worry about it,' he says gently. 'I'll help.'

I look at him and feel an explosion of affection for him. 'Will you?'

'Course I will, Gracie. No problem at all.'

'Oh Matt. Thank you. I really appreciate that.'

'My pleasure.' He lightly touches my hand on my lap. 'I mean that, you know. It's a pleasure to help you. It's a pleasure to be around you. I want to keep doing it.'

'Helping me?'

'Being around you. Whatever you happen to be doing. And if that means helping you in any way I can, then that too. Police reports, witness statements, lifts to the station, court appearances. All the standard coupley things.'

I feel rebuffed for some reason and experience a stab of disappointment. 'Oh.'

'Moving house.' He looks across at me. 'Making dinner.' My disappointment melts away as his voice lowers. 'Foot rubs. Cups of tea. Shopping trips.' He gazes at me from lowered lids. 'DIY.'

'DIY?' I give a little shiver. 'Really?'

'Oh yes. I know how to treat a lady.'

'I think you do. I mean, police reports have never sounded more fun.'

He chuckles. 'I know, right? I can't wait to do all those things with you.'

'Me neither.'

He drops me off at Mum's and I stand at the kerb and watch the car dwindle slowly away. But it's OK. I'm a hundred percent sure he's coming back. He's got to, he's going to have to give a statement.

For the next two hours, someone standing outside our house with their ear pressed to the kitchen window will hear various exclamations from my mum, like 'A safe? In the *floor*?' and '*Thirteen thousand pounds?!*' and some from my dad, which are calmer and less scandalised, and focus more on processing and understanding fully. 'Linton?' he says, nodding interestedly. A short while later, 'Didcot?' I can hear him thinking M25, M4, leave early, miss the rush. Later on, when Lauren and Robbie come home, Mum recounts the whole thing again, and the exclamations are all repeated. Except Mum embellishes it a bit, to make it more interesting. Personally I don't think she needs to add details about Leon's previous criminal history. The diamond smuggling story is certainly a bit much. But they all enjoy it, so I leave them to it.

Much later, when everyone has hugged me and they're all finally happy that I'm stable and not about to start hacking clothes to pieces with a steak knife, I retreat up to my room like a moody sixteen-year-old. I fling myself down onto the bed and let myself think about nothing.

Tomorrow I'll go back to work and start flat hunting. Tomorrow I will restart my adult life. But for now I'm staying a child just a little bit longer. People go through all sorts of things to achieve this: mid-life crises, divorces, negative equity. I've simply had it handed to me. OK, I did have to go through a fair bit to get here, but let's not be negative about this. How many people get to rewind back to their parents' house and start again, just like that? No fallout, no baggage. I stretch out luxuriously on the bed, reaching my arms above my head, and feel exactly like I did when I was sixteen doing this. No worries, no problems, no bills, no responsibilities, just excited about a boy who likes me, and the endless possibilities stretching out ahead of me.

All right, maybe that's not exactly how I felt when I was sixteen. Much more moody and stressing about Geography homework and zits.

But in principle it's the same. I'm going to enjoy my freedom this time round, and nothing is going to prise me out of it.

And lying there, I start to understand what Ryan meant about being a disguise for me. I had made my first foray into the adult world – leaving home, getting my own place, getting married – but I wasn't really ready for it. Maybe I knew that, when I allowed myself to be persuaded away from the flat I really wanted into the one Ryan wanted me to have. It was low maintenance, it was new, it was easy. Then I moved in with him, and married him, and watched his films and ate his food. But as much as I was simply an attachment to him, like an upgrade, to improve his status, so he was for me. We weren't connected to each other like two people in love; we each just thought the addition of a spouse was a necessary step to take at that stage of our lives. Ryan helped me disguise myself as an adult, when I was still hiding the child underneath.

Suddenly my bedroom door bursts open, and standing there silhouetted in the light from the landing, legs planted wide, hands hovering near the pistols at her sides, is Lara Croft. She's breathing hard, her chest rising and falling with it, as if she's just escaped from a tiger.

'What the *fuck*?!' she asks, striding into the room.

'Oh Ginge!' I jump off the bed and run across to her for a comforting hug. 'It's so good to see you.' I step back and take in the costume. 'This looks amazing!'

'Never mind that,' she says, leading me to the bed and sitting down. 'Matt rang me. What the hell is going on?'

So I recount the whole thing to her – the safe contents, Linton, Didcot, Ecuador – and she gasps and sympathises and strokes my arm affectionately.

'So you were never married? And the house is gone? And you're back in your parents' place?'

I nod. 'I've gone back to "Start". Now I just need to roll a six.'

She shrugs. 'That's not such a bad thing, is it?'

'No, it really isn't. It's funny, I'm feeling so positive about everything. Even though this terrible thing has just happened to me.'

'And what about Matt?'

Even the mention of his name makes my tummy clench a bit. 'What about him?'

She looks at me steadily. 'He really likes you.'

That makes me grin like a loon. 'Do you think so?'

'Oh em eff gee, Grace, what's the matter with you? He's liked you for years.'

'Has he?'

She leans forward and raps on my forehead with her knuckles. 'Hello? Anybody in there? Of course he has, you numpty. Since we were teenagers. Why do you think he was always following us around everywhere?'

'Oh!'

'Uh-huh.'

'So why didn't you tell me? I mean, at some point over the past decade there must have been an opportunity?'

'He asked me not to. Told me not to. *Demanded* that I didn't. He knew you weren't really even aware of him, and in his emo state he would have probably killed himself – and then me – if I'd let on. Then, of course, you met Adam . . .'

'Oh.'

'Yeah, not the most observant person in the world, are you?'

I shake my head with a smile. 'I'm, like, the opposite of that.'

'You are.' She gives me another hug. 'But I love ya.' She stands up.

'Are you going?'

'Yeah, Fletch is waiting for me at his place.' She glances down at the costume. 'He really likes this one, so . . .'

'Eeew, I did *not* want to know that.'

Ginge giggles. 'It's the only perk of this ridiculous job!'

I walk her to the door and she kisses my cheek as she's leaving. She's never *ever* done that before. Seems quite grown up. I like it.

Back in my room, I go back to sprawling pointlessly on the bed, thinking about stuff. How odd, how lucky for me, that I got to try out married life with someone who turned out to be the wrong one, and I have no baggage because of it. The only thing I need to sort out is changing my name back on all my bank cards, and cancelling the standing order into our joint bills account. We never fully combined our resources. Adam – no, *Ryan* – was quite vocal about that.

'What's the point of me buying presents for you out of joint money?' he'd said. 'You might as well have bought it for yourself.' It occurred to me at the time that it was more about the thought behind the gift rather than how much it cost, but I didn't say so. I kept quiet and complied and did exactly what he wanted.

My mobile rings and as I roll onto my side to answer it, I resolve never to be told what to do by anyone ever again.

'Get downstairs,' Matt says, a smile in his voice.

'Ah, Matt, I've been downstairs. I'm upstairs now.'

'But I'm downstairs.'

I sit up. 'You're here? Are you inside?'

'Not yet. Come down, I have a surprise for you.'

I go to the window and peer out and I can see his car there but there's no sign of him. He must be at the front door, so I go out of my room and trot downstairs. As I come into view of the hallway, I can see a dark shape through the glass of the door, and I find myself grinning automatically. Too late I wish I'd checked my hair before appearing in front of him but he's seen me moments after I thought I'd become a widow, so now I'm a teenager again, it must be an improvement.

I open the door and he's standing there with his hands behind his back. 'Hi,' he says, grinning.

'Hi.'

'You look lovely.'

Gorgeous butterflies hatch in their thousands in my belly, and my face starts to go hot. 'Thanks, but I'm the same as three hours ago when you last saw me.'

'You looked lovely then, too.'

I grin. 'Thanks. Do you want to come in?'

'No.'

'Ah.'

'I want you to come out.'

'Oh. OK.' I step outside and pull the door closed behind me. 'Where are we going?'

'Nowhere. Well, let's just stroll a little away from the house.'

'OK. So what's my surprise?'

He stops and turns to me. 'Are you ready?'

'No! How can I be? It's a surprise, it's in their very nature that people aren't ready for them!'

He nods. 'OK, yes, good point. Well, all right then. Here we go.' And he brings his hands around from his back and holds them out towards me, saying 'Ta-da!' And for one hideous moment I think he's going to propose to me, and I'd have to say no which would probably mean the end of any possible relationship with him. But I've only just been un-married, I can't get married again, for the first time, straight away. Plus I'm only sixteen at the moment. It would be stupid.

But it's only a split second and then I notice what he's holding out, and it looks like a tiny bouquet of flowers, the way he's presenting it, but it isn't, it's better than that. He's holding out two Cornettos. Mint ones. And as I look at them, and the simplicity of this gesture and the complexity of affection and thought that's behind it, I know that this is the way it should be. And I know I've thrown my six.

For you mum. This is all for you.

For anyone who has loved, lost or found it hard to let go, *Carry You*, will make you laugh, cry and celebrate your best friends.

Daisy has lost her mum to breast cancer. She's at rock bottom and doesn't think she'll ever get back up again. But her best friend Abi has other ideas – and she's determined to make Daisy remember the person she used to be. What Daisy doesn't know is that, thanks to Abi, her life is about to take an unexpected turn . . . and one *full* of surprises.

Beth Thomas's moving and heart-warming debut is available from Avon now.